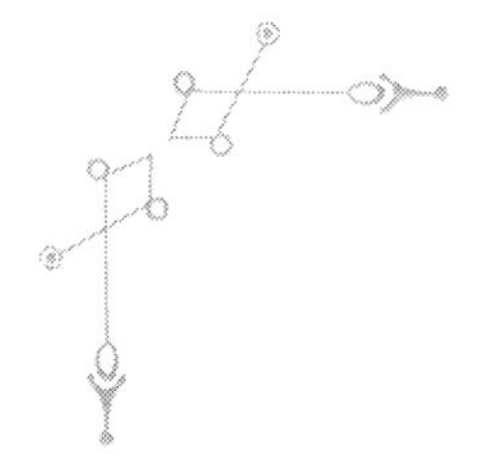

BOOK I

THE CRYSTAL CHRONICLES

ALESSIA DICKSON

FriesenPress

Suite 300 - 990 Fort St
Victoria, BC, Canada, V8V 3K2
www.friesenpress.com

First Edition — 2016

ISBN
978-1-4602-6463-8 (Hardcover)
978-1-4602-6464-5 (Paperback)
978-1-4602-6465-2 (eBook)

1. Fiction, Fantasy

Distributed to the trade by The Ingram Book Company

In loving memory of
Giovanna Conte

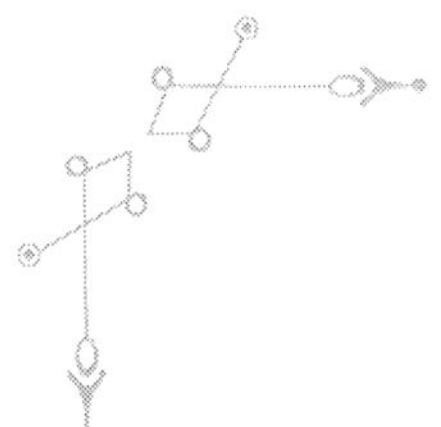
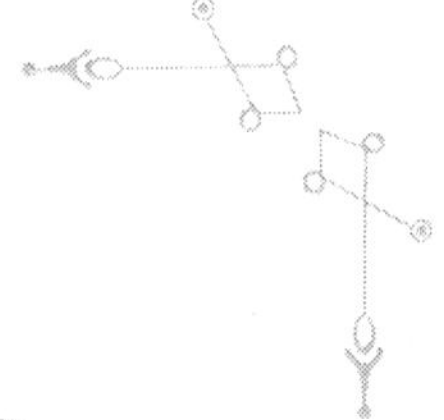

PROLOGUE

Tokyo, 6 years ago

The day Kurt Bell had to kill thousands of innocent people was ironically picturesque. The sun was shining, the people in the city were smiling, and he honestly couldn't remember a time when he had been in a better mood. It was a mood, he knew, that would only brighten as the carefully crafted plans for the day were set into motion. He was rather enthralled by the job, but he just couldn't help being a bit wary of all the blood he knew would be spilt. He didn't want to stain his suit, and besides, he felt so great that the last thing he needed was the depressing look of tragedy that usually accompanied the sight of blood all over his body. Nevertheless, the job needed to be done, and Kurt was just the man to do it.

At a mere twenty-four years old, he was considered a genius in combat, strategic planning, academics, and especially his specific magic type. It came as no surprise that many organizations had attempted to recruit him, but he had disregarded most of them, until he stumbled upon a group worthy his time: the Society, a group with a meaningful goal. To be fair, the Society *was* the most well-known group of the time, to the supernatural community *and* to the mortal world, although they knew it by another name of course. As oblivious to the magic around them as they were to their own inevitable extinction, the mortals blamed the bloodshed and destruction on simple terrorist groups. The Society was so much more than that.

His kind, Elementals—people skilled in practising magic involving any one of the four natural elements—ran the organization, and it was only fitting that he had taken his place among the elite. It didn't take long for Kurt to gain attention within the group and soon he was climbing the status ladder, and approaching the top at an alarming rate.

Kurt smiled, enjoying the cool blast of the conditioned air as he contemplated the task he couldn't afford to mess up. As a rising force in the Society, he was not yet the one who planned these things. He was the one who planned for what was *not* planned. A job like this was hard to tackle and countless things could go wrong.

He quickly threw open the door to the car, in which he had been bottled up for hours, and briskly stepped out onto the edge of a busy road. He hastily fixed his tie, smoothing out any wrinkles that had woven itself into the fabric. His usual pale face now met the harsh unforgiving rays of the sun, and as the light faded to a tolerable shade, he adjusted his sharp eyes. For a moment, he stood observing people as they bustled around, caught up in their daily lives—analyzing, always analyzing. He couldn't deny the repulsive, ill-fated feeling bubbling up in his chest. He scowled. Mortals. They were such useless, weak beings for such an abundant race. They were ruining the pleasant day, and Kurt thought it was almost better that way, as it made it easier to remember what was worth fighting for.

He always thought he was rather fortunate, to be born a Draken—a type of Elemental who specialized in harnessing the magic of the fire element. Since the dawn of time, his people had lived *with* the earth, rather then on it, and since his birth he had watched as mortals multiplied in number, slowly but surely sucking the very life from the planet. He wanted to eliminate them all, one by one, to watch the life fade out of their silly blank expressions ... to watch as their ordinary blood tainted the soil. He wanted to release the fire coursing through his veins.

Luckily he wasn't the only one who strove to see the downfall of the mortal race. It had always been the Society's goal to eliminate mortals, leaving only a small population of supernatural beings. The Society would rise to power and Kurt would be the one leading the world into a new era. They grew closer to their goal with each passing day, although what his subordinates called the "genocide of billions" was no easy feat. Kurt didn't like to think of his goal as genocide; it was merely the healing of the earth, and restoring balance.

Kurt suppressed a rather exasperated sigh, the sun curling the tips of his slicked blond hair almost white. His eyes were as dark as onyx, yet as sharp as the blade he kept hidden under his trench coat. Today he had to execute yet another massacre. He supposed he had to take small steps in order to achieve his goal; he just wished his jobs weren't always so tedious. Kurt had attended so many of these things that he lost track, and the dull, piercing screams of countless humans and Elementals alike lay dormant in the back of his mind, long ago making peace with his nightmares.

Kurt quickly extended his gaze, assessing more specifically this time, spotting his subordinates in the crowd, flawlessly blending in just as he had instructed them to do. Every minute detail of the job had been planned. In exactly three minutes and thirty-two seconds, the clock would strike midday. His workers, carefully woven within the crowd, each concealing an impressive collection of lethal weapons, would begin eliminating the mortals who were unlucky enough to be in the close vicinity. There would be chaos—lots of chaos—as people would return to the earth. The ones still alive would surely be screaming; the mortal authorities, like the police, would be called, and he supposed it would get quite messy.

But as many would be eliminated as possible, and even that was only scratching the surface of the job. One hundred and twelve feet away, a Council meeting was currently being held. Kurt automatically cringed at the thought of the Council, the governing body of the supernatural world. Most were Elementals, and extremely powerful ones at that, and would not stand for the new world Kurt hoped to create. If kept alive, they would be a pressing problem, and perhaps even a threat. Thus, Kurt had readily decided that they would all have to be eliminated. No survivors. He was certain that they would not go easily, but Kurt had faith in his workers. They would do their part, targeting the mortals down below, as he cornered the Council members up above. The plan would be executed perfectly, just like everything else Kurt had ever done.

Less than a minute and twenty seconds to go. Kurt licked his parched lips. What a pity that such a nice day would be ruined by the likes of this disaster. A single gunshot was fired into the crowd and suddenly a bloodcurdling scream reached his ears, followed immediately by more panicked shouts. The chaos began, like a match being set to tinder, and people were running, shouting, and shoving each other out of the way in the hopeless attempt to scramble to safety. He watched for exactly thirty-four seconds, as a total of five bodies fell to the ground in rapid succession, before finally turning away and focusing on his original intent.

His employees were working effectively, each claiming another life before disappearing like mist into the breeze and then reappearing somewhere else to take a few more. Kurt followed suit, lunging forward and running along the path towards the Council meeting, a path he had carefully scoped out weeks ago. There were no flaws in a plan if Kurt Bell had created it. His knife grazed his skin as he moved, the edges of the hilt digging into the flesh along his upper leg. There was no time to pause and readjust the weapon. It was an executioner's duty to be as silent as the very shadows. That meant no stopping, or second-guessing, under any circumstances.

It took less than a minute to weave through the back alleyways and streets leading up to the building. The sirens and screams could be heard in the distance, the cry of pain too loud to possibly be contained. He bounded up the stairs to the back entrance of the building—the bricks freshly laid and the smell of paint wafting through the air. The building was new, intended specifically for this important Council gathering. It would be a grave-site in the next five minutes.

He could hear screaming from inside, and he almost smiled but instead maintained his professional demeanour—even though there was no one in sight to tell him otherwise. An earsplitting emergency siren wailed from the top of the ten-story building, a cry for help that would remain unrequited. His workers had done exactly as he instructed. They had busted open the front door and stormed in, targeting the inferiors on the Council. He would take the most important members—the powerful ones; he wanted the satisfaction of seeing their expressions as they realized he had the upper hand.

With that endearing thought in mind, he backed up a bit, teetering on his feet and kicked down the door. The task would've been impossible for just about anyone else, but for him it wasn't difficult. To be part of the Society meant you had to undergo massive physical and mental training, and his muscles barely uttered protest as they pushed against the door. It fell off its hinges with a pathetic squeak and crashed to the ground, creating a booming noise that announced his arrival.

He stepped inside, stopping at the foot of a winding white staircase that smelled too much like rubber and what he knew to be the metallic scent of blood. He dashed up the stairs, skipping two at a time, and then three, pushed by the forces of his own excitement. He halted when he got to the sixth floor, the level where the meeting was being held. He composed himself before taking in a short breath of air. He was a classy man, and he liked looking his best no matter the occasion—even an occasion like this.

He sauntered down the hallway and quite calmly slipped inside the room on his right, leaving the door slightly ajar. There were exactly twenty people in the room, or rather, there had been—about half of them lay dead or dying at his feet. He looked around and briefly absorbed the sight of a few of his subordinates doing their jobs almost as well as he could have done them. Some of the Council members left alive, the ones who were harder to kill, stood shaking and in shock, while others seemed completely emotionless as he stepped into their line of sight. It was futile to fight back and everyone in the room knew it. The Society had them utterly surrounded, and backed into a corner.

"No need to look so horribly frightened," Kurt said finally, in a tone that almost could have passed as sympathetic. "I'll do you all a favour and end this as quickly as possible."

Kurt surveyed the rest of the room. A man and a woman, very highly regarded on the Council (judging by the clothes they wore), stood in the back, glaring at Kurt with more contempt than he thought they should possess. His lips curled downwards into a frown. What nerve these foolish Elementals possessed, actually patronizing the one with the upper hand!

The woman moved to adopt an attack stance and Kurt reacted swiftly, raising his hands, which were truly the best trigger for magic. Before the couple could attack, Kurt shot four long tendrils of flame, ricocheting between his fingers before flying through the air, coiling around the couples wrists and immediately paralysing their movements. A fire lock. This was Kurt's usual mode of attack, locking and paralysing victims in a personal set of fiery chains. If the caster was powerful, the attack could successfully nullify any other forms of magic, cutting off the victims' circulation for magic to flow. Fortunately, Kurt was as strong as they came.

He moved towards the immobilized couple, more curious than violent at first. He always thought it was nice to speak with his victims, to get a real sense of their character. Memories, after all, were the only thing that remained of a person, and Kurt liked to file them all. The man and woman—he assumed they were a couple by how closely together they stood—didn't even flinch as he advanced towards them.

"I am truly sorry that you two had to be caught up in this mess," he said rather flatly, concentrating on keeping the flames locked around their wrists. The man hissed in pain. Fire did indeed burn flesh, and even Elementals were not spared from that. Shockingly, despite her steaming flesh, the woman regarded Kurt with a sneer. Too bad, Kurt thought, she was a real pretty thing, with dark blue eyes as violent as a storm that pulled him into her defiance as their gazes met. Long, black hair framed her angular face and spilled down her back. Such an alluring Elemental, she was too beautiful to die, yet too important to be spared. Her husband, who was writhing in pain beside her, had dark green eyes that held an impressive level of contempt.

"My name is Kurt Bell and I work for the Society," he said softly to the woman, resisting the urge to reach out and push back the lock of wild black hair that cascaded like a waterfall over her forehead. The couple triggered a faint memory in his archive of faces and names. "Travie." The name rested heavily on his tongue, as he realized who they were.

"You are the famous Travies," he continued, not managing to keep the surprise from his voice. His expression ran sour, curdled by the Travie family's status; they came from extremely powerful bloodlines, ones that had to be eliminated for the good of the cause. The woman remained expressionless as the famous name rushed past his lips, but something in her posture shifted ever so slightly, giving him all the confirmation he needed.

"The Society's goal is to create an ideal world. Mortals and Council members shall not be present in that world. Escape is futile. You and your comrades will be put to rest here." He gestured to the huge window, through which could be seen the swirl of chaos below them in the blood-splattered streets.

The woman released a dry laugh as she realized the horrid truth to his words, but her eyes suddenly looked sad and defeated.

"Run!" The woman's voice echoed throughout the room, authoritative and demanding. Her comrades still alive and mobile reacted to her order, fleeing the room past the other Society members. Kurt made a swinging motion with two fingers, signalling his workers to go after the slew of members who had fled. They moved with silent, merciless obedience.

Kurt smiled, the room now completely empty but for himself and the famous couple.

"Nothing good ever comes out of being a martyr," he said softly, taking a moment to appreciate the couple's fearlessness, and their quick reaction to the crisis.

"Foolish man," the woman spat, coldly. "A stronger, smarter generation is coming. They will walk the earth as the ashes of your organization rain from the skies. I know it is so. My children have been brought into this world, and as you rip my time away from me, I rest in peace with the knowledge that I have taught them justice, and have showed them what's worth fighting for. They will crush you and all that you stand for."

Kurt repressed a sigh. It wasn't uncommon for victims to get cocky and self-righteous before their demise. The man on the other hand remained silent. He held a steely glare, but the mention of his children had a calming effect, and an almost happy expression passed over his face. Kurt decided to grant them their peace in that moment. He whipped a gun out of his pocket, pressed his finger against the roughness of the trigger, and fired once at the man. It was a clear shot to the chest, to be quick, and Kurt had never missed once. The man's limp body hung in the air for a moment, at the mercy of Kurt's fire lock, before he was released and his corpse fell soundlessly, the peaceful look still apparent on his face. The woman produced a desperate gasp, tears streaming down the curves of her cheeks as Kurt turned towards her.

"Don't worry," he said, greedily taking in as much of her beauty as he could. "I'll make this quick." Taking careful aim, he fired the gun squarely at her centre and felt wisps of pity crawl through his veins as he watched her now-lifeless form crumple to the ground beside her husband. He looked at the fallen couple once more before turning around to take inventory of the situation. No survivors. The plan was a success, just as he'd anticipated it would be. He stood for a few moments, committing the whole incident to memory before his workers soundlessly slipped back into the room, their job clearly finished. He gave a curt nod to his workers, who stood quietly, awaiting his next command.

"The project was a success," he said, concealing any remnants of emotion. "Please report promptly back to your stations."

"Over two thousand mortals dead. Over thirty Elementals dead. The plan was successful," Kurt announced one hour and thirteen minutes later, as he and the rest of the parties involved began to arrive at their designated meeting place.

Finally, they all were seated at an oversized table, in a room that was proportionately even larger, mulling over the events of the day. Kurt sat at the head of the table, seeming deep in thought, his expression riddled with tension.

Truth be told, Kurt's plan was conducted flawlessly; plenty of mortals had been eliminated and several Council members executed. After all, the annihilation of a few thousand mortals was hardly more than a drop in the bucket when compared to the overall population. Billions of people walked the earth and it was mathematically impossible that Kurt and the Society would have sufficient time to obliterate everyone. No, they needed something bigger, something powerful beyond measure, but ... the only possibility that lay lurking at the back of his mind was absurd. He hardly thought anyone would disagree with the impossibility of the task, but he predicted none would agree that it was a plausible avenue to explore. He, in his right mind, knew *that* route simply wasn't supposed to be possible, but a difficult route presented a challenge and Kurt liked challenges.

"However, we will need to schedule as many massacres as possible; a few thousand mortals dead is nothing," he continued, suddenly exhausted, the weight of the afternoon wreaking more havoc on him than he cared to admit. The rest of the members in the room remained silent, but many couldn't help but wonder why more scheduled murders would need to be arranged if the project had been a success.

"My dear colleagues, I am afraid our attempts of cleansing the earth is futile," Kurt sighed, raking a hand through his short-cropped blond hair, making him look far older than twenty-four. "We need something bigger, something better if we truly ever hope to accomplish this goal." He spoke quietly, yet firmly.

"There is no other way!" argued a desperate voice from the back. An excited chatter skittered throughout the room.

"Silence!" Kurt thundered after a few moments of listening to their aimless babble. "There *is* another way! Quite possibly the *only* way." The temperature in the room almost seemed to drop, as if waiting for Kurt to announce the severity of the solution.

"Our only chance is the Orb. But as I am sure you all know, it has been divided into four separate crystals and scattered across the globe." He shook his head, frustrated. "The four crystals aren't even accessible without an Orchin, dammit!" His voice escalated, thick with frustration, and he fought to contain his temper. Temper was a flaw and Kurt couldn't afford flaws. He pressed the pads of his fingers to his temple, clearing his mind before facing his subordinates once more.

"The formula is simple, without an Orchin there will be no Orb. An Orchin hasn't been born in centuries. The one thing we need is the one thing we can't have ... but we can keep looking. We can always keep looking for one." He shrugged, flexing his muscles as they contracted against the weariness of his bones. "A pity they're extinct; it would've made our jobs *so* much easier."

A few dared to agree with him, simply murmuring words of praise.

"No matter," he said. "We cannot sit here and wait for an Orchin, though we will look everywhere. We must find other means. I have faith that we can accomplish this; we are the Society!" Kurt was part of the Society, and the Society always got what they wanted. The means of getting there were irrelevant, as long as the end result was the same.

"Our means of obtaining our goal is, at the moment, inconclusive. More information will need to be gathered before making any final decisions. I have decided that, for the time being, we will all stick to carrying out the executions." It was clear that Kurt was almost done talking, as he pressed his thin lips together. "We'll meet soon, I'm sure." He rose from his seat, gazing down at the floor across the room.

"I have a job to get back to after all."

With that, the man was gone, strolling out the door as if the very ground he walked upon belonged to him. The people left inside sat gaping, and those who happened to glance out the window would have seen a black trench coat flapping in the wind before disappearing inside a silver car. None of those at the gathering really knew where the man disappeared to, yet they were aware of the pool of rumours floating around. Most took no heed of the rumours, passing them off as ridiculous. Surely such an important Society representative wouldn't be caught dead doing such a ridiculous job. Nevertheless, there obviously was some motive behind it, some purpose, just like there was behind everything Kurt Bell did. As he liked to say, every detail is important in order to achieve the ultimate end result. And if all went well, a brand new world—the end result to Kurt's madness—would be more than worth it.

CHAPTER I

LIGHT IT UP

"Can you quit it already?" I hissed, to possibly the most annoying person in the world: Tori Mender.

"No!" she shot back, with an air of defiance that almost matched mine, and continued to flick me with her sharp, red ballpoint pen. The tip of the pen grazed my forearms, a nuisance more than anything, but one that I had endured for over an hour.

"Quit it," I whispered through gritted teeth, losing what was left of my thinning patience.

My math teacher, Miss Meeks, looked up from her book and glared. I clamped my mouth shut and she returned to her reading. This was ridiculous.

"I said stop it," I growled, with an amount of malice in my voice that surprised me. It finally dawned on me to move away, so I picked up my battered chair and dragged it forward. I plopped it next to another desk and refocused my muddled brain on what was now a pathetically blank test sheet.

Any possible knowledge I had of mathematics was unreachable now; I couldn't even count the number of times I had been interrupted. I really had no intention of failing math, and I certainly didn't want to endure my parents' wrath about failing a subject, but that seemed completely plausible since I could barely concentrate. I concentrated for all of ten seconds before Tori's weapon of choice got sharper. The tip of her ballpoint was quite sharp, and she dug it deep enough into the crevices of my arm to cause me discomfort.

I glanced up, meeting Tori's dark brown eyes, which were riddled with anger, and a hint of conceit. Her sandy blonde hair framed her normal-looking face; she looked completely average, and yet ... I knew better. She was evil, housed in some plain-looking, blonde form. She gave blondes an even worse name than we already had, which I couldn't help but take a little personally.

Despite how much she seemed to loathe my very existence, I couldn't help but try to make sense of it. Tori's motivations were clear: She craved dominance and wanted to manipulate with her constant pestering. I figured she also adored attention, and I briefly wondered what it was in her life that deprived her of it. But in the end I could feel no empathy, as her current goal in life seemed to be taunting and badgering me until I I snapped.

The flicking continued until the flesh on my arm begun to redden. I would lose this game if I gave her any sort of reaction, so I remained unaffected, pursing my lips shut. Never mind this stupid test, graduating high school would be impossible to finish if things carried on like this.

As to why Tori Mender seemed to hate my guts, I really had no idea. I had no memory of doing anything to scorn her. Quite possibly, she was just a terrible human being, which seemed to be the only possible answer. I fastened my unnerving green eyes onto her cold brown ones again, and somehow, she still had the audacity to continue flicking me.

Until she had developed the wonderful new habit of tormenting me like this in class, gloating in my misery and sucking it up like some addictive drug, I had remained unmoved by her taunting. For quite a while now I had endured an impressive array of insults, and more than a couple of physical attacks. I knew that not fighting back would do more than just hurt my pride, it would make me lose the battle against Tori. My anger and frustration had been building up since the moment I walked into class, and suddenly the solution was more than clear. Quickly, I lunged out of my seat and struck, like some wild animal pouncing on a prey. I snatched the red pen out of her hands before she even had a chance to blink.

Tori glanced down at her empty hand, a smile quivering at the edges of her mouth. I knew she liked it when I reacted. She made a quick lunge to grab the pen out of my hands, but I was faster and dashed towards my seat a couple feet away. With little effort, I tightened my hold and snapped the stupid pen in two, producing a loud cracking noise that reverberated throughout the classroom. The noise earned me a few noticeable stares, but I was beyond caring. I dropped the remains of the pen on the floor and they fell with a clatter. I gave a smug smile. Then she looked down, chuckling softly.

"What?" I practically seethed.

"Look down," she said.

I gritted my teeth, glancing down to where she was so intently focused. My hands were completely covered in red ink from the pen. I could practically hear her congratulating herself on my display of stupidity, and suddenly, without thinking, I snatched her math test off her desk and smeared my red inked palm all over the paper. I furiously rubbed my hands across the entire sheet, and then, to top it off, I very politely (if I do say so myself) placed the test delicately back on her desk.

"Hand *that* in." I said gleefully, as her eyes narrowed into angry slits.

Unfortunately, I saw Tori around school more than I liked, and the teachers had this ludicrous idea that if we sat beside each other we would *magically* become friends. Sitting beside Tori was becoming such a hellish nightmare.

"Miss Meeks!" Tori stood up, slamming one hand on her desk and interrupting the silence. "Alyssa ruined my test!" She held up her red sheet as proof.

I quickly folded my hands on my lap, away from Miss Meeks' prying eyes, but it was too late. It was impossible to deny the claim, so instead I just sat in my seat, jaw clenched, and with glaring hatred in my eyes I retorted back to Tori.

"It's not like you would've passed anyway."

"Alyssa!" Miss Meeks snapped icily, looking up from her book. "Does it even bother you in the slightest that one more complaint against you will get you suspended again?"

I almost winced at the memory of my first suspension, which was the result of another one of Tori's games—one that I had lost quite disastrously. Did I really care if I was suspended again? Not exactly; it was like a forced vacation, but I didn't want another red flag appearing on my transcripts.

"Yes, thank you for asking. It does bother me that I might get suspended again," I said quite calmly. If I was good at anything, it was concealing my emotions. I was exceptionally good at that. Yet, containing them was a whole other problem altogether.

Miss Meeks cocked an eyebrow and pressed her fingertips to her temple. "Well you're treading on a thin line Miss Brooks, so *sit down now*."

It took every ounce of my self-control not to explode with the burning rage I was attempting to suppress.

"Enough is enough," Miss Meeks said. "Do you understand me?"

"Understood." My voice was utterly still and flat, but I could hear the tone of contempt, thinly veiled below the surface. I was so close to exploding, and boy did I want to let it happen, but the idea of getting suspended again wasn't very appealing. There was no point in arguing. Tori had every adult wrapped around her little finger.

Miss Meeks wordlessly held out a new test to Tori, who got up to grab it and then bounced back to her desk. I ducked my reddening face towards my test sheet, trying to tune out the conversations circling the room.

It took a minute to realize that my hands were twitching, so I began taking deep breaths and held myself back from punching her square in the face. Doing so wouldn't exactly prove that I had a handle on my "anger problems," as the teachers called it—which I really didn't have, by the way, but thanks to Tori everyone saw me as an angry psychotic freak.

It wasn't really shocking as to why I spent almost my entire time in isolation ... or maybe I was just unaware of my social disabilities. Either way my life had been lacking any kind of friendship, for as long as I could remember I was always alone. I remember my mother trying to console me, in earlier years, with the excuse that I was "just different." Maybe I didn't want to be different. Sure, isolation stung, but over time I grew mentally and physically stronger and I was used to functioning on my own. I wore my independence like a second skin.

Did I want acceptance? Yes. But, undeniably, I wanted revenge so much more. With a weary sigh, I ran my fingers through the silky strands of my hair and eyed my test one last time, before giving up entirely.

I made a mad grab for my water bottle and uncapped the lid, taking a drink while still managing to maintain my glare. No worthy plots of revenge came to mind so I just continued to stare, at my classmates, hoping that my bright green eyes were as unnerving as everyone claimed them to be.

I could hear Tori shifting ever so slightly in her chair. Then sharp kicks started digging painfully into the back of my knee. The top of her boot was surprisingly sturdy and managed to hurt when she struck my leg. Of course, Miss Meeks was engrossed in her book once again. My peers were busy frantically scribbling. No one noticed anything. They wouldn't even notice if my hair was on fire.

"Tori," I growled, "Remind me again why I deserve to sit in front of the worst human being on the face of planet."

"I ask myself why I get to sit behind you too." She leaned forward on her chair until we were mere inches from each other. "But I guess I'm just lucky."

Before I had time to utter another snappish remark, she took a single finger and pushed over my open water bottle.

Water came pouring out, soaking my whole desk, including my now sodden test, and then sloshed over the edges and doused my clothes. I blinked in disbelief while water dripped onto the floor, splattering in fat droplets.

"I'm going to kill you." I breathed. Her eyes didn't move from my face, which by now was completely red with rage. She leaned towards me and spoke softly into my right ear.

"You're disappointing, Alyssa."

"I'm sorry, is my misery not enough for you today?"

"I thought you were smarter than this ... but you're just worthless. And I can see in your eyes that you know it too."

"*Shut up!*" I roared, unable to keep my flaring anger in check any longer. I rose out of my chair, knocking it over with a loud clatter, and trying to think of a fitting insult. I loomed over her chair as she blinked up at me, the smug look in her eyes veiled by long lashes.

The class went dead silent—twenty-four pairs of eyes staring. At that point I couldn't have been further from caring.

"Alyssa!" Miss Meeks shouted, her eyes wide with the same wariness everyone else had when looking at me. "I will not tolerate this kind of behaviour! Turn around and face me!" I turned, averting my eyes from her stare.

Miss Meeks blinked. "Why are you all wet?"

"Why don't you ask her?" I said, pointing to Tori. I knew I sounded pretty crazy but everyone thought so poorly of me anyway. How could it get any worse? At the very least, I thought, this must be a hell of a show.

"It was an accident!" Tori pleaded. "The lid wasn't on!"

I produced a growl so threatening that it made even the toughest delinquent students scoot away. "She was kicking me!"

"I wasn't!"

"Give it up," I scoffed, "I'm being framed by an egotistical lunatic."

"Miss Meeks!" Tori cried. "She clearly has anger problems!"

"What!" I shouted, waving my arms in disbelief. *"I don't have anger problems!"*

There was a moment of silence that prompted me to take stock of the situation. Horrified, I realized how believable I sounded, and dropped my hands loosely to my sides. I took a deep breath and let it out slowly. "I don't have anger problems," I repeated, with a calmness I didn't feel and that didn't fool anyone.

"I've heard enough," Miss Meek finally snapped. "Apologize right now Alyssa."

There was no way I was going to say sorry to that *thing*. I balled up my fists again, my nails digging into the skin of my palms. I was so profoundly angry I could barely take in any air.

"I believe," I said, dead serious, "that I'd rather be shot in the head."

Miss Meeks' eyes widened. "I said apologize, right now."

I bit my tongue and the room fell into a heavy silence that practically dripped with tension. Miss Meeks waited patiently for my apology, drumming her fingernails against the hard exterior of a textbook. Well, no matter how long she waited, she wasn't going to get what she wanted.

I looked at the clock, wondering how long I was going to stand there. Two minutes? Three? The ticking of the clock did little to reduce the fervour of my rage. I was sick of it all. Then it suddenly occurred to me that my insides felt like they were on fire.

I fixed my glance on the recessed light in the ceiling above Tori's head, trying to distract myself. I felt so horrifically bad; maybe I *did* have anger problems. Regardless, none of this ever would have happened it wasn't for Tori.

I took a big gulp of air and unclenched my fist, finding a reprieve in the heat of my rage. Suddenly I was aware of an incredible adrenaline rush from within me, sort of like pressure that builds up in a shaken soda. The world suddenly went red.

"Alyssa ... ?" Miss Meeks inquired faintly. "Are you—"

Her words were cut short by a deafening popping noise that radiated throughout the room. The noise vibrated the floor and rattled the desks like a localized earthquake.

I whipped around just in time to see the light bulb above Tori's head shatter into a thousand pieces. Startled, I jumped out of the way, and screamed so loud it could have shattered another bulb. The explosion had been instantaneous and violent, as though the molecules in the glass could no longer stand being near each other. Glass flew everywhere like raindrops, but most of it (unfortunately or fortunately depending on how you looked at it) fell directly onto Tori's head. She let out a surprised scream, her hands automatically flying to her head. The glass had already tumbled down, spreading out and decorating her in little sparkling pieces.

I stood gaping, my jaw hanging halfway to the floor. What just happened? All the baffled looks on the students faces confirmed that I wasn't imagining things in my head, this actually happened.

All the anger that I was feeling moments before disappeared, and the fire that was burning through my veins finally extinguished. I felt better than I had in a long time, but most notably, I felt different.

It felt like I had been standing behind a blurred lens my whole life, and it was only now that everything was coming into focus. I saw the individual tiny pieces of glass on Tori's hair and shoulders. The whispers circulating the room were no longer whispers. They were now loud voices that shrieked in my ears, and pounded against my skull. Suddenly just being in this room was too much.

"Tori," Miss Meeks exclaimed, her eyes wide, "are you all right?"

A shadow of mortification spread over Tori's face. "No! Obviously I'm not! A freaking light bulb just exploded over my head!"

Miss Meeks reached down to help Tori out of her chair. Remnants of plaster and glass still tumbled down from above. I glanced upwards into the now giant hole in the ceiling where the light used to be.

"What *was* that?" I finally asked, my eyes wide with disbelief. Any remembrance of my expected apology was forgotten and Miss Meeks shrugged.

"I haven't the slightest idea. Maybe some weird chemical reaction ... ?" Her voice trailed off and the entire room seemed to shift with unease.

"Alyssa, go call the janitor to clean up this mess," she said, waving me away. I still wore a shocked look on my face as I slipped through the classroom door, taking my well-deserved leave. I made my stop at the janitor's office and rapped my knuckles loudly against the wooden door.

"Hello?" I called hesitantly, "Is anyone in there?"

"I'll be right there," answered a gruff but somehow kind voice. I waited patiently and the familiar face of our school janitor appeared. He was a burly man, probably in his late fifties with a mop of curly brown hair coupled with twinkling brown eyes.

"Hi!" I smiled tightly. "There was an accident in our classroom."

"Yeah, what kind of accident?"

"Um," I said sheepishly, "a light bulb exploded." He looked at me incredulously before giving a genuine hearty laugh.

"Kid," he said smiling, "go back to class."

"No! I swear! A light bulb really did explode, right over a student's head!"

"You're sure?"

"Completely sure."

"You better be," he said, giving in and grabbing a bucket of cleaning supplies. I led the way down an array of winding hallways and back into the classroom. He followed me inside, tentatively, and scratched his head as he surveyed the room.

"Hey kid," he remarked, as he glanced up at the gaping hole in the ceiling, "how did this even *happen?*"

"Trust me," I said slowly. "I have absolutely no idea."

"I'm sorry," my mother exclaimed later that night, a deep frown etched into the planes of her face. "Explain this to me again."

I was currently in the process of explaining to my mother why I seemed to be in such a great mood. I was rarely this happy, and the mere mention of the incident had me grinning.

Her face was blank as I quickly retold the story, and when I was finished, I caught a flicker of another emotion behind her eyes, it looked like panic.

"So what?" I asked, more amused than anything, glancing at her fidgety body movements. "You don't believe me?" How could she? How could anyone, if they hadn't witnessed it firsthand?

"You're this happy because a light bulb exploded?" she inquired, ignoring my question.

"Yes," I nodded. "Right over this girl's head. And I was angry with her too. Should've seen the look on her face. Serves her right." At that, my mother's eyes went impossibly wide, her mouth dropping open in shock. The look was almost startling, and I was about to ask about it when I was interrupted by my father, who chose that moment to breeze through the kitchen.

"Eric!" my mom said in a clipped tone, shooting my dad a look that was completely foreign to me. He didn't even bother acknowledging my presence. He seemed to instantly understand the nature of my mom's look and nodded quickly. There was a moment of awkward silence as they both looked at me.

"Um," I mumbled, a bit unnerved by the horrified looks, "what's wrong?"

"Alyssa do you mind stepping outside for a few minutes while your father and I speak privately?"

"Actually, I do mind but thanks for asking."

"Alyssa please," my dad said, "your mother and I need to have a talk."

"You can talk with me here," I challenged, crossing my arms defiantly.

My dad did not look amused with my suggestion, and motioned me toward the doorway with a wave of his hand. When I didn't move, he glared. "It'll just be for a few minutes."

I didn't budge and he sighed, moving himself out into the hallway with my mother trailing behind. I frowned, peering after them with my curiosity most definitely piqued. I was almost tempted to follow them, but with the open design of my house, there was nowhere to hide and eavesdropping was definitely not an option.

"No Eric, it's time," my mother suddenly hissed. I whipped around, half expecting them to be whispering right behind me. Yet they were still conversing in the hallway. I frowned. I heard my dad shush her, and then it got quiet again. Despite having extremely sharp hearing, their hushed voices were so low now, that they were practically inaudible. Only if I really concentrated could I make out some of their faintly whispered words.

"Sienna," my dad said, "if she knows who she is, she could ..." I didn't catch the last part of his sentence as it faded out, and I grinded my teeth together in frustration.

"We've known what we'd have to do ... ever since that day," my mom replied earnestly. "We did what was necessary ... had to keep her safe ... can't feel guilty."

"What will happen?" My dad questioned.

"She'll ... no choice but to go to Magnorium," my mom answered, sounding impatient. "We knew it was coming ... held off as long as possible ... you know that." I slid deeper into the cushion of my chair, biting my lip. Who were they talking about? Me? What was Magnorium? Was I just flat out losing my mind?

"She won't know anything ... too far behind." The conversation resumed, and I recognized the tone of my dad's voice. It was something I'd had aimed at me dozens of times. Absolute pity. Parts of the conversation were fading out, and I tried desperately to piece it together and understand.

"You'll have to ... and deal with her ... done explaining."

"I know," said my mom in a tone of defeat.

"And you know what could happen ... directly, for the first time. It could ... you'll have to ..." My fathers words sounded frantic.

I couldn't hear anything else for a long moment and then my mom's voice rang out, sharply.

"Fine!"

"*Alyssa!*" Her voice was suddenly very loud and I jolted as my tender ears adjusted.

When they both came strolling back into the kitchen, they seemed off somehow ... distracted and almost wary. This wasn't at all how my parents acted, and that could only mean that something was seriously wrong. I ran through a series of worst possible scenarios, but none seemed plausible. Their odd conversation seemed cryptic, almost like a puzzle to sort out ... except I had no pieces.

"We have something to tell you," my mom said, rather nervously.

"Are you busy?"

"Since this seems rather urgent, I guess not."

She awarded me with a tight smile and quickly sat in the chair beside me. I suddenly felt ridiculously out of place, which was terribly wrong since this was my own home.

"What we are about to tell you is absolutely the truth, and we would appreciate it if you could try to understand the best you can. You might be a bit confused at first, but that's okay."

I could think of nothing else to do, except nod. "All right."

The silence that followed seemed to last too long for comfort so I urged them hastily on as I wanted plenty of time for explanation. "Um, can we get on with it please?" I braced myself to hear that I had four months to live, or that I had inherited a mental illness-something terrible like that.

"Alyssa, are you familiar with the four natural elements that are a key part of our world?"

"What?" I blinked, taken aback. "Is this a rhetorical question?"

"No," my mom replied slowly, her voice full of patience. "Do you know of these four natural elements? They are mentioned mostly in legends and myths you may have read about."

"I don't know what you're talking about!" I exploded. "And I'm not here for a lesson on mythology!" What was the point of all this?

"Just please, explain what you're talking about!"

"Well," she continued calmly, ignoring my outburst. "The four natural elements are earth, air, fire, and water. These elements are said to be the most important aspects of our existence, and life as we know it."

"Interesting," I muttered, cocking an eyebrow. "What does this have to do with anything?"

"Other than our very existence, nothing at all," my mom shot back. I pursed my lips together and let her continue. "Just like the four natural elements there are four special groups living on earth that are directly linked with these elements. Each individual group embodies one of these elements." The more she talked, the more her voice evened out, growing slowly steadier.

"These people have powers based on the root of their element," she continued. "For example, if you belong to the water group, your powers will be strictly water based."

I was quiet for a moment, drawing my hands into my lap. I felt an unrestrained smile curling at the edges of my mouth, and I laughed dryly. Had my parents gone mad overnight or was I just the crazy one?

"Are you saying that magic exists?" I asked, with an underlying air of humour dripping from my tone. My parents both remained undeterred by my patronizing demeanour. They looked so serious that the smile faded from my face.

"You might not believe it," she whispered firmly, "but yes, magic does exist."

"That's funny. You two are doing great." After a few more moments of silence, with no one proclaiming the punchline to this joke, I grew annoyed.

"Knock it off. I don't have the time for this and it's rather frightening to think that the two of you do!"

My mother shot me an imploring look and I gulped. "This is our history, Alyssa."

"Yes, you established that already. Is this a secret history lesson that school forgot to teach?"

"Alyssa—"

"What exactly are you saying?" I interrupted. "That magic and supernaturals actually exist?"

"Yes," my dad said, with a nod of his head. "These special groups of people are known as Elementals."

The level of seriousness on their faces had me re-examining the situation. They truly did not appear to be joking. The parents I knew weren't like this. Were they simply delusional, or did I really not know my parents at all? What was going on?

"Prove it," I snapped, deciding to take the conversation as seriously as they seemed to be.

"*We* can't prove it to you, sweetie," my mom said quietly.

"What?"

"It's been this way ever since you were born. We were going to tell you years ago, but we decided to wait until you were a little older. So now, I guess ... you are old enough. Well, actually—"

"If you don't tell me what you're talking about in the next ten seconds, I'm out of here!" I half shouted. "And I may not come back, so you better be quick!"

My dad shook his head fiercely, laying a hand on my arm. I bristled under his touch; somehow it had never felt more foreign. "You don't understand."

"That's perfectly fine with me, because I don't think I want to."

"Alyssa, your mother and I are both Elementals, and that means you're one too."

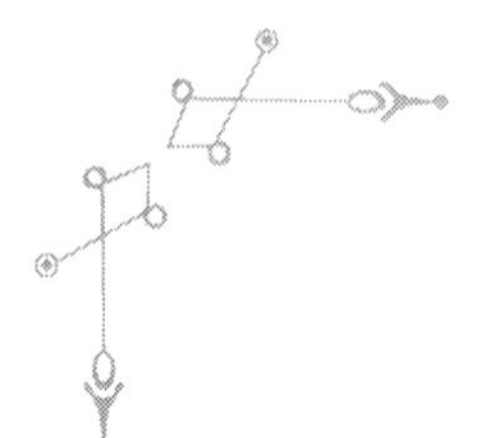
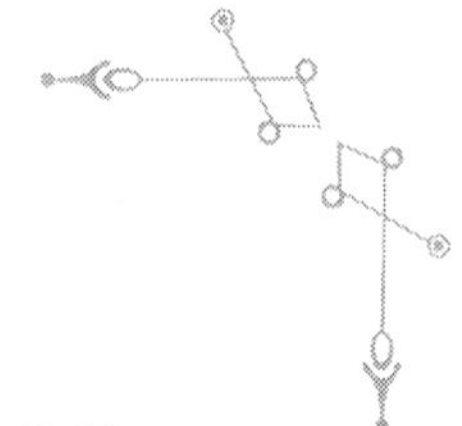

CHAPTER 2

THE TRUTH IS IN THE FIRE

After that surprising proclamation, I figured it would be safe to take my leave. I hastily jumped out of my seat and tried to make a break for the doorway. My father was lightning fast and clamped a hand around my wrist, hauling me backwards into my seat. I blinked, petrified of his iron grip.

"What are you doing?" I whispered.

"Just listen to what we have to say," my mother begged. It seemed like I wouldn't be leaving this room of my own free will.

"It's not like I'm going anywhere apparently. So go ahead. Speak."

"So ... Alyssa, it's important to understand that, while there are four natural elements, there exists five distinct groups of magic."

"So what are these five groups?" I asked sarcastically.

"Four of the five groups have a name that corresponds with the element they represent. The first group embodies the magic of earth, they are known as Terrans, meaning *land* in Latin. Remember when you were five and that bird crashed into the window? You were so upset, because you thought it died, but if you remember correctly, it was fine the next day? Terrans have the ability to heal properties of the natural world, such as animals. I'm Terran!" she exclaimed, with a proud grin.

I could only reciprocate with a scowl. The memory of the bird was foggy, but existed in my mind nonetheless.

"The second group, Skyros, represent air magic. The third natural element is fire and this group is called Drakens. The fourth group called Aquarians represent the natural element of water. Your father is an Aquarian. Remember that summer when there was a really bad drought? Why do you think our property stayed so green?"

My mouth hung open at this point, as my brain replayed the hazy fragments of my childhood.

"Lastly, the fifth group which is the most special of them all are called Orchins. They are special because they are so rare. They have the power of all the elements combined, which is why they are more powerful than anyone on earth. Unfortunately Orchins are extinct. The entire race was eradicated by other Elementals centuries ago. They felt threatened by the Orchins' dominance and power."

"Wow," I commented dryly. "That sucks. Genocide rarely works out. Can I ask you a question now?"

"All right."

"Okay, well it might be a bit shocking, but I truly want to know. Are you ready to hear it?"

"Go ahead." My mom smiled tightly.

"Are you crazy?" I snapped, my voice dripping with sarcasm.

"Your father and I are very serious."

"Well, at least I still have the decency not to be."

"Alyssa, do light bulbs just explode by themselves?" my dad interrupted.

I refused to meet his gaze. Even if he was insane, he was right. Light bulbs don't just explode by themselves.

"Eric!" my mother hissed, slamming a hand across the table. "Not yet—"

"Please, Sienna, she was raised as a mortal, so she thinks like a mortal. We're not getting anywhere like this."

"Hey! I'm right here—"

He held up a hand, cutting my next sentence off. "That was you today and we can prove it."

"What?"

"Listen to us!" my mother half-shouted, her loud voice echoing throughout the room. "Alyssa you were born a Draken, an Elemental of fire. Drakens are notorious for making things explode when angry. I take it you were pretty angry when it happened?"

I gulped. I *was* technically angry, but wasn't I always when Tori was involved?

I snorted, trying to hide my unease with a laugh. "I'm a *dragon?*"

"No. A Draken."

"So let me get this straight. I'm a Draken, Dad's an Aquarian, and you're a Terran?"

"Yes. Both parents have to be Elemental to produce an Elemental offspring."

"This is ridiculous!" My voice was steadily rising.

"I know this *seems* ridiculous," my mom whispered. "But it's the truth."

"The only truth here is that you're crazy."

"Sienna, we shouldn't have raised her as a mortal," my dad said. "I told you!"

"You know what could have happened if we didn't!" my mother shot back.

My jaw dropped at the unexpected outburst. My parents never fought. My mother glared at my father with an amount of venom I had never seen before. He scowled, rose from his seat, and wandered down the hallway into his office. He returned a moment later with a simple white slip of paper clutched in his hands.

"Now what is *that*?" I said, rolling my eyes.

"A spell. One of many from a textbook."

"Sure it's a spell. Just like you have a winning lottery ticket in your pocket, right?"

"Think of spells like training wheels. Spells help channel one's power and help you guide what you want to do with your powers. When you're not using a spell, your magic is harder to control. For example, if you wanted to light that chair on fire, a spell could channel your power, so that you don't set the whole house on fire."

I blinked, digesting his words. "Spells don't exist." I scoffed. "That's all pop culture."

My parents shared a knowing glance.

"Our magic is ancient," my dad explained, "and Elementals have coexisted with mortals since the dawn of time. A very long time ago, our culture was known and accepted by the rest of the world. Where do you think all the legends and stories come from?"

"So, does that mean I would only be able to do Draken spells? Like magic that deals with fire?"

"Exactly," my dad nodded. "Spells start you off, make you familiar with your powers, and then once you master the spells, you train to do magic without them."

"Right," I sneered.

"Read it," my dad snapped.

I quickly skimmed the paper. Whatever. It was just a bunch of random words written by two lunatics.

My father grabbed a candle off the centre of our table and nodded.

"Would you like a lighter?" I said mockingly.

"Outside," my dad commanded, motioning with his hand. "You're going to light this," he said firmly. "Read the spell and it will light. Magic is in your blood."

"You're insane!" I finally screamed, losing my carefully kept temper. My parents didn't even flinch, despite the intensity in my voice.

"Just read it!"

"If nothing happens, *then* you can think we're crazy."

I glared at them. It was a fair deal, and one that would end in my favour.

"Fine!"

I trembled as I got up from the table, storming outside into the backyard. My parents followed and stood side-by-side, blocking the door in case I tried to run. What was I, some sort of prisoner?

"Alyssa you have nothing to fear," my dad said, trying to be comforting. The paper almost slipped out of my hands. Right, I had nothing to fear besides the crazy people who had raised me all my life.

My mother plucked the large candle out of my father's hand and placed it on the grass, far away from the house. I swallowed as they both stepped backwards.

"What am I supposed to do?" I asked quietly.

"Do you know how to read?" my father answered coldly, clearly getting sick and tired of my attitude.

"Yes."

"Then read it." I stared stubbornly at them as they blocked the entrance to my house. My parents had completely lost their minds, and neither of them were going to let me leave until I obeyed. So I unfolded the paper from my sweaty palm, squinted, and began to read slowly.

"Send this wick ablaze, I shall not wither from this flame,
satisfy the needs of man, and simmer my dying rage."

I finished reading with a sigh, crushing the paper in between my fingers. The anticipation hanging in the air was palpable, but the night wore on as usual. They had wasted almost an hour of my time, and suddenly I was so terribly angry that I could barely speak.

"That might've just been the stupidest thing I have ever done," I growled. "Now you better let me walk through that door—" An incredible piercing sensation erupted in my chest. Suddenly there was pain. Pain everywhere. It was a pulsing throb, which in moments spread throughout my entire body. I keeled over, collapsing onto the grass, my face slamming into the mud. My body seemed to enter a state of paralysis for a moment, and the only coherent thought I had was that I could very well be dying.

After a few excruciating moments, the pain slowly melted away, and when I could force enough air into my lungs, I got up off the ground. The world was a giant red blur as it slowly shifted back into focus.

I screamed. The candle hadn't moved from its original spot on the grass, but it was most noticeably on fire. In fact it was burning furiously, as was the patio and most of the backyard. The flames were huge, vicious talons that curled up towards the sky, sending smoke shooting past my head. It took a while to register that *everything* around me was ablaze, and even longer to question why I wasn't burning alive. Except that, in this moment, I had no fear. The flames were mesmerizing, singing a sort of hazy lullaby that was entrancing. My father was standing at the edge of the doorway unmoving, and suddenly my mother was beside me with a fire extinguisher.

She calmly pulled the pin and pressed down on the nozzle, projecting the frothy foam everywhere. I cowered behind the extinguisher, watching in shock as the substance tackled the flames into non-existence. Within minutes, any remnants of the raging fire was gone but I was left with the haunting memory. That fire came from nowhere! Nowhere! Flames aren't supposed to ignite from uttering a ridiculous arrangement of words!

I was so confused, but more than that, I was profoundly tired. An incredible weakness washed over me, my legs turned to jelly and I crumpled to the ground with a painful thud. I laid on the grass, staring up at the starry sky, confused. Why was I floating?

A sudden panicked voice yelled my name, but I couldn't turn around to see who it was. I was paralysed in body and mind and if I could've felt anything it would've been terror. Someone was violently shaking me and I opened one of my eyes, relieved to find that I could still see. But my mother was hovering over me with an expression I didn't like, so I shut my eyes instead and slowly drifted off towards the impending darkness.

When I finally awoke, I found myself neatly stretched out across the couch. I frowned, blinking up at the white ceiling. What happened? I heard my parents shuffling from across the room, and suddenly it all came flooding back. I bolted upright, my vision blurring, and rubbed my eyes groggily. I had so many questions ... so many things that didn't make sense. If those memories were real, how could it possibly make sense?

"Mom?" I whispered timidly.

"Eric, she's awake!" my mom exclaimed softly, nudging my dad.

"Alyssa?" he asked, his voice infuriatingly calm. "How do you feel?"

"Like I just blew up half our backyard."

"Honey," my mother said, in a tone I no longer found soothing, "what do you remember?"

"Fire," I murmured, feeling a dangerous combination of fear and vulnerability: two things, I vowed a long time ago, I wouldn't let myself feel again.

"What happened?"

"You passed out for over an hour."

"An hour!" I exclaimed bewildered. "No, that's not possible—" I glanced up at the clock, only to fall short in the middle of my sentence. A whole hour had actually passed.

"Well, thanks for not calling an ambulance or anything."

"The situation is quite difficult to explain," my dad answered, moving to sit next to me.

"What else do you remember?"

"Everything," I snapped. "I didn't hit my head, I just blew up the backyard." Saying it aloud almost made me cringe. But who was I to deny blatant proof that was right in front of my very eyes?

"Do you understand now?"

"Do I want to? No, but I'm going to have to," I answered truthfully, the words tumbling out of my mouth before I even realized I was going to say them, "because this conversation is clearly far from over." I sighed and looked at my mom. "Can I ask you a question?"

"Go ahead," she answered, smiling.

"Am I ... are you ... are we human?" Funny, in that moment, it was the only thing I wanted to know.

"Well, first, Elementals usually refer to humans as "mortals", although I don't know how that started. It's not like we're immortal. Lord knows we die just like they do. However even though we look like humans, we are not human."

I nodded, squeezing my eyes shut. Did I even want to be a part of a race as cruel as that anyway? Yet there were so many good things about being human. Being able to love, the feeling of sadness, the feeling of anger ... sometimes, human emotions were the only thing that made me feel alive. But as long as I could still feel, I would always be a person, right? It felt like my personal identity, or what little I had of one, was being shattered piece by piece as my parents answered more questions. I didn't know if I would be able to rebuild.

"Was everything you said true?"

"Yes."

"So I'm a Draken, one of the five Elementals," I said, testing the foreign words. My parents exchanged an undecipherable look.

"Yes, you are," my dad answered. "But there's more."

"How much more?" I inquired, my stomach sinking. I didn't know how much more of this I could take.

"A lot more," he muttered. "Let me explain in further detail. 'Supernaturals' is a broad term used to classify beings that include Elementals and numerous other creatures."

"Like what?"

"The list is endless. Witches, Demons, Spirits, stuff like that."

"Wow," I commented dryly. "It's like a giant Halloween party, isn't it?"

My father glared. "This isn't a joke."

"Oh, I wasn't joking. This is a lot to process."

"We're not done," my mom interjected, rather unsympathetically. "Alyssa, you must understand a few things from here on out. First, Elementals have their own government system and revealing our magic to mortals is a serious offence." They looked at me sharply. I had made the light bulb explode over Tori's head. Me. But it all happened so fast, and most importantly, she deserved it.

"Hey, you can't you go blaming me for today," I warned. "A little heads up would've been nice."

"You need to take this seriously!" my mom snapped. "Our kind are always in danger. There are traitors and corruption everywhere. Be careful."

"I *can't* be cautious of things I know nothing about," I said solemnly. Her expression clouded over, as if recalling a slew of haunting memories. I could see her jaw working furiously to contain a temper I had never seen from her before. She took a shuddering breath.

"There are evils in our world, evils that have yet to be brought down by the bravest and best of our Elementals. We call that evil the Society. The Society is the most powerful Elemental organization on the planet. They're a gang of murderers who are obsessed with eliminating all mortals and any supernaturals they see fit. You will need to be taught about these things, and be extra cautious."

"Well what exactly can I do?" I asked, eyes round with disbelief.

"The things you can do, Alyssa," my mom smiled, "are unfathomable. The possibilities are endless."

"Then you can teach me everything you know, right? If there's more, I want to learn it." I was almost excited at the thought.

They both paused. "We're not going to teach you, you're going to get proper lessons at a special school."

"What? I go to a school, thanks." The tension in the room spiked, and suddenly they were looking at me almost apologetically. It was a look I didn't like.

"There's a school in Arizona, called Magnorium," my dad explained gently. "It's a special school run by Elementals who take in kids like you. It's just like real school, except half the time they're teaching you magic, and the other half they teach mortal subjects. Magnorium helps train Elementals to live in the real world. We're going to send you there. It's for the best, honey." My head was spinning out of control, taking in all this information with no proper place to store it. I didn't understand. They were sending me away? To some foreign boarding school?

"You have to go there or else something like this could happen again. Next time you could seriously hurt someone. Magnorium is the only school in the world that teaches you how to use and control your powers."

"So what you're saying is that I have to move to Arizona?"

"You really have no choice in the matter. All Elementals attend at some point. It's a requirement," he added, as if reminding me that I *had* to go anyway would somehow make me want to go more.

"Did you go there?"

"Yes and so did your mother. It's a great school."

She nodded vigorously. I didn't trust their judgement. I would never trust anything they did or said ever again.

"But," I swallowed nervously, "I don't know anything about magic."

"That's why you're going."

I looked around the room at my normal-looking kitchen, and my parents who were quite the opposite. When I reflected on my life, when did this home or going to school here ever bring me any happiness? It didn't, and it never had. I had never felt contentment, only a routine that had been drilled into my head over the years.

Yet now things beyond my wildest imagination existed, and suddenly I had an arsenal of power at my disposal. I wanted to learn more. I needed to. Would it really be such a loss to pick up and leave this world behind? Could I blame myself for *wanting* to start completely fresh?

I sighed, rubbing my temples. "I am *so* confused. You drop this Elemental bomb and now you're just going to ship me off to some weird boarding school?"

"Yes." Neither of them looked or sounded very sorry.

If they truly sent me, I would be the epitome of unprepared, and it would be their fault. Hell, even now I wasn't entirely sure this whole thing wasn't a dream. But even still, the idea of staying home seemed oddly unappealing.

"I guess it beats going to school here," I finally said, with a tight smile. I couldn't deny that I felt frightened, being plunged into a world I knew nothing about. "But don't you think you should show me a bit more of this magic stuff before you send me—"

"Unfortunately there isn't time for that."

"Then make some time."

My dad cleared his throat, refusing to meet my gaze. "I'm sorry. We already called for someone. There is no more time. You leave in three days."

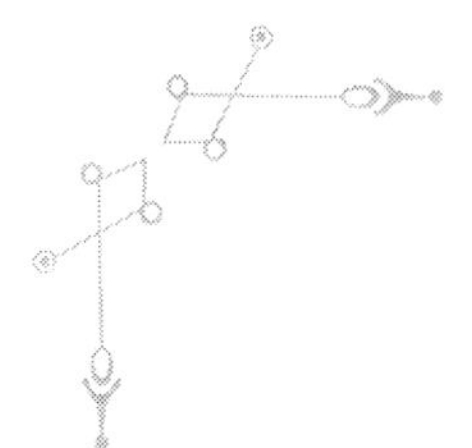
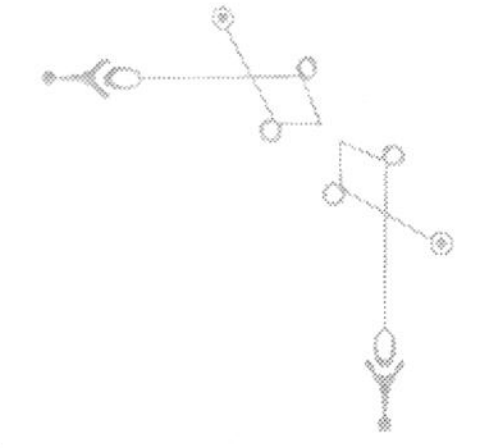

CHAPTER 3

SURFS UP

"I don't think this is very fair at all," I complained to my mother early the next morning. I had woken up to find that reality remained unchanged: I was still a Draken and still leaving in three days—two if I didn't count the day that had already started.

"Two days isn't a very long time."

"I'm sorry honey, it's protocol. Do you have a lot of people to say goodbye to?"

I flushed, moving the spoon around in my cereal, distractedly. It was sad that I had not made friends in my sixteen years of life. I was just another face in an always-moving crowd; no one would miss me or even remember me after a few days. It was my fault. I had done nothing to stand out.

"I guess not." Maybe it really was for the best that I was leaving. "I just don't really understand how I never noticed any of this before." I couldn't keep the cold accusation from my voice. Was I really that oblivious to the things happening around me? My parents had said that my anger had been the outlet to releasing my magic, but I had been angry plenty of times before.

My mom sighed, pulling a chair out to join me at the table. "Power sets in at different times. Some Elementals develop their magic through training while for others it comes naturally. Emotions are always a trigger for magic. And that's what happened to you. We wanted to hold it off for as long as we could."

"Why?"

My mom smiled tightly, wringing her hands together. "We wanted you to have a normal childhood. It's a dangerous world out there. We didn't want you to be part of it until you absolutely had to." Their intentions may have been good, but it certainly wouldn't help me in the long run. I couldn't avoid a birthright, even a birthright I never knew I had.

"You'll be fine at Magnorium Alyssa; I know you will. It's a great school. Speaking of which, you're going to be late for your last day."

"Is going really necessary?"

My mom frowned. "Yes. Now hurry up."

I groaned inwardly. There was no point in stepping a foot back into that school. It had brought me nothing but stress and self-loathing. The only person who would suffer from my absence would presumably be Tori, as she would have no one left to torment. I frowned. *Tori.*

"Alyssa, are you coming?"

I shot up from the kitchen table, a faint smile playing at the edges of my mouth.

"Yeah, I'm coming."

By the time my mother dropped me off before first period, I was convinced that my idea was a good one. Coming to school only to get revenge on Tori through my magic wasn't the best direction for my moral compass, but at this point, I no longer cared. I had enough of enduring the taunting, the insults, and the fights. Before, I had no real defence mechanism, but now I did, and this one could be utilized on command if I just figured out how.

I practically sprinted through the twisting hallways, charging into the girls' bathroom. Just as I predicted, Tori stood in front of the mirror, delicately applying a thin coat of lipstick. She came here every morning without fail. I would know, because more than a few times she had almost submerged my head in one of the toilets.

The door slammed shut behind me and Tori glanced up, capping the lid on her lipstick.

"Alyssa?" She laughed, seeing me in the mirror, and whipped around to face me. "Perfect. No one's here. You really have great timing."

I calmly leaned a hand against one of the greying walls of the bathroom. Usually I avoided bathrooms during the school day, especially this one, but I wasn't threatened anymore. "I just dropped by to tell you that I'm transferring. I just thought you should be the first to know."

Dim surprise filtered across Tori's face. She shrugged dismissively. "Can't say I care about your leaving, but I do care that you don't forget about me." She took a step away from the mirror, dropping her knapsack on the floor.

I stilled, folding my arms across my chest. "I wouldn't do that if I were you. Do you want another accident to happen like yesterday?"

"What?" she snarled. "Oh I get it, you're implying it was a prank? Please. You of all people couldn't pull off something like that."

"Yeah well," I grinned impishly, "I'm full of surprises."

Tori rolled her eyes. "Alyssa, with you, what you see is what you get, a very weak and pathetic excuse of a human being."

I growled, her insult obliterating the last of my nerves. Suddenly, a red, searing burst of fury ran through my veins. The little voice of logic in my head, the one that faintly remembered my parents warning me about exposing my magic to humans, was drowned out by the buzz in my ears. I didn't even think. My hands were suddenly moving, shoving Tori's petite frame into the open stall.

She stumbled backwards before regaining her footing. Her eyes flashed with malice, and she opened her mouth to say something, but this time I was faster—much faster.

My anger built, reducing my self-restraint, and I finally let it go. There was a hiss, followed by a huge booming explosion, and suddenly Tori was screaming. The pipes connected to the back of the toilet rumbled before exploding into tiny little metal pieces. Water and metal shot up from the now-destroyed pipes like a geyser pelting down on Tori's head and ricocheting off the stall partition.

Meanwhile, the toilet in the stall was hissing and overflowing, spilling water across the tiled floors, leaving puddles forming at my feet. Tori flailed her arms, trying to regain balance on the slippery floor, and then she fell backwards, slamming her body against the toilet. Water dripped from the ceilings ... nothing had been spared from the blast. She was completely soaked, and only when I caught my breath did I realize what I had done. The pipes, which had exploded, were completely gone, replaced by a huge gaping hole in the back of the wall. The toilet itself was mostly destroyed, and most of the bathroom was wet, including where I was standing, but not me. I was completely dry.

I gasped in disbelief. Tori lay in a rumpled heap at the base of the toilet, struggling to get to her feet. She propped herself on her elbows, and when our eyes met, the colour drained from her face. Her mouth flapped open and closed, while I struggled to gather my own bearings—my heart thumping wildly in my chest.

"You know, maybe I shouldn't change schools," I said. "I feel like we've made a real bond." The anger that had seconds ago all but consumed me, turning me into a raging monster, began to simmer. All that was left was a grudge—a seemingly ever-present grudge.

She sputtered, shell shocked, leaning to the side and spitting violently. "G-get away from me you freak!"

I sneered at her. Even in the midst of her fear she was cruel. And even though I was leaving, I knew that she would continue to inflict pain ... only this time on someone else.

I took a step forward, and she scrambled backwards. "What I just did back there is nothing compared to what I'm going to do to you if I *ever* catch you hurting someone again. And even if I'm not physically here, I'll always be watching." I glowered down at her and her small frame trembled. I raised an eyebrow.

"Would you like me to repeat that? Or do you understand?"

She was silent, face whitening all the way to the tips of her hair. I leaned in closer, until we were mere inches apart. I had never felt more superior in my life, and I was frightened to find that I liked the feeling.

"I said, do you understand?'

"Yes I get it!" she exclaimed, hands trembling.

"Good." I composed myself after a moment, smiling. Suddenly the years of torment were worth enduring just to see the look on her face in that single moment.

She swallowed, clenching her jaw tightly. Her breathing was shallow and rapid, but somehow she managed to stumble to her feet. She cowered deeper into the stall, noticeably adding distance between us. "What are you?"

"That's a great question," I answered. "When I figure it out fully, I'll be sure to let you know." I recognized the shadow of horror that passed over her face, but I didn't stick around long enough to allow her to respond. I jumped over a few forming puddles, yanked open the door, and dashed down the hallways into the sea of students.

I couldn't tell where I was running towards as I zipped through the hallways; all I knew was that I wanted to leave that bathroom far behind. I couldn't get the look on Tori's face out of my head. Fear. Fear so strong it wove itself deep into the brown murky haze of her eyes. I, too, was afraid. The anger I held for Tori before I released my power was immeasurable. Anger combined with magic couldn't be a good combination. In that moment, I had truly wanted to rip her apart, and now with these strange powers, that could very well be possible. And I had no doubt that if I were placed in a similar situation, I would do it again.

On the morning of my departure, everything was calm. I woke up calm, without an ounce of fear about leaving my home behind. I suppose it was hard to miss a home when it had never really felt like one. Life here was uneventful—a melting pot of days and weeks and years. Even the last two days had passed rather meaninglessly. School had ended just as boring as it started, with the exception of the bathroom incident, and yesterday had been all about packing. I decided to bring little with me. If entering a new life was what I was being forced to do, I wanted to do it with no extra baggage.

"Are you ready?" My mother watched me with soft eyes from her place at the kitchen table, twiddling her thumbs nervously. I swallowed. I may not have minded leaving my home, but I was nervous about entering a world that I knew nothing about.

"Ready for something I know nothing about? No. But I'm going anyway, so what does it matter?" I tried not to sound bitter. I couldn't even speak about what I did to Tori, because I knew what I did was wrong. In fact, it was better that they knew nothing at all.

"Attending Magnorium is a privilege," my dad said defensively.

"I never said I didn't feel privileged," I said dryly. It felt like every little thing my parents did or said now made them feel even more like a pair of strangers.

The doorbell rang, reverberating through the silence of the house, and my dad rose from his seat to grab the door. The faint sound of excited chatter carried its way to the kitchen, and he returned a moment later with a strange man in tow.

The man was ridiculously tall; in fact, his height was so staggering that he barely fit through the kitchen doorway. His body was covered in thick, ropey muscle, his wide frame taking up my entire line of vision. Only when I looked up did I meet his eyes, a dull grey that seemed to somehow compliment the shiny baldness of his head. He was proportionately large everywhere except for his head, which was oddly small. I couldn't help but be reminded of a giant egg with tiny eyes, because that was exactly what he looked like. The man held out a meaty hand in front of my nose, clearing his throat.

"Hello Miss Brooks. My name is Mondo and I'm Magnorium's personal escorter."

I nodded, tentatively taking his hand and hoping it wouldn't break mine. "Hello."

The scowl on his face prevented me from forming another intelligent thing to say. He swooped down to grab my duffel bag from the floor, and swung it over his shoulder.

"So you're the newbie. That sort of thing is rare, but hey, Magnorium takes in everyone."

"What?" I asked curiously. "My case is rare?"

"Most Elementals are aware of their powers and develop them intentionally from a very young age. Very few people keep their children in the dark, it's seen as a disadvantage. Besides most children come to Magnorium at thirteen. You're a bit overdue."

"Great." I muttered.

"Hope you don't mind some company. Got another kid waiting outside. Couldn't believe it when they told me, two transfers in the middle of the year! Double the pay for me!"

I almost sighed in relief. At least I wasn't going to do this entire thing alone.

"Another transfer?" my dad inquired curiously. "Who?"

"The last Reeves kid. I practically had to drag him from his house kicking and screaming. You must know why. You follow politics don't you?"

"Yes," my mother remarked. "Poor boy."

"Yeah, the kid's got a mouth on him though. Sure hope you two get along better than I have, Brooks, because we got a pretty long flight."

I blinked up at him curiously. "A plane?"

"Magnorium's private jet. Hope you don't mind the air, Draken. You have two minutes. I'll be out in the car." He gave a curt nod to both my parents before turning and swiftly striding outside.

I bit my lip, and turned to my parents, who both wore identical nostalgic expressions that made me squirm. We weren't exactly on the best of terms, but I would still miss them.

"I'll see you in the summer, I guess."

"Be careful, but have fun sweetie. You're going to do great."

I smiled tightly, pulling my mom in for a hug and then my dad. I parted from them one last time as they walked me to the door.

Parked in the driveway, and looking ridiculously out of place in my neighbourhood, was an expensive, black BMW. I forced down the nerves that were rising to the surface and opened the door, opting to climb in before Mondo drove away without me.

I slid into the backseat, and a boy (presumably this Reeves kid) sat in the seat directly across from me. He had a mass of striking blond hair, and was looking at me with mild amusement. Our eyes clashed, and I was suddenly hit with blue ... so much blue that they consumed my coherent thoughts. His eyes were of the deepest blue, with flecks of gold. Somehow, his eyes made me feel like I was looking up at sunlight from under the waves.

"If you are not an Aquarian, then the elements really have a sense of humour," I blurted. Just looking at him, I felt like I was being swept away in a tsunami. His blond hair was all mussed and he pushed away a few stubborn strands that were hovering near his eyes. He looked like the type of person who should never, under any circumstances, leave the beach.

He laughed easily. "The elements aren't creative at all. Was it the eyes? It's usually the eyes." There was something almost calming about his voice. In fact, I felt more at ease in the car than I did in my own home. Mondo pulled the car out of the driveway and the boy steadied himself, turning to face me. His face was all angles, sharp and prominent, as if sculpted by the hands of an artist.

"It's a dead giveaway," I said, my lips curling into a smile.

"Well, if we're going by this highly stereotypical eye theory, then you're Terran."

I shook my head.

"Skyros?"

"Nope. Draken."

"Okay Draken, tell me, why is there another transfer student besides me in the middle of the year?"

"I can tell you a hilarious story about that, but then you have to tell me your name, Aquarian. Elementals do have names, right? Or do they just call you by your element?"

He smirked, the edges of his mouth deepening into a pair of dimples. I fought the urge to stare, and decided to just jump right into my story.

"I learned about magic three days ago. So when I say I really don't know if I'm dreaming or not, I'm not kidding. My parents thought keeping me in the dark was a great idea, but it seems like a really awful one now."

He leaned back against the plush headrest, eyebrows raised. "What happened?"

I smiled impishly. "Made a light bulb explode over this girl's head. It wasn't intentional, but I am so glad I did it."

"You must've been surprised."

"Surprised is an understatement," I scoffed. "You should've seen the look on my face."

"Yeah well, Draken magic has a lot of perks. Exploding things, making body temperatures almost as hot as me—"

"Oh really?" I laughed.

He nodded, though it was very clear that he was kidding. "Familiarize yourself with heavy sarcasm or I don't think you'll make it to Magnorium," he paused. "I'm Haven Reeves by the way."

I frowned, finally making the connection. Reeves? That name had been on fliers, posters, television ... they were one of the most famous wealthy families in America. He must've seen my expression shift and smiled dryly.

"Two things we need to establish. One, I have a girl's name because my parents were too plastered to figure out my gender, even though technically speaking it *really* isn't that hard. Two is that I am bundles and bundles of old money, and unfortunately, belong to a family that no one ever shuts up about."

"I didn't say anything about that," I said.

"Yeah," he gestured with a finger, "but you were going to."

"Fine. I was also going to say, if it makes you feel any better, that Haven is actually a unisex name."

"That is just so comforting. Can I know your name now?"

"Alyssa Brooks."

"Well, Alyssa Brooks, welcome to the world of things that shouldn't be possible, anarchy for a government, and a crazy terrorist group running around murdering people. But not necessarily in that order."

He extended his hand and I took it. A flash of ink caught my eye, and I glanced down at his wrist to see a number written on the inside of his wrist. It was etched in thick, black ink but didn't look to be a tattoo. Before I could get a closer look, he withdrew his hand, drawing it to his side. I looked up questioningly. He shook his head mischievously.

"The third thing we need to establish is that you should never stare at people's wrists. That's just plain rude."

"So does that mean I can't ask what it is?" Whoa. When did I become so blunt?

"I'm afraid not." His face gave nothing away, just a mask of blue with a smirk that was extremely irritating.

"All right," I said evenly. "Then can I ask why you're such an old transfer student?"

"I'm only sixteen! Please tell me I have at least a few good years left."

"Well apparently for a transfer that's pretty old."

"You know, Draken, considering the way your face lit up when I mentioned my age, I'm guessing you're sixteen too."

"My face did not light up," I said defensively.

"Are you not sixteen?"

"Yes."

He clapped his hands. "Excellent. Now, let me tell you something you'll probably never hear again." He paused, glancing out his window at the world zipping by. Then he leaned in, edging closer towards my seat. "I hate Magnorium with a burning passion."

"Hey!" Mondo called impudently from the driver's seat. I turned to look at the bald man as he turned his head towards us.

"There's no disrespect for Magnorium allowed in this car."

"Oh I'm sorry, what am I saying?" he gushed, mockingly. "I absolutely adore Magnorium. In fact, let's speed over the limit even more than we already are, so we get there even sooner!"

"That's the spirit Reeves," Mondo said approvingly before stepping on the gas pedal, shooting us even faster down the freeway. I gripped the edges of my seat as Haven calmly leaned back.

"Anyway there's not really much else to say." He shrugged. "Didn't want to go, so I didn't. But things change. So here we are."

"Do you know much magic?"

"Yeah, I guess you could say that."

"Kid's a genius, Brooks," Mondo interrupted from the driver's seat.

"Hey!" Haven shook his head vigorously. "Don't listen to him; he's a compulsive liar."

Mondo chuckled. "Self taught everything he knows. He's already been accepted in the advanced classes at Magnorium. What did I tell ya? A genius."

Haven rolled his eyes. "I prefer the term 'resourceful'."

"Wow!" I couldn't stop my jaw from dropping. Who was this guy? "Are all Elementals like you?"

A steady beam of light filtered in through the window, illuminating his eyes as he flashed me a brilliant grin. "Please Draken, that's insulting. No one's like me."

"Okay good," I said steadily. "I'd be kind of scared if they were."

"So would I," Mondo said, sharply turning the vehicle into the airport parking lot. I was so caught up in my conversation with Haven that I'd barely noticed the trek to the airport. But Mondo did say we were taking a private jet, and he didn't appear to be joking.

"I've already spent two days with this kid. Got at least another to go." He killed the engine, popping the keys out of the ignition. I looked out my window excitedly. I had never been on a plane in my life. Just how rich was Magnorium?

"Consider yourself lucky big guy. That's time not many have the privilege to enjoy," Haven said, swinging his side door open. I followed suit and stepped into a crowd of bustling people, all moving quickly to get somewhere. It was weird to think that not one of them was going where we were going.

Mondo threw both of our bags over his shoulder, swinging the key ring around his finger. He scanned the crowd of bustling heads for a moment, pulling the pair of sunglasses (which were resting on his bald head) down over his eyes.

"Hey you!" he called, gesturing to the person closest to him: an elderly man wheeling a huge suitcase. He approached the man with a huge smile, towering a good two feet above him.

"Here," Mondo said, removing the key ring from his finger and placing it in the man's free hand. "These are the keys to a brand new BMW. It's parked right behind me. Consider it a gift."

The man paused, looking down at the keys in his hand, his eyebrows furrowed questioningly. Mondo cut the man off before he could say anything, clamped a hand down on my shoulder, and quickly guided me through the swinging airport doors.

CHAPTER 4

A BUMP IN THE ROAD

"I kind of thought you were joking about the jet thing," I said, as the three of us hustled into the airport. Mondo shook his head quickly, manoeuvring through a sea of travellers bustling every which way.

"I don't joke. Now keep up." He flashed me a grin, speeding up his pace and turning down a series of empty hallways. I had never been to an airport before, but I was quite sure there were more than a few lines we should have been waiting in. But we did none of that. I had to run just to stay at Mondo's heels as he expertly led us through doorway after doorway.

"Do you know where you're going?" I asked already confused at the airport labyrinth. I doubted he'd ever even been to this airport, so how could he possibly know where to go?

"Of course." He pushed open the next door, and we stepped outside. We were at the top of a set of stairs that overlooked the tarmac. There were no incoming planes or passengers in this area. A lone jet sat in the middle of the tarmac and the only other person around, besides the three of us, was a smiling employee who stood at the bottom of the stairs.

"Hey Mondo!" the guy (presumably another Elemental) shouted up at us. "She's all ready for you!"

"Perfect," he said casually, tossing our two bags over the side of the railing. The bags landed neatly in the employee's outstretched hands. He disappeared with them, moving towards the back of the jet, presumably to stow them and do some last minute maintenance. The jet was utterly huge and sleek—a mass of white that was momentarily blinding. I tried not to look as astonished as I felt.

"All right. The flight should last about four hours, and there is only one rule. Do not distract the pilot with your yammering."

"Who's going to fly this plane?" Haven asked quizzically. "There's no one here, if you haven't noticed."

"I am," Mondo said, tilting his head down towards us, looking almost shocked at the absurdity of the question.

"Great. In that case, we're surely going to die now."

"Don't remind me why I hate this job, Reeves," Mondo said, rattling the flimsy staircase as he climbed down. After a moment's pause, I followed him down, with Haven hesitantly trailing after me.

The only reassurance, that we weren't the only people left in the entire airport, was the low shrieking of planes taking off in the distance.

I followed Mondo across the black tarmac and he motioned to the white staircase descending from the jet's doorway.

"Get in. We leave in five. I swear, Reeves, if you try and run for it, there is absolutely nowhere you can go where I can't catch you."

"I was only thinking about it," he said with a scowl, as he stalked up the stairs and disappeared inside the jet. I quickly hurried after him. When I crossed the threshold, my feet sank into the luxury of soft carpeting. The plane's interior was even more impressive than the outside. I cast my eyes to the rows of couches and tables. An enormous flat screen television hung neatly on the wall, along with several paintings and assorted pieces of art. There was even a full-sized fridge in the far corner, near what could only be described as a fully loaded bar, with its assorted bottles and fixtures carefully strapped and fastened down for safety in the event of bad weather (apparently the plane wasn't reserved for student use alone). Luxuries like this were too extravagant, almost to the point where it could be considered ridiculous, but that didn't mean I couldn't enjoy it for a few hours. Just like the rest of the students did.

Haven stood shockingly still, looking rather unimpressed considering where he was standing. I really didn't know much about the Reeves family, but I was aware that they were billionaires, which meant that something like this might not be all that impressive to him.

"Oh God," he finally moaned, dramatically, obviously unimpressed with the ostentatious finishings. "This is disgusting."

"I agree," I said truthfully. "But enjoy it for now."

Haven collapsed onto the nearest couch, sinking into the plush material. I hesitantly took a seat beside him; we were going to be spending this whole ride together, so I figured we might as well get comfortable with each other now.

"Look around," he whispered. "What do you see?"

"Money," I answered, peering around the room.

"Exactly. Magnorium tries to impress their students before they even arrive, but it's only to distract you from what it really is." The look on his face showed conviction. He truly believed what he was saying.

"And what is that?"

"A prison."

"All right," I said calmly. "This clearly isn't the right place for you. Maybe you should check in to a good old-fashioned public school."

"Another thing we need to establish, Draken, is that I am ninety percent easy going and like to joke around, the other ten percent is dead serious when it comes to scheming liars like Magnorium. See, they're hiding something, and I am giving myself a period of three weeks to find out what it is."

"*If* it is," I corrected gently. I didn't know what his problem was with this secret school. I had no idea if his accusations held any truth, or if he was simply delusional. Hell, I hadn't even been aware of Magnorium's existence a few days ago, and I *still* wasn't exactly sure where we were going.

The jet suddenly lurched forward with a mechanical hum, practically knocking me into Haven's lap.

"You might want to hold on."

I fought a blush, scrambling back into my seat and preparing for the impending take off. I caught a glimpse of Mondo's shiny head from the cockpit where he was working the controls. I could barely contain my excitement as I felt the jet's front wheels lift off, and then the back wheels graze the ground before leaping into the air like a bird of flight.

"It's your first time on a plane," Haven remarked as I turned to look at him.

I stared. "How'd you know?"

"Because you look way more excited than you should be."

"Well," I huffed defensively, "at least I don't look scared!"

Sitting next to him granted me a good view of his face which now looked slightly paler as he tightly clenched his jaw.

"No. Not scared," he said, "unnerved. I am unnerved. There's a big difference."

"It's your element," I said, as something dawned on me. "Elementals must feel uncomfortable in their counter elements."

"You sure got us figured out pretty quick. But you're a Draken, so what's with you?"

"I don't know." I shrugged. "It's nice. It's like nothing can get you up here."

Haven grinned. The rays of the sun coming through the windows settled a light dusting around his head, making his hair shine brilliantly. It then struck me that I had never seen a better-looking human being in my life.

"In that case," he said, "come look out the window with me." He seemed almost eager, inching over in his seat to move closer to the window. He stared out the small opening, the world zipping by in an array of astonishing blues and fluffy whites.

"You're making yourself uncomfortable," I observed, as his hand tightened its grip on the edge of the couch.

"Even though I'm Aquarian, there's something beautiful in all the elements and it would be a waste to miss it. Besides, you should try to remember that, if you have no fear, nothing can hurt you."

"Lots of things can hurt you," I joked. "Like this plane crashing or—"

"Fear and paranoia are very similar things," he interrupted. "Both of them just so happen to be all in your head."

"Maybe you're scared of fear," I said.

Haven nodded. "As they say, the only thing to fear is fear itself."

"You're quoting a dead president."

"So," Haven smiled, "you'll be surprised to learn that powerful people like presidents are often Elementals. They know fear when they speak of it."

"Fear is an odd thing," I said. "It can be used as motivation or a driving force. Some people just embrace it."

"And I guess that's you, isn't it? You're afraid of being an Elemental, yet here you are."

There was something about the way he looked at me; it was almost analytical, as if I were a puzzle for him to figure out.

I laughed, shaking my head again. "No, this isn't embracing anything. I was forced to come here."

"Then we have something in common, don't we? Draken, do you think you could trust me?"

"Well I don't know," I said evenly. "You *are* trying to make me hate a place I haven't even been to yet, and the only other thing I know about you is that you answer every personal question I ask you vaguely ... so I'd have to go with 'no'."

"Ouch." He clutched his chest, feigning hurt. "I'm just trying to teach you the ropes."

"Yes, you've been helpful," I said dryly.

He still had that impish look on his face, but then suddenly his features changed, hardening into something more serious.

"You need to be careful Alyssa, seriously. I know this all must seem like a dream come true, finding out that magic exists. A lot of the time, it *is* really cool. But there's bigger stuff going on in our world. Bigger stuff than just getting revenge on people you hate."

I reddened. He made me sound childish.

He paused. "Do you know there has been over thirty thousand mortal deaths in the last six months, lives that were taken by a group called the Society? Has anyone broken this to you yet?" He sounded sincerely concerned for my well-being. "I just don't want any more people to die ... especially people like you, who have little involvement with our world."

"That's awful." I swallowed, truly horrified. "How come someone doesn't do something about it?"

"Our government is composed of a bunch of idiots called the Council. And they try. But magic is a weapon. I've seen people utterly destroyed by it." He sounded solemn, bitterness lacing his voice.

"You sound bitter."

He snorted. "I have every reason to be. And it's enough to tell you that I'm right."

I frowned. "Can I ask why?"

"Ask away, but I'm not inclined to tell you."

I threw up my hands as he shifted his eyes back to the window. "You're incredibly frustrating."

"God I know. I pity you really." He kept looking out the window. "You're going to be stuck with me for a while."

"Well, can't say I mind *too* much," I teased, but it was the truth. If I was honest with myself, it was nice to talk to another person without them looking at me like I was invisible. But four hours was a long time to spend with another person. Still, I found that I truly enjoyed his company. He was kind and thoughtful, and his dry sarcasm kept me entertained all the way to Arizona. He was undeniably strange, but I couldn't really dwell on that without feeling like a complete hypocrite.

When Haven destroyed me again in a multi-player video game on the flat screen, I looked out the window and saw that we were descending. My ears were rapidly popping as we changed altitudes, the plane finally dipping down towards the glittering city lights. An airport came into view and suddenly we were descending towards the runway. Seeming very abrupt, the plane's landing gear slammed into the ground. We did bounce a bit, and swerve slightly on the landing strip before coming to a jolting stop. Mondo had flown the plane completely by himself and hadn't crashed it.

A few minutes later, he came back, cranked open the door, and told us to stay put as he descended the staircase that had been rolled up to the door.

A pair of muffled voices could be heard from down below and then Mondo was back, dangling a new set of silver keys in front of my face.

"We're off on another road trip!" He smiled at our exasperated expressions.

"Whatever," Haven said. "I don't know about you people, but there is ground down there and I'm going to go stand on it." Looking much more at ease now, he quickly exited the jet and bolted down the stairs.

"Hey!" Mondo seemed to view this as an escape. He glanced at me. "Reeves, don't you even think about moving!" Then he charged down the stairs after Haven. I followed after them. Mondo practically grabbed Haven by the collar of his shirt, dragging him back in the direction of the plane. This time we didn't even enter the airport.

He saw me, nodded, and then led us from the tarmac, veering to the right into a parking lot where a lone, red BMW was parked.

He didn't handle Haven very gently, shoving him into the backseat and motioning me to get in on the other side. "Your bags are in the trunk. Now let's get going."

I complied without a word, slipping in for another long drive. Mondo popped the keys into the ignition, quickly peeling onto the road. It was truly like he had the whole world mapped out in his brain or something.

"How long until we get there?"

"Oh really, Draken, there's no rush," Haven commented, his arms crossed over his chest.

"A little over an hour," Mondo said, shrugging. "Now can it, kid. Listen to some music, why don't you?" He flicked on the radio, blasting some weird Indie music from the speaker behind me. Haven groaned, slouching down and clearly getting comfortable for the long ride.

I made a point of counting the small towns we drove through, and the streets we passed, figuring it would be nice to know the route to where I would be living for the next few years. After a full hour of driving, we had driven through a grand total of three small towns and driven past only a handful of cars. Magnorium truly seemed to be in complete isolation.

Suddenly, the loud, obnoxious roar of a powerful engine cackled over the dry desert air and I frowned, peering out my window as the sound shrieked even louder.

"What ungodly thing is making that noise?" Haven complained from the other side of the seat. I glanced out the window on the driver's side, meeting the side profiles of two of the most unattractive human beings I had ever seen in my life. Usually I didn't really judge people solely based on looks, but the ugliness of these two guys hit me like a slap in the face.

There were two bikers riding beside us on a pair of Harleys, both middle-aged, with oily, misshapen faces and long grey beards that cascaded down their chests. I could even see evidence of black rotting teeth as the two bikers spoke to each other on their bikes. And that was only what I could see from my somewhat obstructed view. They were both clad in biking wear: Harley Davidson leather jackets and biker boots, as well as a couple of metal chains coiled around their necks.

I withheld my groan of disgust.

"Be lucky this isn't your window," Haven said. "My view is way better than it needs to be."

The biker nearest to the window tightened his grip around the handlebars before revving his engine, burning rubber as he sped off farther up the road. Mondo grinned devilishly from the front seat before slamming a foot onto the accelerator, shooting us forward at an even faster rate. The second biker passed us and steered his motorcycle into our lane before racing to catch up with his partner, throwing a taunting glance over his shoulder.

"Well then," Mondo muttered, his grip tightening around the steering wheel, applying even more pressure to the accelerator. Haven clutched his armrest as the car lurched forward in an attempt to catch up with the two motorcycles.

"Whoa there, big guy," Haven said tensely. "This isn't the Grand Prix."

I watched with wide eyes as the second biker suddenly spun his bike around, slamming on his brakes and cutting off the entire road. Mondo cursed as his whole husky frame shot forward as he slammed on the brakes. Haven and I both went flying forward and I flung my hands out to keep from banging my head on the passenger seat in front of me.

Our car skidded for a long, heart-stopping moment, as Mondo swerved desperately to avoid hitting the bike, and then spiraled off the road entirely.

The car wheeled over something large and bounced, landing hard in the desert sand. I looked out to see the two bikers parked at a distance on either side of our car. Our engine was still roaring, and the car's wheels still spun frantically in the sand, unable to find the traction it needed to get away. The distinct smell of gasoline wafted through the air and a loud hissing sounded from under the hood. There was a loud bursting sound and the engine died, the wheels grinding to a halt.

Mondo was shouting, absolutely enraged, bringing his hands down, slamming them again and again on the steering wheel. Haven and Mondo were out of the car before I could even comprehend what exactly had happened. I scrambled out after them.

"Hey!" Mondo shouted, glaring at his destroyed car and charging towards the nearest biker, who stood a good thirty feet away. Haven was standing beside the hood, shoulders heaving. He actually appeared to be laughing.

"What the hell were you thinking?" Mondo snarled, in a way that should've instilled terror in the biker.

Instead, the biker just eyed Mondo warily, not even flinching at the anger oozing from the seven-foot-tall stranger. He pushed his pair of sunglasses to rest atop his head, reached into his jacket pocket, and pulled out a tiny pistol that glistened under the hot Arizona sun.

Mondo's steps faltered, and he halted, catching himself before he crashed right into the barrel of the gun. He swallowed nervously, eyes flicking to the end of the pistol that was practically slammed against his forehead. I sucked in a breath.

"If you move an inch Mondo, we'll shoot."

I froze, amazed at the way the man had to fully extend his arm to even reach Mondo's head with the gun. I stared at the way his finger was laced around the trigger, and the way the tip of the gun dug comfortably into the creases of Mondo's forehead.

"You know these guys?" Haven asked accusingly.

Mondo whipped around, ignoring the gun pressed to his head, and glared at us.

"You two listen to me. If I say run, you run. Got it?"

"We're not leaving you," I suddenly heard myself say. He was our ticket to Magnorium, but it wasn't just that. I wouldn't leave anyone with these guys, not if I had the choice.

"Moron." Mondo's once stoic face was the epitome of panic now, beads of perspiration running down his bald head. "Do what I say."

"Hey shut up!" The biker tightened his grip, almost imperceptibly, around the hilt of the gun. Mondo turned his attention back to the biker, and the gun that still pressed against him. I gulped. One shot could end it all.

The second biker frowned, moving to stand beside his partner. I felt his intrusive glare drift in my direction and he grunted. "You two. Over here. Now."

My legs remained frozen as he scowled at us, and then Haven was beside me, breathing down my neck.

"Just do what they say. Come on."

His words broke me out of my petrified state, and I forced my legs to move in their direction.

"That's some nice kids you got there," the second biker sneered, leaning against his Harley.

The one who held the gun, pointed at Mondo's skull, merely shrugged. "We just need him."

"But we could take her. Ransom her off for good money," the other one suggested, moving towards me. I held my breath as he neared. He drew a sweaty hand over a lock of my hair, letting it run between his fingers. I made a small, barely audible sound of disgust, my knees trembling. He was close, too close; he smelt like dirt and cigarettes ... a smell of the vilest intentions.

"Hey," Haven barked in a clipped tone. "Don't touch her." The man laughed, letting my hair slide from his fingers. I clenched my fists to keep my hands from shaking, and released a breath.

"Ah, I like this kid. He ain't scared. Let's take him instead."

The biker with the gun was having none of it. "I said no."

"Fine." The second man grunted, clearly unimpressed, stuffing his fists into his pockets.

"How'd you two find me?" Mondo asked, through clenched teeth.

The biker with the gun sighed. "Wasn't easy, finding someone who's always on the go."

"What do you want?" I growled, faintly surprised at the firmness in my voice.

The second biker shrugged, circling Mondo indignantly, and kicking up clumps of dust into the dry air. He leaned to the side and spat before answering my question, addressing it to Mondo.

"Our money. Which you took from us. Now we're going to go get it back." He glared, shoving his elbow hard into Mondo's shoulder blades. I winced as the big man clumsily stumbled forward, just barely catching himself.

"Get on the back." He gestured to his partner's bike.

I looked desperately around, scanning the area for any other signs of life, but there weren't any. The entire area seemed devoid of everything but asphalt and dust.

Mondo stilled, and the gun slid down from the slope of his forehead to rest in the gap between his eyes.

"We just want you; not them. Get on."

Mondo's eyes shifted between me, on his right, Haven, on his left, and the gun resting on his face. Wordlessly, he moved towards the bike, slinging a leg over the seat and clambering onto the back.

"Stop!" I shouted, a bout of fury racing through my veins. "You have no right to do this!"

The first biker shrugged. "Sorry kid." He stuffed his gun neatly into a leather pocket. "You got the wrong guy to bring you to Magnorium." He grabbed his helmet, pulled it on, and climbed on in front of Mondo, who looked far too large for the motorcycle, even if he had been riding it alone. His knees stuck up at absurd angles, his feet perched precariously on the black and silver passenger foot pegs.

"Stop!" I screamed, heart hammering in my chest. They were going to take Mondo, and technically I couldn't even call this a kidnapping, because he was apparently going with them willingly! Surely as large as he was, and with his magic (whatever that was), he could have fought them off if he had chosen to do so!

"Shut up," the second biker growled and only then did I notice a matching gun in his hand.

I was so overwhelmingly angry that it hardly registered. I growled. "There's a word for people like you. Cowards. If you're Elementals, fight me without a gun."

There was the sound of a gunshot, and I readied myself for the inevitability of pain, but it never came. Directly below me, just inches from my foot, I saw his tiny black bullet embedded in the sand. My brain tried to convince the rest of me that I was fine, and not dead, but my entire body still shook anyway.

"Next time," the man sneered coldly, as he climbed onto his bike and jump started it, "I'll shoot you dead. Watch your mouth, Goldilocks."

Both engines roared to life. Mondo was silent, refusing to meet my eyes and looking down at his lap. I watched helplessly as they steered their bikes back onto the road, and sped off. They were going so fast that, in moments, they were nothing but a blur in the distance. Rage roared inside of me and I started running, throwing away any logic I possessed. I was chasing after them, running faster than I ever had in my life, waving my hands above my head.

"Stop!" I screamed, pushing my feet harder, pounding them against the scorching asphalt. Somewhere in the back of my mind I knew that it was futile, that I was clearly no match for a motorcycle, but I pressed on.

"Alyssa!" Haven shouted, taking off after me. He reached me in a grand total of twenty seconds, grabbing my arm and hauling me backwards towards the car.

"What exactly do you think you're doing?" He loosened his grip on my arm, but still held on, as if making sure I wouldn't take off again.

"Let Mondo go," he said softly. "Okay? We can't help him."

"We *have* to help him!" I exploded, my heart still thumping crazily in my chest. "We let him go ... with *them!*"

Haven shook his head. "You're definitely brave but incredibly stupid."

I drew in big shaky breaths, and it was only then that the severity of our situation hit. We were stranded in the middle of nowhere. Our driver had been kidnapped. We had no food or water or shelter. It was blazing hot, and if we were stuck here until nightfall, we would likely freeze.

"What just happened?" I whispered in shock, my mouth hanging agape.

Haven scratched his head, confused by the question. "I believe our driver was kidnapped by the twin spawn of Satan."

I shouted at him, infuriated by his calmness. "You realize we're stranded here! Right? That means we're as good as dead!" There were times to be laid back, but this really wasn't one of them.

"Be a little optimistic," Haven answered curtly, staring into the distance.

"Oh, I'm sorry," I growled. "How pessimistic of me. Maybe you can summon a tidal wave and we can surf our way back to civilization. Or maybe, if I tried really hard, using my Draken magic, a map will fall out of the sky to show us how to get to Magnorium!"

"Wow. And I thought *I* was sarcastic." He sighed, running a hand through his hair. "Listen to me Alyssa. We'll be fine. Don't you trust me?"

"No!" I exploded vehemently. "I only met you, like, a few hours ago! What if you're one of their accomplices?"

"Oh God!" Haven exclaimed, looking aghast. "Don't even put us in the same sentence. We're already on the same planet, and even that's too close for me."

"Well you're oddly calm, considering that we're stranded in the middle of a desert!"

"It's because we're close. Look Alyssa, we're so close to Magnorium that we can literally walk there. And we better start moving, because it's going to take a while on foot."

I peered off into the distance, eyes drifting down the long, endless single road. "So are you saying that, if we just follow this road, we'll eventually hit Magnorium?"

"Well, unless Magnorium is actually on the moon, then yes."

I closed my eyes for a breathless moment, trying to calm my jangling nerves. "All right fine. If we see anyone on the way, we ask for help. Remember, we still have no food or water."

Haven grimaced. "We shouldn't be out here too long anyway. Come on start walking."

"What if we don't find anything? I mean Mondo could've lied. Is he even employed by Magnorium?"

Now Haven looked serious, a muscle ticking in his jaw as he considered it, drumming his fingers against his jean-clad knee. "I suppose that is entirely possible."

"What if those guys were working for the Society? I mean, they knew what Magnorium was!"

Haven shook his head. "A lot of people know what Magnorium is. Let me tell you, Draken, the Society is a million times worse than those guys could ever dream to be." He started walking down the road, not even bothering to wait for me to catch up.

I hurried after him. The only thing we could do was stay together. We walked down the road in a comfortable silence for a good while, the only sounds being the crunch of dirt under our feet. How could this be happening? Actually *happening?* I had no idea where Magnorium was, but we needed to find it. And fast.

After a full hour of relentless moving under the sweltering sun, I was hot, tired, and my feet ached—not to mention my worries about being stuck out here at night. Also, something odd started soon in our walk. At first all I felt was a dull vibration in the pit of my stomach; it quickly spread down and through my limbs. I dismissed it as exhaustion, dehydration, or paranoia, but it could no longer be ignored.

I slowed my pace behind Haven and finally stopped, leaning towards the ground, closing my eyes and taking a deep breath. I felt shaky; there was a feeling tugging at me, pulsing angrily in the centre of my gut. I needed to sit. Haven stopped walking as soon as he noticed, kneeling down beside me.

"I think it's about time we take a break," he said gently, drawing his knees into himself and resting his chin atop them.

"You don't feel it?" I whispered.

"Feel what?"

"Tugging?"

"No definitely not."

"Okay," I said steadily, attempting to keep my face stoic. "It's clearly just me then."

"Tugging?" he asked again, with a small smile.

I sighed. I knew what magic felt like: the sweet feeling of adrenaline pulsating through your blood. This did not feel like magic. "Yes."

"Well that's a new one. I think you're just nervous. Try taking deep breaths."

I took his advice, concentrating on drawing in air through pursed lips, and then letting it back out. The exercise did little to ease my jittering nerves. I clambered back onto my feet anyway and we started walking again. After a few minutes, Haven sucked in a breath, his eyes narrowing. "Look Alyssa! The road forks."

I quickened my pace to where he stood, a couple of feet away. Ahead of us, the road split into two long curving roads, which really did nothing to clue us in as to where we were, because each one was devoid of any sign of life.

"Which one?"

"I don't think it really matters, at this point," Haven sighed, running a hand through his hair. It was too hot and dry out here; it felt like my brain was melting. It was hard to think logically or focus on anything. "I mean we're bound to come across something or someone at some point, right?"

"I guess," I sighed.

He shrugged, turning to the road on the right, and started walking. I gathered my bearings and trailed after him. Then suddenly I was screaming, and not even realizing I was screaming; the only thing I could feel was the sensation of movement, as though my body were being twisted almost entirely in half. We needed to go the other way. I was literally unable to take another step in the direction we were going.

"Alyssa?" I didn't even realize I was on the ground, until Haven was there beside me, a hand on my arm. "What's wrong?"

"We need to go back!" I whispered.

"What? Why?" His blue eyes were wide—wide with questions mixed with worry. I couldn't think. I could barely speak, consumed by this feeling ... this consuming, foreign force of a feeling.

"No." I clamped my hand around his wrist in panic. "We need to go back right now."

He swallowed nervously, eyes flickering down to the grip I had on his arm. "Calm down. You're just panicking, okay? You're having a panic attack."

I shook my head vigorously. "No, I'm not. We need to go back."

"Come on Alyssa, get up! I can't leave you here!"

"We need to go back." I was so completely adamant about going back that I would've picked him up and carried him the other way if I could have stood up.

He scrambled to his feet. He was probably annoyed, but when he spoke he was gentle. "All right fine. I'm just going to walk down there a little farther to see if there's anybody around. Okay? Don't move from this spot."

He turned to make sure I hadn't moved, before quickly jogging down the road. The road sloped, curving downwards to catch the golden rays of the sun. A minute later, he disappeared from my sight.

Suddenly, Haven yelled out my name, and in the arid desert, it really seemed to echo, amplifying my alarm. I was on my feet before I could even register my body's actions charging down the road. The feeling, which had kept me enslaved by the side of the road, heightened, and I contained my own cry of pain, pressing onward. Haven was charging towards me almost as quickly as I was charging towards him, except he was grinning, a relieved look on his face.

"Alyssa!" He caught my arm as we met and I skidded to a halt. "Come on. Let's go."

"Go where?" I asked, confused.

The grin slid off his face and he frowned. "What do you mean where? To that trailer parked by the side of the road!"

"What?" I snapped my head around, scanning the area. "Where?"

"Are you blind?" he exploded in a way that seemed very oddly out of character. "Right there! Come on! Right there!" His grip slid down to wrap around my wrist, and as he pulled me forward, I pulled back. I saw nothing and rewarded him with a blank stare.

"Haven," I said, gently pulling away. "There's nothing there. I think you're seeing a mirage. Can an Aquarian get dehydrated?"

"No!" he snapped, looking at me like I was crazy. "Look, it's right there!" His voice was laced with annoyance and I bit my lip, exasperated.

"You're hallucinating."

"I'm not hallucinating!" he shouted defensively. "There are people there who can help us! Come on!"

I took a tentative step forward. Something was wrong. "Haven, stop," I said quietly, with finality to my voice. "Please. There's nothing there! I have a really bad feeling about this. Literally." I could feel the wrongness of it in my gut.

"I'm not the one having the hallucination!" he seethed. "You are! Snap out of it Alyssa; come with me! I can't leave you here alone!"

"God," I muttered under my breath, "it's like you're under a glamour spell or something." According to my mother, who had given me the run down on dangerous magic before I left, glamour spells were a type of Skyros magic. They put unknowing people under trances, in which one sees things that aren't actually there. Glamour spells were frightening. If a powerful Skyros cast it, it would be hard to tell what was real.

Haven's head snapped up, blue eyes wide. "What did you just say?" he asked, more softly this time. Just looking at him, I realized that the theory seemed completely plausible.

"Haven," I said quietly. "This is a glamour. You're under a glamour." He looked doubtful. "Listen to me. You think you see people, but I don't! It makes sense!"

"Why would someone put a glamour spell on this road?" he asked, looking dazed.

"It would convince people like us that this is the right road to take!"

"But why would there be magic in the middle of nowhere?" he asked again.

I grinned as the pieces fell together. Suddenly it all made sense. "Because," I exclaimed, "someone wants us to think that going down this road is the right choice! That means the other road is the right one to take! Haven, I bet the other road will lead us to Magnorium! This has to be a test! They must want us to use our magic to find Magnorium! Come on, let's go down the other road!"

He still didn't budge and looked at me accusingly.

"Please!" I begged. "This isn't you. Concentrate and you will see that nothing is there."

He sighed, closing and reopening his eyes. "I still see it. Listen Alyssa, if it's really a glamour spell, why isn't it influencing you? No offence or anything, but you just learned about magic. Powerful Elementals are the only ones who can see past glamours and even that takes years and years of training that even I don't have."

I shrugged, not having an explanation.

"Do you really see nothing?" he asked.

I nodded my head firmly. "Do you have any idea how to see past a glamour?"

He nodded, surveying the barren ground, before letting out a frustrated sigh. "There's a way. But it's hard. I don't know if you'll be able to do it, or if we're even compatible."

"Compatible for what?"

"All right. Here's your first magic lesson, from yours truly. Each person has their own style of practising magic; everybody has their own sort of magical energy. Since we're all a type of Elemental in the end, sometimes we can share energies." He paused, casting his gaze over me. "Okay you look really freaked out, but there's not much else to it."

"So we'd be, like ... connecting?" I asked sheepishly.

"Theoretically yes. We'd have to be in contact and we'd be temporarily sharing power. If you see past the glamour, and if you do this right, so will I."

"All right," I said nervously. "Let's try it. But I make no promises."

"That's all I can ask for," Haven said gratefully. "When we transfer magic, you're going to feel something foreign. That's my energy. Don't reject it or else it'll hurt. Just try to accept it, okay?"

This whole thing sounded so complicated. I was in way over my head. "Haven," I said sarcastically, "your instructions couldn't be more clear."

He rolled his eyes, grabbing my hand before I could protest. It fit neatly in his palm. "When you think you can't do something, you should just do it anyway. Even if you fail miserably." He said as he squeezed my hand reassuringly.

He was right. I had done magic on two separate occasions; I could do it again. I closed my eyes, trying to follow what he said, but it was hard. His instructions were too vague.

I had never actually willed my magic before; it had always been triggered by anger. But I was willing it to come now—willing that unmistakable sweet feeling of power to surface. We stood immobile for a few minutes, and I was so grateful for his patience. If I didn't share my energy, we might never get to Magnorium. That single fear struck a chord, and suddenly the arm that intertwined with his was tingling, thrumming with the adrenaline of magic. Like Haven said, there was something else present. A wave of calmness and peace washed over me. It was Havens magic. Not that I'd be telling him, but his magic felt wonderful. He squeezed my hand tighter this time, as if feeling the connection too, and opened his eyes.

"The glamour's gone!" he breathed in shock, stumbling backwards and breaking our connection. Wait. I did it?

"What do you see now?" I asked curiously.

"Nothing really. It's flashing in and out ... faintly." His eyes narrowed and shook his head. "You helped me see through it."

"I guess I did."

He kept looking back and forth, as if to make sure it was really gone. "I don't know if you're aware of this Draken, but your magic is overwhelming."

"That sounds like a bad thing. Sorry. Didn't mean to consume you with my absolutely fantastic energy."

"No Alyssa, seriously," he whispered, oddly solemn. "I never felt anything like your magic before. You saw through a glamour! You must've been lying when you said you've had no training."

I shook my head. "I honestly haven't."

His analytical eyes bore into mine. It was clear he didn't believe me. "Who are you?"

"What?" I asked, perturbed at the question. "I thought we already went over this in the car."

"Yeah well, let's review, shall we? You didn't know about magic until three days ago, yet you saw through a glamour and shared energy."

"Sounds about right," I said, crossing my arms over my chest defensively.

He shook his head stubbornly. "Who are you?"

"Um," I said slowly, "who do you expect me to be?"

"I don't know. But if you're employed by Magnorium, or you're a prodigy of the Society or the Council ... or something ... let's just put our cards on the table now."

"Haven!" I snapped. "I'm just an extremely confused sixteen year old who also happens to be an Elemental. Is that enough cards on the table? And I'm about to turn around and leave you here if you don't shut up, because we are so close to Magnorium I think I'm literally feeling it."

He clamped his mouth shut, shrugging. "Nicely said."

"Thanks," I said, irritated. "Do you interrogate everyone like this?"

"No," he said dryly. "On some occasions I just yell at them."

"Well can I yell at you?"

"Another time, for sure."

I rolled my eyes, quickly walking towards the other road.

"Hurry up." I was walking so fast that he was having to sprint to catch up. "You know this must be a test, right?"

He looked at me sharply. "This *is* the sort of thing they would do. But I am in no mood to pass this test with flying colours. We should just stay out here and become runaways."

"You know, the scary thing is that I can't tell if you're joking."

"Didn't I tell you that I am ninety-nine percent easy going?"

"I thought it was ninety actually ... but you were probably joking."

He looked at me and laughed, a genuine sound, and one that made me smile.

We picked up speed as the road sloped downwards. The terrain was becoming hilly. I noticed that the texture of the ground had gradually begun to look different, a more golden brownish colour, with pockets of soil instead of sand and more greenery. It was like we were slowly crossing over from a barren dusty wasteland and back into the world again.

For ten minutes we jogged, side by side, in silence. It came to a point where I was no longer aware that I was even moving. My legs were moving by themselves, like a magnet attracted to a steel force field. Suddenly, the asphalt road narrowed and came to an abrupt stop at the edge of freshly cut green grass that looked ridiculously out of place. A looming shadow cast its way across my face and I looked up.

A long cobblestone walkway wound through the grass, snaking up to the front door of a huge building about two hundred feet away. The building was enormous, with ornate peaks and a Corinthian-style design. Two tall white pillars climbed their way to the top of an archway, complimenting the huge brass door. The main building was large, at least ten floors, but despite its enormity, there were still smaller buildings attached to it with long narrow corridors. The stones that adorned the buildings were almost luminescent, with a silver glow shimmering off of them. And the gardens—the gardens were breathtaking. Patches of bright flowers in every colour dotted the grass, and huge trees reached towards the sky, which was an odd sight considering the entire estate sat nearly smack-dab in the middle of the desert. Everything was perfectly groomed, right down to the trimmed hedges and the pristine walkways that peeked out from between the cobblestones. The building sat in the middle of the lush garden like some sort of extraterrestrial palace.

Suddenly I was overwhelmed. There was so much magic here that it made me dizzy. I could sense at least a hundred unique individuals;

it was like the very air was colliding with different energies. Haven stiffened, and when we finally recovered from our shock, he shot me a look.

"Oh joy," he deadpanned, "It seems we have found it."

"Alyssa Brooks and Haven Reeves," exclaimed an overly enthusiastic voice behind us.

"Welcome to Magnorium—school for Elementals."

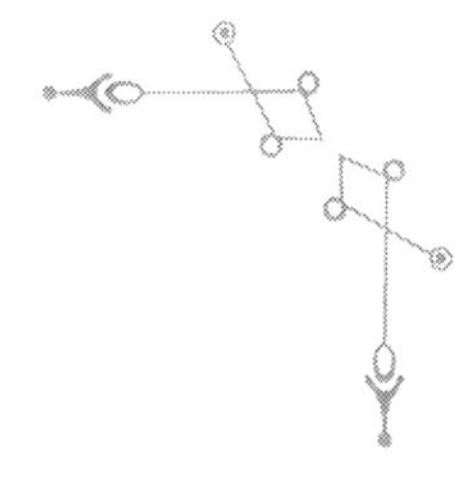

CHAPTER 5

ARRIVAL

After Mondo was kidnapped, needless to say, we were both a bit anxious. I jumped at the sudden sound of the stranger's voice, and spun around to meet two elegantly dressed adults. A man and women stood side by side, about ten feet behind me. The woman was quite short and delicately built, and wore a humbling grey dress that fell practically to her ankles. If I squinted, I could see a little crest over her heart. Grey eyes met mine, and her lips curled into a mad grin. She stepped forward, an old calloused hand outstretched.

"Welcome to Magnorium! My name is Mrs. Musk and I am second in command here at the school!"

I took her hand and gave it a firm shake, smiling at the enthusiasm that practically oozed from her voice.

"Glad to be here!" Haven exclaimed, with a smile that was a bit too wide. She released my hand and took his, shaking it and looking pleased. If she actually knew him, she might've been able to detect the falseness in his voice. She released Haven's hand from her grip, stepping back and making a sweeping gesture toward the man behind her. Distracted, he was staring up at the peaks of the building, and only when Mrs. Musk gestured did he turn.

"This is Mr. Bell—"

"Kurt actually," he interrupted, without showing any emotion. "I prefer to be called by my first name." Kurt stuffed his hands into the deep pockets of his suit.

This man, I thought, was the epitome of propriety. He sported a mass of blinding blond hair that was smoothed over and gelled neatly. His oval face and long pointed nose were just like the rest of him: sharp. His eyes were as black as night and emotionless as they looked over at Haven and I, as if just noticing that we were standing there. The longer I looked at him, the harder I tried to guess his age; he didn't look old at all, perhaps in his mid twenties or early thirties. I detected a slight English accent when he spoke, which was fitting—he didn't look very American.

"Ah," Kurt mused, pulling his sleeve back to hastily check his watch. "Look who finally joined us! Mr. Reeves."

I frowned. Kurt knew Haven?

Haven stiffened. "Kurt. Nice to see you again." He extended his hand politely.

"Yes Mr. Reeves," he accepted Haven's hand, shaking it slowly. "I believe the last time we spoke was at the funeral, was it not?"

"That was it." Haven pulled his hand back, and wiped it on his pant leg.

"Well, I remember Jason quite well. He was one of my best students. Pity what happened to him."

"Well you *should* remember him. You were the last one to see him."

"Yes, the memory is quite vivid. And your parents? Still as pleasant as I remember them?"

"Oh yes," Haven replied in the driest tone I had ever heard. "They're even more pleasant than the last time you spoke to them."

"Yes well," Kurt sighed, running a hand over his hair. "You Reeves have always been something. Maybe we can resume this conversation later in my office?"

"I might take you up on that."

"Excuse me," I interrupted. "But who are you?"

Kurt turned, as if finally deigning to acknowledge my existence.

"Kurt is the headmaster here at Magnorium!" Mrs. Musk chirped excitedly.

He looked down his nose at me. "Name?"

"Um. I'm Alyssa; it's nice to meet you—"

"Not your first name. First names hardly matter."

"Oh," I said blushing. "Brooks. Alyssa Brooks."

"Hmm ... Brooks. Never heard that one before." He scrutinized me for about fifteen seconds and then, as though finding nothing to comment on, pulled out his mobile phone. I, quite frankly, tried not to be offended.

"Well," Mrs. Musk said, trying to fill up the awkward silence of the moment, "congratulations! You two found this school in record time! You're going to be forces to reckon with, but I already knew that about you, Haven dear!"

Kurt looked up from whatever he was typing on his phone and glared. "Don't inflate their egos," he snapped. "Remember, they are your subordinates, as you are mine."

She frowned but nodded and regained her professional composure.

"Anyway Mrs. Musk, I'm terribly busy. See to it that they are settled in," he commanded with a distracted wave of his hand, before heading up the path that would lead him to Magnorium's huge front doors.

"Oh my God!" I practically shouted, suddenly remembering what had brought us here in the first place. "Our driver was kidnapped!"

"Oh that," Mrs. Musk said calmly.

"Yes, '*oh that*'," Haven echoed, not believing her callousness. "*Oh*, he might be hurt. *Oh*, he's missing. *Oh*, he might be dead!"

"While you three were on route to Magnorium," she said, "two men abducted him, leaving you two stranded in the desert; is this correct?"

"Yes ...?" Haven answered leaving room for her to explain.

"Well that was all a test! You both passed!"

Haven and I looked at each other, blinking. Was she serious?

"I knew it!" I exclaimed, clamping down my shock as it quickly turned into anger. "You scared me half to death! I thought Mondo was going to die! They shot a gun at me!"

"Yes, we had to simulate a believable situation."

Haven shook his head, mortified. "I think a written test would have done just fine."

Mrs. Musk sighed, almost appearing apologetic. Almost. "Don't get the wrong idea you two. We had to see if you were worthy."

"Worthy!" Haven practically exploded. "I didn't even want—"

"You need to understand, Kurt and I need to see if you had enough magical skill to study here at Magnorium," she said, cutting Haven off. "We give each potential student a certain period of time to find the school, and if they are not successful at locating the school, we retract their admission. Students who fail the test are not ready, because their powers are weak. We used to let everyone in. It was required in fact. But this school is now meant for students like you two, who need training in managing their powers. If any student gets injured during the test, we go and retrieve them immediately. We were monitoring you both the entire time. It was completely safe."

"That's ridiculous," Haven said bluntly.

Mrs. Musk smiled tightly, looking up at the school fondly. "We are not a regular school; our standards are much higher."

"Are you telling me that every student has gone through the same test Alyssa and I went through?"

"Of course not!" she answered. "The test varies with age, ability, experience, and other circumstances. The test is always different."

"So you hired the bikers to fake Mondo's abduction?"

"Yes, and rest assured, your personal belongings left behind in the car are being retrieved by Mondo as we speak."

I managed a weak smile. "So we passed?"

Mrs. Musk laughed. "You two passed with flying colours! You set a school record!"

"A record?" Haven asked, curiously.

"You two located the school in less than two hours—one hour and forty-seven minutes to be exact. That is the fastest time ever. Our two most powerful students here at Magnorium found the school in three hours. That was the previous record. My dears, you were magnificent!"

"You're saying that other students have wandered out in the desert for *more* than three hours!" I shouted, horrified.

"Much longer than that," Mrs. Musk said casually, as if it was of no consequence. "But since you're not quite human, there was never any real threat of death."

I blinked, still digesting the fact that I was *actually* right for once.

"Gee thanks. Like I said, glad to be here," Haven muttered, crossing his arms over his chest.

"And we're so glad to have you, Haven!" Mrs. Musk said warmly, completely oblivious to his sarcasm.

"Well follow me, you two!" She gestured for us to follow her onto the long cobblestone path, weaving through the very impressive, manicured front yard.

"Haven," I muttered, as he walked beside me up the path. "Why does everyone know you?"

"They don't," he said with a smirk. "Not many people do."

"I don't mean in that way—" I said.

"Oh. Well when your family consists of a bunch of rich psychos, word kind of gets around. And contrary to popular belief, I am actually *not* a psycho."

"Really? Not even a little bit?" I asked jokingly, climbing the slew of stairs that led up to the front door.

"Well, maybe a little a bit."

"Alyssa, Haven, welcome to Magnorium!" Mrs. Musk announced, grabbing the handle of the door and swinging it open. The inside of

Magnorium looked just as impressive as the outside. The flooring was marble, and the walls decorated with intricate paintings, pictures, and plaques. The ceiling was huge, and arched, sloping upwards to meet a dazzling chandelier in the very centre. The whole front entrance really resembled a hotel lobby, but when I looked to the side, I saw hints of school life. Off to the right, I saw posted signs, pointing the way to a gymnasium, a pool, and the cafeteria. The cafeteria's doors were actually in sight, and open. In the first ten seconds of standing in the doorway, I found that this new atmosphere somehow comforted me. It was a mess and in complete chaos, with students bustling about—some running, others screaming. As the huge main door slammed shut, a few students in the cafeteria turned to stare.

"It's rare to have new arrivals this late in the year," Mrs. Musk explained, leading us down a winding hallway.

"Where are we going?" Haven asked.

She answered with only a smile, turning down into the maze of hallways. Everything seemed different. There were the echoes of voices—teachers lecturing on foreign things I had never heard of before. The school looked different, smelled different, even the energy in the air was one of excitement. I had never seen so many people happy to be at a school. I followed Mrs. Musk as she cheerfully led us to a chestnut-coloured door at the end of the hallway.

"This is my office," she exclaimed proudly.

Haven looked at the door, and then squinted, leaning closer. "Well I think someone broke into your office."

"What?" Mrs. Musk muttered distractedly.

Haven pointed. "There are scratch marks on the face of the lock here. The scratches aren't faded into the steel; they look pretty prominent. When was the last time you were in here?"

"Wait, what?" Mrs. Musk huffed, trying the handle, which (as Haven predicted) turned loosely. She rushed inside and I followed, with Haven trailing behind me. The office looked pretty normal given the circumstances. There was a huge oak desk in the centre, accented with elegant chairs. Huge glass cases, brimming with awards, and huge filing cabinets lined the walls. The only thing I could definitely say was out of place was the girl sitting in Mrs. Musk's chair. She was seated behind the desk, with two feet propped up lazily against the wood.

"Um," Haven said loudly, stopping in the doorway. "I'm sorry. You look quite busy. We can come back if this is an inconvenient time for you."

The girl looked to be a student, dressed elegantly in the uniform, maybe about our age. She tilted her head in our direction, cocking an eyebrow. Everything about her was striking: her straight, long black hair, her angular cheekbones, her huge grey-blue eyes ... even the way she had her feet planted on the desk was striking. The girl practically exuded confidence as she sat up, carefully folding her feet back under the desk, and leaned forward.

"Well this is interesting. I just love newbies."

"What in the world?" Mrs. Musk started, her voice slowly rising in volume. "Miss Travie, what do you think you are doing?"

The girl seized me up with a sharp glare, completely ignoring Mrs. Musk's question. "Who are they? Well actually, that's clearly what's-his-name, because it's about time, but who's that?"

Haven stepped into the room. "I *am* what's-his-name, more commonly referred to as Haven Reeves."

"Alyssa Brooks," I supplied.

"Element?"

"Draken," I said coolly.

She gave an odd little smile. "I didn't know Drakens could be that cold. Ouch."

I stared. Who was this girl? "And who are you?" I shot back. "The welcoming committee?"

"Miss Travie would you care to explain how you broke into my office?" Mrs. Musk seethed, practically fuming.

"Badly, that's how." Haven rolled his eyes. "You did a lousy job. Try to be discreet and not wait around next time and you might just get away with it."

She pointedly ignored his comments and introduced herself. "I'm Amber Travie, Skyros, and currently the most powerful Elemental here at Magnorium."

"That's great." I said, detecting the arrogance that accompanied her grin. "I currently am the most confused Elemental here at Magnorium."

"Excuse me!" Mrs. Musk finally shouted, storming over to her chair and motioning Amber out. "But this is *my* office, and if you don't get out in the next ten seconds, you're getting detention!"

"I'm here for a perfectly good reason. I want to teach the battle strategy class."

"You want to teach the ..." She didn't even finish her sentence, rubbing her temples tiredly. "And why is that, Miss Travie?"

"Well," Amber announced calmly, getting out of the chair, and then circling the room fervently. "The current teacher is useless."

"Excuse me—"

"I can do a much better job! At the rate we're going at, no one's going to be prepared if the Society attacks."

"Magnorium is perfectly safe." Mrs. Musk rolled her eyes, and took her seat.

Amber slapped her hands on the desk and leaned towards Mrs. Musk, drumming her fingernails on the wood. "Oh really? I'd say Magnorium's suffering from a serious invasion of controlling sociopaths. How many mortals died last month at the hands of the Society? I might be a bit off, but I believe it was around fifteen hundred. Forty Elementals died—"

"Forty-two actually," Haven muttered. I turned to stare at him, and could feel Amber's piercing gaze doing the same.

"And two students," she finally concluded, with a sickening grin. "But sorry, didn't mean to scare you guys, especially you Draken.

You dress and look so much like a mortal, it's distracting me. Do you think you can turn around or step outside for a moment? It's a matter of life and death here."

"Wait, *what* is happening?" I asked, blinking. "You actually want me to wait outside—"

"This isn't a debate!" Mrs. Musk interrupted, slamming her hands down on the desk. The noise was startling and jolted the room into a still sort of silence.

"You two," she gestured to Haven and I, "sit." She pointed to a set of chairs. "And you," she pointed at Amber, "out! Now!"

Amber groaned dramatically as Mrs. Musk got up and led her towards the door. "No one ever listens to me!"

"Perhaps if you knock next time, I might. I have one more piece of news for you, Miss Travie," Mrs. Musk said, sounding almost amused. "You record has been broken. These two passed the test in less than two hours. Just thought you should know. Good day."

Amber blinked her grey-blue eyes in astonishment. *"What?"*

"Good day," Mrs. Musk repeated firmly, just barely getting Amber out of the way before slamming the door. Haven and I looked at each other in shock. Mrs. Musk sighed loudly, collapsing back into the folds of her swivel chair.

"I don't know what I'm going to do with her. But if you think *she's* bad, wait till you meet her brother. The Travies will be the death of me. Anyway, let's go over a few rules, shall we?"

We both nodded.

"First rule, school starts promptly at nine o'clock and ends at four, Monday through Friday. You are required to wear your uniform during school hours only. Breakfast is at eight, lunch at twelve, and dinner at seven. All meals are served in the cafeteria, which is located in this building. The boys' dormitories are on the fifth, sixth, and seventh floors; the girls' are on the eighth, ninth, and tenth."

She picked up two stacks of paper and books, and handed one to me and the other to Haven. "In here you will find a map of the school, your class schedule for every day of the week, your dorm assignment, and other important information. Oh yes, no magic classes on Monday and Tuesday; these days are reserved for mortal schooling. On weekends, Magnorium offers a variety of different activities. Please explore. We have a pool, recreation room, bowling alley, movie theatre, and a mini-mall for students. Curfews on week-nights is ten o'clock, but feel free to stay out as long as you like on weekends. Don't break these rules and we should get along just fine. Here you go," she said, handing me and Haven our uniforms, which were neatly folded in garment bags.

"Now follow me and I'll take you to your rooms." She stood up, folding her hands together, and led us back out into the hallway, glaring at the lock on the door as we passed.

I wriggled my class schedule out from the pile of books, and started scanning it. The mortal classes were standard, but there were a bunch of Elemental classes I had never heard of. "AVERAGE" was printed in big, bolded letters at the top of my Elemental schedule.

"Interesting word choice. Not the one I would use," I said frowning, as Haven peered over my shoulder.

"There are three levels of magic at Magnorium," Haven explained. "Basic, average, and advanced. The majority of Elementals are average; advanced is what you want to train to become."

I glanced over his shoulder as he quickly tried to stuff his schedule away, but I still caught the word "ADVANCED" in bold on the top of his paper. He winced.

"How did you become advanced if you haven't even trained here before?"

"Long story. But I taught myself a lot."

"You must be a damn good teacher then."

"I didn't just want to *have* magic, you know? I mean, why have magic if you can't make a difference with it?"

"Oh I don't know," I said, quite childishly, "maybe because it's the coolest thing I've ever seen!"

He laughed, darting through a blockade of students to keep up with Mrs. Musk. "Hey, we still have Math and English together," he said, shrugging.

"Nothing's magical about that."

"I happen to find numerical equations very magical."

"Mr. Reeves," Mrs. Musk interrupted, guiding us into the glass elevator past its double doors. "We will be going to your room first, located in the advanced dorms."

"So you have specific dorms just for the powerful kids," Haven commented dryly. "I can just feel the equality here, can't you?"

"Excuse me Mr. Reeves, but you students have separate dorms, a whole separate floor actually, as a safety precaution. You could potentially harm the other students."

"You feel the urge to harm anyone, Haven?" I asked with a frown.

He nodded, shifting his weight back and forth, from one foot to the other. "Oh yes. If I'm not detained immediately the whole school might blow up."

"Please, don't make me question why I decided to work with teenagers," Mrs. Musk muttered under her breath, as the elevator doors slid back open. The seventh floor was impressive. I stepped out onto plush carpeting, and noticed expensive chandeliers dangling from the ceiling. There were only about eight double doors on the entire floor, which meant that the rooms were bigger than normal, and there probably weren't many really powerful kids. The ambiance didn't match at all with the atmosphere; the hallway practically shook with loud music, mostly emanating from the dorm at the end of the hall.

Mrs. Musk forehead crinkled in irritation as she stormed down the hall. "Zack Travie!" she shouted furiously, pounding a fist against the solid wood door. "Open this door right now!"

A string of rude words floated over the sound of the pulsing music, and a moment later the sound-system switched off. There was a loud rustling from inside the room, and then the door opened about a foot and a teenaged boy stuck his head out.

"Mrs. Musk!" he exclaimed enthusiastically. "Now what brings you here on this lovely day?" The boy had huge dark green eyes, which just seemed to spark with mischief, and the hair that fell across his eyes was jet black. His sharp facial features and his mannerisms reminded me of Amber. This was clearly her brother—her ridiculously attractive brother.

"Zack," Mrs. Musk hissed, using the same exasperated tone that she had used with his sister. "You have a new roommate!"

Zack eyes narrowed and he stuck his neck farther out the door, his dark bangs resting lightly on the fringe of his dark eyelashes. "Wait. Seriously?"

"Very *seriously*," she said, making it sound like a foreign word. "Now may we come in?" Zack's eyes flickered to Haven before coming to rest on me. "You don't want to come in," he drawled, with a smirk.

"I don't know," Haven said, leaning against the wall. "I *kind of* want to. I mean, I do live here now."

"Well I wasn't expecting guests!" Zack announced, before slamming the door in Mrs. Musk's face.

"Zack Travie, open this door right now! I have a key, you know!"

Zack's laughter couldn't be contained, and carried right through the door and down the hallway. Then a loud, heated discussion could be heard from inside the room. The actual words were muffled, but finally, the doorknob turned again and the door opened a few inches. Zack peeked out the opening.

"So darling," he said, in his rough raspy voice, "who are you?" He looked at me through the crack, with one dark green eye. "Mortal? You look like one. The shocked look on your face looks almost as mortal as your clothes."

I defensively glanced down at my t-shirt and jeans. Did I really look that much like a mortal? What did that even *mean,* anyway?

"So, do you Elementals not wear clothes then, and just run around naked?" I asked, raising an eyebrow. Mrs. Musk caught the door with her foot before the conversation could continue and roughly pried it open.

"That's enough Zack. Come on in, Haven. Alyssa you too." Mrs. Musk stepped inside and we followed. The room was ridiculously huge. It was big enough to host a huge party, which was what it seemed to be doing—a party with a population that was sixty percent female. Twenty or so girls, who looked about my age, were sitting on various chairs and couches around his room, with red plastic cups in their hands. In fact, the only boys in the room were Haven, Zack, and a few other guys that I had never seen before. Suddenly, I was struck by the realization of how good-looking every single Elemental seemed to be. But it wasn't the normal sort of good-looking. Their good looks were almost extraterrestrial—too exotic and perfect to be real. For a moment, I wondered if I looked like that too, but I wasn't about to ask anyone.

"Well, this is awkward," I observed.

"Oh you're telling me." Haven whistled, surveying the assortment of strange girls in his new room.

Mrs. Musk's face was aflame as she took a glance around the room. "All of you," she seethed, raising a wavering finger to the doorway. "Out. Now!"

It took all of ten seconds for everyone to respond to Mrs. Musk's clipped tone, and shuffle out the door faster than I could even blink.

"Told you I wasn't expecting guests," Zack answered with a shrug, staring at his empty room in disdain.

"Really?" Haven said, amused. "Seems like you had a lot of them."

"Got to do something to pass the time," Zack said, slamming the door shut with the heel of his shoe. "So, Alyssa, right? If you prove yourself to be smarter than you look, consider your first party at Magnorium to be in here and hosted by yours truly."

"Gee thanks," I said dryly. "This overwhelming sense of kindness must really run in your family."

"Oh, so you know who I am," he muttered, leaning against the wall. "Guess I underestimated your intellect."

"You're Zack Travie, Amber Travie's brother. Since she's the most powerful *person* here, you're probably the most powerful *boy*."

"Well, aren't you just the full package," he muttered with a smirk.

I rolled my eyes. "I can practically feel your arrogance; you might want to tone it down a bit."

"I can't," Zack said, with fleeting sadness. "And being this good-looking sure doesn't help."

"Really?" I growled. "It sure doesn't help when you're this much of a jerk."

Zack made no retort, a huge and legitimate smile breaking out across his face, even reaching the crinkles of his eyes. "All right Alyssa, you've earned a formal greeting." He winked. "Not many people get one of those. I'm Zack Travie, Terran." He extended his hand and I had to return the smile, accepting his warm, smooth hand and shaking it firmly.

"I'm Alyssa Brooks, Draken."

"So ... newbie?"

"Very," I said dryly. "I didn't know about magic until three days ago."

"Hmm ... Let me extend a formal welcome then. And you," he paused, looking at Haven, "you don't need a welcome because I know exactly who you are." Zack grinned, circling Haven curiously. "Your family at least. I've seen them on TV. How much money do you people have?"

"Oh thats real subtle," Haven said sarcastically. "'I've seen your crazy family on the news and just how rich are you?' Just write that on my gravestone."

"Children," Mrs. Musk interrupted with a sigh.

Zack held up a hand with an annoyed sigh of his own. "Just give us a moment, would you?"

"Oh, of course!" she exploded sarcastically. "Just let me know when you're ready! You clearly run this school anyway."

"Thank you!" Zack said, ignoring the tone and folding his hands together.

I gaped as she actually complied, scowling and cursing under her breath as she lowered herself onto one of the couches.

"So you've got a name?" Zack asked smugly. "Or would you prefer 'roomy'?"

"I'd prefer 'roomy' actually. Sounds more intimate."

"So what'd you do to land yourself in this room anyway? I almost killed someone, but that's just me."

"Almost?" I interrupted, eyeing Mrs. Musk, who looked quite irritated with her lips drawn together firmly. I was thoroughly confused. She was second in command; students couldn't order her around, even ones who almost kill people. Right?

"Yeah," Zack said. "The key word there is *almost*. So what'd you do? Flood a school? A town? I just love you water freaks! You're not going to hang out at the pool all day, are you?"

"That depends on whether or not you spend all your time outside, Terran."

"Hey, that's just stereotyping," Zack laughed, a few wild strands of his black locks falling over his eyes. He shook them away. He was so laid back that almost every second sentence was a mockery of some sort. He was extremely hard to take seriously. After living and interacting with serious people all my life, standing with these two was like a breath of fresh air.

"So you two came together? What was your time? Mine's three hours," he exclaimed proudly.

"An hour and forty-seven minutes." I grinned, stealing some of his smugness. "I guess that makes us the holders of the new record."

Zack frowned, trying to contain his shock. "Wait, what? You're lying! No one gets here that fast; we're in the middle of nowhere, if you haven't noticed. Did you fly here?"

"I can't tell if he's being serious. Is he being serious?" I muttered, turning to Haven.

Haven smirked at my cluelessness. "He's joking. Only very powerful Skyros can fly. We were just lucky."

"You do realize," Zack said slowly, his dark green eyes almost blackening, "that my sister may or may not kill you, and I am in no way responsible for her actions."

"Amber." I nodded. "Lovely family you got there. The resemblance is almost uncanny. Twins?"

"God no. That would mean I actually had to share something with her. I'm almost eighteen. Probably older than you two, which means by default I'm always right, and no, you cannot argue with me."

"You are?" Haven said, amused. "Well then proving you wrong is going to be fun."

"You know," Zack glanced at me, "I'm starting not to hate him as much as I did ten seconds ago."

"I hope so because you're going to be stuck here together."

Zack smirked, surveying his room proudly. It really was a nice room—almost too nice. Zack's giant bed was the centerpiece and everything else worked around it flawlessly. There was a comfortable-looking sitting area, complete with a huge flat screen. The room had its own kitchen in the far corner. It was decorated in sharp contrast to the rest of the building; everything in this room was new—the newest models, the most modern styles.

"Well, that all depends on him." He looked back at Haven. "Do you mind partying until three a.m. with a few strangers, sleeping during daylight hours, and trying to brainwash yourself into thinking you don't live at a school?"

Haven shrugged. "Can't say I mind too much."

Zack clapped his hands together loudly. "We shall get along splendidly."

"I'm Haven Reeves, by the way, Aquarian."

Zack smirked, folding his arms across his chest. "Haven?"

Haven scowled, muscles quickly working in his jaw to contain his irritation. "Yes."

"Well okay then!" Zack said amusingly. I tried not to stare. This guy was all energy, never standing still, as though he had a severe case of ADHD. "Thank you my dear Mrs. Musk. I will be happy to show this guy around!" he exclaimed, grabbing Haven by the shoulders.

"I already know my way around," Haven mumbled under his breath, but he was smiling.

Zack huffed. "Fine, then let's go work on some brotherly bonding."

"You two clearly have a lot to discuss. Zack, it's always a ..." Mrs. Musk's voice trailed off as she rose to her feet, trying to figure out how she wanted to end that sentence.

"Pleasure?" Zack guessed, with another huge grin.

She rolled her eyes. "Not the word I'd use. Entertaining. I suppose. It's always entertaining, Mr. Travie." She spun on her heels and stalked out the door, gesturing for me to follow. "Come along Alyssa."

"Hey, come back soon!" Zack hollered mischievously, as I made my way towards the doorway, wondering how I could possibly *not* come back.

"I do see a visit in your near future," Haven called, following me to the door of his new room.

I rolled my eyes. "You do?"

"Yes," Haven said quite seriously, leaning against the inside of the door frame as I stepped outside. "I forgot to mention that one of my hidden talents is seeing into the future." Then he smiled and swung the door closed before I could figure out if he had been joking that time.

Mrs. Musk was already heading back towards the elevator and I scrambled to catch up, hopping in just as the doors slid shut.

"What floor are we going to?" I asked curiously. According to the school, I was average, so where did that put me exactly? She looked at the piece of paper in her hands and shrugged.

"Eighth floor." As the doors finally slid open, Magnorium's hierarchy began to form in my head. Clearly the more powerful you were, the more luxury you lived in. This hallway was dim and narrow, and the walls in need of a serious paint job. The dorm room doors were significantly smaller than the ones on Haven's floor, and the rooms much closer together. They must have packed a lot of kids into this hallway, I thought. Mrs. Musk, who seemed unperturbed by the unfairness of it all, moved to the left of the hallway, unlocking one of the many doors. I followed her hesitantly inside.

This particular room had a wonderful scent of decaying food and week-old laundry. The room wasn't big at all—tolerable for two, but certainly not three. The floor was bare, covered in harsh grey tile, and the walls didn't exactly match any of the décor, being an ugly shade of orange. There were only two small beds rammed up against one wall. The rest of the space was occupied by a small television and a small table. I didn't see a bathroom or even a closet. I recoiled in distaste.

"This is your new room!" Mrs. Musk exclaimed, seeming excited for me.

"Great," I said dryly. "It's so cozy."

"I'm so glad you like it!" Mrs. Musk gushed, apparently not noticing my sarcasm. I nodded, with my eyes still scanning the room. To make matters worse, the room was horrendously messy, with clothes and other items thrown about. I felt claustrophobic just standing in the doorway.

Mrs. Musk pressed a key into my hand. "Here is your key, Mondo will be by later to deliver the stuff left out in the car. This whole room will be rearranged later to fit your accommodations. Any other questions?"

I shook my head mutely.

"Good," she smiled sincerely. "I'm sure you will settle nicely here. After all, this is where you truly belong!" And then she was gone as quickly as she had come, leaving me alone for the first time that day.

The events of the last three days suddenly rushed up to greet me, and what I once thought as fantasy was now becoming a reality. I was stuck here. I reminded myself to breathe, drawing in big gulps of air. I was fine. So what if my room was ugly? The school was still like a palace, and I didn't even need to spend that much time in here anyway.

"Who the hell are *you*?" an angry voice yelped. The door was open again, but this time a blonde girl stood behind me in nothing but a pink bathrobe, wet hair plastered to her skull. I didn't even hear the door open. The blonde looked royally ticked off, her mouth hanging open. To be fair, I'd be angry too if a random stranger was suddenly in my room.

"Hi," I said quickly, hurrying to explain myself. "My name is Alyssa Brooks, Draken ... I'm a new student here. Is this your room?"

"Would I be standing here if this wasn't my room?" the blonde drawled, looking increasingly displeased with every second that passed.

"Oh. Well I guess we'll be living together now. I'm your new roommate."

The girl frowned, blinking her long lashes.

"Roommate?" she growled, as if me standing there was completely incomprehensible.

"Yeah, Mrs. Musk assigned me to this room no more than two minutes ago!"

"We don't get assigned new roommates."

I shrugged. "Sorry. I really *was* just assigned here."

The blonde finally seemed to process what that meant. She took one last look at me, muttering an impressive slew of curse words under her breath. I have to admit; it wasn't the nicest welcome I could've gotten.

"Um," I mumbled, shifting awkwardly on either foot. "Call me old fashioned, but do people still introduce themselves nowadays?"

Her answer was a murderous glare, as she stomped back towards the open doorway.

"I'm Emma, Aquarian." Sticking her head out into the hallway, she screamed, "Rachel! Come here!" And then she started laughing. When Rachel finally barged in, I knew this wasn't going to be good.

Rachel stormed through the doorway, and it took all of ten seconds to come to an indisputable conclusion: *She* clearly had anger issues. This girl was large but short, clearly leaving her less space to store her fury. Her hair was a mass of wild red curls that almost made her head look like it was on fire. Her face was dotted with freckles, and her eyes burned with malice and anger that was clearly unjustified towards a complete stranger. In that moment, she reminded me very much of an enraged Little Orphan Annie on steroids.

"Who the hell is she?" she half-shouted.

I blinked, taken aback at her murderous tone. "Alyssa Brooks, Draken. I'm your new roommate."

Rachel's frame shuddered, as she drew in deep gulps of air to calm down. She looked like a burning fuse on its way to an explosion and she'd only been in the room for ten seconds.

"Why are you in my room?" she seethed.

"I'm a new student," I answered, and then repeated myself slowly, careful not to make things worse. "I'm your new roommate."

Rachel growled, a low, almost inaudible noise. "I don't want a new roommate."

"This is Rachel. She's Draken, like you," Emma remarked casually, moving to stand protectively next to her friend. "If you haven't already guessed. This is our room."

If all Drakens threw major tantrums like this, my own episodes were seriously missing from my memory. Sure, I could get snappy on occasions, but I was not in any way like this girl.

I gulped down the lump that was starting to form in my throat. "Look I'm sorry ... I mean, it's not like I have any choice of where I'm put, so—"

"Just get out!" Rachel interrupted, arming herself with the closest thing on her dresser: a clear vase.

"Hey now," I said, quickly raising my hands in surrender. "Just calm down. We'll compromise okay?"

Her grip tightening around the glass was enough to tell me what was going to happen next. She swung her arm back, and then hurled the vase straight at my midriff. I sidestepped, yelping in surprise as the item smashed into the wall, literally an inch from my hip. She was *actually* aiming to hit me, and yet she was grinning, her ugly face twisted in some sort of sick satisfaction.

"You think I'm going to leave just because you can throw glass vases?" I growled, taking a tentative step forward, the glass crunching underneath my shoes. "Try a bit harder."

"I said get out of this room!" she roared, shuddering with hate. She flexed a clenched hand, smiling as five identical flames, no bigger than two inches long, sprouted from her fingertips. I tried not to look as shocked as I felt. I knew Drakens could easily manipulate their magic like that, but to see it up close made it so much more real.

"I bet you couldn't even do this if you tried," she exclaimed, proudly admiring her fingers. "You're just a little amateur, aren't you?"

I didn't trust myself to speak. Clearly there was no reasoning with these people.

In one swift motion, Rachel raised her fingers to her lips, blowing the tiny flames off of her hands and sending them slamming into the wooden dresser, which promptly exploded into flames. The smell of burning wood immediately filled the tiny space, smoke curling its way up to meet the ceiling.

"Rachel!" Emma growled in annoyance, moving to the other side of the room where three identical fire extinguishers were hanging from the wall. It took a tug to get one free, and then she pulled the pin from the locking mechanism and squeezed the lever, blasting the dresser in the frothy white liquid. The fire was almost instantly extinguished, and parts of the dresser reduced to crumbling embers, leaving a strong smell of burned wood and chemicals.

I shook my head at the steaming mess of wood and foam, staring at them in shock.

"What is *happening?*" I exploded angrily. "I've been standing here for *one* minute and I didn't do anything *wrong!* There isn't anything anyone can do to make me leave this room, but I'll sure as hell stay out of your way as long as *you* stay out of *mine!*"

"This just isn't acceptable newbie," Rachel sneered. Her face was beginning to redden, and lacy blue veins on her neck and chest were becoming dangerously prominent.

"Hey, calm down," I cautioned, "you're going to pop a blood vessel!" It was a legitimate concern; blue veins were starting to actually protrude from her fair skin as she clenched her jaw. Surprisingly, my statement didn't calm her down. Instead, she snarled, rewarding me with a disgusted glare. "I won't have her in our room. I'm going to find Mrs. Musk. Emma, watch her."

"Watch *me?*" I said, aghast. "Someone needs to watch *you* before you turn into a raging monster and *kill* someone!"

She was already gone by the time I even finished my sentence, which was probably for the best. Emma still stood behind me, glaring. I could feel her cold brown eyes on the back of my head.

"Are all you Elementals insane?" I shrieked, turning to look at her and crossing my arms over my chest. What was wrong with the people here? Blowing up furniture? Breaking into offices? Having parties in the middle of the afternoon ... ? Was the entire population of Magnorium crazy?

"Most of us are," Emma said softly, a warning edge to her voice. "Now listen to me, Alyssa. We both know you're going to be stuck here. So ... you might live here now, but this is still *our* room, got it? Don't make Rachel angry, and it should be fine."

"Is that even possible?" I snapped icily.

Emma hesitated, considering. "Not quite sure. She's already mad that you're another Draken, so the odds are probably quite low actually." She gave me an impish half smile, one that made me scared to guess the intentions behind it. "Draken or not, welcome to Magnorium."

CHAPTER 6

THE FIGHT BEGINS

After unpacking most of my stuff, it was nearly seven o'clock. Emma and Rachel had quite rudely stormed out of the room together hours ago, and I was left alone with myself to survey the room and make it my new home, despite how unwanted my presence was. I remembered that dinner started at seven, which meant I needed to get down to the cafeteria now.

I frantically dug through the huge pile of stuff that Mrs. Musk gave me and pulled out the school map. Magnorium really seemed to be an endless twist of unforgiving corridors and empty rooms.

All the mundane insecurities, which I kept telling myself I was resilient to, came crawling back. Who would I sit with anyway? I glanced at the mirror on Emma's dresser and held in a sigh. I looked somehow bland; maybe I'd expected my appearance to change when my whole life did. Disappointingly, I still looked the same as I always did.

I folded the map, stuffing it into the pocket of my faded jeans. I walked out of my room and locked the door, soaking in all the details of my foreign surroundings. The dormitory hallway was somehow empty. Signs of life, or fun for that matter, were nonexistent. It was too quiet on this floor—the complete opposite of the upbeat atmosphere of the powerful dorms.

There was whispering behind me, and I turned around. Two girls stood behind me, sizing me up as if I were a new specimen that was unworthy of making my stand in the hallway. I gave them both a once over, and seeing as they were apparently devoid of friendliness, I continued to the elevator and pushed the down button.

The shiny doors slid open and I stepped inside. The two girls moved quickly, lunging into my elevator and glancing at me curiously.

"Hi," I said, experimentally, flashing them both a small smile.

One of the pair spoke up, raising an eyebrow. "So what, you think you're the new Amber Travie now?"

Having only met this Amber once, and judging her from that one run in, I was startled that anyone could possibly compare me to her. She clearly held a notorious reputation for her power. But to put it simply, she was rude, blunt, and arrogant, all in that order.

"Um ... what?" I asked, peering at the pair curiously.

"You're the girl who holds the new record, right? Do you think you're the new Amber or something?"

I laughed. I sensed that the competition to best each other was fierce, and that maybe Haven and I had miscalculated that little detail.

"No, definitely not." I said, with finality to my voice. "I'm average. I just got lucky. Our test was really obvious."

"She came with Haven Reeves," her friend whispered, smacking the other girl in the arm. The girl's eyes went wide.

"Haven Reeves? That guy's really dangerous."

"Yeah, gorgeous and dangerous," her friend added with a smirk.

"Okay," I rolled my eyes. "I really don't remember him threatening to kill me or anything." I was growing curious. Everyone seemed to be commenting on Haven's status.

"So can you tell me what the deal is with this Amber girl?" I inquired, desperate for any more pieces of information about Magnorium's social hierarchy. They seemed more at ease with me since I told them I was an average. One of girls grinned, her eyes clouding over with admiration and something else I couldn't quite place.

"She's amazing. The most powerful person ever to attend Magnorium! People say that when she gets older she's going be the end of the Society!"

I raised my eyebrows at these new pieces of information. I had to admit, I gained a little respect for the girl. I mean being powerful enough to wipe out the most evil organization on the planet ... well she had some serious goals to live up to.

"That's some pretty high expectations."

"Sure is!" the other girl chattered excitedly. "But she even said she would do it herself!"

I smiled at the two of them just as the elevator arrived at the ground floor.

"Hey welcome to Magnorium, Alyssa!" one of them hollered as they exited the elevator, disappearing into one of many long twisting hallways. Surprised that they knew my name, I strained my eyes to find the two again in the crowd of strangers, but they had disappeared.

I set off into the labyrinth of hallways, following the steady flow of people to the cafeteria. Unfortunately, I was late, which really didn't look good—it being my first day and all. When I finally trudged my way to the double doors of the cafeteria, Mrs. Musk was waiting for me. She was still practically oozing enthusiasm about the school, which I found very comforting at the moment.

"Ah there you are! Fashionably late I see!"

I muttered an apology and she smiled, patting me on the back. "So what do you think of the place?" she asked, spreading her arms out wide.

"It's incredible," I offered up, which was the honest truth.

Mrs. Musk laughed easily, surveying her school. It was clear that she loved it here. "Ah that's exactly what I thought when Kurt hired me! Of course, nowadays I can't enjoy it nearly as much since Kurt's got me practically doing his job," she muttered aloud, with a heavy sigh, glancing toward the back of the room, where he was sitting alone at a table, eating his dinner and fiddling with his cell phone. "I swear to you, that man is nocturnal," she confided, seeming almost excited by the opportunity to gossip. "This could be his breakfast most days. We hardly see him, which I suppose isn't a bad thing but I do wish he wouldn't leave me to do most of his work."

I laughed at that and she ushered me inside the cafeteria.

"So here is the eatery. There are five rooms, each one named after an element. Feel free to eat wherever you'd like besides the Skyros room of course; that one is off limits I'm afraid. Oh, I'll be introducing you and Haven to the rest of the student body at the end of supper. It's not every day that we get such exciting arrivals! Enjoy your meal!" she gushed, practically floating away, disappearing into another room.

I looked at the cafeteria, giving it a proper inspection and growing even more impressed than I'd been before. The flooring was a sleek marble, and the rooms decorated with long granite tables. Kids sat at the tables, chattering excitedly and stuffing food into their mouths. There were five dining rooms—the four basic Elemental ones connected to the central Orchin room, in which the food was also served—each decorated uniquely to reflect their element. I wanted to look around a bit, especially drawn to the room Mrs. Musk had specifically said was off limits. I immediately wandered into the Skyros room, curiosity getting the better of me.

This room was pretty, with light blue hues filtering down from the ceiling and casting a calm glow over the rest of the room. There were four guards positioned at the foot of the doorway, and when they saw me, they glared.

"Sorry, can't sit over there kid."

I nodded innocently. "I'm just walking by." The difference between this room and the others was the lone long table that stretched from one side of the room to the other. About twenty or so kids were seated there, among them being Amber, Zack, and Haven. Maybe this was some sort of elite, powerful thing?

Haven was surrounded by a bunch of guys and girls, all competing for his attention, but he seemed not to be listening. Zack was on the far side of him, and he had that steady look of amusement that never seemed to waver. Our eyes met and he smirked, rising from the table abruptly.

"You look like you're lost," Zack announced, standing up and spreading his arms out wide as he approached.

I shrugged. "I'm not lost. I know I'm not allowed to be in here. So what *is* this? Some powerful kid internment camp or something?"

Zack rolled his eyes. "I wish that was a joke."

"What?" I laughed and frowned at the same time. "Really?"

"Yeah. Powerful kids have to stay at this table. Something about safety precautions." He was eyeing the doorway to the other rooms bitterly.

"That's ridiculous. You mean you can't even see your other friends in the other rooms?"

"No. I hate it, and Haven over there doesn't look too happy either. We don't all hate it though."

"Zack?" Amber called icily, from her spot opposite Haven. She was frowning at her brother, while managing to glare at me.

"Like her." Zack sighed and led me toward the table. "Come on and meet my sister."

"We've met."

Amber rolled her eyes, at the both of us. "It's Alyssa right? You're the one who's rooming with that girl with the anger problems. Rachel, is it?" she asked, with an impish smirk.

"Yeah. Hi Amber," I said, remembering the conversation about her in the elevator. "I'm not even going to ask how you know that, seeing as I was only placed there about an hour ago."

"It must be exciting in that room," she continued, ignoring my response.

"Yeah. Things get quite heated," I muttered dryly. She laughed as though I'd just made the funniest joke she'd ever heard and took a dramatic slurp of her drink.

"I'm not that funny," I said, irritated.

"Oh I know. It just proves what I've always said. *'That's what you get for being average.'*" She looked at her friends around the table. "Am I right?"

"Excuse me?" I cocked an eyebrow.

"All the inferior Elementals get the bad dorms and bad roommates." The twenty or so people left around the table murmured in agreement with Amber. They seemed to hang on her every word, fascinated and adoring. It was then that I realized Magnorium wasn't so different from regular school. Maybe in normal school, status was based on popularity or looks, but here it also seemed to be based on power. It seemed that Amber had a sufficient dose of all three. It was clear that everyone here at this table loved her, other than possibly Haven.

"What do you mean 'inferior Elementals?'" I asked curiously.

"Let's not talk about that."

Haven groaned, motioning me over with a flick of his fingers. "If you two are going to argue about Elemental hierarchy, then come sit. You're small, we can hide you over here."

"Haven, this might be your first day, but you know the rules," Amber said, in a clipped tone.

"Yeah so? Rules are meant to be broken.Don't tell me that you of all people actually follow the rules." He seemed to be the only person, other than her brother, not intimidated by Amber. She glared at him.

Zack smiled at Haven, shifting on his feet. "You know, I'm starting to really like you."

"Haven, this rule I can't help but follow," Amber said. "You know it's a safety precaution. You of all people should understand that. Magic is an experiment to you."

Now it was Haven's turn to glare.

"What are you talking about?" I interrupted, confused.

Amber sighed. "Well, we're the powerful kids," she gestured to her whole table. "Only the powerful kids sit together during meals and room together. We're dangerous, so it's about guaranteeing the safety of the other students. Everybody else can sit with whomever they want and wherever they want."

"Does that mean if I sit here, you're going to kill me?" I joked.

She didn't laugh. "Do you know anything or are you really just the amateur newbie everyone thinks you are? The reality, *Alyssa,* is just because you attracted attention for beating my record, it doesn't mean you're anything special. To be honest, if it's true what they say about you, you're too new to *all* of this. Someone like you won't last here. You'll be begging to go back home."

My cheeks reddened angrily. She was right. I really didn't know anything about Magnorium, or magic. But I couldn't let this completely arrogant stranger insult me just because she thought I was weak.

"So no, you can't sit here," she continued, "even if you wanted to. Zack and Haven are the wrong people to be making friends with, Draken."

Haven stared at Amber, looking appalled. "You listen to me, Travie—"

Zack held up a hand, cutting him off and addressing his sister. "Amber, be quiet."

"No! Zack, it's true and you know it." She pointed her spoon at me. "What's the point of even keeping people like them here? It's not like any of them can help me!"

My face flushed an even deeper shade of red, and a few others around the table whistled at my embarrassment. "Power shouldn't define you," I finally growled.

Amber shook her head, a faraway look in her eyes. "Here it does. I train to be the best of the best. With my power, I can go places, and change things, but what can you do? Look, it's nothing personal, but all averages are pretty much useless!"

"I see what this is about Amber, and it sounds pretty personal to me," I breathed, narrowing my eyes. "You're upset that I broke your record. Well, putting me down won't lift you up, but if you're so shallow that it makes you feel better, then go for it. You might think I'm an amateur, but an amateur couldn't break the powerful Amber Travie's record, now could she?"

She glared at me with her stormy, grey-blue eyes.

I continued. "Stop looking at me like I'm something that's stuck to the bottom of your shoe, because that only makes me want to prove you wrong ... and since you're *still* looking at me like that, I guess I'll have to do just that."

"New girl has some guts!" another onlooker observed. "If you had any guts you would quit following people like her." I motioned to Amber, who seemed to be stunned into silence. "Now go grow a pair and sit at whatever table you like."

With that I stalked icily past the guards, leaving an astonished Amber Travie and her powerful friends all equally silent at their stupid table. I couldn't believe the nerve of that girl! What right did she have to treat people like subordinates?

I was definitely not venturing back in there anytime soon.

I stormed my way over into the Orchin room instead, where ladies were handing out plates of steaming hot food. The line was steadily increasing, so I hurried to get a place, trying not to look as isolated as I felt. Magnorium seemed to operate purely on the class system—which such a sophisticated institution shouldn't allow. I stood alone in the lineup. Maybe I really was just a foreigner who'd crossed into a world in which I had no place.

"Hey look who it is!" snickered a familiar voice. I turned around, recognizing the distinct and patronizing tone. Rachel and Emma were standing behind me, irritation stamped on their faces, as if my very presence was a nuisance. I couldn't believe how cruel so many Elementals seemed to be.

"Look," I begun tiredly. "We're roommates now; we shouldn't hate each other. So what do you say?" I extended a hand with a smile, willing to be friendly, although not exactly friends. My hand was met with empty air, and I awkwardly let it drop back to my side and turned back around, tired and resigned to the animosity.

"Don't come back to my room tonight, Draken," Rachel growled, her hot breath lingering on the back of my neck. I moved away a bit, holding my tongue and staring straight ahead.

The long line kept moving, and after what felt like hours, I was ravenous and finally at the front. Behind me, Rachel tapped her foot impatiently as I peered over at the trays. There was so much food behind the glass that it could've fed a small country.

The lady behind the counter sighed. "You're holding up the line, kid."

I snapped out of my haze, and finally decided, choosing from one of the dozens of options. Before I could tell the lady my decision, someone's hands grabbed me tightly by the shoulders, and threw me out of the line and onto the hard floor. I landed hard, scratching my legs on the corner of the display case during my descent. I snapped my head up, infuriated and staring at the person who had attacked me, who not surprisingly was Rachel. She was carrying on like nothing happened. All I could do for a moment was blink up at her, as I gathered my bearings. Physically I was fine, other than my sore legs, but my ego hurt, and some people farther down the line had the audacity to snicker. The line continued on normally, as if shoving people was a common occurrence. No one offered to help me up as I sat there. None even looked my way. That was it. Forget cruel, all Elementals were insane. I surveyed the huge lineup warily and tried to contain my flaring temper.

Rachel stepped away from the lineup, a tray of food clutched in her hands. Without even thinking, I stuck my left foot out, right in front of her. In one swift motion, she collided with my outstretched limb and her tray of food clattered to the floor. A second later, she toppled as well, losing her balance. A few people nervously sucked in gasps of air, as if aware of Rachel's temper problems—which I suddenly remembered as she jumped to her feet, her face bright red. I scrambled to my own feet and stood looking at her.

"You idiot!" she screamed furiously. "You're dead!"

"You think you can just push me around because I'm new?" I shouted.

Someone cheered. "You tell her newbie!"

"Fight me, you coward!" she shouted, advancing towards me. "I'll teach you how to really use Draken magic!"

I couldn't help it. I laughed. She looked so comically ridiculous, with her face beet red and splattered with her dinner; I just couldn't suppress my amusement. Rachel looked at me incredulously, and as if provoked by my nerve for laughing, picked up a handful of spaghetti from the nearest tray and whipped it at me.

I saw it hurling in my direction the moment it left her hand. I ducked so fast I didn't even realize I had moved until I was kneeling on the floor. The ball of spaghetti continued to sail through the air, past where I had been standing, and hit some poor girl behind me straight in the face.

I had never moved so unconsciously fast in my life. Rachel's eyes practically bulged out of her head.

A shot of excitement, a rowdiness I couldn't quite contain, raced through me. "What? You really thought you could hit me?" I teased, not even recognizing where the boldness came from.

Suddenly a splatter of vanilla pudding whizzed past my ear, hitting Rachel in the shoulder with a messy splat. I turned around. The girl who got hit with the spaghetti was angrily squelching her meal in her hand. The temperature in the room seemed to drop drastically, as everyone's eye shifted back to Rachel.

She let out a low growl, swiping a meatball off the tray and whipping it at the girl behind me. The girl lunged sideways and the meatball flew past and hit some other kid in the back.

Worry began to creep its way up my spine. If this continued any longer it was going to turn into a major—

"FOOD FIGHT!" someone exclaimed, gleefully.

"What! No!" I shouted. "Everyone stop!"

Nobody stopped, and my pathetic plea was ignored. In just a few seconds, the whole room erupted into chaos, with kids screaming, gripping wads of their food, and whipping it around barbarically.

"Get the newbie!" Rachel declared.

Everyone stopped and looked at me, bringing attention I really didn't want. Most of the school wasn't actually aware of my existence yet, so I shielded my face, ducked, and ran like a bat out of hell for the other rooms.

The fight was spreading like the plague through the entire cafeteria, and I was quick to dodge and maneuver around people's airborne dinners. It was complete chaos, and I moved towards the exit doors as quickly as I could, only to find two students blocking it deviously, with wads of food in their hands.

Everywhere I looked there was food flying through the air. I felt like a caged animal and desperately looked around for any signs of authority, of which there apparently were none. I finally spotted Mrs. Musk in the Terran room, but there were no signs of Kurt, who seemed to have disappeared into thin air.

Mrs. Musk was shouting, making futile attempts to stop the rampage, but no one was listening. She stood up quickly, only to be knocked back down by an airborne apple. Some of the most powerful Elementals in the world resided here and no one could stop a food fight started by a bunch of teenagers?

Food decorated the walls and slid from the ceiling and I watched as some people started ganging up on others. Rachel's name was being chanted, back in the Orchin room, and I picked up the pace, moving faster, ducking, and dodging, and knowing that I had to get out of the cafeteria before Rachel came after me to fry me to a crisp.

With all the excitement happening all at once, I didn't even notice as my body collided with another person, who seemed to be moving just as fast as I was, at least not until the collision sent us both flying back. Untangling myself from the other person, I quickly regained my composure and looked up only to meet a pair of glowering, stormy eyes. *Amber Travie.* She had a furious expression on her face, as if she suddenly realized that I was the core of her misery. Swiftly, she grabbed ahold of my sleeve and yanked me forward, forcing me to stand in front of her.

"You!" she seethed.

"*You!*" I answered, imitating her cold, drawling voice. "What do you want, Amber? Have you come to boast about your powers again?"

"Talk to me again like that, Draken. I dare you." Her eyes flashed dangerously. "Do you want to find out why I'm the most powerful person here?"

I laughed. "It's no wonder you're so strong; you carry around an ego that's bigger than me!"

"Alyssa! Alyssa ...!"

My name was being chanted in the other room now, and not just by Rachel but by a bunch of other Elementals with loud voices. I swallowed nervously. Rachel was raising an army against me.

"You've hardly been here for more than an hour! What did you *do*?" Amber asked, staring through the doorway to the other rooms, in shock.

"I did nothing!" I glanced at her quickly. Even Amber, as powerful as she was, couldn't escape the flying food and was covered in numerous sauces and juices.

"Everyone in this cafeteria is covered in food, and you are perfectly clean! What kind of magic are you using?"

"If there's magic to protect me from a food fight, I'm definitely using it," I said sarcastically.

She rolled her eyes. "I'm curious; what can you even do? They say you're as close to a mortal as they come."

I glared. "What can *you* even do?" I snapped. "Can you just talk big or are you as powerful as everyone says you are?"

"Oh I'm worse," she replied, with a devious smirk.

"Alyssa Brooks!" Rachel shouted, interrupting our little conversation and appearing in the doorway. "Fight me or you'll be covered in *this*!"

I surveyed the concoction in her hands: an appealing blend of spaghetti and potatoes.

"No thanks!" I yelled back.

Beside me, Amber gave a genuine hearty laugh, amusement making her face light up. "I was debating whether or not to kill you where you stood, but I think I'm going to let Rachel do it for me."

"I knew you had a sense of humour in there somewhere!" I hollered over my shoulder, moving past Amber, and barrelling straight into the Skyros room, the guards nowhere to be found.

My stomach growled, with all this food flying around I still hadn't had anything to eat. The irony of this whole situation was funny, and I knew I was going to laugh about it later. Much later. There were footsteps thudding behind me and I peered over my shoulder, finding Amber stubbornly trailing after me.

"Why are you following me?"

"For someone who is utterly defenseless in every way possible, you've got guts ... when you have absolutely no reason to have them. It's kind of refreshing."

I recoiled, shocked at the first thing Amber had said to me that wasn't entirely an insult.

"Thanks," I offered up awkwardly, coming to a screeching halt in the Skyros room. My eyes were immediately drawn towards Haven and Zack, who were both comically covered in bits of green, and yet somehow still gorgeous. They looked like Calvin Klein models for the salad bar.

"Am I allowed to come in this room now?" I asked, diving for cover in the back corner. This room was the calmest, as the majority of the students hadn't dared to venture inside yet, keeping the numbers fairly low.

"No, but *I* can finally leave it. It's been a great first day here. Really," Haven said calmly.

Amber raised an eyebrow. "You want to go out into that?" She gestured to the rest of the cafeteria.

"This isn't fair," Zack muttered, not even flinching as a wad of food whizzed by, splattering onto his broad chest. "Who started this without me?"

Amber glared, but the faintest smile of amusement quirked at the edges of her mouth. "She did."

Zack blinked. "Wow. Starting food fights without me? And here I thought we made a real bond today, Draken."

"It was an accident," I answered.

"Yes great idea," Haven said. "Always make it look an accident."

"You should duck," I whispered, anticipating something strange. I dropped to the ground, but no one bothered to listen. I was astonished to see an overly ripe banana zip by my head and hit Amber squarely in the chest. She glared angrily, scraping off the remains.

"I said 'duck' didn't I?" The three of them stared at me.

"How did you do that?" Zack asked curiously, which would have been a great question to answer if only I knew.

"I have eyes on the back of my head."

Before he could give an equally dry response, Rachel appeared in the doorway, covered head to toe in dirty smearings. Out of everyone present, she looked the worst, which made the most sense, since she was clearly one of the most disliked people in school.

"Alyssa Brooks, I know you're in here!" she shouted, her eyes maniacally ablaze. She clearly had no self-control. No one here seemed to.

"All of you are crazy," I muttered under my breath. Thinking fast, I looked around wildly, and before she could spot me, I dropped onto my hands and knees and crawled under the long table, taking momentary refuge. Rachel's signature black boots grew closer and closer, and I scrambled backwards as I heard her ask about me.

"Alyssa? She's under there," supplied Zack helpfully, rapping a knuckle on the top of the table. I gritted my teeth, vowing to kill him later. Rachel ducked quickly, wiggling into the small space. Our eyes clashed and she charged forward as fast as she could go, considering we were stuck under a table. I crawled desperately backwards. Technically I could bolt out from under the table, but she wasn't worth outrunning. I lived with her, so what was the point really? I stopped backing away, and we almost collided as I came to an unexpected halt. Surprise dashed across her eyes and then her features curled into a sinister grin.

"This is uncomfortable; we're stuck in a very small space together," I blurted, squeezing my eyes shut and preparing for the blast, "just like in our room."

She laughed. "And you call yourself an Elemental."

Just then there came a thunderous voice. "Stop it! All of you! Drop everything!" The tiny pause that followed was all I needed. Suddenly letting Rachel pulverize me didn't seem like the best option, and taking advantage of the moment of confusion, I scrambled out from under the table.

I emerged to see an extremely angry Mrs. Musk. She stood at the centre of the room looking utterly furious, not even bothering to maintain a calm or professional facade. It seemed that she had finally gotten her bearings and started to act, bringing in two huge goons to stop the chaos. She also apparently came armed and ready, as in her hand she clutched some odd weapons I had never seen before. They looked exactly like arrows, except made of clear glass, with the tips sharpened to deadly-looking points.

Everyone in the room took one look at the mysterious weapons and stopped what they were doing, backing cautiously away from Mrs. Musk.

"Stop!" she thundered again, her voice reverberating off the walls.

A moment later, Rachel scrambled out from out under the table as well, and all eyes shifted to her ... and then to me. Mrs. Musk looked at both of us, sighed, and took a deep breath.

"What is the meaning of this? Anyone who throws one more piece of food is getting a gentle reminder of what *these* do!" She gestured with the glass arrows, waving them wildly around above her head. I did a double take at their incredibly sharp-looking, pointed ends and decided that I didn't *want* to know what they did.

Would Mrs. Musk actually shoot one of us? Considering how everyone paled the moment she gave the warning, I assumed that the answer was '*Yes,* she actually *would* shoot at us'.

Realizing that people still had food in their hands, she roared once again, with a fierce growl in her tone. "I *said* to put down that food! Now! Drop it!"

As everyone moved to drop the food they still held onto the floor or trays on the table, Rachel took advantage of the momentary confusion to catch me off guard. She rushed at me unexpectedly, throwing herself forward clearly meaning to tackle me to the floor. The way she was moving made it clear that she intended to cause more than a few injuries.

Fortunately she never got to lay a single finger on me.

Mrs. Musk reacted quickly, grabbing one of the arrows in her right hand. Her grip tightened around the unusual glass weapon, and in an instant, she whipped it straight at Rachel. The arrow spiralled neatly through the air, with perfect accuracy—demonstrating a level of skill that could only be the result of years of practise. The entire room watched in awe as it sailed through the air.

In that instant, I realized that Rachel was going to get seriously hurt because of something I technically had started. Sure she was cruel, rude, and angry, but despite how much it pained me to admit it, I was partly responsible for this. A shot of adrenaline zipped through me, like a bout of protectiveness, making me spring into action before I even realized what I was doing.

"No!" I yelled, lunging to tackle Rachel and knock her out of the way.

This time it was Mrs. Musk's turn to watch, dumbstruck, as I sailed through the air with my hands outstretched. I was a second too late. The bizarre weapon sailed past my open arms and buried itself smoothly in Rachel's neck. My body connected with hers and we both crumpled to the floor, a look of complete surprise flying across her face. The arrow quivered in her neck briefly, before blood started oozing around it. Rachel slumped forward against me, instantly motionless.

I was dimly aware of making some sort of strangling noise. Was she dead? My hands immediately went to her pulse, ready to start CPR if needed. Her heart beat steadily in her chest. I didn't like her, but I certainly didn't want her dead, and hearing her heart beating strongly, I let out a true sigh of relief. I took her unconscious head in my hands, gently placing it on the hard floor. Then I slowly stood back up. The silence in the room was palpable.

"Is she crazy?" a voice whispered a little too loud. I didn't know if they meant Rachel or me, but either way, I felt my face turn crimson.

Finally Mrs. Musk's goon approached the scene and pried Rachel off the floor, slinging the Draken's limp body over his shoulder. My jaw dropped as he stalked out of the cafeteria without another word. I had seen enough! Furious, I jumped forward, spinning on Mrs. Musk.

"How could you just shoot someone like that?" I shouted indignantly. At this point, I didn't even care if I got swatted down with another arrow. I was absolutely disgusted. "Wouldn't just yelling at her suffice? You just can't go around shooting glass *arrows* at people!"

Twenty jaws dropped, gaping at my bluntness. Mrs. Musk frowned at me as if *I* were the one who was crazy.

"Those arrows are dangerous; you shouldn't have tried to interfere!" she chastised. "Though it was a noble act, you shouldn't be so foolish dear. These weapons aren't to be taken lightly; they're what we call Power Arrows. They're special weapons designed to bring down Elementals. It drains our powers and knocks us unconscious for a short while, like a tranquilizer. Rachel's magic will return in a few days."

"What right do you think you have to take someone's powers away?" Magic felt like taking shots of pure adrenaline, and I involuntary shuddered at the thought of going back to having no magic running thickly through my veins the way it did.

Mrs. Musk ran a tired hand through her greying hair. "Miss Brooks, I know that you're new to all of this, but please, no more questions unless I am the one asking them ... and I just have one for you." There was a long pause that put everyone on edge.

When she finally asked her question, I winced as all the eyes in the room slowly swung in my direction.

"Who on earth started this whole thing?"

I wasn't aiming to be noticed at this foreign school, but blending in and becoming invisible now—the way I always did—did not seem like an available option.

"Miss Brooks?" Mrs. Musk purred, questioningly. "This is not a good way to end your first day. Care to explain?" I noticed the way her fingers danced delicately over the rest of the arrows. I gulped.

"This was not my fault!" I replied quickly, which sounded hollow even to my ears.

"Judging by the last five minutes, Rachel sure had it in for you."

"It wasn't my fault!" I insisted, averting my gaze.

"She was chasing you," Mrs. Musk pointed out.

"Yeah," I said, "I was aware of that."

"What did you do Miss Brooks?" she sighed, seeming to see right through me. "And I suggest you tell the truth, because we have the means of *making* you tell the truth."

I swallowed nervously. "She shoved me and I fell, so I tripped her and she started throwing food around." The simplified version of the truth sounded completely plausible.

"You provoked someone with obvious anger issues then?" Mrs. Musk asked.

I reddened. When she said it like that, I sounded like the crazy one. "I was not provoking anyone, I was defending myself."

"By tripping her?"

There was nothing I could do or say that would justify my cause at this point. It was better that I shut up and accepted my punishment. "Yes."

Mrs. Musk glared and the look on her face made me feel utterly ashamed. Here I was in a school like Magnorium, given a privilege that very few others had, and I was running around starting fights.

"You will be punished, as will Rachel. Detention. In the library."

"What? Come on, that's too soft!" Amber Travie called. She was ignored, something she clearly wasn't accustomed to.

"Regardless of whose fault this all may be, your retaliation will be punished!" she continued. "You are going to sort our books in alphabetical order. You will do this every day for the rest of this week, for an hour a day."

"If I don't need to see Rachel, I'll do anything."

"You might want to watch your tongue Miss Brooks. Around here it might just get you into trouble."

I clamped my mouth shut at that.

"Now everybody get out, at once!" Mrs. Musk shouted in a commanding tone, one that contrasted greatly with her petite frame. "You all should be ashamed of yourselves! Go back to your rooms, and clean up!"

Slowly the crowds dispersed. The rooms were filthy with muck and I was mortified at what my one action had unintentionally caused. This was just great; I got detention on my very first day. Suddenly I was angry, my temper roaring and begging to be released, but I held it in. I was no better than Rachel. I just hid it better.

Obediently, I shuffled my way towards the exit only to get stopped by an icy hand clamped onto my shoulder. Amber stood behind me, her eyes narrowed into tiny slits of suspicion. I really wasn't in the mood.

"The only reason you got such a lenient punishment is because she likes you. Keep that in mind the next time you decide to start something, mortal."

"I'm not a mortal," I seethed.

"Yeah, well you might as well be one."

With that she stormed away and I found myself fantasizing about how nice it would be if a meteor dropped out of the sky and landed on her head. Yet something was off about Amber; something fuelled that fire in her eyes. I wondered what it was.

I walked down the halls attentively, earning stares from the people around me. Some introduced themselves, as if starting a commotion on my first day was a worthy right of passage to becoming accepted. I introduced myself to a jumble of faces that all blurred together after a few moments. Then Haven appeared, seemingly out of nowhere, beside me.

He seemed to have ditched his entourage of fans and stood, inspecting me. There was something about the way he looked at me, like I was the only other person in the world. Whenever he was thinking, he was fully concentrated. It was unnerving. He was blocking my entrance to the elevator, and I crossed my arms against my chest.

"You've got a lot to learn."

"Thank you for stating the obvious," I rolled my eyes.

"You need to blend in Alyssa. That means no starting food fights and no challenging authority."

"What's your deal with this place?" I asked bluntly. "I mean, look around. It's nice!"

He groaned dramatically. "Exactly what I told you on the plane. They buy you!"

"Well it's working," I said. "Maybe you're just used to it."

"Careful now," Haven said defensively. "I'm rich, not spoiled; there's a difference."

"I'm just saying, maybe you need to relax a bit."

"I relax every other weekend, but thanks for the concern."

"Are you going to let me go into the elevator?" I asked, beginning to get a bit annoyed. I didn't want to hear conspiracy theories about Magnorium.

"You don't draw attention to yourself here; that can get you killed. Did you not just see a student get an arrow in the neck? Yeah it's magical and all that, but it's still an arrow *in her neck!* You have to *know* the rules before you can start breaking them, Alyssa. Just a friendly reminder."

It was hard to tell when he was being serious, but before I could ask him, he disappeared into the elevator, the doors sliding shut before I could join him.

I eventually made my way back up to the eighth floor, unlocking the door and discovering that the room had been completely rearranged, with a third bed added and a dresser. It looked even more cramped than it did before. Emma sat alone on her slate bed, covered in food and glaring. Rachel was nowhere to be found, gladly, but I couldn't shake that feeling of guilt.

"Going to take a shower?" I muttered bravely.

She scowled at me. "You started a food fight!" she accused, every word sounding like an insult.

"No, Rachel started the food fight."

"Because of you, my best friend got shot by a Power Arrow and now she'll be in the infirmary for at least a week!"

"Look I'm sorry. Okay? I never meant for it to happen!" That was all I seemed to ever do, apologize. What did I have to apologize for? Standing up for myself?

She continued moaning, throwing up her hands. "Now I'm going to have to spend a week with you, all by myself!"

"I'm not looking forward to it either!" I retorted dryly, unzipping my knapsack. "But there is a major conflict here. For example, you're friends with a maniac—"

"Shut up!" she growled.

"Or you'll what? Want to get library duty with me?"

She gritted her teeth. "That's it. I'm going to the lounge!" she announced with a sneer, hopping off her bed and storming out, slamming the door loudly.

I blinked. Well, at least now it would be peaceful. Lights out wasn't till eleven, and to burn through some time, I called my mom and completely lied, telling her I was having a great time. Then I began to examine some of the strange textbooks—the ones about magic.

There was a battle strategy textbook, the history of magic, a spell book, and a few others. I studied each one, extracting as much information as I could; I needed it, considering how behind I was.

At around eleven o'clock, the lights turned off automatically, putting my studying on hold, and so I reluctantly crawled into my new bed, sinking under the plush comforter. I lay awake for hours staring up at the ceiling.

Emma came back around midnight, despite the curfew, and I was a bit wary of sleeping in the same room. It didn't exactly seem like the safest thing, but sometime in the early morning, my body surrendered despite my wishes, and I drifted off into a light dreamless sleep.

An extremely loud and unexpected alarm jolted me awake at exactly seven the next morning. I lay awake, peering around for a moment and trying to remember exactly where I was. When it finally dawned on me, I forced myself out of bed, feeling a thrum of excitement. Today was my first real day at Magnorium.

I found Emma already out of bed and ready to go, looking fresh and neatly trimmed. She took in my tousled hair and lost expression and smirked. "There's an alarm to wake you up."

"Is that the best you can do?" I shot back.

I quickly slipped into the Magnorium uniform, the softness of the fabric resting comfortably against my skin. Compared to other school uniforms, it wasn't horrible. A tight pencil skirt hugged my curves neatly, with the simple white blouse accenting the style. I let my hair cascade down my shoulders and hurried to stuff all my textbooks into my knapsack. I grabbed my key off the nightstand, making sure to put it in my pocket, because if I ever forgot, or lost it, I doubted my roommates would ever let me back in. It was nearly eight by the time I was completely ready.

This time it only took me a grand total of five minutes to retrace my steps and find the cafeteria. There was a steady flow of students ahead of me as I walked towards the overly large double doors. Once again, Mrs. Musk stood at the entrance, joined by Haven.

"Alyssa," Mrs. Musk called, a relieved expression noticeable in the corners of her tired eyes. "It's about time you bothered to show up."

"Sorry," I apologized, squirming under her strict gaze. "And I really am sorry about last night."

"Morning Alyssa," Haven said, meeting my eyes slyly. "Isn't it a nice day to not be wandering around the desert?"

"That's the spirit, Haven!" Mrs. Musk exclaimed approvingly.

His arms hung loosely at his sides, and I couldn't help glancing down at his wrist. The ink I had seen imprinted across his wrist the day before was still there, but the number had increased by one. What was he counting? He watched me study his wrist, making no move to hide it.

"It went up since yesterday," I observed. "What is it?" I revelled in my own boldness, leaving plenty room for him to explain.

"Please Alyssa, I've only known you for a day. Can't let the cat out of the bag yet. I still don't trust you."

"Hey!"

"All right, it's time to go in," Mrs. Musk interrupted. "Alyssa, thanks to the incident you stirred up yesterday, there wasn't a chance to introduce you properly to your peers. Now come along you two; it's not very often that we get new arrivals." She grinned excitedly and beckoned us to follow as she disappeared behind the fancy doors.

"All students!" Mrs. Musk called out, "report to the Draken room immediately!" She led us to the front of the room, and Haven took a stand beside me. I watched shyly as the student body trickled in, forming a huge circle around us. From my books, I knew that there were never very many young Elementals at one time, but even with all of us gathered in one crowd, there couldn't have been more than a hundred and fifty of us.

I scanned the diverse faces, trying to memorize every little detail about the room and the people, until my eyes came to a crashing halt. A frail old lady wheeled herself to the centre of the room. The woman emitted confidence, which was odd considering that she looked half dead. The crowd had parted instantly, split down the middle to make a path for the woman, a deep and profound respect etched deeply on their faces.

The woman in question looked to be about eighty years old or so, and sported a mass of pure white hair that stuck up wildly in all directions. She scanned the room with a pair of beady brown eyes sunk deeply in their sockets. Her skin was disturbingly translucent, with the sickly pallor of candle wax. I could barely make out her thin-lipped mouth, but could tell it was moving. The woman was chattering excitedly to Mrs. Musk, and the life and joy in her tone surprised me. She was clad in a baggy grey shirt and pants, which practically enveloped her frail frame. She looked like a heap of wrinkles desperately strewn together, and I feared that, if I touched her even slightly, she would shatter. I tried not to stare at her as the crowd settled down.

Mrs. Musk awarded her students with a bright, warm smile that immediately eased the mood and then gestured to us with her small hands. "Ladies and gentlemen, it pleases me to say that yesterday we had two new arrivals, Alyssa Brooks and Haven Reeves, Draken and Aquarian!"

If my existence was unknown yesterday, even after the food fight I had caused, it was surely known now. I got the feeling that Haven was pretty well known already, but being scrutinized by so many sets of eyes was a bit overwhelming to us both.

"Alyssa and Haven," Mrs. Musk went on, somehow growing even more enthusiastic, "found the school in one hour and forty-seven minutes and hold the new test record!"

There was a moment where the entire room lapsed into a stunned silence. They looked at us almost disbelievingly, and then back to Mrs. Musk. Apparently achieving the old record had been no easy feat. Amber and Zack's three-hour time had given them huge bragging rights and resulted in two super-sized egos.

The cheering started in the back of the crowd, slowly moving forward until it reached us at the front. My ears were ringing from the enthusiastic clapping and whooping. I felt the need to shy away and blend back into the crowd. This record really was no big deal, but I was embarrassed by the way everyone was eyeing me so seriously

"If you see these two around, don't be afraid to say hello!" Mrs. Musk said, still smiling brightly, seemingly unaware of our humiliation. Finally, our big debut moment was over and Mrs. Musk shooed the crowd away, directing them back to their meals. Her attempts appeared futile as the entire student body swarmed, peppering the two of us with rapid questions and declarations of praise.

"Are you the new Amber and Zack?"

"All four of them should fight!"

"Tell us how you did it!"

The questions were relentless and my head was spinning at the commotion. The room was loud—too loud—and I couldn't distinguish one voice from the next.

"Excuse me!" Someone yelled from deep within the unsettled mob.

"Excuse me children!" the same voice hollered a second time. The mob immediately quieted down and the old woman from before slowly wheeled herself in my direction, coming to a stop at my feet.

"Well I suppose that took long enough?" The strange woman's gaze finally locked onto my own and she smiled. She extended a hand and I shook it cautiously, afraid that I would somehow hurt her.

"I've been meaning to introduce myself. My name is Elda."

"I'm Alyssa Brooks," I said, smiling politely.

"Oh believe me, I know. That's quite a record you two got there."

I smiled warmly. "Thanks, I guess. Are you a teacher here or something?"

"I teach battle strategy for the advanced. I know, that's surprising with this bloody wheelchair."

I narrowed my eyes. I noticed her weight leaned to the right, which probably meant her left side must have been wounded or damaged, and was likely the reason for the wheelchair. She had quite a few scars running along the exposed skin of her body: on her neck, her arms, and her chin. Some looked older than others, which implied that she wasn't just old, she was old enough to have survived quite a few battles. I remembered Amber complaining only yesterday about her battle strategy teacher. Was this her teacher?

"Your little friend here is in my class, and I expect him to stand out." She motioned to Haven, who suddenly looked very interested in the floor.

"Don't get too hung up on me," he said modestly.

"Nonsense boy, you're a prodigy. You already broke the Travie boy's record."

"Alyssa figured it all out," Haven shrugged, easily admitting his part.

"You're the powerful one," I teased.

"I've been wondering about that," he said. "What haven't you told me?"

"Everything you haven't asked me," I retorted.

"Ah, I forgot how amusing you youngsters could be. I'll leave you to yourselves then. Nice meeting you Alyssa, Haven."

"Nice meeting you," I echoed, watching as she wove herself through the maze of tables and chairs. Finally, I turned back to Haven, who had his arms crossed over his chest and was looking up at the ceiling.

"So," I said, "are you as good as everyone says you are?"

"Well, if you threw me in a pool I wouldn't drown, so I guess that makes me all right."

"Fair enough. I guess you better go; you're due at your table. I'll see you around, Haven."

"See you," he replied, reluctantly retreating into the Skyros room.

About thirty minutes later, the bell for first period rang, and a crowd of about a hundred and fifty bodies dispersed, heading to class. I fought my confusion as I got swept along in the chaos, trying to find my first class: spell casting.

I found it easily and ventured inside. A class of twenty students, all around my age, sat in identical rows. It looked much like a class in any other normal school, and the familiar scene was somehow comforting. A middle-aged woman stood at the front of the room, already speaking.

The room grew quiet, the door slamming behind me. A bunch of students looked up, recognizing me from last night and this morning.

"Hi," I said nervously, smiling warmly.

The teacher frowned. "You're Alyssa Brooks," she muttered in an irritated voice. "You're going to cause me quite a bit of extra work. You have years of catching up to do." She motioned to an empty desk right in the front row. She was right. Everyone else was so far ahead of me, how could I possibly hope to catch up?

"I'm Mrs. Abott, your spell-casting teacher." She nodded to me and then looked back up at the class. "As I was saying before Miss Brooks walked in, we will be focusing for the next little while on type C spells. Would anyone like to explain what that is to Alyssa?"

A bunch of hands eagerly shot up and I sunk farther down in my chair.

"There are four different levels of spells or magic: A through D," the girl sitting next to me happily supplied. "A being the easiest spell to cast, D being the hardest, needing more energy and concentration." I had never heard of such things. I was going to be so lost.

"Exactly," said Mrs. Abott.

The next two hours progressed like that. I tried absorbing everything Mrs. Abott was saying but it was difficult. At times, she might as well have been speaking some ancient language I'd never heard of.

"To conduct a spell you must begin with clearing your mind and summoning up all your energy. Your hands are your biggest asset when performing magic. They're like an outlet; they act as a release. Alyssa, do you understand?"

I nodded mutely, so overwhelmed by this point that I doubted I could've grasped two plus two.

"You have to want your power," she said. "Believe it will happen."

I nodded again.

"Doubt," she continued, "is the greatest obstacle Elementals have to overcome in order to cast spells. Conducting difficult spells depletes your energy. But eventually energy is restored as magic is all about balance. Balance your energy with your magic and know your boundaries."

I watched quietly as my classmates tried summoning their magic for a type C spell. None succeeded, even though it appeared no one was doing anything inherently wrong. Maybe that was why we were classified as average, good but not good enough. I wondered what I could do, if I really tried. For now I was content with being an observer. That was good enough.

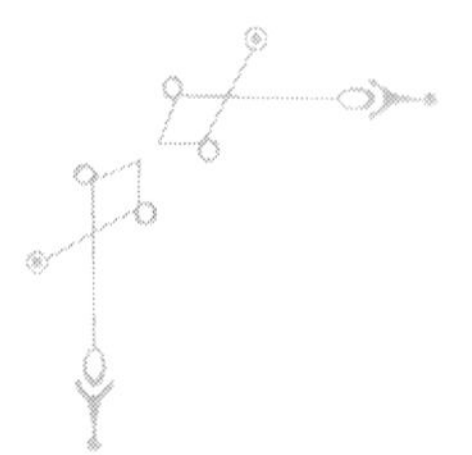
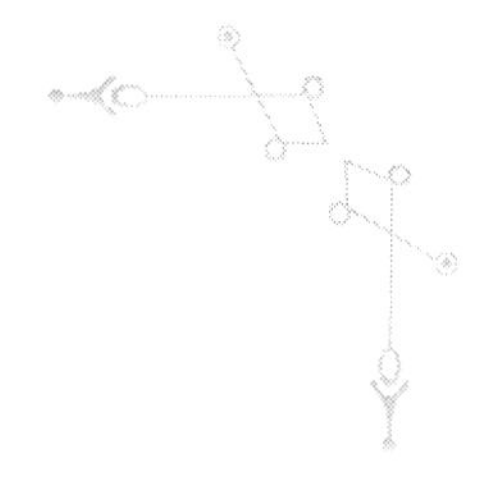

CHAPTER 7

THE ORB

My first full day at Magnorium passed pretty uneventfully considering the circumstances. I sat through a set of four classes, growing more lost by the minute. If I could pick one similarity between Magnorium and regular public school, it would definitely be the level of friendliness, because both types of teenagers, human or not, were equally unfriendly. However, that didn't stop me from trying, though my attempts were becoming less enthusiastic each time.

I walked into what was considered the most boring magic class at Magnorium, the History of Elemental Artifacts, and quickly decided that everyone was sorely mistaken about it. A teacher, with a weird-looking goggle contraption strapped to his head, smiled and stopped me right as I walked through the door.

"Alyssa Brooks?"

"That's me," I said.

"Perfect. I'm Professor Tate!," he exclaimed reaching into a bin he held strapped to his side. He dug through the contents, pulled out a matching head contraption, and placed it in my hand.

"Put this on."

"Why?" I asked. "This is a history class, isn't it? We're not time travelling, are we?" I was only half joking about that.

His blue eyes practically bulged out of the mask.

"*Just* history class?" he scoffed. "Please. A couple of years ago there was a little accident in my class. Since then, Mrs. Musk wants these things used in order to satisfy some safety protocol. Nothing's getting through here!" he said, and as if to prove it, slammed his fist against his plastic eye-coverings.

"Understood," I said quickly, slipping the contraption over my face and securing it as it tried to fall over my eyes and down to my chin.

"All right then," he said, stepping dramatically aside and motioning me forward. "Welcome to History of Elemental Artifacts!"

Smiling uncertainly, I moved past him, entering the class curiously, and meeting the gazes of twenty other pairs of eyes, identically concealed behind plastic goggles.

I slid into an empty seat and studied the long, makeshift table at the front of the room. Odd-looking items had been placed in a line on its surface. Some I vaguely recognized from overheard gossip in the cafeteria, or my quick perusal of my textbooks, but most I had never seen before. I knew all of them did something special though, and by the looks of them, could be pretty dangerous.

"Can any of you lovely people please explain to Miss Brooks what exactly these toys are?" Professor Tate asked, taking his place behind the long table, facing his class, and grabbing one of the objects at random, admiring it in his hands.

"Elemental artifacts!" a voice cheerily called from the back row.

Pleased, he nodded. "Since the beginning of time, Elementals have been the strongest of the supernatural beings. Our wit has always defined us. Each of these items have been collected over the years by Magnorium. Each of them has a purpose. Each of them should not be touched unless you are directly instructed to. Miss Brooks?"

"Yes?" I piped up loudly.

"Catch!" he called casually, tossing a small rectangular-shaped box at my head. I yelped, scrambling to catch it and sighing in relief when it landed safely in the palm of my hand.

"What is this?" I asked curiously, running my fingers over the smooth wood of the box.

"It's a bottomless box, used for storage. Go on, open it."

Curiously, I shifted the box between my two hands. It felt hollow, like it was empty. I popped the lid off the top of the box with relative ease and stared inside. The box looked empty, and true to its name, was bottomless. When I looked inside, all I saw was blackness peering back out at me.

"It's empty," I said, with a frown.

Professor Tate laughed at that, rolling his eyes. "They told me you were going to be quite a bit of work. Maybe a lot more work than they anticipated."

My cheeks burned. I couldn't even count how many times I had heard variations of that same heartwarming message, and it was only my second day at the school.

"It's actually quite full, Miss Brooks. It only looks empty. That's the point. Created by Terrans, who infused it with magic, this box can hold an endless amount of weight and bulk."

The box wasn't very wide, maybe about the length of my hand, but when I moved to reach my fingers through the opening, my whole hand slipped through.

The air inside of the box felt soft, almost like it was coated in silk. I reached deeper inside, my hand brushing against something rough. Interestingly enough, I felt no bottom. I kept extending my hand until I fit my whole arm inside.

I fastened my fingers around an object I could feel deep in the box. Even though the object was far too big to conceivably fit through the small opening, it did so without even grazing the sides of the box as I pulled it out. A foreign-looking textbook I had never seen before tumbled onto my desk.

Professor Tate smiled, satisfied, as I put the book back inside the box and replaced the lid.

"If you were wondering, Miss Brooks, that particular item you're holding is used as an extension of Magnorium's library."

"You better take it then," I said, carefully tossing the box back to him. He caught it, only to drop it back carelessly onto the table.

"Now let's take a look at this thing here," he said, and moved on to showcase the next item. He grinned, holding up what looked like a large metal urn. The urn was decorated, quite disturbingly, with images of young women, their faces twisted and screaming in horror.

"You guys should hold an auction," I said, frowning at the urn in his hands.

Professor Tate ignored the comment. "This urn captures the screams of Banshees, the wailing women of death. Banshee screams can be quite a useful weapon." Wordlessly, he replaced the urn on the table and lifted off the heavy lid. A horrible sound escaped, almost like the noise itself had been imprisoned, which is exactly what had happened.

The sound invaded my ears—a sound that I dearly hoped could never be replicated by a living organism. It screeched, and wailed ... an inhuman cry of terror and agony. Just listening to a second of the horrid sound sent me spiralling into a state of impending terror. My vision blurred, and I slammed my hands over my tender ears to block out the noise.

Professor Tate quickly slammed the lid back on, cutting off the terrible wailing abruptly. I uncovered my ears reluctantly, as he grinned.

"Music to my ears." The class moaned, not appreciating his humour. "Now, this baby right here," he continued moving on down the table, "is an indestructible sword. Quite useful."

I stared down at the shiny metal curiously.

"This pen-looking thing," he declared dramatically, snatching what really did look like a black ballpoint pen off the table, moving out from behind the table, and approaching the class, "sucks the very life out of your soul and stores it." He slammed it down onto my desk for good measure.

I practically jumped out of my seat.

"Kidding," he announced quickly. "It's a pen." I let out a sigh of relief. "One that you should be using, Miss Brooks, to take notes." He pivoted on one foot and headed back to his table, motioning to the items, pointing them out one after the next almost as quickly as he could describe them.

"This vial right here contains dust that allows one to change shape. This candle is a passageway for talking to deceased supernatural beings. These glasses show the user their worst fear. It's almost as if it springs to life in front of them. We use these for training." He drew his hands together and sighed.

"Well you get the idea. These artifacts have proven themselves to be quite useful over the years. Any questions? Miss Brooks, you look particularly overwhelmed."

My eyes were dancing as I stared at the arsenal of objects. I didn't know whether to be fascinated or terrified that such things existed. Perhaps it was safe to be a bit of both.

Out of all the things he showed us, he seemed to have missed one, a small globe that sat directly in the middle of the table.

"What does that thing do?" I asked curiously. The class murmured and I almost sensed a wave of excitement roll through the room.

"This thing?" Professor Tate asked, snatching it off the desk. "This is a replica of an artifact we do not actually have in our possession. As such, it doesn't do anything."

"A replica of what?" I asked curiously.

"The most powerful known Elemental artifact."

"Wow," I commented. "Where's the real one?"

He laughed, amused by the question. "It hasn't been made yet my dear. Or perhaps remade would be more accurate. I'll let you in on an Elemental legend. What I have here in my hands is what is known to supernaturals as the Orb. Created by the Orchins a very long time ago, this artifact has more power than any other weapon ever created."

"Cool. Maybe it's good you don't have it then."

He ignored that comment, his eyes unfocused as he had already launched into a deep Elemental tangent.

"Legend has it that the Orb is split into four parts, four rare magic crystals scattered across the globe. Only when these four crystals are brought together do they create the Orb. By right of creation, the wielder of this Orb must be an Orchin, which as we all know is impossible. This little Orb in my hands is said to have power that can launch the world into eternal light and demolish any foe or army."

"Sounds unreal," I said quietly.

Professor Tate glared, tightening his hold around the replica. It was translucent, a colour that almost seemed to shimmer against the light. It looked a bit bigger than a golf ball. Compared to the other artifacts on the table, the Orb looked ridiculously out of place.

"Unreal? Is it unreal that Elemental treasure hunters have died looking for the Orb? I spent a year of my own life tracking down the crystals!"

"Did you ever find them, sir?" a girl behind me asked curiously.

"Yes I did, in fact!" he practically shouted, clapping his hands together loudly.

"Yeah, where are they?"

"First one's in the Amazon jungle."

"Excuse me for saying," I interrupted cautiously, "but the Amazon jungle is a pretty big place."

The others murmured in agreement.

"Our results are vague, but not inconclusive. We're so close! So close to figuring out the location!" he exclaimed with a wave of his hand.

I could suddenly understand the reasoning behind his eccentric behaviour. He was a treasure hunter. Well, an Elemental treasure hunter, one who fed off of conspiracies and theories. So many people,

I suddenly thought, were fuelled by what *could* be. Driven mad by stories and legends. It was almost comforting that some myths were actually true.

"What's it matter even if you do find it? It's not like any Elemental can just go and take it. It's dangerous and impossible," another kid pointed out.

"Even if you won't be able to take it, you'll still make history," I said, trying to be supportive.

His face was lit red with passion, and it looked like he was seconds away from blowing a fuse. "Exactly. Unlikely people doing dangerous things that are deemed impossible *make history*. And if I can teach you one thing, it is to make history. Ask yourself, what makes you different than the other people sitting around you? Why should they remember *your* name? That is why I want to find the Orb—the Orb that so many say is lost to the world."

I was quiet. He might as well be mad. He was, after all, fascinated with magical items and in my opinion, dedicating your life to hunting down artifacts didn't exactly count as making history.

But living life the way I was doing it didn't count as making history either. I was born with special powers, but what have I done with them?

Suddenly worrying about fitting in with the rest of the Elementals here didn't seem like such a big deal, because really, what actually made me different? Nothing. Even amongst the mortals I had been ordinary. I had not done a single thing to impact people's lives. I had done nothing to give people a reason to remember my name. Well other than starting a food fight, which was just humiliating, or breaking some record that didn't even mean anything. Hell, I couldn't find a reason why anyone would remember me. It was pitiful, but I knew I was pretty much unidentifiable. And in that moment, nothing else was more startling.

"You should really stand back," Mr. Garcia, my supernatural training teacher, said to the class. There were so many weird things at Magnorium, but my Supernatural Training Class—a class dedicated solely to exploring the world of other supernaturals—went beyond the normal sort of weird. "*You're probably going to lose your mind in my class, mortal girl,*" is what Mr. Garcia had warmly said to me on the first day.

The class was the epitome of the unfathomable, and so far the only thing it had really taught me was that everything I previously thought was not real, was in fact, very real. There were about a thousand possible ways to die when dealing with other supernaturals, but apparently if I listened very carefully to Mr. Garcia, and tried not to cross paths with any other beings, I should be fine. Other than that, this class had also succeeded in scaring me into not going outside ever again.

"Miss Brooks, you should know that Trolls have a tendency to get quite nasty."

"Wait, what?" I exclaimed, staring at the violently shaking, brown cardboard box in his hands. "That's what's in there?"

"Obviously," he said, rolling his eyes as if I were ridiculous for ever thinking anything else. It had been two weeks since I first came to Magnorium, and while it had taken time to get used to the mass chaos, I didn't think I'd ever get used to the magic.

It was humiliating; I was failing all of my magic classes. In fact, the only classes I was passing were my mortal ones, which probably made me the worst Elemental ever. It was useless to even try anymore. Even after the extra hours of training and tutoring. No matter what any teacher did or said, I hadn't produced an ounce of my magic since taking the test with Haven. Everything here was just so unbelievable, like Trolls stuck in damn boxes. It was like travelling to a distant planet where I was the alien.

"You scared Alyssa?" someone behind me whispered, causing an outbreak of irritating laughter that echoed in the stillness of the forest.

"No," I snapped, eyeing the claw marks that were starting to reach through to the outer shell of the cardboard. "But I think you should let it out."

"It's not a pet, you idiot. It's a Troll."

"Perfect," Mr. Garcia said cheerfully. "Alyssa you can come and open it up for us then." He set the jerking box down on the soft grass. It was protocol for all of our classes to be held outside. Things tended to get a bit unpredictable.

Even though the school grounds were in the middle of the desert, a beautiful forest was able to grow. Terrans could make anything grow anywhere, so it was like we were standing smack in the middle of a rain forest. Light filtered through the zigzagging splashes of the tree branches overhead, casting dappled shade on the clearing. The natural grass greens and pretty pink and blue flowers wrestled with the sun's rays, making this forest my favourite place in the whole school.

"Open it fast; they bite," Mr. Garcia said, with a wild look in his eyes, stepping back a few feet for good measure.

"Do I have to do any magic?"

"No, we're just going to talk to it."

"Trolls speak English?"

"Alyssa," a guy behind me snapped, nudging me forward with his foot, "they can speak any language; now go and open it." The class fanned outwards as I approached the box on the ground. It was taped shut, with two small air holes poked on either side. Whatever was inside was clearly not happy, and appeared to be kicking and punching at the box's sides. As far as I knew from our lessons, Trolls were not on the list of beings that would kill you on a whim. But even still, it didn't mean they had to be treated like an inanimate object and locked up in a box.

I knelt on the damp grass, the moisture seeping through my skirt. The box was shaking, its sides heaving against the force of a small weight moving around inside. I grabbed the box with my hands, to stop the harsh movements, and gently pried the tape off.

As soon as I ripped the tape off, a small body shot out from the front flap, crashing onto the grass. The crowd behind me laughed and I leaned curiously over the lump on the ground.

To put it simply, the Troll looked like a small gorilla whose DNA was mixed with a human's. It was small, the top of its head barely reaching my knees, but quite thick, and just as ugly as the folklore described. The flesh on the Troll's face, hands, and feet, was a pale brown, earthy colour, and practically blended in with the rest of the forest. He or she (if there even *was* a gender differentiation) was absolutely covered in hair. Long, coarse black hair cascaded down its small chest, all knotted and decorated with smears of dirt. Its small eyes glared, darting back and forth, and its abnormally large nose looked ridiculous in proportion to the rest of its body.

The Troll hissed and groaned, which reminded me of Rachel on a good day. The Troll began to shift, untangling its limbs, and when I looked down, the creature was gone.

"*OW!*" I yelped, feeling a sudden searing pain on the side of my ankle. The next thing I knew, my feet were being swiped out from underneath me by long twisted fingernails. I wobbled unsteadily, crumpling to the ground in a heap. I touched my ankle curiously, finding a row of sharp, incisor-like bite marks beginning to spurt blood. It bit me?

"Oh God," I groaned. "I'm going to get Troll rabies."

I struggled to get to my feet, but the Troll turned, gnashing its razor sharp teeth angrily. It stomped quickly back towards me on its tiny little feet, jumping up onto my stomach and pushing me back down. I gasped as its surprising weight pressed its bony bare feet deep into my diaphragm. Its oddly shaped nose was now mere inches from mine, and its drooping face, looking like melted candle-wax, left me absolutely speechless.

"I hate you Elementals, always thinking you can push us around!" the Troll complained in a low throaty voice—a voice that sounded like it was uncomfortable speaking anything at all. "Well you can't! You can't!" It jumped up and down, landing roughly on the soft flesh of my stomach, knocking the wind out of me.

My head hit the ground hard, at the mercy of the little thrashing Troll, and I groaned. "Um ... Mr. Garcia?" I had no idea what to do. Or what to say. Or how to calm the Troll down.

"This is a hands on exercise, Miss Brooks," Mr. Garcia called, his voice floating over from where he stood, a good distance away.

"Eh!" the Troll yelled, sending globs of green spittle flying into the air over my head. "You can't push a Troll around!"

"We're sorry!" I gasped.

"Sorry?" It waved a long, twisted grey fingernail in front of my nose and screeched, "SORRY! Do we look like pets?"

"No!" I said quickly, trying to think. What did I know about Trolls from the lessons? They were aggressive. They were greedy ... and dimwitted ...

"Well that's what it feels like!" Indignant, the Troll jumped off my stomach, stomped over to the cardboard box and then kicked it across the clearing with one stubby foot.

I scrambled to my feet before it could climb onto me again, backing away from the little rampaging creature. The rest of the class backed even farther away, giving the creature some room. It was so angry, and so fast, that it was hard to even keep track of it.

"Ow!" I yelled again, feeling a hard yank at the side of my head. The Troll had jumped up, climbed my shirt, yanked out a little handful of hair, and then jumped back off. Now it stood behind me, puffing its chest out, eyes glittering with gluttony. In its hands was a thick strand of my hair. The Troll was running it through its long, pointed fingers.

"It looks like gold," it said, eyes flashing. "So shiny, like gold."

"Hey!" Mr. Garcia shouted from about ten feet away, with the rest of the class huddled behind him. "I've got gold for you!"

The Troll turned its short stubby neck, eyes lighting up in curiosity. He hobbled over to my teacher, staring up at what looked to be a piece of shiny gold costume jewellery, a necklace, in his hands.

"Is that real gold?" the Troll snarled, baring its long pointed teeth and making a wild jump at the piece of painted plastic. It got about three feet into the air, which was pretty impressive, before landing back on the ground with a thud.

"Yes! This is real gold! And you can have it if you talk with us for a few minutes."

Drool was pooling at the edges of the Troll's grey lips, and it frowned in confusion. "What do you want Elemental?"

"Hey, it looks like a monkey," a voice giggled behind me.

The Troll growled, a feral look on its small face. "I'm not an it! I'm clearly a *he!*"

"Clearly," Mr. Garcia stated, swinging the cheap costume jewelry around his fingers. "Look at his lower esophlin."

I had no idea what an esophlin was. All that I could see was his long tangled hair that concealed virtually every body part.

"Tell my class what you are." Mr. Garcia knelt and bent at the waist until he was somewhat level with the Troll's grotesque face.

"I'm a forest Troll. I live here with the rest of my kind. I hate you Elementals. You're all so loud and ugly."

"Hey, we built your forest, Troll!" someone called from the back.

The Troll gnashed his teeth, threateningly. "No it's ours! Not yours! Ours!"

That's right, I thought. Trolls were very possessive over territory.

"Now now," Mr. Garcia said, chastising the small fuming creature. "No need to yell. Tell us what you do all day."

The troll looked offended, his two large canine teeth protruding past his lower lip.

"We do whatever we want! The Sprites are always fun to play with, but they don't make good stuff like you Elementals do," he squawked, eyeing the necklace and greedily making a sloppy attempt to snatch it out of Mr. Garcia's hand.

Mr. Garcia pulled it away disapprovingly.

"Give me the shiny thing!"

I couldn't help but notice how much the Troll seemed like an indignant human toddler.

"Not yet. First, tell us what you eat, Troll."

The Troll licked his thin lips, looking around at the small clearing hungrily. "Bugs, worms, the good stuff."

"Any skills?" someone piped up, staring down at the unruly creature in disgust.

"Pretty good at stealing things. I got a whole collection of your trinkets! And you know what else we do? My kind supplies your kind with whatever you desire. At a price of course." He laughed—a loud hysterical burst of amusement.

"How helpful," another voice muttered.

Mr. Garcia nodded. "They keep the forest healthy. It's why Kurt has allowed them to stay."

"We don't answer to Kurt Bell," the Troll argued.

"It'd be best if you do," Mr. Garcia said smugly, swiping the Troll off it's feet, and grabbing the wriggling creature by the hair.

"Put me down!" the Troll screeched, eyes lit with anger, thrashing his feet and arms. Mr. Garcia ducked a swinging foot and tightened his hold around the Troll's hair causing his small body to still.

"You see kids, Trolls are a non-magic species; they look like a smaller version of mortals. This tells you their gender," he said, pressing his hand roughly down on the slightly bulging stomach of the creature. The troll whimpered at Mr. Garcia's invasive exhibition of his body, treating him as though he were some sort of specimen.

I swallowed, feeling ill. "I think that's enough. Stop it."

Mr. Garcia shook his head, a crazed look in his eyes. "I haven't even shown you his reproductive organs yet."

"You stupid Elementals, you all think you're so strong just because you have magic!" the Troll screamed in his gravelly voice. "You think you can just stick us in those monstrous square machines? The Sprites won't even come out now thanks to you!"

He aimed a futile punch at Mr. Garcia's head, which didn't come anywhere close to making contact. The poor creature finally seemed to give up, and just hung there, dangling by his hair like some sort of limp corpse.

"I said, I think that's enough!" I growled. "Let him go!" This was sick. Trolls were a species. No better or worse than us, or mortals, or anything else that lived in this forest. The class was snickering, staring at the dangling Troll in amusement.

"Do you actually find this funny?" I asked, astonished, whipping around and looking accusingly at the huddled crowd. Twenty pairs of eyes stared back at me like I was crazy.

"It's just a Troll, Alyssa; they're harmless."

The forest Troll responded to that, growling and speaking up angrily. "Just a Troll! We strike fear into hearts of the other supernaturals!" He made a mad grab for the costume jewellery in Mr. Garcia's other hand.

"Well I think we've seen enough of your kind." Mr. Garcia raised his arm up higher, bringing the dangling Troll up with it. "Trolls are known for their fascination with human items, their aggression, their stupidity, and their uselessness. That concludes our lesson."

He released the Troll from his grip, and I watched as he fell, crashing to the ground and landing painfully on his grotesque face. Mr. Garcia took a step backwards, tossing the piece of shiny costume jewellery to the ground. The troll snatched it up quickly, admiring the sparkly sheen on the plastic.

"There's your gold. Go share it with your friends."

The Troll shook his head, scrambling to distance himself from us. "I'll be telling Master you kidnapped me! You stupid Elementals!" he huffed, staring at us with contempt, which I had to agree, was well deserved. I wanted to see cool creatures from storybooks and legends. Not torture them and grab them by the hair.

When I looked back, the Troll was nowhere to be seen, having disappeared into the forest like mist, gone as quick as it appears. I peered down one of the long twisting paths, partially concealed by thick branches, which led into the deeper parts of the forests. I wondered what else lived in there, and what else we'd be torturing this year.

"Hey!" a voice cried angrily from the back of the crowd. "My watch is gone!"

"My bracelet!" another one yelled. I looked around wildly. The oddly shaped creature was nowhere to be found. I suppressed a grin.

"Idiots. No getting it back now. Trolls steal." Mr. Garcia said, looking quite unbothered by it. "They run the black market, and do a pretty good job of it too. Anyway class, considering that you're all a bunch of inexperienced wimps, next week I think we'll be paying a Sprite a visit."

"Can you guys tell me the answer to this equation?" my math professor asked our class the next day.

I sunk lower into my seat, trying to hide behind my math book. Mortal subjects were usually my forte, since I was hopelessly failing all my magic classes, but today I just wasn't into it.

Behind me, Haven and Amber's hands both shot up. I rolled my eyes. The only people other than me who actually excelled in mortal classes were the people who also excelled at magic. I guess the universe just went all the way with prodigies. It wasn't fair. Why couldn't I just have an *ounce* of magical skill?

My professor surveyed the class, and sighing, motioned to Haven. "Mr. Reeves?"

Haven smiled smugly and then proceeded to answer the question perfectly. Irritated, I turned around and snapped at him in an angry whisper, trying not to look as annoyed as I felt.

"Do you have to be good at mortal classes too?"

He wasn't even looking at what we were doing in the textbook! In fact, after observing Haven in mortal classes, I realized that he never seemed to be listening, yet somehow he got amazing grades. I knew I shouldn't blame him for being intelligent, but after the frustration of failing again and again with my magic, I was on edge.

He had his nose buried in some sort of file, eyes narrowed in concentration, but he looked up at my question, and answered distractedly, keeping his voice low to keep from drawing the attention of the professor. "Obviously, it's part of being an annoying, cocky prodigy ... or so people tell me."

"That is very true," Amber agreed with a whisper from her desk in the next row, beside Haven's. She was leaning sideways towards us a bit to be heard, while still appearing to pay attention to what the professor was talking about. Despite Amber's reluctance to speak with anyone below advanced level, she *was* stuck with us in mortal classes.

"I was joking," Haven mumbled, casting a sideways glance at her.

She grinned. "I wasn't."

I glared. Sometimes I really wished mortal classes were as segregated as the magic classes were. "You never even listen to anything the teacher says."

"Yes, he answered, "that'd be a waste of my time." There was a small smug smile working at the edges of his mouth.

"What are you looking at anyway?" I muttered, leaning closer to his desk. Anything that Haven was studying so intently had to be good.

"Oh this?" Haven asked, raising an eyebrow. He pulled it free from his pile of stuff, flashing it in front of my face. I squinted. Wait. It had my name on it!

"Is that *my file?*" I asked, astonished.

He nodded calmly. "Yup."

"Haven!" I practically hissed, wanting to smack that smug grin off his face. "What's *wrong* with you?"

"Don't be offended," Haven said, looking quite unashamed. "I also have Amber's."

"Wait, what?" Amber asked curiously, whipping her head around to stare him. "Where did you get that?"

They had to pause briefly, as the professor's attention seemed to be turning their way. When he finally returned to the blackboard and resumed his lecture, Haven sighed. "You're not the only person who can break into locked places Amber."

"I feel weirdly violated right now!" I said, aghast, and reached swiftly towards his desk in an attempt to snatch my file. He fended me off easily, and made a chastising noise with his tongue.

"I'm only borrowing it."

"Please Haven," Amber said quietly, rolling her eyes and tossing her black hair, "if you want to know something about me, just ask."

I still couldn't believe what Haven had done. "You're such a stalker!" I seethed. "What do you possibly want to know that you think I couldn't tell you? And anyway, I'm sorry to say, you probably picked the most boring file out of everyone's at the school!"

Haven's eyes flashed, and I couldn't believe the suspicion that nested there.

I shook my head. "What have I done for you to not trust me?"

Now he almost looked apologetic. "I can explain."

"I sure hope so,"

"Look, what you told me when we first met just doesn't add up. You saw through a glamour when even I couldn't! You couldn't be that strong, not when you were raised as a mortal. I thought you were employed by the Society or something."

"Her? Some sort of Society spy?" Amber gave a breathy laugh, not even bothering to entertain the theory. "Oh please Haven, I thought you were supposed to be smart."

"Hey!" I exclaimed, mildly miffed at what seemed to be an insult. "I *could* be working for the Society for all you know!"

Haven ignored me and shook his head firmly. "Amber, you weren't with us. You didn't see how it happened. She did it almost effortlessly."

"I didn't need to be there," Amber said. "Look at her. A bug is stronger than she is."

"Shut up!" I hissed, my cheeks flaming red, mainly because I knew her comparison wasn't that far off. "You don't know me. You don't know anything!" Wishing that there was more merit to that statement made me even angrier.

"Hey," Haven said, more gently this time. "Don't underestimate people Amber. That's exactly how people lose battles. You can never judge a person until you've been through all they've been through. Anyway, she's not employed by anybody. Maybe our test was a just a freak incident. I know you don't like that I took your file, Alyssa, but now I know I can trust you. Aren't you glad?"

"No," I said, firmly. "And I don't think I'm going to trust *you* ever again."

"Hey now," Haven said defensively, raising his hands in surrender. "In our world you can't blame me for checking to make sure."

I blinked, and then stared at him. Suddenly, I could see Haven's biggest fault, laid out in front of me. "You know what your problem is? You're too curious, you always have to be right, and you're obsessed with making *sure* you're right. But you know what, Haven? I've heard that curiosity might just get you killed around here."

I didn't know what came over me. Haven was, if anything, my only friend. But nothing gave anyone the right to go snooping into other people's lives. He could've asked me first!

"Miss Brooks!" the professor snapped, making all three of us jump. I turned around sheepishly to meet the curious stares of the entire class. "Could you, very kindly, stop harassing Miss Travie and Mr. Reeves? Or shall I just send you on a walk with our guards over there?"

I glanced at the side door, where two security guards were stationed. They both sneered at me, their hands moving (not so discreetly) towards their weapons.

"Sorry," I said, not even bothering to try to find the energy to defend myself.

"It's my fault, sir." Haven assured him quickly.

"Oh you're definitely right on that one," I hissed under my breath.

"Nonsense Mr. Reeves. That is why we have guards here; we don't want anyone harassing you or Miss Travie."

I couldn't stop my jaw from dropping halfway to the floor.

The professor's phone rang right at that moment, a shrieking, annoying sound that kept him from personally experiencing one of my outbursts. I held my tongue. I *wasn't* going to make something explode in this classroom. But this was ridiculous. I might not have a lot of magical ability, but I wasn't worthless. Right?

"Yes Kurt, right away!" our professor exclaimed, practically beaming. Ending the call, he slammed the phone back onto his desk and hurried to collect some papers that were strewn across the table.

"Kurt needs to speak with me. It's urgent."

"But sir," a girl in the front row interjected, "we were in the middle of the lesson—"

"Sorry class!" he said almost apologetically, hastily zipping his book bag shut, his scolding of me long forgotten. "Miss Travie, please take over from where we left off."

"Wait, what?" Amber started to argue but was cut off by the rough slamming of the classroom door as the professor made his exit. I blinked, completely shocked.

"And that," Haven said calmly, his voice sounding very loud in the stunned silence of the classroom, "is why none of us ever end up having mortal jobs."

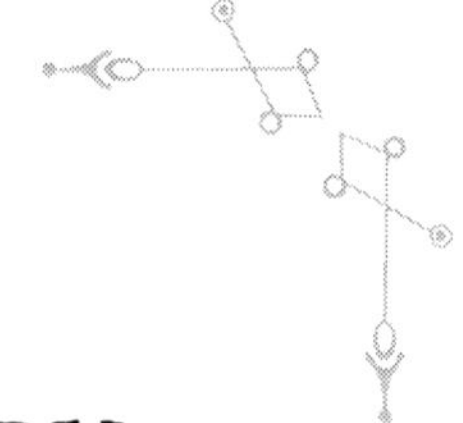

CHAPTER 8

THE MYSTERY BEGINS

I woke up early the next morning to a dull light filtering through my window and settling on the back of my eyelids, stirring me out of a restless sleep. I peered over at my sleeping roommates, who for once looked peaceful. Rachel had recovered and left the infirmary over a week before, and while she still glared at me with cold hatred, I suspected she was forbidden to harm me again. Although, that didn't stop the two of them from being cruel to me. But I could handle cruel. I had always handled cruel.

I slipped out of bed, got dressed, and made my way tiredly to the cafeteria. I could tell right away that something felt off. I couldn't quite put my finger on it, but the atmosphere in the school today seemed dreary, blanketed by a heavy silence in the hallways that felt very out of place. Even early on a Saturday morning, there were usually at least a few students up and about, laughing or complaining in small groups as they made their way to or from the cafeteria.

I opened the heavy doors to the cafeteria, surprised to find what looked to be the entire student body crowded together and facing the small raised stage near the back wall of the Orchin room, from which minor announcements were usually delivered. There was a certain aura of fear that seemed to hang heavily over the room. Even I fell victim to it, and started growing increasingly uneasy.

I entered the sea of bodies, picking up bits and pieces here and there about word having been passed around the dorms that everyone needed to gather here for an important announcement of some sort. My room, I assumed, had simply been overlooked. Either that or all three of us had simply slept through the call. In any case, the consensus seemed to be that it wasn't anything good. I wriggled my way to the front of the crowd, where I stumbled across Mrs. Musk, who was right in the midst of the commotion.

Her cheery disposition was gone. Instead, a look of anger mixed with fear was evident on her face. She clutched a sheet of paper in her hands, her knuckles whitening as she stepped up onto the small stage and turned around to face us. Behind her there was a large TV on a stand. The screen was black at the moment, but everyone was staring at it uncertainly. Waiting.

What the hell was happening? I raised my eyebrows, turning quickly to the girl standing beside me.

"What's going on?"

The girl glared at me, as if I'd just committed some unspeakable act by even asking, and shook her head, ignoring my question. Everybody was looking at each other accusingly, and you could have sliced the tension in the room with a knife.

Finally Mrs. Musk cleared her throat, as all eyes in the room slowly turned towards her. Whatever news she had obviously wasn't going to be good. Why did Mrs. Musk have to bring such obviously bleak news to the students of Magnorium? Where was Kurt? I looked around, trying to catch a glimpse of the man, but he was nowhere to be found. Kurt's presence was lacking, as it always seemed to be, and I wasn't sure how well Mrs. Musk would be able to keep us all in line. As the last stragglers arrived, and the cafeteria doors slammed shut for the final time, she spoke, opening her mouth with a grim expression.

"Students," she exclaimed, her voice taking on an authoritative tone, one that demanded complete and utter attention.

"Thank you for your cooperation in gathering here this morning; it pains me to say that I have unfortunate news for all of you." I looked around as everyone's expressions darkened. They all seemed to have a good guess of what Mrs. Musk was about to say; whereas I was, once again, ignorant.

"It has been decided," she sighed, "for your overall safety, that this news shouldn't be withheld. I am sure all of you are aware of the tremendous threat the terrorist group called the Society poses to our community." She glanced at the sheet in her small hands. This had to do with the Society?

"I'm sure you're also aware of the Council, our government—an organization dedicated to protecting supernaturals and mortals alike. They fight groups like the Society to keep our world safe, and all supernaturals." She seemed to take a moment to gather herself before clearing her throat and continuing.

"Most of you know of the Society's 'Plan of Purification' ... their goal to achieve the eradication of all mortals and gain control over supernaturals. The Council has always stood in the way of this. For this reason, the Council has once again become a target of the Society.

"I know a lot of students here have parents who sit on the Council, but this needs to be said. Yesterday, there was a massacre at a Council meeting in London ..." she breathed a shaky breath, and for just a moment, her cool professional facade weakened once more.

Her eyes narrowed as she fixated on the sheet of paper, seemingly unable to meet the eyes of her students, no doubt realizing that, for some of them, what she was sharing would tear their worlds apart.

"The fax came in early this morning. The Council's security forces were quickly overpowered and the Council members present were left to the mercy of the Society. No one at the Council meeting was spared. A total of fifty Council members have been confirmed dead." She looked up from the sheet, swallowing hard and surveying the distraught faces of her students.

"Immediately following the attack on the Council, the Society attacked a mortal cultural centre." She pulled a small remote from her blouse pocket, wordlessly flicking on the screen behind her. The screen hummed to life, with a fuzzy montage of images slowly coming into clear focus and making my stomach drop into my shoes.

Rubble littered the pavement, and half of a giant metal scaffolding, which was all that seemed to be left of a once tall building. Glass, bricks, and mortar ... pieces of insulation, shingles, and enormous wooden splinters were all leaning in towering heaps, and crumbling slowly to the ground. But the absolutely destroyed buildings weren't the worst of it. Bodies of men and women, alike lay dead ... everywhere. The once green grass, of a carefully cultivated lawn, was coated in red blood as thick as paint. In the pictures, corpses and limbs lay crushed under heavy pieces of rubble. Horror and pain were printed firmly across the faces of the dead ... dust and soot covering them like dark shadows.

The scene changed. A young man, his mouth unhinged and his eyes wide in pain, was clutching his shoulder where a deep wound leaked blood. There were bodies upon bodies among the wreckage, most dead, some wounded, but all with the same look of terror and pain on their faces.

I gasped at the next picture. A snake, coiled around a staff, was painted in blood on a slab of concrete that was clear of rubble. It was the Society's mark. I knew as much from textbooks.

There was a shocked silence as the screen continued playing through the haunting images. "Twenty thousand mortals dead ... another thousand injured," Mrs. Musk said quietly. "It is pure speculation as to how the Society managed to take so many lives at one time. If they are in possession of a new sort of weapon, we do not know of it yet."

Her voice took on an almost desperate tension as she realized what had to come next. "The following is a list of Elementals who did not survive the attack." She swallowed hard. "The funeral arrangement details will be forthcoming ... and grief counsellors will be available around the clock for anyone needing help, or guidance, or ..." Her voice trailed off then, and in a moment, when she started reading out names, her voice shook worse and worse with each cry of pain and devastation that erupted from the crowd. I barely heard the names, only the sobbing and screaming. I turned to find a girl huddled in the corner with tears running rapidly down her cheeks. Then another was sobbing. And another ...

As the students in the crowd broke apart into small groups, holding up and comforting the shattered among them, my stomach lurched. Utterly sickened by what had happened, I clenched my hands into fists. Just how many kids in here had parents who sat on the Council? Parents who had been at that meeting and were now a part of that terrible list?

I looked up angrily at the sheet in Mrs. Musk's hand. We were living under the constant threat of terrorism! We were being *ruled* by it! Someone had to do something!

I'm not sure how long it had been since the last name had been read out, but Mrs. Musk's voice suddenly rose up above the painful cries of the crowd. "I think a moment of silence, for all those we have lost, is in order."

Everywhere I looked, faces were white. Even above the sadness, and the agony of those who had lost loved ones, there was fear. I could practically smell it mixing with the tears to create something truly horrible. We all had good reason to be afraid; this Society was unpredictable, powerful, and clearly merciless. They operated on their own judgement.

Who knows, I thought, someone here could be next ... even someone powerful like Amber, Zack, or Haven. They were the most powerful people here—people the Society would want out of their way. After a respectful amount of time had passed, Mrs. Musk brought the image of the painted snake back up, and cleared her throat.

"The Staff of Asclepius. The symbol for the Society's purification plan. The message they were sending with this attack is all too clear.

"*Anyone* could be a member of the Society, and I want all of you to be extra careful. Society agents are clever and deceptive, and have clearly infiltrated human and supernatural establishments and organizations. If you see anyone or anything that is at all suspicious, I want you to march straight down to my office at once. Are we clear?" She received a murmuring chorus of agreement, the chatter in the room quickly growing louder.

"What's Magnorium going to do about the Society?" a courageous voice finally yelled from deep within the crowd. The voice was backed up, as more and more people seconded the pressing question. Mrs. Musk looked down at them apologetically, and the answer was clear. She was going to do nothing.

How could they do nothing?

"We are a *school,*" she explained. "None of us here are equipped or prepared to fight the Society. The protection of supernaturals and mortals alike is a duty that belongs to the Council!"

"So what? We just watch as more of them are murdered! That's bullshit!" screamed an angry yet recognizable voice. My head snapped around and I spotted her. Amber stood in the middle of the crowd, her eyes completely ablaze and more intense than I ever remember seeing them. Her fists were clenched, just like mine, and she was breathing heavily.

"You're all cowards!" she screamed fearlessly.

Mrs. Musk eyed Amber tiredly, running a hand through her steadily greying hair. "Please calm down Miss Travie. No matter how much you want to, it is not your place to fight the Society. You're a child!"

"I haven't been a child for six years!"

"Miss Travie—"

"Who will fight if I don't?" She pointed an accusing finger at her, looking nowhere near calming down. "You're a coward! Kurt is a coward!" She turned to her peers, exuding a fierce and unmatched determination. "Why are we really at the mercy of the Society?"

Amber looked angrily around, infuriated by the blank, weak stares she was receiving. She growled, producing a low, almost inaudible sound before storming out of the room, slamming the doors behind her. Zack followed suit. Finally, as Mrs. Musk called feebly after them, more students followed. Swept up in the emotion of the moment, I joined them too, glancing over my shoulder at Mrs. Musk, who was standing alone in the cafeteria, still clutching that piece of paper. The fearful expression never left her face for even a moment. I figured that, if Mrs. Musk looked afraid, then there was good reason to be.

Outside the cafeteria, there was shouting and angry voices cheering Amber on. I struggled to look past the sea of bodies. About fifty feet away, in one of the open-concept student lounges just down the hall, another crowd was forming—this one in a circle around a central table. People were banging their fists on the other tables and screaming at the person who was standing on top of the centre table, and feeding the fire. I craned my neck over the crowd, not entirely surprised to find Amber standing above them all.

Man, I thought, that girl sure is persistent. I joined the crowd, staring up at the fearless girl. She was certainly a sight to see. The fiercest, most infuriated expression was on her face, making her look like she was out for blood. I knew whose blood she wanted spilt.

"We need to fight the Society!" Amber shouted. "Who's to say we're not *next?* The Society could be anyone! *Anywhere!*"

As she spoke, she slowly turned, addressing the crowd surrounding her table, looking up at her with admiration. "If we don't do something, they'll always stay in power! They're close to *winning!* Do you *want* to let them have control?"

Amber shuddered, taking a second to try to rein in her temper, which was quickly spiralling dangerously out of control. She might've looked crazy, but her words were truer than everyone realized. I knew that, if we didn't do something about the Society, we would be living in fear forever.

Someone piped up from the back. "We're just going to get killed if we fight back!"

Amber's face reddened. "We're going to get killed either way! You people don't get it, do you? *No one* is fighting for us! If we don't fight for ourselves, we're all going to die!"

She paused for a second to let that sink in. "Haven't you had enough?" She was meeting people's eyes now, trying to speak to them as individuals, rather than just as a mob. "Haven't you had enough of wondering if you're going to be next?"

The intensity of her message was escalating as her voice deepened with passion. There was so much emotion in her words, more emotion than even she probably realized. I figured that there had to be a story behind it, and wondered what it was.

"They killed our parents! They killed our leaders! What right do they have to pass judgement on *anyone?* They're not Gods! I swear to you, I won't stop until I've ripped every last member of the Society to shreds! I'm the most powerful Elemental here, and I'm going to kill them! Who's with me?" Her powerful voice seemed to vibrate off the walls and made everyone in the room shiver.

No one dared to agree, all too afraid to be targeted. Seconds passed, and Amber's fiery passion was met by cold, fearful silence. Amber's hopeful face fell as she looked at her unwilling peers, shaking her head.

"Cowards."

"Save yourself, Amber! The Society's going to have you killed if you don't stop!"

She made a dismissive sound, deep in her throat. "Over my dead body!" She laughed humorlessly. "If no one sacrifices, how can we expect to live freely?"

No one would meet her eyes; no one wanted to join her in such a dangerous cause. But, just because they were scared, it didn't mean they should deny what was right.

A surge of jolting anger shot through my body. If I was an Elemental, and if I really was gifted with power, then I should use it to make a difference. So, before I even knew what I was doing, I was speaking—my voice cutting sharply through the tense silence.

"Innocent people are dying! All of us have magic, but what's the point if you can't use that magic for good?" I spoke loudly but firmly, and hoped that my words might spark a rebellious streak in someone else, the same way that Amber's words had inspired me. My statement hung in the air, and slowly heads turned to face me, surprised to see the new girl speaking up.

I was publicly opposing the Society, something my parents had expressly told me not to do. But at the moment, it felt right. I *knew* it was right. Someone had to stop them, and it might as well be Amber and I. Her words *had* ignited a spark inside of me—a spark that had been waiting to be lit. I needed a passion in my life ... a reason to live. I needed to give myself a reason to wear my name, and maybe this was my chance.

"*Alyssa?*" She said my name like it was a question. I looked up at her, giving her a half smile and meeting her stormy grey-blue eyes.

She shot me down with a snarl. "You're practically mortal! What do you know about fighting?"

"Try me!" I shrugged. "Look Amber, no one is against you here. They're just scared to face the Society. After all, who here would be stupid enough to provoke the Society, except for maybe you?" I grinned at her for a second and then shook my head. "You're right though."

I pushed my way through the crowd, and jumped up onto the table beside her. On the one hand, I felt ridiculously out of place. Amber was powerful; I was a nobody—a random average. But I was also the only one, out of all these Elementals, brave enough to take a stand with her.

She cocked a disbelieving eyebrow at me. "You're serious?" she asked, with an especially bewildered look.

"I'm with you Amber. The only thing we can do is fight back. The Society needs to fall." I looked at the crowd. "And if none of you are brave enough to help us ... then we'll do it ourselves!"

Heated debate erupted in the crowd, as it tried to figure out if we were pathetic or courageous for thinking we could even try to bring down the Society. The noise level grew louder and louder, and eventually was silenced by a loud whistle. I spotted a mass of shining blond hair in the crowd.

Haven couldn't stand anywhere without being noticed. He demanded attention without even saying a word, and when he *did* begin to speak, everyone's eyes were fixed on him, hanging on his every word. He gave me a crooked smirk, raising a single dimple at the corner of his mouth, but similar to Amber, passion lit up his eyes.

"There's a difference between being stupid and being brave." He strode confidently through the crowd until he was standing practically under our noses.

"You *are* stupid *and* naive if you think you can take on the Society by yourself," he said, nodding in Amber's direction. "And you ..." His voice trailed off as he looked at me, his huge blue eyes blinking and a bemused expression on his face. "I don't even *know* what to think of you. You're just plain crazy for even *considering* agreeing to help her." I opened my mouth to send a witty retort his way, but he held up a hand, cutting me off. "But you're brave too."

He looked back and forth between us. "If you want to destroy the Society, or anything really, you don't use brute force. You need to be strategic or else they'll just cut you down." He grinned at us. "Lucky for you, I've got some ideas."

"What are you saying, Haven? Are you actually going to help me?" Amber snapped at him, though I thought she sounded hopeful.

Haven winked. "What do you think I'm here for? To learn what I already know?"

Amber gave him a warm, genuine smile at that, and jumped down from the table, approvingly. I mean why wouldn't she? Haven was one of the most powerful students here; those two alone could probably take on the whole Society. I quickly followed suit, jumping down and eyeing Haven carefully.

"Those three are going to get us all killed!" someone snapped, deep within the crowd. "They're crazy!"

"Crazy people with crazy ideas end up changing the world," Haven whispered as our eyes met. As soon as the idea that we were clearly crazy was brought to the discussion, the crowd dispersed almost immediately. They doubted us, and wanted nothing to do with anyone who dared to oppose the Society. A small part of me couldn't blame them for walking away. Why *did* I do this exactly? To validate my existence?

Someone clapped loudly, and I turned.

"I think you might've forgot someone important!" Zack stood behind us, chuckling, his arms folded comfortably across his broad chest.

"Zack!" Amber snapped, but a fondness she couldn't hide crept up into her voice. "Where the hell were you? I looked like an idiot up there all alone!"

Zack laughed, tapping his sister on the back. "That's why I stood and watched."

"I knew there was a reason I liked you," I said.

Zack scoffed, good-naturedly. "One of many I'm sure."

"Are you saying you're going to help us or not?" Haven asked.

"Yes," Zack said, his voice deepening, all signs of humour draining quickly away. Without any warning, his eyes were ablaze with anger, similar to his sister's. "I hate the Society just as much as you do," he growled, "and I'm not going to stop until they're all dead." With that, he glanced at each of us in turn, nodded, and slowly let himself smile again as his eyes settled on his sister. "Aren't you glad we're all on the same page now, Ember?"

"Very," Amber finally said, smiling softly at his use of his childhood nickname for her. She looked over at me, almost seeming embarrassed.

"Thanks for what you did back there, Draken." She fidgeted a bit, twisting her rings on her fingers and looking at the floor.

She was certainly unusual, and clearly lacking basic social skills, but so was I. She sounded sincere, and so I accepted her thanks all the same. "I meant what I said Amber."

She gave another one of her rare smiles. "I know. See you around, Alyssa. We gotta go."

"We do?" Zack asked.

She clamped a hand on his shoulder, and dragged him away down the hallway, past milling students looking lost and afraid.

"Bye, I guess." I watched them disappear. I had offered my help. Would Amber actually take it?

"Hey Alyssa," Haven said, "do you mind if we go up to your room?"

I had almost forgotten that he was standing behind me. I turned to look at him. "What do you want?" I asked, still annoyed from math class the day before.

"Relax, okay? I just need to ask you a question. It won't take too long; I promise." His tone was oddly teasing but his eyes were sharp. If he wanted to talk to me, of all people, I figured there must be a really good reason.

So I complied, nodding, and he took off eagerly down the hallway. I followed him to the elevator, which we rode in comfortable silence. We got off at my floor and I led the way. Since it was Saturday, we only passed a few people in the hallway. They stared at us as we went by. There was so much segregation that seeing Haven Reeves on the average floor was almost unbelievable. I suddenly felt ashamed.

I swung open the door to my room, relieved to find it vacant. I think part of me was afraid that they'd still be here, sleeping, and I'd have to be the one to break the horrible news to them. A meeting between Haven, Emma, and Rachel probably wouldn't have gone over so well either.

Haven sighed as we entered the privacy of my room, closing the door softly behind us. He ran a hand through his blond waves, and I tried not to stare at the gesture, which always made me far too aware of his good looks.

"So Alyssa, I'm not going to lie. People are almost never who they say they are, and you can never be too careful, you know? So I took your file, because after the test I seriously thought you were employed by either Magnorium or the Society."

"Gee thanks," I said sarcastically. "I guess I should be flattered then."

He smirked. "No. But surprisingly, you don't hate me as much as other people do. You're smart. You're fast. And, as I figured out from your file, you like breaking rules."

"We came all the way up here for you to analyze my file ... which you stole?"

"No," Haven said earnestly. "I'm just pointing out that we could work well together. How would you feel about coming on an adventure with me?"

I looked at his bright blue eyes, which seemed to contain a permanent spark—as though absolutely everything interested him, and asked, "Could we get in trouble?"

"Not if we don't get caught."

I grinned, considering what he said. "Sure. Sounds fun."

He plopped down on my bed uninvited and I dropped down next to him.

"Seriously," I said, "you've already broken into an office to steal files. What do you have in mind that you haven't already done?"

"Well I *have* already broken into ninety percent of the locked rooms in this school, including Mrs. Musk's office, which was really boring by the way. But tonight," he announced, a little too casually, "we're going to break into Kurt's office."

"Is breaking and entering your hobby or something?" I asked, more than a little shocked. Considering that he stole a heap of student files, I thought that it might just be.

"Yeah. You really should try it sometime."

I shrugged. "It seems like you're pretty confident on your own."

"No," he shook his head stubbornly. "I need your help. You need to search the office while I hack into his computer."

"Oh my God," I jumped up off the bed, astonished. "You're like ... a criminal."

He held up a finger. "I'm not a criminal. I've never gotten caught. I figure that if I *am* going to be one, I might as well be a good one."

I sighed. "Why do you want to do this?"

"Magnorium is hiding something and I want to know what it is! I told you that I was giving myself three weeks to find out."

"What do you want to know Haven? If you're so sure about this, then tell me. What do you think they're doing here?"

Almost subconsciously, he glanced down at the black ink that was etched firmly across his wrist. A silence settled over us, and I watched as Haven's expression blanked, as if he were somewhere else entirely. "I guess if you're coming with me, you should know."

The light settled onto his face, outlining the curve of his mouth as it dipped downwards into a frown. "This school is like prison. And the only reason I came to prison is to find out what happened to my brother."

"You have a brother?" I asked, and then quickly kicked myself, remembering our first meeting with Kurt and something about a funeral, and sat back down beside him.

"No," his voice deepened, and for once he didn't seem playful at all. He seemed mournful.

"I *had* a brother. He practically raised me. My parents were insanely rich and never around, so I didn't see them much. My brother took care of me up until the time he left for Magnorium. That was the last time I ever saw him." I was quiet. This didn't sound like it ended well.

"He was extremely smart and could master anything. He had a major temper and always got into fights. I remember sometimes, when he was still at the house, he'd come home bleeding and beaten up. He never offered any explanation, but he didn't have to. Anyway, when he was old enough, he was dumped here, just like we were. Then, at the very end of his first year, Kurt came to see me." His voice stilled.

"Kurt took me aside and told me my that brother had died, and handed me some stupid accident report as proof of his death. The cause of death was undetermined, but that's crap. There was no proof at all of his death ... no witnesses. Nothing. Just a report claiming that he was dead, filed by Kurt. Dead or alive ... people just don't vanish."

For a fleeting moment his voice wavered. He seemed vulnerable. I was surprised to find how much it made my heart ache.

"I was ten. I didn't go to Magnorium at a normal age, because I was sick of magic. I didn't want to learn something that had gotten my brother killed."

I understood. The one thing in his life that mattered had been ripped away like a page in a story, and well ... denial was to be expected, wasn't it?

He seemed to sense my quick scepticism, and he glanced down, his shoulders heaving with humourless laughter. "And now you're thinking, 'he must be in denial' ... right? Still grieving after six years?"

He looked back up, meeting my eyes without any uncertainty at all. "He's not dead, Alyssa." He repeated himself then, sounding so convincing that I had to believe him. "He's not dead!"

I gently took his wrist into my hands, tracing the ink tenderly with my finger. He shuddered a bit at my touch.

"What does this stand for?" I asked softly, meeting his eyes.

He pressed his lips together, but then his fingers brushed against mine, following my movement and tracing the outline of the number, his expression blank.

After a long moment, he spoke. His voice sounded gruff with emotion. "Sometimes the past ruins people ... because unlike the future, it'll always be there, ingrained in the very back of our minds. But you can't let it change you ... So I didn't. Every day since my brother's disappearance, I've written the number of days on my wrist. It reminds me to find out the truth. And maybe it's stupid, but it's better than letting it go." He said the last part rather dryly.

For a moment I was at a loss for words; I'd never seen him speak so genuinely. I was touched that he allowed me to see all of him, even if it was for only a second.

"Listen Alyssa," he said, gently pulling his hands away, "all I know is that he's gone, and Magnorium is somehow responsible. Something weird is going on here and ...." his voice trailed off unexpectedly as he looked at me. "I sound so pathetic to you ... so delusional right? Dammit!" His words sounded so broken, like shattered glass.

That's when that overwhelming feeling, that protective quality I seemed to possess, tugged on my heartstrings.

"No," I said firmly, without any room for debate. "Haven, that isn't what it sounds like at all!" I had no words that could possibly make him feel better, so I opted for action instead. I embraced him tenderly, sliding my arms around his broad shoulders and settling them at the small of his back ... and hoping that my innocent gesture was at least a little comforting. He tensed for a moment and then relaxed, hugging me back before reluctantly letting me go.

"I'm so sorry, Haven. Really. What was his name?"

"Jason," he said, laughing bitterly. "He got the normal name. I got stuck with 'Haven'."

I lowered my eyes to the ink on his wrist and then back to up to his face. His mouth was drawn in a hard line.

I sighed. "I really hate saying sorry to people who've lost someone, you know? Because I'll never know what it was like to lose that person, and me saying sorry won't bring them back. Would you tell me your favourite memory of him? I mean, if you had to pick? I want to know what he was like ... if it's not too painful for you, I mean. If I really understand what he meant to you, then I can begin to understand the weight of your loss ... and maybe then," I said softly, "you won't have to keep carrying it alone."

Haven was speechless and looked at me with wide, shocked eyes. "Um my ... my favourite memory?" he stammered, sounding very un-Haven like. He closed his eyes and shook his head a bit. When he looked at me again, he looked thoughtful, a calm expression passing over his once-troubled features. "It has nothing to do with magic or Elementals or anything like that. It was the summer ... I was seven and my brother was teaching me how to ride a bike. I wasn't quite getting it, and it took hours, but he didn't give up on me." He paused, remembering.

"Then what?" I asked, before I could stop myself.

Haven smiled fondly. "After hours of trying, I finally started riding properly only to crash straight into a stop sign."

I laughed. I couldn't help myself.

"Jason laughed too. He picked me up, put me on his shoulders, carried me home, and threw me into our pool. But what came after is what I remember most. He kept trying, day after day, to teach me ... and after a couple of weeks, I told him I would never be able to do it. He told me, 'You don't give up on people you love, even when they give up on themselves.' Of course, he eventually taught me how to ride a bike properly, but it took a damn while ... and I was a stupid and annoying seven year old."

I smiled at the image of a little Haven teetering around on a bike, and suddenly I could almost understand why he never gave up on Jason, even after six years.

I smiled sadly at him. "When you have memories of a person, they're never truly gone. They stay with you as long as you live. You know that right?" I said, astonished at my boldness, and the fact that I actually seemed to be helping him. When did I become an expert on people's feelings?

Haven seemed shocked into silence. When he finally managed to close his mouth, which had been hanging open while I spoke, I thought he looked at least a little more at peace, looking at me as though he was seeing me in a whole new light.

"So, will you come with me?"

Of course I would. How could I not after he just showed me a piece of himself—a real piece.

"I'll tell you what, Haven, we're going to find out what happened to him, and then we're going to find out if anything *is* going on here." I was surprised to discover how strong and sure of myself I felt, when usually it was the polar opposite.

He extended a hand to push a stray hair back from my eyes and smiled. The gesture seemed sincere and natural, but despite the innocence of it, I blushed all the same.

"Thank you," he said. "Really." There was no backing out now. "Meet me outside my dorm at eleven?"

"Eleven," I echoed, and he shot me another look before standing up, gratitude still present in his crystal blue eyes.

I stood up too, and watched as he let himself out, closing the door softly behind him. I stood there, stunned at what had just happened. I had agreed to go trespassing into our principal's private office. Trespassing anywhere wasn't a forgivable act, even in the best of circumstances, but here it would be significantly worse ... if we weren't careful. I just prayed that Haven wasn't kidding when he said he was good at not getting caught.

After my conversation with Haven, the rest of my day passed quite uneventfully, at least in comparison to the rush of the morning's events. I couldn't believe I had agreed to do this. Despite my doubts, I never backed down from anything and that's precisely why I found myself ready to go right before eleven.

I twisted the doorknob slowly, opening the door just enough to let myself out. Fortunately the hallway was vacant, allowing an easy journey to the elevator.

I entered the elevator and got off at the seventh floor. There was no curfew, as it was the weekend, and eleven o'clock was still early. Loud music was blaring down the halls and people were yelling to each other.

Rolling my eyes, I knocked on Haven and Zack's dorm door. I wondered if Haven had trusted his roommate enough to invite him along or even tell him where he was going, though I had the feeling that no one knew exactly *what* Haven did. I got my answer a moment later when Haven alone opened the door, the shadows outlining the well-defined contours of his face.

"Hi," I said. I didn't have to worry about being quiet on this floor; anything I said was going to be drowned out by the music anyway. His eyes were so bright that they practically lit up the dark, turning the shadows an electric blue. He eagerly ushered me inside. Zack wasn't there, but his stuff was thrown messily throughout the room. I almost laughed at Haven's side of the room, which was freakishly neat.

"He's at a party," he answered, with a distracted wave of his hand, as if reading my mind.

"Thought they were all held in here?" I joked.

"I kind of kicked everyone out. This whole school practically lives in here, and I had plans. After the news this morning though ... I think they're really just going through the motions. Trying to take their minds off everything. Can't imagine it'll last long."

He was quickly rummaging through a drawer filled to the brim with a variety of odd-shaped metallic trinkets.

"Um ... Haven, what are those?"

"Oh these?" He grinned slyly. "I collect them. They're ... uh ... stuff for picking locks, hacking computers, cutting through metal ... you know, the necessities."

My eyes went round. There must've been about thirty different tools in there, many of which he seemed to be taking with him, stashing them in various pockets.

"Where'd you get them?"

"Please Alyssa, it's not like I stole them. I bought them."

"Where?"

"The black market."

"The black market *here?* The one that the Trolls run?"

That seemed to startle him for a moment. "Hey, there are black markets everywhere. Why, do you want something?"

"Uh ... no thanks."

He shrugged, pulling out a long metal rod with a jagged edge at the tip.

"Gee, I see you thought of everything. What's that supposed to be, a dagger?"

He laughed. "A lock pick. Don't worry. I won't let us get caught." There was something in his voice—a firmness that made me believe him. "Thanks for doing this, Alyssa."

A moment of understanding passed between us and there was suddenly no need for words. "I was beginning to get bored at night anyway," I said. "You ready?"

"Yeah one sec." He moved towards the nightstand next to his bed, opened a drawer, and pulled out a very small pistol, quickly stashing it in one of the few empty pockets left in his loose, black, cargo pants. I shook my head. I didn't even want to know what would happen if I brought a metal detector in here.

"So," he began, "you're going to just follow my lead. I mapped out the route security guards take each night, and if you follow me, we're going to avoid them. When we get in, let's search the whole place. Anything that looks suspicious or odd, we're taking with us. If anyone is going to get blamed, it's me? Got it?"

I frowned, there was no way I was taking orders from him. "I don't think so." I stood up abruptly and opened his door. The noise levels were already settling down substantially.

He studied me for a moment, standing in the doorway.

I rolled my eyes. "Well, are you coming or not?" I was anxious to finally do something that brought a rush ... something to remind me I was still alive. I needed all those moments I could get these days.

"I said, I'm leading," he muttered, quickening his pace to get ahead of me and padding down the hall into the elevator.

We rode our way downstairs with companionable silence blanketing the air around us. I really had no idea where we were going. I just had to trust him. So I followed him closely as he expertly moved through the twisting hallways. It seemed like he knew exactly where he was going. He hadn't been here for that long, but then again, he had been planning this for a long time. The school was larger than I anticipated, and as if sensing my confusion, he slowed his pace and made sure I was following.

"Can you keep up?" he whispered.

"Yes," I muttered, despite trying to ignore how unnerving Magnorium was at night.

He led me to a stop at one end of a long, isolated corridor. I strained my eyes trying to see. It was almost pitch black. Unexpectedly, Haven clamped a firm hold around my wrist, and I jumped a bit. He led me down the corridor and stopped in front of the last door.

Haven wrestled a flashlight from one of his seemingly bottomless pockets, and illuminated the space around us for a moment. I observed the single, pathetic lock on the door—a hopefully futile attempt to keep trespassers out. Haven grinned as he realized this.

I frowned. "I'm surprised his office doesn't have heavier security, if he's so suspicious."

"That would make *him* look suspicious, like he had a reason to keep others out. He's the principal; he's supposed to be ... approachable." He wriggled the jagged piece of metal out of his pocket.

I tried the door experimentally.

"It's locked," I whispered. "I mean we could use magic, but the only thing I could probably do is burn a hole through it."

He cocked an eyebrow. "Nothing is ever locked if you have the right tools." He gently nudged me aside and leaned over, sticking the metal piece into the lock. He messed around for a moment, jiggling the inner components of the lock.

"There isn't much to this actually," he said calmly, moving to a different angle and digging deeper into the lock. "The secret is flipping the inside set of pins until they align." Suddenly, his face lit up at a soft click and he slid the jagged piece back out.

He shrugged. "I told you I didn't come here unprepared." Then he swung open the door, smugly, barely making a sound. "After you."

I eagerly stepped inside, getting my first glimpse of the private quarters of the strange man.

Haven quickly followed suit, shutting the door softly behind him. He clearly had no worries about getting caught and flicked on the nearest light switch. Light flooded into the large room, and when our eyes finally adjusted, I soaked in the sight of the somehow disappointing office. I didn't know exactly what I was expecting, but definitely something more interesting than what was actually here.

Haven took it all in, fervently circling the room.

"Wow," I muttered, glancing at the mundane desk, chair, filing cabinet, and bookshelf. "This is disappointing."

Haven shook his head quickly, the first signs of madness peeking through the light in his eyes.

"No, this is exactly what they *want* us to think; that it's all normal! Why the hell does it look so empty? Does this guy work *at all*?" He spun around angrily before plopping dramatically into Kurt's swivel chair, spinning on its wheels.

"I am Kurt Bell, and *you* are my subordinate," he mocked intimating Kurt's signature monotone and spinning the chair faster and faster.

"Feel free to take it up in my office," I mocked, getting into the spirit, flashing back to our first meeting outside of the school all those days ago.

"And *we* took you up on that," Haven joked, before halting his final spin behind the desk.

"Can you search the room for me? I'm going to hack into his computer," Haven snapped forward and casually pulled out a minuscule computer chip. He popped it into the opening of Kurt's desktop computer and I watched as the screen hummed to life. He slipped on a pair of latex gloves, to conceal his fingerprints, and started frantically clicking away at the keyboard. This guy really knew what he was doing.

I didn't want to say anything, but it seemed like the only thing Kurt was guilty of was being extremely boring. But Haven seemed determined to find him guilty of something, and it seemed like he wasn't going to listen to what I said. For his sake, I spun around and got to work, going to the desk drawers first. I knelt down beside Haven and tried the first drawer, not surprisingly finding it locked.

I peered at the jagged metal pickpocketing tool sticking out of one of Haven's pant pockets. Without a second's hesitation, I snatched the object out of his pocket and stuck the jagged edge into the keyhole. I twisted it around, mimicking Haven's movements from the office door. I felt the sharp edge hit a row of pins, and after manipulating them a bit, heard a satisfying soft click. Haven glanced down, surprise flying across his features.

"Hey, did you just pickpocket me *and* pick that lock?" he asked, dumbstruck.

I shrugged slyly, sliding the drawer open. Quickly rummaging through the contents, I thumbed through what appeared to be a leaflet of boring legal papers. After repeating the whole process with the only other drawer in the desk, I realized that there was nothing noteworthy in the desk. I stood up and moved on to the filing cabinet. I unlocked it with ease, feeling like an old pro, and sorted through a stack of what, most likely, was at least a thousand student files.

"Magnorium needs to keep records of all Elementals who attended the school, dead or alive. Everyone's in there," he said, frowning as he glared at the screen. "This computer has no password or security. And it's practically empty."

I shrugged. I spotted my file near the beginning of the stack, and quickly grabbed it out of curiosity. I was awarded with a boring single piece of paper, with my picture stamped across the centre and some bits of seemingly useless information. It was nice to know where I stood in the grand scheme of things. I deposited my file back where I found it and kept flipping. I spotted my parents' files but didn't stop, flipping down through the alphabet, searching for Haven's file and his brother's.

"I found your file," I called out to him. I quickly scanned the single piece of paper. Like mine, it had his picture and some family information, which I filed in the back of my mind. It said nothing about a deceased brother. I put his file back and started hunting down his brother's. Jason Reeve's file was mysteriously missing, and after triple checking, I was sure. It had been removed.

"Haven, his file isn't here," I said in a quiet, still voice.

He snapped his head up, his blond waves falling into his eyes. He swiped his hair back furiously, blinking fast.

"Are you sure?" In a moment, he was up beside me, frantically searching through the stack of files. He sighed, taking a deep breath. "Dammit. Why do you think he removed his file?"

"There *is* something he doesn't want anyone to know," I said apologetically, cocking an eyebrow and closing the drawer softly. "There's got to be *something* here, Haven."

I moved to the bookshelf next, picking up the first book and determined to find at least one piece of evidence. I quickly thumbed through the pages of a number of random books, ranging from textbooks to encyclopedias to dictionaries.

Haven's computer chip beeped just as I grabbed the last book, and he slid the chip out.

"I have his whole hard drive on this chip, though it's odd there isn't much on the computer itself," he said, carefully pocketing the item.

I furrowed my brow as I snapped the final book shut. "I got nothing," I said solemnly. His eyes darkened drastically, changing from an electrifying, sky blue to a violent, stormy blue that seemed to seize his whole expression.

"No!" he snapped. "There's *got* to be something! I *know* there's something!" He snatched the book out of my hands and started flipping through it.

"There ... there's *got* to be something in here! He needs to give me my brother back!" Before I knew it, his voice had escalated to an unnatural pitch, and for once, Haven Reeves—one of the most laid-back people I had ever met—lost it. His grip tightened around the spine of the book and he whipped it hard at the back wall. The book flew through the air and ricocheted off the wall with a bang that seemed to echo throughout the room.

I stopped dead in my tracks and stared at the book on the floor.

"Did you hear that?" I whispered to Haven cautiously. For once, he looked unfocused, the anguish of loss running through his expression.

"No," he muttered, refusing to meet my gaze.

I quickly sidestepped to the wall the book had been whipped at, pressing one of my sensitive ears against it. I knocked experimentally. It echoed.

"It's hollow," I whispered disbelievingly.

"What?" Haven snapped back to reality immediately, pressing his own ear to the wall. He pressed a hand to the wall applying pressure cautiously, and feeling it give a bit. "You're right. It's too thin to possibly support any beams. And why isn't there a window! Look! We went to the end of the hallway, right? Shouldn't this be an exterior wall? This wall must be a fake. There's something behind it!" Just like that, his eyes gleamed and the enthusiasm was back in his voice. He reached into a pocket and pulled out what looked like a long metal baton.

"What ... is that a metal detector?" I asked, as he activated the device, pressing the red button on the side.

"The black market. For the right price, the Trolls will sell you anything you could possibly want."

Haven moved around the room cautiously, waving the metal detector over the walls. I jumped when it beeped, and Haven paused, standing just behind Kurt's desk. My eyes darted every which way, trying to find the source, until my eyes landed on a lone painting hanging on the wall above the desk.

"There," I pointed suspiciously at the painting. "It's off centre, and it's the only bit of decoration in the room."

It took less than a second for Haven to reach the painting, and take it down. Set into the wall was a small flashing screen with a keypad. My jaw dropped.

"Finally," Haven breathed, relieved.

"You're relieved to find a password-protected, screen?"

He grinned slyly. "Yes, because I think I know the password. Well, I have a pretty good guess."

"How could you *possibly* know the password?"

"Because if there's something locked, that Kurt doesn't want us to find, what do you think it could be?"

"I don't know." I said dryly. "Nude photos?" I moved over to where he stood and peered over his shoulder at the blinking screen.

"Not exactly." He looked awfully smug. "If I'm wrong, I could probably dismantle it anyway, but that would take time that we do not have."

"Is this one of your Magnorium conspiracy theories?" I asked quizzically.

Haven didn't answer, sucked in a breath, and quickly typed in nine letters A-S-C-L-E-P-I-U-S.

I remembered that symbol—the face of the Society. The snake and staff.

I watched with my mouth hanging open as the screen flashed green, making a pleasant dinging sound. I couldn't believe it. Haven actually guessed the correct password in one try.

"Do you work for some sort of Elemental FBI?"

Haven burst out laughing before being cut off by a loud and unsettling noise. Part of the hollow wall slid open to reveal a large archway that opened into darkness. I practically jumped out of my skin.

Haven was ecstatic. He practically ran into the other room, dismissing the danger that usually follows when one trespasses into unknown, dark places. I quickly followed anyway, before the door could shut behind me ... which it did, as soon I entered the other room.

I had never seen Haven fight before, but something about the determination and fire in his eyes reassured me that he could handle anyone who came at us. Even though it was dark, it was easy to see that the secret room was much more spacious than Kurt's office. You could almost hear it in the way our footsteps echoed. Haven fished out his flashlight, turned it on, and then gasped, stumbling backwards.

"Look!" he hissed, adjusting his flashlight for a wider beam, one that spread evenly throughout the room.

The room was *extremely* large and had a huge desk in the centre. Unlike the first room, huge stacks of papers and reports littered the workspace and a more advanced computer sat on the desk. The room certainly looked used but was still elegant, and clearly intended for someone with a lot of power and authority—Kurt himself, one would assume.

"Alyssa ..." Haven's voice trailed off as he pointed at the far wall behind the desk, drawing my attention to what he had already noticed.

I felt the blood in my veins freeze. A hanging tapestry hung on that wall, with a giant, detailed snake carefully woven into the fabric, its scaled body coiled around a large staff. My stomach lurched. There was no mistaking the symbol. The symbol of the Society ... the same symbol I had seen painted in human blood on the concrete in London.

Haven seemed to be having trouble breathing. "The Staff of Aspeclius. Originally a symbol representing healing, until the Society adopted it years ago ... Something about 'healing the natural world' by getting rid of mortals. Nothing like a band of terrorists trying to be justifiable." He was trying to sound lighthearted, but the colour had drained from his face.

And that wasn't all. There was a huge map on the far right wall. Red markers had been placed strategically in different locations across the globe. As I looked closer, I saw that the biggest one had been planted firmly in London, the location of yesterday's Council massacre. A huge television screen hung from the ceiling, and an array of weapons—Power Arrows, guns, knives, and other things I had never seen before—filled a huge bin beneath it. There was another archway at the back of the room, apparently leading to yet another passage ... leading somewhere I was very tempted to explore.

"So his real office is behind his fake office," Haven breathed, eyes narrowing. "This is wonderful."

"Wonderful?" I exploded, aghast. "We're standing in an office clearly belonging to the Society! A bunch of people running around and murdering people!"

"Do you know what this means Alyssa?" he said mystified. "This means Kurt, our headmaster, is a member of the Society! Which means Magnorium could very well be involved too!"

I opened my mouth to respond, but instantly clamped it shut when I heard murmuring voices echoing close by. I didn't know where the voices were coming from. My heart raced at the thought of someone discovering us in here. Haven's reaction was instantaneous; he grabbed my hand and frantically threw open the door to our only possible hiding place: a small coat closet. It was a tight fit for two people, but it was our only option. He pushed me inside first and squeezed inside behind me, his body pressed tightly against mine. He shut the door just in time, as two voices came in through the back door.

"Not a word," Haven whispered, pleadingly.

We didn't dare move a muscle. He had clamped a hand over my mouth, just in case, and I hoped he could see me glare through the darkness. It was hard to concentrate on the severity of the situation, or anything really, considering how closely we were squished up against each other. I could feel the thump of his heart, his quick breaths against my neck. The coat closet had a weird, repellent smell, like expensive cologne. It smelled like Kurt.

I could pick out two voices, both male, in a heated debate of some kind. I struggled to focus on the voices so I could identify the men.

"These attempts are futile! You heard what Kurt said," one voice snapped at the other.

The other gave a low grunt. "I don't understand the point of working like a dog every day."

"What don't you understand? The purification plan is failing. We need to think of a new alternative or all that we worked for will be lost."

"But what we need is the one thing we can never *get!*" the other voice argued, sounding quite irritable. "Just get the damn laptop." There was some quick bustling around as the two men retrieved what they had come for. "They are bloody extinct! Even *he* can't do anything about *that!* He should just give it up, and stick to the plan. Nothing else is going to work."

The voices grew muffled, as they retreated slightly, and Haven shifted position, ever so slightly, trying desperately to make out what they were saying.

"Don't question his orders. Just go along with it; you know he's right."

"He might be right, but you know how impatient he can get. He said he's had a breakthrough."

"How many times have I heard that?"

"Apparently not enough to shut you up."

The two voices continued arguing as they exited the room, their voices growing more and more distant. I hadn't the slightest idea what was on the laptop they came in for, or where they were possibly going with it ... or even what they were talking about really. But Haven seemed to have some ideas. His grip had tightened around my waist almost subconsciously, pulling me even closer, as if protecting me. I suddenly felt an almost overwhelming urge to get out of there. The heat and the thick cologne smell were suffocating.

Haven pulled me back when I reached to push open the closet. "Not yet," he whispered. We stayed where we were for another few minutes, making sure that the two strange men weren't coming back.

Who were they? Society workers? Who exactly employed them? Magnorium? Did this mean Magnorium was bad? Were we in danger? This whole time, Haven had been right ... and I hadn't believed him.

After a tense extended silence, Haven finally deemed it safe enough to venture back out into the room. He pushed the door open slowly, quietly untangled himself from me, and stepped out. I quickly followed, the fresh air hitting me in waves.

Haven pressed his finger to his lips, signalling me not to speak but just follow him. I nodded and trailed behind him as he walked towards the exit leading back out into the fake office. Something beeped as we neared the exit and for a moment I was sure it was an alarm, but it was only a motion detector. The door slid open, welcoming us back into the fake office. As we passed through the doorway, the wall slid neatly back into place. Haven quickly hung the painting back over the keypad, and when he finished, he looked at me calmly.

"We should probably get out of here. Like right now."

I gave a curt nod, following him back into the empty halls of the school, which were somehow comforting now and refreshingly familiar.

Haven checked his watch, swearing.

"It's almost one!" he whispered. He no longer sounded calm, but possibly on the verge of panic. "Alyssa, the guards make their rounds of this hallway in five minutes. How fast can you run?"

"Faster than you," I answered, still half in shock.

Haven exhaled, turning to face me. "Yeah right. Just follow me quickly."

Then he broke out into a run, moving fast and dissolving into the shadows. I broke into a mad run after him, not wanting to lose him. Back home, I had a lot of spare time on my hands, and had always enjoyed going for runs, enjoying a solitude of my own choosing. I never thought I'd be using my running skills to fly through hallways in the dead of night, but I was grateful for those skills now. I practically flew through the air, sometimes feeling like I really was flying, and in minutes he led us to a skidding stop at an unfamiliar elevator.

For a fleeting moment, I wondered how he had turned out so untamed, so free, coming from such a refined and wealthy setting. Simply having been raised by his brother, instead of his parents, hardly seemed like explanation enough. I wondered if it was, perhaps, an Aquarian trait, but wasn't curious enough to ask.

"You're fast," he exclaimed, composing himself with more elegance and grace than a sixteen-year-old boy should have.

"You're not bad yourself," I said, a bit breathlessly. We entered the elevator, enjoying the ride up in comfortable silence once again, neither of us feeling the need to fill the void with chatter.

We got off on my floor first and I practically floated down the hallway toward my room, still mulling over everything we had seen tonight. We got to my door, but neither one of us moved to say goodbye. Our eyes locked, silently saying everything that neither one of us were willing or ready to say.

"Are you usually this right about everything?" I whispered, finally breaking the silence.

"Usually," he said quietly. "I knew Kurt was weird, and even possibly evil," he chuckled a bit at that, "but I wasn't exactly expecting him to be part of the Society."

I could see the curve of his mouth outlined in a small smile. "Are you *smiling?*" I asked, astonished. "Are you usually this happy when you find out that the head of your school is murdering innocent people?"

"No, but now we know I was right. And so now we can try to stop him. I still don't know what happened to my brother, but we need to do something about this first. Are you prepared to do something, Alyssa?"

"Of course I am," I said, a bit surprised. "I thought you understood that when I stood up with Amber."

"You didn't know, at that point, that the threat was a two-minute walk down the hallway," he pointed out, a bit breathlessly. "I want you to be careful, okay? Blend in, and please, no more starting food fights or political uprisings." There was a pleading edge in his voice, and his blinding blue eyes seemed to gaze right through me.

A small smile playing on my lips, I shrugged. "I'll try my best."

"Your tone isn't very reassuring ..." his voice trailed off and I finally noticed how close we were standing. I hadn't the slightest idea how we got like that, but I made no attempt to back away. We were standing so close that, when I shyly looked away, afraid of what he might see in my eyes, I could see every little crease in his shirt, and noticed, for the first time, the way his muscular arms and shoulders stretched against the fabric.

He leaned in, and for a split second I was sure he was going to kiss me. My heart thumped against my chest and the air between us crackled with heat. But instead of kissing me, he moved his hands in a fluid motion and I glanced down to see my room key (which had been in my pocket) in his hand, as he carefully put it in the keyhole and twisted it to unlock my dorm door. He pickpocketed me! Before I had time to formulate a comment, I felt his lingering breath cascading down the slope of my neck.

"It's late," he said, very softly in my ear. "You should sleep." He pulled back as quickly as he'd leaned in. I was glad that it was so dark in the hallway, because I could feel the crimson in my cheeks.

"You can't tell anyone what we saw today," he said, seriously. "And we need to talk about this again before we do anything."

"Oh ... okay," I stammered. "You know where to find me."

Then suddenly he was on the move again, giving me a quick nod over his shoulder before disappearing completely down the narrow hallway. I had to pause for a moment before going in. I needed to compose myself and calm down.

I unlocked the door to my room and silently crawled into my bed. Not surprisingly, I couldn't fall asleep, replaying the events of the evening over and over in my mind. The people responsible for the killings they had showed us ... they ran our school! Were we in danger here? Who was Kurt really? Was Haven's brother actually dead?

That question still remained unanswered and I winced, remembering Haven's anguish when talking about him. I hoped we could find the truth, to finally put Haven's fears to rest and give him the proper closure he'd been robbed of.

It wasn't as safe at Magnorium as I had first thought, and I knew I had to tread cautiously. I wasn't really certain of much of anything these days, but one thing I *was* certain of was that life at Magnorium just got a lot more intriguing.

It felt like I had only closed my eyes for five minutes when there was a loud, frantic knocking at my door. I muttered something unintelligible and flipped over, exhausted.

"Who the hell is that?" Rachel sat up in bed, her red hair all mussed with sleep. She pounced out of her bed with a glare, strode to the door in her too-tight tank top and crumpled-looking drawstring pants, and swung open the door.

"Morning," greeted an amused voice.

"I-I ... um," Rachel stammered, sounding mortified. I cracked open my eyes, frowning.

"Is Alyssa Brooks in there?"

I bolted upright in my bed, glancing at the clock. What was Haven doing here at six a.m.? Then the events of the previous night came rushing back and I blinked remembering.

"Uh ... what?" Rachel muttered again, looking at him incredulously.

Haven sighed, leaning against the door frame and peering lazily into the room. "Alyssa; wake up."

"Haven!" I exclaimed, jumping out of my bed. "Why are you here so early?"

He frowned, pointing at my window as if that explained it. "It's daytime."

"Barely!" I exclaimed. "It's six a.m.! On a Sunday!"

"Can I come in?"

Rachel stood in the doorway, looking at me in shock. Seeing as she wasn't budging, Haven rolled his eyes, squeezing past her and strolling into the room.

"*You* know Haven Reeves?" Emma asked from her bed, sounding confused with sleep, and dumbfounded.

"Yeah," I answered distractedly.

"How?"

Before Rachel could speak up, dismissively reminding her that we had arrived at the school together—and likely point out that it wasn't as if we were friends or anything—Haven spoke up.

"I'll tell you how," Haven said, sounding completely serious as he approached me, staring into my eyes. "She mistook me for a training dummy and nearly fried me to a crisp. Mrs. Musk wanted me to detain her immediately. This one's a monster." He glanced over at Emma as he slapped his hands down on my shoulders. I jumped at the contact. "Better not make her angry."

"Yes," I said seriously, nodding at the look on their horrified faces. "I almost charbroiled him. I guess I owe him a favour or two."

"Would you two mind stepping outside for a few minutes? I don't think you want to hear or witness this favour. You know what I mean?" He actually had the *audacity* to wink at them. They both looked astonished at this point, glancing back and forth from me to Haven, who was smiling smugly.

I cleared my throat uncomfortably.

"I cannot believe this," Emma said, finally recovering from her surprise. Shaking her head angrily, she climbed out of bed, tugging at the hem of her t-shirt, and tensely adjusting her sweatpants, which had become twisted as she slept. "Come on Rachel." Then, with an awkward glance over her shoulder, Emma led Rachel stomping out of the room.

Haven made a noise that sounded like a laugh, followed them toward the door, and then slammed it shut behind him. He quickly glanced through the peephole, and nodded.

"They're gone. Finally. Great roommates you got there. I see why you never want to spend any time in your room."

I crossed my arms over my chest self consciously. I was wearing my favourite, comfiest nightgown—faded and worn through in places—and smiled despite the situation, remembering everything he had said to Rachel and Emma. "You have a great poker face."

"I do try," he smiled and nodded his thanks. "Anyways, sorry for waking you up, but I couldn't sleep, so I wanted to come here."

For someone who'd barely slept, I couldn't believe how bright and alert he looked. But then, he always did. "You're thinking about what we found yesterday?"

Haven looked thoughtful. "I just don't know what to do about it, Alyssa. I mean, do you think we're the only people who know about this?"

"Well," I said, taking a seat on my unmade bed. "Considering I don't know many other people who trespass as a hobby, I'd say probably yes. The only students anyway."

Haven smiled tightly. I think it was the first time I had seen him look genuinely nervous about anything. "I don't want any more people to get hurt or killed by the Society. Especially since we know about Kurt." Tentatively, he took a seat next to me and looked up, meeting my eyes. He seemed like he was genuinely waiting for my opinion.

I bit my lip. "Well," I started, "what if we reported him to the Council or something? Or at least told Mrs. Musk? We could expose Kurt and the rest of the Society"

Haven shook his head quickly. "We don't know who we can trust. She could be working with him ... the whole school could be. *That's* why I like making sure that people *are* who they say they are. I don't even know how to contact the Council, and besides, why would they believe us? Magnorium is one of the most highly regarded institutes in the supernatural world. And even if they *did* believe us, the Council is losing their fight against the Society as it is."

"Maybe we should keep it to ourselves then," I said quietly. "Just for now. Just until we figure out a better way to handle this—one that won't end up getting us killed."

"We *can't* just do *nothing!*" Haven exploded. "Innocent people are dying, and here we have found one of it's members, and possibly their headquarters ... and we're going to do *nothing?*"

"Haven," I said softly. "Just how far are you willing to go to protect those other people? At the cost of your own life? How would dying help *anyone?* Because Kurt *isn't* just some weirdo. He's a part of the Society. He could be the actual leader for all we know! He *will* kill you or *worse*, if you expose him or fight him openly."

He looked up fiercely. "Kurt took my brother. Now that we know who he really is, I don't even want to imagine what could've happened to ..." He swallowed. "I don't want anything like that to happen to anyone else again. I don't want more people's lives to be ruined because of the Society. And yes, I would do anything to make sure that they *don't* hurt anyone ever again. Even risk getting killed."

He shuddered. "Maybe I should just go downstairs right now and kill him with my bare hands." He genuinely did not appear to be joking, and I wasn't exactly sure that he wasn't going to do just that, if I did not calm him down quickly.

"Listen to me," I said steadily. "You need to be strategic, not reckless. Isn't that what you've always said? What can we do that would make the most sense? Us getting killed won't help anyone."

He took a deep breath and exhaled slowly, gripping the coverlet of my bed tightly in his hands as he repeated the process a few times, calming himself. "Okay. You're right." He looked at me for a long moment and then nodded. "Give me two weeks. I'll see what else I can find out about Kurt. Then we'll decide what to do."

"That's fair," I echoed. "We definitely need more information first."

"Right," he said, a bit unsteadily.

"Haven," I said, recognizing the look in his eyes. "Be careful, okay? Don't do anything stupid."

"I can do stupid things as long as I'm smart about it. I mean, breaking into Kurt's office was pretty stupid."

"I'm being serious. Promise me that you'll be safe."

"I promise," he said, jumping off the bed with a wild glint in his eyes. Reassurance was definitely not his strong suit. "I'll talk to you later; I got to go." He strode quickly towards the door, grabbing the doorknob.

"Wait!" I said, jumping up to stop him. "Go where?"

He was already gone, slamming the door behind him.

I stared at the closed door, worry knotting in the pit of my stomach. I could only hope Haven liked keeping his word as much as he liked breaking the rules.

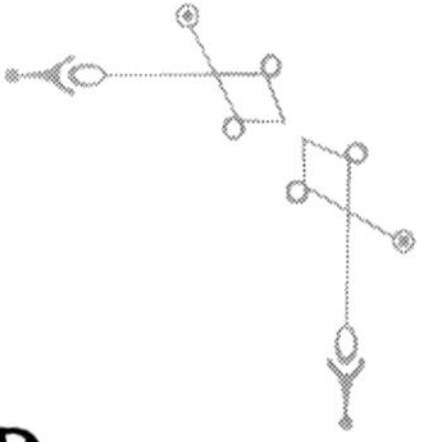

CHAPTER 9

TURNING UP THE HEAT

"Alyssa Brooks?"

I snapped my head up from the comfortable crook of my arm and looked up at my spell-casting teacher, Mrs. Abott. "What?" I asked, fatigued. "I mean ... yes?"

She held in a sigh, rolling her eyes at my lethargic demeanour. I'm not a total delinquent. I *wanted* to dutifully reassure her, as she gave me an icy stare, but at the moment, I just didn't have the energy. I was failing her class, and struggling to stay awake during today's lesson. Mrs. Abott's lips moved, as she started to say something, and her eyebrows rose, but my mind was already wandering. I struggled to focus.

"Are you even listening, Brooks? I asked what is the classification of this spell?" I frantically pieced together remnants of the lesson and squinted at the writing scrawled across the white board in black ink.

"Type D. It's too long and complicated to be anything else," I mumbled the pathetic answer, hoping that I was at least partly right. Mrs. Abott nodded slowly, looking even more irritated than normal by my presence in her classroom.

"Correct." An idea seemed to occur to her. "Brooks, since you *are* paying attention, I guess you wouldn't mind trying to demonstrate a spell for the class?"

"Can I please pass?" I asked as politely as I could. She glared. I was almost tempted to tell her what I knew—what no one in this room probably knew. *Magnorium is corrupt. The Society is here.*

"I don't remember giving you that option, Miss Brooks."

I didn't say what was on the tip of my tongue. She was opting to embarrass me, so there was no point. I got up, made my way to the front of the room, and stood beside the large wooden table that often held spell books, magical implements and outdated overhead projectors.

The kids around me barely held in their laughter. I bet they were remembering the previous day, when I had lost it and stood on that table, screaming at them.

'Stupid new girl.'

'She's all talk.'

I could hear them saying these things and more. Well I'll show them, I thought, suddenly feeling sure of myself. I'll show all of them, even if I have to stand here all damn day.

"As you know, Type D spells require a lot of energy and concentration. Most pupils simply lack the skill and the power to conduct this spell, so ... Miss Brooks, you certainly will not be able to do this. But one can learn just as much from failure."

This seemed like an odd teaching approach, since she had reiterated over and over that belief and confidence were the most important tools for spell casting, but clearly she was trying to teach me a different sort of lesson.

"The spell I want you to attempt is called '*Magnus Lumen*' ... meaning 'big light'. If you do it correctly, you will start a fire on your own body. Gradually, this spell spreads across your body until you become completely engulfed in flames. Powerful pupils can do this without the use of a spell. They do it using only willpower, but we're taking baby steps here."

"I'll try my best," I said, scanning the wording of the spell. I needed to prove what I was worth, to them and to myself. So ... how did I do this again?

"Go ahead, Miss Brooks. And make sure to keep the flames under control."

I ignored her sarcasm. It was nothing new, but it would end here. My lips parted to form the words, which rolled off my tongue easier than I expected.

"*Fire powers, thy sight protect me through day and when day falls down to night.*

I gathered every ounce of my might, determined to produce at least a wisp of my power. I knew it was in there somewhere ... even if I hadn't exactly seen it these last few weeks.

I call on my inner fire, this light I was given rests in my soul."

My voice was satisfyingly strong—a ray of hope that would not be denied. I didn't even have to finish the last sentence to know that something had shifted and clicked into place. The sensation was comforting, a warmth that travelled through every pore of my body. Suddenly, I felt zapped with a million watts of electrical energy and I shook, stumbling backwards.

A single flame burst from my fingertips. Then another, and another ... spreading until my entire body was consumed in fire. The flames were stubborn, but I held onto my instructions to keep it under control. I willed it to remain with me, embracing me alone, and repeated the command in my mind until it was ingrained in my skull. I felt no heat and my vision was oddly unaffected. Yet when I looked down, my body vanished ... hidden behind long talons of flames.

I did it. And it was about time.

The people around me were murmuring in excited whispers, gaping at my unexpected success. I smiled through the fine curtain of bellowing smoke that was rising up around me. Mrs. Abott's scowling face morphed into one of complete and utter shock at my immediate success.

"Quite impressive, Brooks! You have more skill than I anticipated. It should've been near impossible!"

I squinted experimentally, flexing my fingers. No matter what I did, or how I moved, I couldn't evade the flames. They wouldn't let me go. It was exciting, exhilarating, and more than a bit unnerving.

"How long will I stay like this?" I asked, surprised that my voice carried over the fire, sounding steady and calm.

Mrs. Abott shrugged dismissively. "Not too long I'm afraid. It's no easy feat that you've managed the spell on the first try! Give it another minute, and try not to move around."

Of course, I did precisely what I was told not to do, daring to move an inch from where I was standing. A minute ticked by. Then four. Then eight. I let my arms drop loosely to my side, still flaming vigorously. Getting increasingly uncomfortable with the silence, Mrs. Abott used the opportunity to talk about the spell, watching me "burn" and trying to look calm. As time passed, the look was getting less and less convincing. I looked to my teacher and then back to the class, who were still sitting in front of me—staring.

"Is it going to go away?" I asked, the rush of magic still running through my veins.

"You mean, you can feel that it's not?"

I frowned, my fingers still tingling from the flow of power. "No," I answered.

Mrs. Abott nodded, looking relieved, which prompted me to clarify my answer.

"No, what I mean is ... *yes*, I can feel that it's *not* going away."

My answer seemed to do something to her. Worry was suddenly etched across the wrinkles and crevices on her aging face.

She looked around nervously, and said, "Something is very wrong." That was all. Not a word of praise or explanation. She simply bolted to the telephone, mounted on the wall across the room. She fumbled with the receiver and then started quickly dialling a number. Someone answered and she started explaining the situation in harsh, clipped words. I edged a bit closer, hoping to eavesdrop.

"Don't move!" she screamed, her voice bouncing across the barren walls as she waved a finger sharply at me, as if to ward me off. I sucked in a breath, jumping backwards.

"What's going on?" I asked, looking at the clock worriedly. It had been over thirty minutes since I had set myself aflame. I didn't know all that much about magic, but I was fairly certain that Elementals didn't use their magic for this long. It wasn't supposed to be possible. Our bodies weren't supposed to be able to sustain magic for more than a few minutes at a time, and after that ...

I tried not to think about it, which wasn't as hard as it probably should have been. It was hard to focus on anything really. The sweet trance-like state that magic granted was simply euphoric. The looks on everyone's faces were the biggest clue that something extremely odd was happening.

"Class dismissed," Mrs. Abott said, as she hung up the phone, slamming down the receiver. The entire class immediately complied, climbing to their feet. They seemed to be used to odd happenings, although I sure wasn't, but a few of them seemed hesitant to just leave. "Hey but—"

"*Class is dismissed!*" Mrs. Abott commanded, leaving no room for questions. The last of the stragglers scampered out the door. She closed it behind them and locked it.

I turned to her, my mouth hanging open. "What's going on?"

"Don't you wor—"

Her answer was interrupted by someone banging loudly on the classroom door. We both jumped. Mrs. Abott opened it quickly, letting Mrs. Musk slip inside, and then carefully closed and locked it again. Mrs. Musk, sucked in a breath as she strode forward and began circling me.

"Miss Brooks, you really can't turn back, can you?" she asked, with a certain exasperated edge to her voice. "When you overwork yourself for praise, it can be fatal."

"No!" I stomped my flaming foot, reaching the extent of my patience. It was such a shocking sight, looking down at my feet and seeing flames shooting back up at me.

Mrs. Musk's gaze darkened for a moment, which didn't help me calm down.

"No one has *taught* me how to stop this! You think I *want* to stay on fire for this long? Can someone just, *please*, explain to me what I did wrong?"

The level of hysteria in my voice wasn't exaggerated and her gaze immediately softened. "You mean, you are not deliberately using your magic right now?"

"Of course not!" I huffed. "And I barely know how to do that even when I *do* try!"

Mrs. Musk sighed, shaking her head. As she stared into my eyes, I noticed how tired she looked. "I am going to sit right here until you revert back to normal. I have never seen anyone perform a spell for such a long period of time and the people who dared to attempt it have collapsed ..." Her voice trailed off and she seated herself a good distance away. She was staring at me so intensely that I couldn't face it and looked at the floor instead.

I stayed quiet as they both watched me with identical expressions. I didn't move from where I stood, and after about an hour, my legs began to get tired from standing so long.

"Alyssa," Mrs. Abott said, clearing her throat, her voice sounding raspy after over an hour of silence. "Your file says you haven't had any previous training in magic. Is that true? Or were you lying?"

"No! Why does everyone keep asking me that question? I haven't had any training!"

"You're a liar," she accused, rising from her chair. Her step towards me was tentative, but her voice was strong as steel. "I can practically feel your magic pulsating. Why don't you tell us who you really are? Or at least, why you were pretending to be weak."

"Hey!" I exclaimed, trying not to be too hurt by the insulting accusation. "I wasn't pretending—"

"Of *course* you were," Mrs. Abott continued, cutting me off. "*No one* can go from failing my class to achieving total ignition! And then maintain it this long ...? There is *no* way. Musk, have you done a complete background check on the girl? You know that infiltrators tend to be those weird, quiet ones—"

"Excuse me?" I was angry now. "I'm not *trying* to be anything! Especially not 'weird and quiet', but thanks for that! And I'm *not a spy!* If I was, don't you think I'd have to be a pretty *stupid* one to go and do something like *this?"* Now that I had started, I couldn't seem to stop, with all the anger and pain I had pushed down starting to come back up. "*I* didn't lie about *anything!* It was my *parents* who lied to *me* my whole life! Letting me think that I was just normal and *that magic didn't even exist!* I found out the truth three days before I arrived here! *Three days!* That is the truth, and if you don't believe me, why don't you just go talk to them? They're the ones who gave you your information, not me!"

Mrs. Abott had clearly stopped listening, perhaps not used to being yelled at by her students. "Magnorium clearly should not be so ready to take in *everyone,*" she growled. She glanced over at Mrs. Musk. "We get people like this," she gestured angrily at me, throwing a murderous glare my way, "and then we wonder why so many of us are killed!"

"Now let's just calm down for a moment," Mrs. Musk said smoothly, trying to intervene.

I was really on fire now, but it had nothing to do with the flames. Hot anger was bubbling its way to the surface. I grounded my teeth, trying to keep it together.

Mrs. Abott was anything but calm. "I want this girl thrown out of Magnorium as soon as possible! We cannot take *any* chances. Anomalies are *not* to be permitted."

"Shut up!" I shouted, and suddenly it was all too much. The pressure of life here, my humiliation at failing all of my classes, and then somehow being humiliated again for actually doing something right for once ...? For doing it *too* well ... ? There was a huge, shattering burst of sound, and then another and another ... One of the large classroom windows that overlooked the courtyard exploded, shattering into a thousand tiny pieces of glass. Then the window beside it followed suit, raining down pieces of glass in specks.

There was a loud bang above my head and I yelped, diving out of the way. The light above my head shattered—just like the one in my old school all those weeks ago. But this time, one light and one explosion did little to satisfy my anger. The effect seemed to expand outward, spreading through the room. More lights were exploding, spewing glass everywhere.

This was out of control!

Yet as one thing after another shattered, my anger only grew more intense, as memories and painful feelings started rising to the surface. A dormant volcano for most of my life, I had suddenly become active.

Mrs. Abott yelped and jumped out of the way as the light she was standing under exploded.

Mrs. Musk's eyes were very round, as she took a step forward. "Calm down, Alyssa!" she shouted, though not unkindly.

"I can't!" I screamed helplessly, and was terrified to find that I truly couldn't. I felt another wave of energy escape my control and I closed my eyes, not wanting to see. Then I remembered Haven's advice, from back in the desert, about focusing on my breathing. I counted to twenty inside of my head ... and then forty, drawing in big gasps of air and letting them out slowly. When I was done counting, I did feel less angry. I opened my eyes.

All fourteen lights and the two huge windows were completely obliterated. Broken glass covered the floor like glittering pieces of crystal. The explosions left fourteen identical holes in the ceiling plaster, and dust was tumbling down from each one. Having been blown backwards, the desks no longer sat in neat rows. Some were piled on top of each other and others had been destroyed, leaving nothing but large splinters. Even the walls had not escaped damages, with cracks running through them like veins, branching off in all directions. When I looked more closely at the concrete floor, I was shocked to see that it was cracked in places as well. I could see glass dust and tiny shards flowing into the cracks.

It looked like someone had set off a bomb inside the classroom. And I was that bomb.

"I-I ..." I tried to speak, crossing my arms over my chest as I searched for words.

Unbelievably, I was still on fire. The flames were wrapping around me like some sort of thick blanket I couldn't shrug off. I could still feel the effects of my magic very clearly.

"I am *so* sorry! I don't know how that happened—"

Mrs. Abott had been thrown onto the floor during the last wave of chaos and now struggled back to her feet. Mrs. Musk seemed to have kept better balance, but was wobbling a bit on her high-heeled shoes.

"You're a monster," Mrs. Abott spat murderously. "Look at what you've *done!*"

I flinched at her words, my eyes welling with tears. How could I do something like this? They both could've been seriously hurt!

"*Enough!*" Mrs. Musk shouted finally, her voice reverberating off the cracked walls. Shocked, Mrs. Abott looked up, her lips parted in surprise.

"You!" Mrs. Musk yelled at her, not giving her the chance to speak. "You need to leave! Now! Go find Mr. Bell and tell him I *will* be speaking with him today."

"But—"

"No!" Mrs. Musk glared at her. "Leave, right now. I will speak with you later."

The small woman looked like she wanted to say more, but thought better of it. She gave a curt nod, though defiance flashed in her eyes. "Of course. I will meet you later." She stepped over the worst of the glass and exited carefully through the doorway. I was shocked to see that even the door had been thrown off its hinges during the chaos, and was propped awkwardly against its frame. Excited chatter floated in from the hallway, though no one dared to come inside.

Utterly humiliated, I looked at the floor. How did I manage to continually mess up things so badly?

"Alyssa," Mrs. Musk's voice was soft and I glanced up to meet her eyes. "I want you to listen to me. This is not your fault. This is an example of what happens when one is provoked beyond reason, and Mrs. Abott should've known to stop."

"I'm sorry," I moaned. "I'll pay for all of this somehow, I promise—"

"That will not be necessary," she said firmly, shaking her head. "You, my dear, must be very special."

"I don't feel special. I'm a failure," I said, burying my head in my flaming hands.

"Alyssa," Mrs. Musk began, soothingly, "All who have succeeded have failed spectacularly at least once."

"My failure destroyed your classroom!"

"Yes," she remarked quietly, and took another step towards me, "it did. And luckily, Magnorium has far more funds than it needs to fix it."

I looked at my hands ... at the tendrils of fire that danced across my skin. "Why won't this go away?" I asked in a small voice. I raised an arm out to the side, hopelessly, as if to show her what was happening to me. Long tendrils of flames sprouted from the very pores of my skin, as though the ignition itself came from inside my body.

"You have not been trained properly," Mrs. Musk explained. "Your magic is all over the place. Spells are a beginner's outlet to magic and your magic is clearly too strong for you to control it, especially when provoked by emotion."

"I don't understand ..."

"It means," she said, patiently, "that we will just have to wait it out. Your power is shockingly strong, and you do not have the skill to turn it off. Not yet anyway. And so we will wait."

I began looking around the destroyed classroom. "Can't that end up being fatal?" I knew that when magic was used for an extended period of time, it could exhaust a user or even kill them. If I had no idea how to stop my magic, what did that mean for me exactly?

I would burn out, and I would burn out brilliantly ... or would I?

"Yes," Mrs. Musk nodded, making my heart almost stop in my chest. "It can be ..." She saw the fear in my eyes and softened a bit, "but ... if I have learned nothing else, it is that nothing is certain." She was beginning to look beyond nervous, and I tried to swallow my dread.

"I'm sorry Miss Brooks, but there simply *isn't* anything else to be done. We will just have to wait and see. You might want to sit down. We could be here a while."

"Mrs. Musk?" I looked over at her, tiredly. "I never asked, what kind of Elemental are you?"

It had been at least another hour since Mrs. Abott left the classroom, and I had a feeling that a crowd was growing outside, since I could barely hear Mrs. Musk over the chatter. Considering how long I had been stuck in this room, with no one but our vice principal for company, I wasn't uncomfortable. She had managed to calm me down so much that I no longer even cared that I was *still* on fire.

"I'm an Aquarian," she said, smiling.

Funny, I thought, I could tell straightway that Haven was an Aquarian, yet it wasn't so clear with her. I sat cross-legged on the concrete floor—since the desks and chairs had all pretty much been demolished—almost in the exact same place where I had been standing when this nightmare began. Mrs. Musk was sitting opposite me in a place that she had carefully cleared of debris and broken glass, with her legs out in front of her, her ankles crossed and her back leaning against the far wall.

I had nothing to do but wait, in this fireproof room, making small talk with Mrs. Musk.

I studied her for a moment, and then asked, "How long have you been working here?" Magnorium might look very modern, but I knew it had been around for a long time.

"Thirty years." She smoothed down a wrinkle in her long dark skirt, and shook her head. "The way Mr. Bell has got me working, I'll be around another thirty more, just to catch up on my paperwork."

"It must be hard," I remarked, feeling a bit of sympathy for the woman.

"Yes, at times it is." She blinked at me with tired eyes. "You'll have to forgive my colleagues, Alyssa. Nowadays, with the Society posing such a threat ... everyone is paranoid, and becoming more so with every attack. Infiltrators *have* been at Magnorium in the past, and more often than not, our students have paid with their lives." She noticed a flyaway strand of grey hair that had came loose from her bun, and tucked it behind her ear.

"I apologize if that upsets you, my dear, but you must know that the rumours are true ... and I do not agree with sugarcoating things for my students."

"It's okay," I said quietly. "I would rather know how bad things are than be in denial. It seems like half the school is already in it pretty deep."

Mrs. Musk sighed, as if she couldn't believe that we were sitting here having this conversation. Neither could I.

"Just last month," she said, "we lost two of our advanced students to the Society. And the Council has never forgiven me over the incident with Jason Reeves."

"Jason Reeves?" I asked, startled. I sat up a bit straighter.

"Yes, he was Haven Reeves' older brother. He was one of the most promising Elementals of his generation. Everyone knew that the Council wanted to recruit him." She sighed. "He went missing from here about six years ago, but unlike the other students we've lost, his body was never found. The investigation was led by Kurt and myself and was a massive failure. Jason was never found, and even today, I can barely face Haven—that poor boy. Sometimes, Miss Brooks, I wonder if I am the right person for this job." She sounded exhausted, a certain type of exhaustion that must come from managing over a hundred teenaged Elementals for thirty years, and trying to keep them safe.

"I think you do a great job here," I said quickly. It seemed that even the most powerful people needed someone to listen to them. "Tragedy happens. It's in the job description. You can't fix everything; you can only *try* to fix it. And you *do* try. I mean," I gestured to my own flaming arm. "You do a great job handling things like this. I'm feeling much better than I was." I shrugged. "I might not agree with everything that goes on around here," I added, not wanting to be a hypocrite, and certain that she remembered my opposition to her use of Power Arrows at the food fight, "or even everything that you do, but *no one* can deny how hard you work. You deserve your job."

"Thank you, my dear," Mrs. Musk said, sounding so grateful that I couldn't help but wonder how rarely she heard the sentiment. "Right now though, my job is to help you." She seemed to regain her professionalism as she remembered this, and peered down at her wristwatch.

"Alyssa, do you realize that you been like this for more than two and a half hours?" She scrutinized me for a long moment.

"No," I breathed, having lost track some time ago. "How is that even possible? Come on, there has got to be *something* that you can do." I found myself pleading with her, suddenly afraid once again. "Please? You've got to change me back!"

It couldn't have been more than two hours could it?

"I can't ... I am so sorry, Alyssa," she wrung her hands together, clearly wishing that she had some sort of answer for me, "but you're not letting go of your power!"

"But I would really love to let go ... but how do I *do* that?" My voice trembled.

She looked me steadily in the eye, and said, "Alyssa, you are going to be fine." She sounded firm, but her attempts were failing to calm my heart, which was hammering in my chest. "You *will* eventually turn back on your own."

Things started getting sort of fuzzy after that. As I looked down at the flames on my hands, I realized how exhausted I was. I wanted them to go away. I wanted to sleep, but my power kept me awake, refusing to release its hold. I was left enslaved.

I was sure it was nearing three hours, but time seemed to be passing in a hazy, blurry sort of way. I was conscious but oddly so. Everything seemed kind of skewed.

I sucked in a breath, as my eyelids finally drooped in surrender, and the world faded away for a moment. I barely possessed the strength to open my eyes again, or formulate a cry for help as I crashed down onto my side. Mrs. Musk jumped at the noise. The adrenaline and magic, which had kept its hold for three hours of my life, finally released me from its bonds. The flames finally disappeared, as if slithering back inside me to lie dormant, waiting for its next release. I gasped for air, fighting to get up—the whole world wrapped tightly in a murky haze. My hands flew to my hair and the skin on my cheeks. Miraculously, I was not burned ... or bald. I realized then that, even as death had threatened me, some small, vain part of myself had been afraid that the flaming hours might have singed off my hair.

Relieved, I took a series of long slow breaths, to try to slow my heart rate, gathered my wits about me, and ... very slowly ... climbed to my feet.

Mrs. Musk's face paled. "How are you standing?" she exclaimed, forgetting herself for a moment. She sounded genuinely perplexed by this, and I suddenly felt the need to reassure her.

"I'm fine," I mumbled, my words slurring—which should have made it instantly apparent that I really wasn't fine. The whole world was spinning and I realized that I was swaying on my feet. I felt drained of thought, of purpose ... of life.

Instantly, Mrs. Musk was at my side, helping me regain my shaky balance. "Can you make it down to my office?" she asked softly, and I blinked, trying to chase away the grogginess.

I didn't think I could really make it anywhere, but there was no way I was telling her that.

"Sure," I managed to choke out, forcing whatever energy I had left into dragging myself to the door.

This might just have been the most humiliating ordeal of my life, I thought, sloppily reaching for the door handle, before realizing that the door was only leaned up crookedly against the frame.

I turned the knob with a degree of difficulty, and then sort of pushed awkwardly at the door so that it fell out of my way, and stumbled out into the hallway—where crowds of onlookers had gathered to watch. I barely recognized the few shocked faces in the crowd. Amber was there, her eyebrows knit together. Haven and Zack stood behind her. Rachel and Emma were there too and some others ... then they all blended together into a hopeless sea of people, and I couldn't distinguish faces any longer.

Mrs. Musk walked swiftly out the classroom, unfazed by the gathering crowds, and all at once the entire world shifted from a foggy haze to a blinding array of colour. Everything around me was moving too fast and too loud.

My bones turned to liquid and I collapsed. As I crashed to the ground—startling almost everyone into jumping out of the way—I barely registered the commotion and chaos that was happening around me. People seemed to be screaming, and I saw dark greens and then electric blues ... then I felt someone simply shaking me. But all I wanted to do was sleep.

I closed my eyes, succumbing to the exhaustion. I followed sleep down into the darkness, and happily let it carry me away.

"Wake up," an irritated voice hissed. The voice was harsh yet soft all at the same time and I could faintly remember only one person who possessed a voice made up of such different aspects. I felt a rush of breath as the person sighed and then a hand was shaking me unceremoniously. I snapped out of my murky dream state.

I rubbed my eyes vigorously with the back of my fist to clear my vision, only to find Amber staring back at me. For once she wasn't scowling, screaming, or taunting me.

I gathered my bearings, jumping up from the simple padded bench that apparently had been my resting place. I looked around the small, empty room. I had a million questions—the first one being why I had the pleasure of sharing this slightly-too-small space with Amber Travie. I couldn't seem to get them all out fast enough.

"What are you doing here? Where are we? How long was I out? What happened?" I paused when I realized that she was looking at me with amusement and anger at the same time. "What?"

"What do you think you were doing pulling a stunt like that? You should be dead. Do you know that? Do you have a death wish?"

"I wasn't trying to *pull* anything," I answered, thoroughly confused. "Where's Mrs. Musk?"

Amber sighed, running a hand through her perfectly kept hair. "Mrs. Musk and Kurt are both waiting for us."

"Us?" I asked raising an eyebrow. "Last time I checked this doesn't have anything to do with you."

She held up her hands, looking almost like she was surrendering. "Apparently it does. I was told that they needed to talk to both of us. They sent me to wake you."

"How long was I out?"

"Five hours."

"Five hours!" I yelped, eyes widening. No, that was impossible.

Amber shook her head, irritated. "What do you expect Alyssa? You practically killed yourself doing that sort of magic for that long. I don't even know if I could do that, although *I* wouldn't be stupid enough to try! To be honest, I don't even know how you're not dead!" She crossed her arms across her chest accusingly. "Who are you?"

"*What?*" I practically squeaked, stunned into silence by the fact that I was apparently going to have to go through this yet again.

"Who are you?" she repeated, her eyes narrowing with suspicion. "I've never seen magic like yours. What you did was impossible. You're average ... 'normal' ... and no normal person in their right mind would challenge the Society, much less jump up on a table and declare war." She stared at me and I just stared right back at her for a moment. Her eyes held accusation and confusion. I just couldn't help myself. I laughed. Hard.

"This is ridiculous. First Haven, then Mrs. Abott, and now you! You think I'm a spy or something, right? Everyone around here must really have a higher opinion of me than I thought. I hate to disappoint you, but I'm really just average, and exactly who I say I am."

"I don't believe you," Amber said flatly.

I snorted. "That's what they said too."

She opened her mouth to respond but was cut off by harsh knocking at the door. She shot me a single look that told me we would be resuming this conversation later.

Kurt and Mrs. Musk stood in the doorway, expressionless, and I figured that they must've had years of training to hide their emotions so discreetly. I gave Mrs. Musk a small smile and tried to look anywhere but at Kurt. I was afraid that he would hear my heart pounding in my chest. All I could think of was the snake on the wall of his secret office and I half expected him to say something about it at any given moment, but of course he didn't. He didn't even look at me suspiciously. He carried on just like he had the first day I met him. He was dressed impeccably, in a slick black suit, and nodded a greeting.

"About time you came to," Kurt said, and gestured us to follow him with a single, demanding finger. He led us into a connecting room, which I recognized as Mrs. Musk's office—the place I had first come with Haven (and apparently the first room he had broken into).

Mrs. Musk motioned for Amber and I to each take a seat, in the plush chairs across from her desk. For a long moment, Kurt and Musk simply looked me up and down, as though they were sizing me up. No one dared to speak. Not even Amber, who had a notorious reputation for challenging authority.

"How about we begin with what you did today," Mrs. Musk finally said, breaking the silence.

I fumbled with my hands as I looked into her eyes.

"I want you to know that I wasn't trying to earn praise or brag or show off. People keep suggesting that but that isn't what happened." Kurt's eyes darkened and I tried to quell my nerves. I just had to act normal. I was telling the truth here, so I focused on that and took a breath.

"My teacher wanted me to read a spell off the board. So I did. It was one of the first spells that actually worked for me. It was supposed to light your entire body on fire. I waited for the effect to wear off, but it didn't. I wasn't trying to prolong the spell. I wanted it to stop but it just wouldn't. How long did it last anyway?"

"Exactly three hours," answered Mrs. Musk.

"Three hours!" Kurt slammed his hands down on the desk, chuckling. "Really, this is quite funny. That her enormous power almost went undetected, I mean."

"What?" I laughed. "Oh no, you don't understand. I'm ... uh ... well I'm failing all of my magic classes. This was just a fluke and I'm sorry for the trouble and all the damages and—"

"Listen Brooks, I have seen many things in my lifetime, but never have I seen anyone pull off what you did today. Physically and mentally, Elementals can only do magic for a limited period of time. Using magic for too long is exhausting and can potentially kill us. Now, the more power you possess, and the more stamina you have, the longer you can do magic. You have had basically no training. It should not have been possible for *anyone* to do what you did ... but for *you* especially. You really *should* be dead and yet here you are ..." His voice trailed off and I had never seen anyone look so intrigued. It was as though he felt the need to understand how everything in his world worked, so that he could control it.

"To put things into perspective for you, your powers are on par with, or likely even exceed, Miss Travie's here ... and that, my dear, is something not to be taken lightly."

Amber glared as she absorbed this information. "You're joking."

Kurt cast a sideways glance at Amber and I sensed his amusement at this situation. "Oh my dear, I am *not* joking. Surely you cannot argue with the evidence before us."

"What does this mean then?" Amber said almost frantically, running a hand through her dark, silky hair.

"Well technically, this means that Alyssa is now the most powerful student here," Mrs. Musk piped in, unapologetically, and then leaned towards me, speaking earnestly. "I should've known from the start, but must admit that I saw a non-pedigreed lineage, combined with a lack of training and experience, and assumed a lack of power ... accepting your 'fluke' theory, when I should have known better! You found the school in less than two hours, Alyssa. And it was *you* who saw through the glamour, yes? You are so powerful that you must be able to *feel* magic. There is so much magic in our area that, when you got stranded, you felt the energy and it led you here!"

I blinked, startled. That is exactly how it happened.

"This is ridiculous!" Amber exploded, glaring at me. "Her? Powerful?" Her stormy eyes flashed and darkened. "No one has ever had more power than me! Everyone here *knows* what I'm capable of." She glared at me once again. "I'll give you the choice of asking them or finding out for yourself."

I reciprocated the glare. "Are you asking me to *fight* you?" I asked, raising an eyebrow.

Amber sneered. "You can hardly call it a fight if it was with you."

Kurt burst out laughing. For a moment, I was stunned at the genuine pleasure in his voice. We all stopped to look at him.

"Oh my, no ... don't stop on our account, please. I can't tell you how much you're going to enjoy this next bit Travie," Kurt paused, leaning forward until he and Amber were locked in a cold, silent stare down. "Since Brooks' power now surpasses your own, it's only fitting for her to move out of her current dorm. I am personally moving Alyssa into *your* room. And if you have any problems with these new arrangements, you can take it up with me."

He took a breath. "Now, Travie, your fifteen minutes of fame has officially ended. Let's see how long yours will last Alyssa."

I met his look with a steady one of my own. "I told you, I'm nothing special Kurt."

He grinned, flashing his ridiculous white teeth. "No. Where you come from is nothing special. Your parents are nothing special. Average, if that. So what really interests me is where your power possibly came from."

I bit my lip. I really didn't know.

Kurt stood up abruptly, brushing off any remnants of the conversation, as though he had more important places to be.

"Musk, I want this all arranged for her. Move her stuff into Travie's room, along with any new textbooks she may need. Create a new schedule, and equip her with a private tutor. I want her skills developed and pushed to the max. Congratulations Brooks, we're going to find out how far you can possibly go." He made his way to the doorway.

"Oh and Musk, don't forget to notify the student body about this little discovery. I'm sure this will satisfy their curiosity." With that, he left the room, his presence managing to linger long after he was gone—the presence of someone with power.

Amber still sat staring at the doorway, a shocked expression stamped across her delicate features. I wasn't really surprised. I doubted that anyone ever talked to Amber that way. I had a feeling that the people in charge here didn't like her too much.

"You little—"

"Amber please!" Mrs. Musk held up a hand. "You can sort out your apparent problems later." She swiftly opened up a giant, locked cabinet, plucking out a single key and placing it in my outstretched hand.

"For your new room. Amber can show you the way, I'm sure."

Amber made some sort of noise that gave me the feeling I'd be finding the room on my own.

"The powerful dorms, room 1003. That's the tenth floor, room three, just in case Miss Travie decides to be inhospitable and not show you the way." She sat down in front of her blinking laptop, and after typing for a few moments, printed out a single sheet of paper.

"Your mortal schooling schedule will remain the same. Here is your new Advanced Elemental Training schedule. There are fifteen advanced students now, with whom you will share all classes, so make an effort to get to know them."

She paused for a moment, as if remembering something. "You will also now be required to sit in the Skyros room during meal times. So Miss Brooks," she smiled, "do you have any questions?"

Did I have any questions? Here was my chance to address at least one of the things that was wrong with Magnorium. But should I take it? I wasn't going to lie to myself and say that Haven's hatred for Magnorium hadn't passed over to me after last night. A little bit of it had. Magnorium treated the advanced better than everyone else, like the rest weren't even worth a second glance, and it was wrong.

"Yes actually. I would like to know why you think it's okay to treat the advanced better than everyone else, giving them nicer rooms and better treatment? Do you think that they—or I guess I should say 'we'—are better than the kids with less power?"

Mrs. Musk flinched—actually flinched, her cheeks reddening. I didn't falter. She *knew* this was wrong. She cleared her throat uncomfortably.

"Alyssa, I recognize that many things here are unfair. Unfortunately I have never, and will never, run this school," she said firmly, with no room for argument. "Mr. Bell does."

"Maybe that could change."

"One day," she said softly, "I hope that it might."

I sighed and nodded, forcing a tight smile. Clearly there was nothing more at the moment that I could possibly do. "All right then. Thank you for everything Mrs. Musk. Really."

Amber rose, copying my move and nodding in acknowledgement to Mrs. Musk, who gave a pained smile in return. I followed Amber out into the hall and gently closed the solid oak door, clutching my new schedule and room key.

I was powerful. Was this really happening? I had almost reached the conclusion that I was an absolute failure. I couldn't even pass a single magic class. And now I was supposed to have more power than people like Amber or Zack? Judging by the sour, defeated look on Amber's face, this was real whether I liked it or not. It was like the world was forcing Amber and I to be become friends ... or bitter enemies. I wondered which way it would go.

"This wasn't intentional," I said to fill the silence. I almost laughed at the absurdity of it all. "I mean, I did *one* spell."

"Yeah whatever. That one spell was done extremely well."

I rolled my eyes, moving back towards the elevator.

"Where are you going?" Amber asked curiously.

I froze. Most of the time Amber spoke to me in a vicious, insulting tone. To hear her speaking to me in a normal tone like this was refreshing.

"I'm going back to my old room, I guess. Want to come?"

She shrugged nonchalantly, but her eyes betrayed her. She was pleased. "Fine, but only because you'll get lost without my help."

I smiled at that and she followed me quietly all the way up to my dorm. When we reached the dull narrow hallways of the average dorms, Amber wrinkled her nose in disdain.

"This really *is* unfair."

I nodded, swinging open my dorm room door one last time. The room was vacant. Emma and Rachel, who I guess were now my *old* roommates, were nowhere to be found. This made things easier. I did a quick sweep of the room, stuffing my belongings into bags, and was out the door in less than five minutes. I had to hold back a grin. Being powerful did have its perks, as selfish as they might be. I would no longer have to see Emma and Rachel's snarling faces in the morning, and I would get to sit with Haven and Zack, who were really my only two friends here.

"Follow me," Amber said, before turning curtly towards the elevator. I hurried to catch up with her. The elevator opened with a chime on the tenth floor and I stepped out. Plush chiffon carpeting squished beneath my shoes. The long hallway had seven pairs of white-marble double-doors, three on one side and four on the other. An elaborate gold chandelier hung from the ceiling and the thick textured wallpaper practically screamed extravagance. It made me so upset, after where I had been staying, that I wanted to hurl something at the stupid chandelier above our heads.

As if she could read my mind, Amber's eyes lowered, and she looked almost ashamed. I followed her to the end of the hallway and she opened the door to her room. My jaw dropped to the floor as the door swung shut behind me. The room I was standing in looked like a million-dollar penthouse from some sort of five-star hotel.

The room was designed around the two huge, four-poster canopy beds that looked fit for royalty. Brightly coloured chairs were arranged in a corner and sat on plush, beige wall-to-wall carpeting, along with a huge oak desk with books piled high. There was an expensive but comfortable-looking sectional sofa in the centre of the room, in front of an entertainment unit that showcased a huge flat screen television and stereo system. Unlike the dorms on the average floor, this room had its own bathroom, which I assumed was also luxurious, although I couldn't see it from where I stood gawking. Matching chests lay at the foot of the beds and matching nightstands were on either side, each with its own reading lamp. There was even a full-size fridge and a microwave in a small kitchenette area. A huge chandelier was the final touch that brought the room together, glittering but not too dazzling. Despite the abundance of furnishings, the room wasn't even remotely cluttered. This was just too luxurious, and for what? Just for the powerful kids?

"How do you like it?" she asked.

I scoffed, swallowing the lump in my throat. "It's disgusting," I said honestly, not really referring to the room itself.

Amber glanced at me before laughing weakly. "That's not the reaction most people have," she said softly, "but I think I know what you mean."

"I guess I wouldn't mind living here though, as long as I don't let myself think about it too much. So, when did this stuff get here?" I asked, pointing to the second bed.

"It's always been there. I usually keep my books and things on it."

"Do you really live here alone?"

She folded her arms across her chest, sighing. "Well I used to."

"But it's so big," I said, emphasizing the enormity of the space with my hands. "It's too big."

"Yeah well, it was nice. I had it all to myself. There are only fourteen of us left after last month's attacks—well I guess fifteen now, and more than half of those are boys, so some of our rooms are just sitting empty up here." She looked up at me, saw my disturbed expression, and quickly went on. "Yes, I know that's sick. These beautiful and spacious rooms are sitting empty while the other students are crammed in like sardines. I get it."

She had misread my expression. I'd actually just come to the realization that Amber and Zack would have known the two advanced students who had been killed last month ... and probably others since coming to Magnorium. I decided not to stir up painful memories by pressing for details, knowing that she would share them when and if she was ready to do so.

"I just thought living here by yourself seems lonely." I said quietly.

Her stormy grey-blue eyes went into overcast mode and she suddenly became very interested in the floor.

"It is. But I'm *always* alone ... whether I'm with people or not. No one understands what I want to do and it scares people ..." her voice trailed off wistfully, as if this were something I could never hope to understand.

I gave her an almost soothing smile.

"Lucky for you, I've had a lot of experience with being alone." I could hear the bitterness in my voice, and could practically taste the sourness of my words. "In any case, you *won't* be alone anymore. I'm here." I grinned at her. "And you won't be able to ignore my presence either. I can be really annoying when I want to be."

"Oh trust me, I know. You're almost on the same level as my brother." She paused for a moment and decided to let me off the hook. "Almost."

"Well then, I feel *extremely* bad for you."

Amber laughed at that, and I stopped completely to just listen. Laughter was one of those few sounds that could make me do that.

There was something so raw and natural about laughter and I could tell Amber didn't do it often.

"Honestly Draken, I think I was wrong about you."

It was in that moment I realized I might have been horribly wrong about her too.

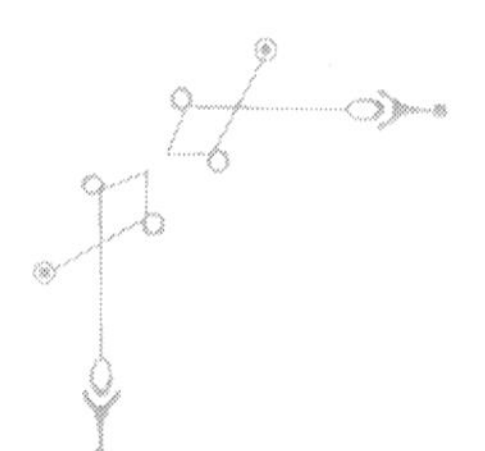
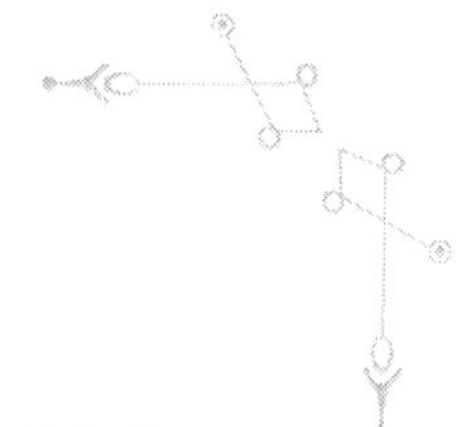

CHAPTER 10

APPREHENSION

Amber, I quickly learned, was a very lonely person encased in a thick armour of ice. I spent the majority of the first night in my new room working endlessly to melt it away. I still wasn't exactly sure if she liked me, but for now, being tolerated was a step in the right direction. I was in no position to pass up friends, as flawed as they may be, and the more time that passed, the more I discovered that I actually enjoyed her company.

Amber and I strode into the cafeteria early the next morning for breakfast—on time for once in my life. I entered the mass chaos, no longer feeling intimidated. There wasn't a single person in the entire cafeteria who didn't turn to stare at me as I entered.

"Why are they looking at me?" I mumbled to Amber.

She raised her eyebrows. "Well, you did faint in front of the entire school."

I laughed, my face reddening. "Oh God."

"It was funny ... well, sort of ... "Amber's voice trailed off, moving towards the Skyros room.

I realized with a jolt that I would now be following the same set of rules as the rest of the advanced students. The security guards at the doorway nodded at me and I stopped moving.

"I don't want to sit at that table; it's stupid."

Amber sighed, "you belong with us now, like it or not."

Then, before I could argue any further, she clamped an iron grip around my wrist and all but hauled me into the Skyros room, leaving no room for debate.

I took a quick inventory of who I would be forced to spend time with for the remainder of my time at Magnorium. Zack and Haven were there, and about ten other guys and girls who had never before looked once in my direction. Now my presence was almost too prominent. Immediately a hushed silence settled and all eyes were on me. None of them said a word, simply shifting over and making room for one more. They'd probably heard the news by now; Mrs. Musk had practically broadcast it, so inevitably, everyone was aware.

"Hi," I tried almost experimentally, standing awkwardly at the foot of the table. Startled faces started breaking out into reluctant smiles, until everyone at the table was urging me over to come and take a seat with them. It felt so weird to suddenly be the centre of attention. It was almost suffocating, and for a moment, I really empathized with Amber—who must've had to endure this gawking for years on end.

I felt a sudden yank on my shirt and the next thing I knew I was being pulled down onto a chair in between Zack and Haven.

"So," Zack said, happily munching his food. "Hit me with all you got, Draken!"

I poked him lightly in the chest. "Don't make me try."

Zack held up his hands in surrender. "All right you got me. I'm practically shaking over here."

I smirked.

"So just for the record," Haven muttered, using his spoon to point at Amber across the table. "I was right about her first."

"Yeah," Amber said. "But that's not fair. You took the test with her."

"When I get an impression about someone, I'm never wrong."

I shrugged, leaning my elbows on the table. "I don't know about that. You *did* accuse me of being a Society spy, and stole my file to check on me."

"*That* was a precaution," Haven said, but he was smiling. "So what do you know ... Alyssa Brooks is the most powerful Elemental here at Magnorium. You must be crazy strong."

I snorted. "You guys are strong too."

"No, not all of us." Haven said.

"Really?" I asked skeptically, getting lost in his eyes—like the ocean, they were always in chaos, always moving, never at ease. He bowed his head, his lashes casting shadows on his smooth, tanned skin. "I'm strong because I don't have the option *not* to be. Zack's strong because he likes the bragging rights. And Amber's strong because she likes to fight."

"I *do* like my bragging rights," Zack agreed, nodding.

"And I *do* enjoy fighting," Amber murmured.

"You always have options you know," I said softly.

"Not always. Could you stand up right now and go sit somewhere else?"

I shrugged. "If I wanted to I would, but I don't think I want to,"

Haven made a sour face. "They just took away your freedom! Everyone else is afraid to talk to you. And we, unfortunately, have *these* lovely people to talk to all day." He gestured down the table at our peers.

Amber glowered, taking a bite of her cereal. "It's not that bad."

"Oh it's bad." Haven said. "But now it sucks for all *four* of us."

"Haven doesn't like to be controlled or told what to do," Zack said, shooting a rather fond look in his roommate's direction. "But seriously dude, *stop* being so obsessive. I'm trying to forget we live in a school here!"

"Anyway," Zack continued. "I saw you fall. Pretty funny actually, you were steaming."

"Gee thanks," I said trying not to blush. "I *did* stay on fire for three hours, but I'm glad you found it amusing."

"No, I mean I found it funny because you were *literally* steaming," Zack grinned.

"I was?"

"Like a volcano, Draken." He whistled. "And now, since you're rooming with Amber, I would just like to warn you ... there is no guarantee that she won't kill you in your sleep."

"If I really wanted to hurt her, she wouldn't be sitting here right now," Amber said casually, spooning her cereal.

"Excuse me!" I interrupted. "But how defenseless do you think I am?"

"Well so far you can set yourself on fire and make things explode around you, almost killing yourself in the process," Zack supplied, "so pretty defenseless actually."

"It's a valid question though," a voice piped in from farther down the table. "Can you fight, Draken?"

"Yeah," another girl commented, sounding snarky. "She'll probably get eaten up in battle strategy." There was a murmuring chorus of agreement and I stood up abruptly, my commotion momentarily silencing the table. I was tired of people telling me what I could and couldn't do.

"We'll see about that." I'd had enough of the advanced for one day.

"Where do you think you're going?" Zack called, moving to follow me as I quickly moved towards the cafeteria doors.

"How do you stand them Zack?" I asked, with a mad gesture towards the Skyros room. "I mean you've been stuck with them for what ... your *whole* time here?"

"You mean how do I deal with their arrogance and their constant whining, while they continue to judge every single thing I do?"

"Yes, that's exactly what I mean."

"Well," Zack said. "I've had practise. I've been dealing with one of them for about seventeen years. The advanced are all kiss ups really."

"Kissing up to who?"

"To me obviously. I have many god-like qualities." I rolled my eyes. "Seriously Alyssa, it's not rocket science. They just follow around the most powerful person."

"Does that mean they're going to follow *me* around now?" I asked with horror.

He grinned, his dark green eyes glittering. "Like a flock of sheep."

I stared back towards the doorway in disdain. "Great."

"Everyone loves a good leader, darling." He smiled as I pushed open the doors to the cafeteria, heading back out into the swirling chaos of the morning. "Speaking of which," he continued, "you're going to have to let me lead you to your next class."

"I can get there myself, you know."

"Um ... no." He grabbed my wrist as I turned down the hallway towards my first-period math class.

"You're going the wrong way. Today's Elemental schooling, not mortal."

Right. I had almost forgotten about the midweek switch. I shrugged in explanation. "Old habits die hard."

For once, Zack seemed to be right, and I was in no position to pass up *any* form of hospitality. I also had no idea where my new set of classes were located. So, I followed his mop of messy black hair as he quickly took off down the hallway in the opposite direction.

It was only my first day as an advanced and I already had enough of the fourteen awful elite students. Sure they were welcoming during breakfast, but that facade had quickly worn off. Following them into two new classes allowed me the chance to see how incredibly rude they were to the rest of the student body, as if I could forget my own treatment as an average. They pushed them out of the way, shot them dirty looks over their shoulders, laughed at them behind their backs ... It was ridiculous, and had been enough to make me want to ditch lunch and hide in the library. Which was exactly what I was doing.

Other than the forest, the library was my favourite place to go in all of Magnorium. Perhaps that was because the rest of the school looked so foreign, whereas the library looked very mortal. I wondered if 'mortal' was an actual category of interior design around here.

Huge oak bookshelves climbed towards the ceiling and covered all four walls. The centre of the enormous room was filled with books, in countless cases with countless shelves. Rows and rows of books stretched as far as the eye could see. There were so many books that it made my head spin with a sort of giddy excitement. Old books, new books, books on magic, books on mortal science ... there was every conceivable title under the sun in this one library. I just couldn't believe it.

Back home, when I had way too much time on my hands, I remembered reading for hours upon hours, alone in my bedroom. It was nice—a sort of solitary peacefulness—but back home I was alone far too often.

Coming to Magnorium was a shock to my system. Here, I was never alone; there was always someone yelling at me, or insulting me, or talking to me ... it was the complete opposite of what I knew. I could never get a moment to myself. I missed just sitting in a comfortable armchair and immersing myself in a story. Especially because, at Magnorium, it literally felt like I was living in one.

Besides that, it was comfortable in here. I had a feeling that most Elementals didn't read; they probably preferred combat training over books and that was just fine by me. I was sitting in a comfortable armchair under a large, stained-glass window that just seemed to sparkle with blues and reds. The cherry hardwood floor, covered in places by expensive Persian rugs, made the whole room feel quite cozy. There was also music playing in the background, real classical music, which was nice, because music didn't seem to exist in any other part of Magnorium. I was in the middle of reading a really interesting book that I'd found when the library door opened and Zack and Amber stormed inside.

Clearly they were looking for me, because when I tried to hide behind the book I was reading, Amber pointed loudly and hissed my name. The two of them walked over to where I was sitting and I withheld my groan, looking up as they approached.

"What are you doing in here?" Amber asked curiously, and dropped loudly into the seat next to me, apparently oblivious to the fact that she was in a library.

"Clearly not *reading* or anything like that," I said sarcastically, shutting my book. "What brings you to this mortal neck of the woods?"

Zack smiled, dropping into the armchair on the other side of me. "When you weren't at lunch we thought you were going to ditch being an advanced and try to switch back levels."

"And leave all of you lovely people? How could I?" I drummed my fingers on the cover of the book. It made me happy, that the two of them had cared enough to come looking for me.

"What are you reading?" Zack whispered, taking the book out of my hands before I could protest.

I sighed, not looking forward to the judgement I was about to receive. "Poetry."

"You like poetry?" he asked, sounding flabbergasted and examining the old fragile book in his hands. "*Old* poetry? Jeez, this book is like centuries old." He thumbed through the yellowed pages and then closed it, disinterested. "This is barely written in English anyway."

"'I would challenge you to a battle of wits,'" I quoted smugly, "'but I see that you are unarmed.'"

"Where's that from?" Zack asked, sounding genuinely curious.

I grinned. "William Shakespeare."

"Who?" Amber asked, sounding bewildered.

I made some sort of choking noise. "Did you guys not listen at all in mortal history class?"

"We don't have mortal history class." Zack handed me back the book. "There's not really any point; it's like learning about an alternate universe we're not part of."

"Okay," I said, trying not to gloat, knowing things that these two didn't. "So how did you know I was here? And why is it so important that I'm at lunch anyway?"

"We *didn't* know," Amber said, shrugging. "We checked other places and since Zack likes it in here anyway, here we are." She rose to her feet, her nose wrinkling as she surveyed the room.

"I'm going to go see what Haven's doing. He wasn't at lunch either." She looked at me. "Any idea where he is?"

I shook my head. "When it comes to Haven, I never know for sure."

"Well," Amber shrugged her shoulders, "I don't really like it in here. It's too quiet. I'll see you guys after lunch." She threw her straight black hair over her shoulder and headed out. I watched her go in a whirl of movement. It really seemed as though Amber *never* rested, not even for a moment.

"Amber has two modes," Zack said, practically reading my mind. "Fighting and not fighting ... and when she's not fighting, she's *thinking* about fighting. If she can't win something or beat something up, she gets bored. I think Magnorium drilled that into her head," he added, almost as an afterthought. I glanced at him as he drew his knees up to his chin, leaned his head back, and closed his eyes.

"Amber said you liked it in here?" I asked, conversationally. It occurred to me that I didn't know much about Zack or Amber, or even Haven really. They were my friends, I realized with a start, but I barely knew anything about them.

Zack's eyes popped open. He looked so at ease sitting there, even more so than he did normally. Just looking at him made me remember how attractive he was, with his striking black hair and green eyes.

I leaned towards him a bit, so I could keep my voice low as we talked. "Do you like to read too?"

Zack gave a snort. "Of course not. But I like the music they play in here. Magnorium blocks like half of the Internet, so I can never listen to a wide variety of good music. Not like the kind they play in here."

"*You* like music?" I asked, before I could stop myself. I didn't mean to sound so shocked, it was just that ... I guess I wasn't expecting Zack to like things that were so mundane.

Zack shrugged, the black strands of his hair falling into his eyes. "I like hard rock the best. I'm only familiar with music that I listened to back home. My dad used to play records for me." He looked like he was about to say something else, but the words seemed to catch in his throat.

I frowned, realizing that I didn't know much about Zack or Amber's past.

"Hey," I said, nudging him with my foot. "If you like music, then you're in the right place. All the artists come to Las Vegas. That's not too far. Why don't you go to concerts on the weekends?"

Zack laughed again, but this time it seemed sad. I had never seen Zack sad before. He smiled at me, but it didn't reach his eyes. Something inside of me ached in reaction to the look on his face.

"Advanced aren't allowed to leave the premises on weekends."

"What?" I shouted, bolting upright in my chair, my book almost sliding off my lap. "Why not? Why didn't anyone *tell* me that?"

"Everything is about safety here." Zack rolled his eyes. "It's another safety precaution. They don't want us mingling with mortals until we are finished our training, just in case we hurt them. And they don't want us out and about in the real world, because that makes us easy targets for the Society. And we all know how much the Society likes killing powerful people." He sounded humourless, speaking with the voice of someone who had given up long ago.

"That's awful," I whispered, so repulsed by Magnorium that I almost couldn't stand it.

"Sometimes I think about running away you know. But Amber loves it here."

"Zack–"

"You know, sometimes I wonder what I would do with my life if I wasn't an Elemental. I think I'd want to be a musician," he said with a nod, "or at least learn how to play an instrument, like the guitar or the piano."

"You still can," I said soothingly. "Nothing's stopping you. You can do anything you want to."

He shook his head sadly. "Not here you can't. My potential and all the things I could've loved were crushed the day I was born into an Elemental family. I was handed a dagger and a gun and taught to fight."

"Zack," I said firmly. "You *are* who you want to be. Not who they make you. You are a person. You're not a warrior, even though you can fight as one. You should be able to do the things you love."

"I do love music," Zack agreed, closing his eyes for a moment again. The melody of a soft cello playing floated comfortably in the background. "But my potential, or what could've been, will never *be* ... not here at Magnorium. The best I can do is come to the library on occasions and just listen to music instead. It's relaxing all the same."

"I'll change that," I vowed, suddenly so angry I could barely speak. "I'll change things for you. For everyone. You'll learn how to play a real instrument. You deserve a life just like I had."

I had a life of freedom—a freedom where I could do what I wanted, and explore the things I loved. And only now, speaking with Zack, did I realize how little I had done with that freedom.

"You're so passionate," Zack remarked, looking at me oddly. I almost blushed. "There's a shortage of passionate people here," he continued. "I almost forgot that someone else could be as driven as

Amber. Haven is that way too. When did I become completely surrounded by you people?"

"'If music be the food of love play on'," I quoted again, smiling at his confused expression as he tried to decipher the words.

"Is that another quote by your dead mortal writer?"

"That dead mortal writer happens to be the most famous writer of all time."

Zack shrugged, leaning forward until our feet were almost touching. "He's right. Let music play on. But he uses too many confusing words."

I laughed. Explaining mortal culture to Elementals was extremely amusing.

"Hey Zack," I whispered, setting my book carefully down on the nearby table. "I went to a Pearl Jam concert by myself a few years ago. I videotaped it. Want to see it? It's on my phone."

Zack's face lit up adorably, and he grinned, the smile crinkling the corners of his eyes. "Now that, darling," he said, and I could hear him trying to control the level of excitement flooding into his voice, "is something I would love to see."

"Great," I said, rising from my chair. "Because we have an hour to kill before we have to go to class, and I usually never have anything cool to show anyone."

Zack was already on his feet, beckoning me to follow. I followed him quickly out of the library, trying not to smile at his enthusiasm. It was so odd, I realized, how such small things could bring someone else such joy. Knowing something small that I had could make someone that happy, made *me* happy—the happiest I had been all day.

It really was impossible not to hear the circulating rumours about the fights that went down in the Advanced Battle Strategy class—the widely anticipated fights. There were stories of the entire room being ripped apart, or participants receiving permanent injuries. There was even talk of a death. None of the rumours floating around the school were particularly pleasant; so when I walked into my first ever battle strategy class after lunch, and saw Elda sitting there in her wheelchair in front of the room, it was more than a little intimidating ... and intriguing.

I quickly followed Amber inside and sat down, raising my eyebrows questioningly. It might have been ironic, that the teacher of this class was an old lady in a wheelchair, but tons of people swore she was the best teacher at Magnorium.

"So I have decided," Elda announced, clapping her rough hands together, "that in honour of our new transfer—thank you, Alyssa Brooks—it is about time to have another team battle." That seemed to spark something in the rest of the class and they erupted in excited chatter.

"Most of you know the rules for this particular type of fight. Four students, whom I see fit to battle, are chosen. These students will fight in the training room," she motioned to the room directly behind her. Elda's classroom was split into two sections, a normal classroom and (connected to it) an enormous training room, with a huge safety glass window, through which the fights were watched by the non-participants. "The objective is to be the first team to press the red button at the far end of the room, using any strategy you see fit. To be clear, killing one another is *not* a strategy that I see fit." She paused for a moment, clearing her throat.

"In the past, these fights have been known to get quite violent, so please be careful."

I gulped, realizing that the rumours I heard might actually have some substance to them.

"When I announce the teams," she said "please join me up here. Team number one ... Alyssa Brooks and Zack Travie!"

I thought my name had just come out of Elda's mouth, but then again, I wasn't exactly sure. I mean ... it wouldn't make much sense to throw me in the midst of a heated fight, unless Elda wanted to see me squashed like a bug. The sound of Zack's easy laughter seemed to confirm that my name *had* been called, and the expectant look on the faces of the other kids told me clearly to get a move on.

"You do know she called your name, right?" Zack inquired casually, as I looked around. He was grinning at me. Things had changed between us since our conversation in the library, but still I only managed to blink up at him. "It's your lucky day to be paired with me," he boasted, "because I don't lose."

"That's funny, because I wasn't planning to either," I said, trying to get over my shock. I stood up abruptly, sending my chair flying and exuding more confidence than I probably should have. Elda grinned.

"Team number two ... Haven Reeves and Amber Travie!" Elda exclaimed enthusiastically. I couldn't stop my jaw from plummeting towards the floor, because Amber, Haven, and Zack *alone* were killing machines. I did not want to find out what it would be like if we were all together in one room. The likelihood that I could stand any ground against them was slim.

"Elda, are you sure about this?" Amber tentatively voiced the question that was on everyone's mind, genuinely worried for my safety. "She has raw talent, but she has no combat training."

"She's been deemed the most powerful person here for a reason," Elda said, dismissing Amber's concerns with a wave of her hand. Kurt might've deemed me that same title, but in no way did I agree with the assessment.

Elda's wishes certainly weren't up for debate, however, so I had no choice but to reluctantly follow the rest of them into the training room.

"You have exactly five minutes to converse and devise strategies with your teammate," Elda said, setting a timer on her watch.

I struggled to wrap my mind around the sheer size of this room, which was about the size of a football field, and carpeted with soil and green grass. Everywhere I looked there were elements of a natural landscape. I couldn't quite figure out how it could be contained within the confines of the building, but I didn't have time to worry about it. My eyes danced across the room, analyzing any possible strategies that could give me some sort of advantage.

I quickly closed my eyes, tapping into my other heightened senses. If I listened closely I could hear the distinct sound of rushing water, an indication that some sort of reservoir was present underneath the ground. I wondered what Haven, as an Aquarian, would be able to do with that. I noticed that even the air felt slightly different in here—fresher, almost more pure. Thick sheets of metal lined the impenetrable walls, and judging by the various scorch marks, were meant for no other purpose than conducting electricity. This room was perfectly crafted to give each Elemental an ample opportunity to win. About a hundred feet away, a bright red button on the back wall was encased in a huge glass box.

"Alyssa," Zack called over to me, distancing himself from Amber and Haven, who were whispering to each other in low voices. Zack followed suit, leaning in close. "You have no idea what you're doing, do you?" he whispered, amused.

"What on earth would give you that idea?" I asked, dryly.

"Don't worry," he reassured me. "I can handle most of it. So ... the trick to winning a battle is to catch your opponent off guard, right in the very first moment. When we start, I'm going to surprise them, so make sure you keep your balance."

"What?" I asked curiously.

Zack grinned. "I have a few tricks up my sleeve. This fight is going to be fought with a couple of perfectly timed earthquakes."

"*Earthquakes*?" I hissed, my eyes going round. I had little idea of what Terrans were capable of, but the idea of causing actual earthquakes was just shocking, despite all I had learned thus far.

Zack nodded, shifting his feet. "Yeah. Try not to be too close to me. Are you a fast runner?"

I gave a curt nod. "Yeah."

"Good. I want you to run as fast as you can towards the button. I'll try to fend off Amber and Haven."

I smiled tightly. I wanted to help, but really ... what good was I? I would probably only get in the way.

"I can help too you know," I said, trying to think positively, though I had no idea what I could do. "I'm good at improvising."

"The reason why Elda offers team battles is because she wants Elementals who control different elements to work together, so that their *elements* can work together." He looked at me gently. "That can really only happen after years of training or after you know how to work with someone really well. Haven and Amber's elements won't work together well, and they're both too stubborn, and haven't known each other long enough, to work well together as a team. If I had more time, maybe our elements could work together, but you don't have the training."

"Two minutes," Elda interrupted.

"Anyway," Zack shook his head, "they're going to lose, because what you're going to see is two extremely powerful people using their powers individually. And you're going to run like hell. I'll handle Amber, and hopefully Haven isn't as good as everyone thinks he is. Got it?"

"Yeah," I said quickly, though my head was swimming.

"Good." Zack withdrew just as Elda cleared her throat to speak.

"The fight begins when the buzzer sounds," Elda announced, her loud voice reverberating off the endless stretch of metal walls. She raised a bony finger in my direction, pointing me to a marked starting point on the floor. She automatically did the same with the others, Zack on my right, and Amber and Haven on my left. It was clear that the three of them hadn't fought in a long time and were eager to get started.

Being involved in this fight wasn't the greatest idea even in the best of circumstances ... and these were far from the best.

"Once again," Elda said, "there are no rules in this particular type of battle, just please refrain from severely harming each other." Elda didn't really appear to be joking, even though her thin lips had curled into a smirk.

"Have a splendid fight." This was the last thing she said before wheeling her frail body on over to the exit and safely removing herself from the room. The steel doors slammed shut behind her.

I reminded myself to take a breath. And then another. I *probably* was going to be fine. I may not have known them for very long, but I held a sliver of hope that no one would take it too far. I tried to ignore the fact that I knew little to no magic, as well as the fact that everyone was watching me through the window.

For a breathless second no one moved from their positioned stance, silently going over strategies and attacks they could use to their advantage. I mean, that's what I would have been doing too ... if I had any strategies or attacks. The sheer anticipation of what was to come had me perspiring slightly.

Time seemed to stop completely, but the buzzer sounded anyway.

It wasn't until that exact moment that I realized just how clearly I did *not* deserve the title Kurt had bestowed upon me. I was completely and utterly out of my class. Regardless, I was expected to fight as an equal.

So I would.

Zack remained true to his word. He leapt through the air with agility that rivalled even a Skyros. His sudden movement startled us all—even me, and I had been expecting something of the sort. He landed on his knees, slamming his fists into the grass. Then, the ground beneath us tilted. This tilting of the ground sent Haven and Amber toppling over onto the grass. Fortunately a moment was all I needed to gain some ground.

Zack laughed as if on cue, all the while screaming, "Alyssa go!"

So I went. I regained my full balance, taking off in a burst of speed and stamina. Amber was quick to jump to her feet, zipping through the air and landing in my path. Her usual stormy grey-blue eyes were now clear like a cloudless sky. It seemed like fighting was the only thing in the world that made sense to her.

"Do you think you can win with a mad dash? I don't think so," she chastised, with a click of her tongue. There wasn't enough time to think of a witty response. Almost appearing bored, she raised her hands to eye level and flicked her wrist. There was a soft rustling and then a giant blast of wind hit me straight in the face. Disoriented, the sheer power of the wind knocked me right off my feet, blowing me backwards and spinning me around in the air. I landed hard on my knees, shook my head to clear away the dizziness, and jumped back up.

I went straight for her, angling my elbows just like I had been taught to do in my Average Combat class, in order to deliver the fiercest blow. My fist should have connected with her face, but connected with air instead. I withdrew, with a frustrated sigh. She moved too fast. But my reflexes were quick too.

I ducked, dropping my head to my knees just as she took a swing of her own, her fist swinging fast through the air and just missing my cheekbone. As her forward momentum carried her past me, I lit my entire body into flames and slammed my elbow into her backside.

The impact of my elbow sent Amber crashing towards the ground, crying out in surprise. My entire body was engulfed in huge talons of flames, just like the first time I had done it in the classroom. There was no spell or even much thought needed this time. It was purely instinctual and somehow seemed to work much better that way. I extinguished myself, momentarily breathless with exertion.

Suddenly something incredibly sharp whizzed by, hitting my side. The object stung a bit and I suddenly felt an icy cold sensation. I turned around to see an onslaught of tiny sharp ice pellets hurtling through the air in my direction. I ducked just in time, saving myself from their sting. There were too many unbelievable things all happening at once. I couldn't keep up with it. But just like Zack had predicted, Haven and Amber weren't blending their elements together. They were fighting individually.

Just a short distance away, Haven was wrestling with Zack in hand-to-hand combat. Haven managed to wriggle free from the hold Zack had on his arm and took a swing, aiming a punch straight at Zack's jaw. The sheer force of Haven's single punch sent Zack flying backwards. Haven's reflexes were stunningly quick and in a flash he rolled away and was charging towards his fallen teammate.

That was when I realized that Amber still lay on the ground with her shoulders heaving, attempting to get up.

Haven reached her quickly, helping her to her feet. I didn't even think about what I did next. I transferred the concentration of my magic down into my palms. This time I didn't want my whole body to spontaneously combust. My hands burst into flames, and carefully aiming, I shot a tendril of flame, straight out of my bare hands, spiralling in their direction.

It looked surreal, but at the same time, felt completely natural. It felt like throwing a rope. The talons of flame ripped from my hands, hitting the ground near them—the earth lighting up in a brilliant flash of red, yellow, and gold. The grass caught fire, greedily sucking in the purity of the air and growing larger by the second.

I was concentrating too hard to be stunned, but the fire was completely under my command. I only had to think about what I wanted it to do, how I wanted it to behave, and that is exactly what it did.

I directed the flames to create a ring, essentially trapping Amber and Haven right where they stood. The fire fanned outwards, looping around in a circle like a row of torches. The flames were vicious, climbing to about fifteen feet, obstructing my view of the pair completely.

"Finally I get to see your magic!" Amber's loud voice carried over the billowing flames and smoke, still managing to remain cocky, even though she seemed unnerved by my trap. "I thought I'd never see it!"

All I could hear was the antagonizing sound of their laugher, daring to make light of my best work to date. A pulse of air radiated from within the circle of smoke and flame and I watched dumbstruck as Amber manipulated the air currents, launching herself about twenty feet into the air.

The shift in the air was almost visible, like a blast of fresh air on a crisp winter morning. Amber flung herself over my head, landing on her feet with more grace and agility than most birds of flight. I was so captivated by seeing someone fly that I forgot to fight back.

Luckily, before she had a chance to execute another move, Zack settled for a good old-fashioned tackle, and quite mercilessly, forced Amber to the ground. She went down, growling and wrestling with her brother.

I gulped. That left me to deal with Haven. He was still trapped inside my ring of fire, as I had yet to release my hold on the flames. Unfortunately, our elements were anything but compatible. They cancelled each other out, something Haven could use to his advantage. Even though I couldn't see him, I could detect his energy—strong, powerful, and fierce.

The ground beneath my feet shook, but this time it wasn't Zack's doing. The ground under Haven's feet split open, viciously spewing a giant wave of water up into the air. The water was airborne for a moment before gravity took its toll. Then it rained down on my flames, instantly extinguishing them.

Haven's smirk was pretentious enough to make me seethe. He stood still, almost like some sort of viscous animal waiting to strike. Then he leapt forward.

Deep gashes were etched into the skin on his forearms and wrists. They looked almost looked like intentional cuts ... except I didn't remember anyone doing anything to create injuries like that.

I gasped. Huge rings of water shot out from deep within the long slits in his arms, as though he were *made* of water. The water didn't drip, but rather immediately solidified into ice. How he did that, I couldn't even fathom.

Two scythe-like blades, made of solid ice, hung from his arms, each extending to a fine tip. The blades really appeared to be an extension of his body. The blades were made of ice, but they would hurt nonetheless if I didn't dodge.

Haven swung his arms towards my face, wielding his blades with more skill than I thought possible. Instinctively, I threw my hands in front of my face in a pathetic attempt to block, although I knew they would do little to protect me from the two giant blades of solid ice. He struck the side of my face, while the other blade of ice smashed into my waist. The sheer force of the impact sent me crashing to the ground about five feet away from where I had been standing. I laid on the ground, struggling to get up—my body throbbing and cold.

Fortunately it was at that exact moment when Zack struggled to his feet, a murderous look in his eye.

"You're dead Reeves," he growled, and then the entire world tipped upside down. His attack had felt different before, as though he was just tilting the ground in an awkward direction. This was something else. The world actually *seemed* to tip upside down. As the earth exploded, throwing my body against a huge wall of dirt that had formed from the once flat ground, I lunged away from Haven and towards Zack, worried about being caught in the middle of a forming barrier.

The enormous wall of dirt grew up past my head, eventually reaching about forty feet into the air. It crossed the room from one side to the other, completely trapping Amber and Haven on the other side.

"That's amazing," I exclaimed, staring at Zack, in shock.

He winked. "That's just the beginning."

The wall shook as a strong wind heaved against it. I didn't know much about Skyros magic. But I knew Amber was conjuring concentrated blasts of air, shooting them against the wall to break it down.

I knew that Amber could launch herself over the wall, as it didn't quite reach the ceiling. But Haven would be left pretty much trapped. The only thing they could possibly do was hope to break it.

The wall trembled a little as it endured another blast of wind. The force sent little pieces of dirt crumbling down, the dust settling in my hair. I held my breath as Amber sent yet another blast, making the wall shudder violently this time. As if realizing the inevitable, Zack clamped a hand around my wrist tugging me backwards.

With one last mighty explosion, the wall shuddered and came crashing down in huge crumbling masses of dirt. Haven and Amber both took off sprinting, jumping over the pieces of dirt onto smoother grass. Haven recomposed himself, facing Zack with a sly grin on his face.

For a breathless moment all was still. Then the patchy earth beneath my feet cracked open, filling up with water from deep underneath the ground. Haven smiled triumphantly as his element bled through the earth, sloshing its way into my shoes. I jumped backwards.

Suddenly a concentration of water shot up from the ground, smashing into Zack like a giant tidal wave. The impact of the wave sent Zack crashing to the floor, a look of surprise frozen on his face.

This water wasn't like normal water. Haven was clearly in control of it, and as it washed over Zack, it trapped him inside a compact oval of water.

"What the hell is that?" I shouted, shocked.

"I hardened the water molecules. He can't break free. It's like a glass casing of water," Haven shouted over the chaos.

Zack pounded against the walls of his watery cage in a futile attempt at gaining his freedom. Like Haven said, it was like the walls were made of glass.

Zack was trapped inside a giant water bubble with no oxygen.

"Are you going to drown him?" I shouted, panicked.

Haven shrugged, amusement flying across his face. "Don't worry he'll be fine after this," he muttered, and raised a single hand in preparation for yet another attack.

What could I do? I didn't have any more attacks and everything was happening too fast.

As Haven gestured with his hand, the entire water cage spiralled away as though it had been pushed. Zack flew through the air at an alarming speed and hit a wall with a bang, the glassy bubble bursting immediately.

Haven had not chosen to spare Zack the impact, and I watched completely shocked as his body smashed into the metal wall and crumpled to the floor, soaking wet. A puddle of water formed around his sprawled form.

All the commotion of Haven's foreign attack almost made me forget about Amber and I was unprepared when she came charging at me full force.

A popping sound shrieked through the room and what felt like a sharp slice of air came shooting towards me. It felt like being sliced with a real knife, although it spilled no blood. It was so violent and sudden that the air knocked me backwards into the nearest wall. I let out a small groan, flashes of pain shooting up my spine. I began to panic as I realized that I couldn't move. I was locked in place and I had no idea how to get free.

Amber eyed me with a steely gaze, as if making sure not to break concentration. The more I attempted to move my body, the more she hardened the air around it.

"Really Amber?" I barely managed to squeak out—even the simple task of speech challenging.

"It'll be a miracle if you get out of this one!" she exclaimed. I gritted my teeth, attempting to move just a single finger. It almost felt like I was pushing against an invisible wall, but the harder I pushed the more room I had to move around. For a few precious moments, I was preoccupied with pushing against the force to free one of my hands.

I bit back a smile as my wrist flexed forward, moving a few inches. A few inches was all I needed. I wrestled with concentrating my power into my palms, which tingled, growing hot.

I glanced at Amber's shoulder, the only thing I could hit at the angle open to me for a blow. With considerable ease, I aimed and shot a compacted ball of heat straight out of my palm and into Amber's shoulder. The shot fired so fast that there was no time to even catch a glimpse. It embedded itself into Amber's shoulder and she fell to her knees, gasping in surprise.

The second her concentration was broken; I fell to the floor, released from my heavy bonds. Before giving her yet another chance to retaliate, I aimed another compact ball, this time at her ankle. The shot whizzed out of my hands as soon as the thought even processed.

Surprisingly I could shoot them at a much faster rate now. Then just like that I was shooting two, three, four ... all in a matter of seconds, straight at Amber's vulnerable body. I had given her no chance to move. She was forced to lie there uselessly, taking all my hits. She bit her lip, masking any discomfort that my tiny smoldering blasts of heat could possibly bring about. It probably hurt. But all I could think of was the objective to win ... and suddenly nothing could stand in my way.

Haven's cries soon broke me out of my trance and I turned sharply to see Haven and Zack pummelling each other with their fists. Haven used his odd ice blades as offensive weapons, but whenever they made contact with Zack's arm, instead of piercing it, the ice kept shattering.

Zack pulled his arms back to reveal an almost metallic sheen to his skin.

"Zack," I shouted horrified. "What is that on your arm?"

Zack glanced upwards for a moment. "It's armour made of the earth's minerals!" he hollered. "This isn't show and tell Alyssa, if you haven't noticed!"

Zack brought another armoured fist down on Haven's cheek, which sent the Aquarian crashing to the ground.

I surveyed the current situation. With Haven down for the count, Amber was proving to be as persistent as I thought she would be. She was stumbling back to her feet after taking the onslaught. I tried to meet Zack's eyes from across the room, but he wasn't looking at Haven or me. His entire concentration was focused on Amber.

Four long cylinders of mud sprouted from the ground around Amber. She screamed as the mud cylinders reached upwards, finally reaching the ceiling. She had no time to escape.

In an instant, dirt began to fill in the four sides, forming a rectangular dirt cage. Amber's cursing could be heard well after the walls were complete, trapping her inside. It wasn't a very big trap but it was effective. She pounded against the walls from inside and I winced for her as the steady material held. While I knew this was somehow cruel, it could give us the advantage we needed to win. Zack had disabled her ability to fly, and now, inevitably, it was two versus one.

"Alyssa go hit that button for me, will you?" Zack yelled, hunched over and trying to regain his strength. Haven was forcing himself up onto his knees but another hard punch to the side of his face sent him slamming back down into the mud.

There was no need to tell me twice. In seconds I was flying across the room getting very close to the button that lay behind the thick glass. Without even thinking about it, I raised my arms, calling on my power. It responded instantly and I focused on shattering the glass. I could feel my power pressing against something hard. I pushed just about as hard as I could and a giant crack snaked its way down the middle of the case, followed by the deafening sound of it shattering.

Millions of tiny glass shards flew through the air. Some of the tiny pieces flew towards me, scraping my skin as they passed, but

I hardly noticed. The red button sat bolted to the wall. Someone was screaming, so I wasted no more time, lunging forward and slamming my body against it. Immediately, a blaring siren rang, shrieking throughout the room and signalling the end to the fight.

It was over. I caught my breath—my pride absolutely immeasurable. I had won my first fight ever, and against some of the strongest people at Magnorium! Just not dying would've been great, but actually winning? I almost didn't believe it.

The next moments were a blur of commotion. Everyone was shouting. I hazily made my way back towards Zack, who had a triumphant look on his face.

Haven was on the ground gasping and Amber was beside him covered in watery mud. I looked around for the cage Zack had created, and was rewarded with the sight of a huge wet lump of earth. Zack too was soaked from head to toe and had streams of water running down his back.

"We won!" he shouted loudly, just in case anyone who was watching didn't already know. My grin was contagious and a giant smile eased its way onto Zack's face.

"I have to say that kicking their asses was kind of fun," Zack laughed. Haven and Amber both staggered to their feet and we all made our way to the exit. Despite his loss, Haven was smiling, running a hand through his muddied hair.

"Good fight." he said, holding his hand out to Zack. Zack took his hand, giving it a firm shake. Amber merely nodded, an approving look on her face.

"Nicely done," she said simply, and I knew that was as close to complimenting someone as Amber was ever going to get. I quickly surveyed the room and the remnants of the battle we had graciously left behind. Half of the floor had been reduced to a watery mess; the other half was split open, with uneven cracks running through it. In numerous spots on the walls, the sheer impact of our bodies had left actual dents in the metal.

I took a minute to catch my breath and gather my bearings regarding what exactly had just happened. The aftereffects of the adrenaline were quickly wearing off, replaced with the feeling of utter exhaustion. That came as no surprise.

It was a known fact that the more magic you performed the more it would take a toll on you. I wasn't the only one feeling it. Sure I was tired, but the three of them looked like they could barely stand. Zack looked by far the worst; after all, he had used the most magic. His body swayed back and forth, practically teetering against my weight. Before anyone had a chance to voice their concerns, the door to the room slid open and Elda wheeled herself in.

"Now *that*," she exclaimed excitedly, "is precisely what I want all fights to be like. Well done, all of you. It was a close fight, but the winners are Zack and Alyssa!" My peers' cheering could be heard well outside the metal room. Zack and I grinned at each other as we followed Elda outside into the classroom.

For once I held my head up high, too proud of myself to possibly be shot down. People were cheering. Others were counting stacks of bills. They had actually placed bets on us and the majority weren't in my favour. For a moment, this whole thing seemed comical—that I had actually cost them money.

Elda slowly wheeled herself to the front of the classroom. She still had that grin on her face. "Thank you for that entertaining fight. Tomorrow we'll be picking up right where we left off. You four are dismissed. Go clean up," Elda exclaimed with a wave of her hand.

I followed Amber out the door with Zack still leaning heavily against me. Once we were all out in the corridor, Amber gently looped an elbow under her brother's arm.

"Is he okay?" I asked, genuinely beginning to get worried.

"I'm fine," Zack muttered, trying to regain his own footing. Amber rolled her eyes, tightening the hold she had around his arm.

"It isn't healthy to use so much powerful magic in one go. It's dangerous even for someone like him," she explained. I nodded.

Magic, like all things, was to be used in moderation. Abusing it in fights wasn't particularly healthy for anyone.

"Well that was fun," Haven commented casually. "We should do it again sometime."

"Was burning yourself out worth it Zack?" Amber asked smugly.

"Please," he snorted dismissively, "hangovers are worse than this. And that look on your face Amber, when you lost?" he laughed, with a slight wheeze.

Amber rolled her eyes but couldn't quite mask the worry hidden there. "I'm going to help this idiot upstairs."

"I can get there myself!" Zack snapped, failing to shoot her down with a glare. Amber's scrutinizing look put his glare to shame and she shook her head stubbornly. "Shut up and walk."

He seemed to be walking fine by himself now, but she would have none of it, making sure he really was all right. Amber could be cold sometimes, but anyone could see the undeniable love she had for her brother.

Haven, who was creating a muddy puddle under his feet, reluctantly trailed after them to get cleaned up, which left me standing all alone in the hallway. Since I was also covered in mud and wanted to wash off, I headed toward the confinements of my own room.

I arrived moments later, winded just from the walk to the elevator. Suddenly a nap looked quite inviting and I didn't give it a second thought before peeling off my muddy school uniform and collapsing onto my huge bed, officially exhausted.

Rolling over, I felt something brittle brush up against my side.

It was a simple white manila envelope, with no address or any identification.

I didn't remember Amber mentioning anything about a letter, and besides it was on my bed so I thought it was acceptable to assume that the letter was mine. Someone sent me a letter?

I ran my nails over the flap curiously, gently prying it open. A smaller piece of paper slid out of the envelope into my awaiting hand; the entire thing was covered in eloquent handwriting, in black ink. I immediately spied my name written on the top left corner of the paper, drawing my eyes, which danced frantically over the words that followed.

Dear Alyssa Brooks;

Please do not be startled by this letter. From what I understand, you are sixteen years old. Your parents are Sienna and Eric Brooks. You are Draken. You only just learned about magic recently ...

My eyes ventured farther down the page, my heart thumping wildly in my chest. I couldn't fathom any reason why someone would take the time to write a letter like this in the first place, and even more unnerving was the fact that someone must have broken into this room just to ensure I received it.

I have a theory, an experiment if you will. I need you to be my test subject, and only you will be able to fill my curiosity. I fear your life has been built upon webs of lies, woven to keep you safe. If this is true, each day that passes increases the incredible danger you are in. Please come to the training room tomorrow at exactly midnight. I will deactivate any cameras and other surveillance. I am not your enemy or anyone you should fear. However, if you don't come voluntarily, I will have to resort to forcing you for your own good. Please do not be alarmed by this letter. Here are your instructions: Do not tell anyone about this message or you will regret it. Remain calm. Do not contact any authority figures. Come to the training room alone. I am eager to meet with you, Miss Brooks.

For a dizzying moment, the words formed pools on the insides of my eyelids, swimming in one giant inky puddle. The letter's intent did not fully dawn on me until after I had reread it about five times. I clutched the letter in my sweaty hands.

Surely, this was strange even by Magnorium standards. I didn't know whether to laugh it off as a sick joke, take it seriously, or simply shred the letter to pieces. I just had to think logically.

Sure, there were a few people in my life who disliked me, like Tori, Rachel, and Emma, but it was improbable that any of them would go to such extensive lengths just to make a fool out of me. What did this person want to know? Why was I, out of the hundreds of kids here, the only one who could do it? Nothing about this odd letter made any sense, and I found it rather creepy. I could only draw one conclusion, after a few minutes of fruitlessly trying to wrestle with the motive behind it.

Someone must be following me, or at least watching me closely enough to gather some of my information. But who would really be that interested in watching me of all people? Kurt? I conceded that Kurt could be a possibility. I mean, after all, Haven and I *did* break into his private space, but I was sure that as the principal of Magnorium, and a Society member, he had better things to do with his time.

Other than him I couldn't think of anyone who would have a reason to toy with me like this. What did this person intend to do? Were they serious about their threats, if I chose to be uncooperative?

There were so many things I didn't know, so many things I was unsure of. But nothing would satisfy me more than the truth. Prank or not, someone was on the other end of this message. I wanted to find out who. Most of the Elementals I had come across didn't really make jokes. I was afraid that this truly wasn't a prank.

So I would cooperate with this mystery person. I would meet them at midnight tomorrow, just like they had requested. I closed my eyes, and laid back down on the bed, gently tucking the letter under my pillow. I couldn't let Amber find it. It had already been such an exciting week, and I wondered why nothing ever stayed boring at Magnorium, even for a moment.

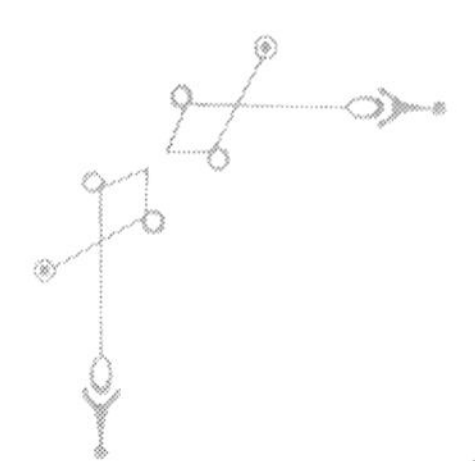
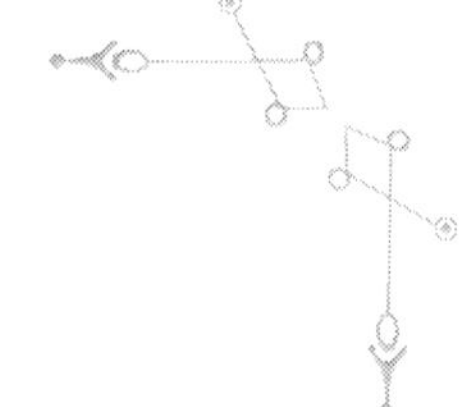

CHAPTER 11

VERACITY

It became apparent, the next day, how agonizingly slow time could pass. I had spent the majority of that night lying awake stuck in my own mind, conjuring possible scenarios of what was to come.

I glanced up to check the time during my very last class of the day, withering under the unforgiving hands of the clock. For the last hour, I had been counting down the minutes until the day was over.

"What's the matter with you?" Amber hissed, elbowing me in the side. "I mean you have this weird look on your face, and it's not even the weird look you have every day."

I shot her a look. I couldn't believe that it was today of all days that Amber decided to pay attention to me. If Amber noticed something was off, I really had to work on my discretion. Somehow this realization made me smile.

"Nothing," I said simply.

She knitted her eyebrows together before shrugging. At that precise moment, the bell rang, graciously relieving me from the tediousness of the school day. In seconds I was out of the class and halfway to my room, with Amber trailing behind me curiously. The evening passed as per usual, and unbeknownst to Amber, her very presence sent the clock ticking faster, and in no time it was practically time to go.

Since our mornings always seemed to start ridiculously early, Amber was out like a light long before midnight, which left me time to think and saved me from worrying about her prying. When it was almost midnight, I carefully got up from my bed and crept my way to the door. I stuffed the stupid letter deep into my pocket, and as silently as I could manage, opened the door, slipping out into the shadows of the hallway.

This person sure wasn't one for convenience, because this whole plan was certainly a pain in the ass to execute at night. Daylight hours would've been just fine with me, and the fact that I might set off an alarm or be caught on surveillance had me on my toes. Regardless of these possibilities, I continued onwards down the hallway, opting to take the stairs. It would be quieter without the noise of the mechanical elevator.

Thankfully I knew my way around the school by now and didn't need any sort of light to help locate the unmistakable training room. After all it was by far the biggest room in the whole school. I went in through the outer classroom, which had been left unlocked, and halted at the entrance, glancing up at the huge steel doors. I had only been in the training room the one time, but it was really nice, specially made to contain the effects of our magic.

I tried the door handle. The room was unlocked, just like the person in the letter had promised. I swung the heavy door open and tentatively ventured inside. The lights were on, and I only took a couple of steps forward before a distinct voice rang out from behind me.

"I must say, my dear, I am glad to see you."

"*Elda?*" I practically squeaked. Maybe I could've found humour in this situation if I was in the mood, but standing here in this empty training room in the middle of the night, was nothing short of infuriating. How could Elda be the person who wrote that letter? I had only left her class a few minutes before finding it. I looked expectantly towards her, waiting for an explanation, but she merely smiled.

"You came."

"Well, from your letter, it sounded like you *required* my presence, whether I wanted to come or not," I snapped.

"Forgive me for being unpleasant," Elda said softly, "but it was of dire consequence that I speak with you."

"Was a letter really necessary? I *am* in your class you know."

She nodded sheepishly. "I could not have spoken to you during class without risking being overheard or asked to speak to you after class without attracting unwanted attention."

"So, what about this experiment you wrote about? I thought you were a teacher."

"I am. A good one too."

I was still confused. "Are you some sort of scientist as well?"

"Hardly. But I have been around for a while, long enough to gather information and recognize an anomaly when I see one." She brought her calloused hands together.

I dug into my pocket, ripping out the crumpled letter. "I don't understand exactly what you want from me. In your letter you said you had a theory."

Elda drummed the edges of her worn fingernails against the side of her wheelchair, seemingly deep in thought. "All I want is to run a series of tests on you."

I gave a short laugh. "That doesn't sound too good."

"Nothing ludicrous, I assure you. Just a physical test, a mental test, and then a few tests of your Draken abilities. Please Alyssa, just humour me."

"What *is* this theory of yours?" I asked stubbornly, staring at her thin hands, and the skin that was practically clinging to her bones there. She looked far too frail.

Elda smiled, flashing her worn and broken teeth. "You wouldn't believe me if I told you dear."

"Please Elda, just humour me," I mimicked, not budging from where I stood.

"I'll explain later, I promise."

I recognized the look in Elda's small brown eyes; it was a look I had worn many times before. There was nothing stronger than the human desire to understand. Elda was no exception. I could clearly see that she wanted to know something very badly, and somehow I could help. I inwardly cursed my own curiosity, and averted my gaze.

"Fine." How bad could a couple of tests be? She was my teacher after all.

Elda smiled, beckoning me to follow her farther inside the huge training room. The room was now set up with some sort of metallic, and likely indestructible, material from floor to ceiling. There were mannequins set up around the room, and lots of machines—training equipment that I had never seen before. I frowned.

"Tell me more about these tests."

Elda shook her head, drawing her hand down to tap the large oak table beside her. It was a weapons table, but there was a huge basin of water sitting on it, filled to the brim.

"If you wanted me to go swimming," I said raising my eyebrows, "we should've met at the pool."

"Please no questions about that yet."

"All right," I answered, growing weary of the secrecy. "I have a better question then. Who are you really?"

She sighed, pursing her lips together. "You know the answer. My name is Elda and I teach your battle strategy class here at Magnorium. If you pass my tests, and I am actually correct in my theory, I will also be a genius."

I blinked. I hadn't expected the humorous conceit from someone so old.

"Now," she said, "could we kindly postpone the rest of your questions until later and proceed with the tests?"

I scowled, but nodded. Elda smiled her old woman smile again—almost humouring me, as though I were a small child. She pointed across the room, where a sleek treadmill sat.

I eyed the machine wearily, stretching my half-sleeping muscles.

"No thank you," I said, before she could even get a word out. If it was possible for someone like Elda to pout, she was doing so.

"Please?" she asked, with an impressive batting of her eyelashes. "It's necessary to draw conclusive results. The tests will run in order. First will be physical, second mental, and third magical. Then you are free to go, and you will get an automatic A in my class. Deal?"

"You drive a hard bargain," I said, moving to climb up onto the treadmill. I peered down at the black screen that was mounted in the centre.

"I guess I'm going for a run then?" She wordlessly held up a tiny black remote control, pressing one of the buttons. The treadmill lurched forward all at once, skipping any sort of gradual speed. It shocked me into moving and I grabbed onto the handlebars, practically losing my footing.

"I will be controlling your speed, time, and elevation. Keep moving until I say otherwise."

I didn't have time to shoot her a glare, because it was moving too fast. I always considered myself pretty fit physically, but this was a speed I wasn't used to.

"You see Alyssa," Elda continued, feeding the small remote back and forth through the gaps of her fingers, "a person's magical skill is often directly linked to physical and mental strength. And at the current moment, you are the most powerful person here. So I am curious to see how far I can stretch your strength."

"Well I'm flattered to contribute," I said, pounding my already-aching feet against the treadmill. When I had decided to sneak out here, I wasn't expecting a jog. "Did you run this test on Amber and Zack too?"

"Oh no. I cannot deny that the Travies are powerful, but a lot of their power was developed through years and years of extensive training. Let me put this in perspective for you dear. You have done in weeks what the Travie family did in years. This is why I am so fascinated."

I almost went flying off the end of the treadmill staring at Elda. "I don't find myself overly fascinating."

"Oh but if I'm right ... you will." She drew her lips together. "Keep running."

I reluctantly obliged, concentrating on balancing my speed and my heart rate. After a while, I got used to the speed and I ran for a good hour before Elda clicked another button, drawing the machine to a close.

I hopped off the machine, hardly even winded. This, in itself, surprised me. Either I was more fit than I originally deduced or I was just running well on the adrenaline of sleep deprivation.

"Sit." Elda commanded, wheeling herself back over to the table and patting a battered and worn metal chair. I slid into the seat and Elda moved her wheelchair directly across from me. For a moment, the room was quiet and we looked at each other.

"Alyssa, that machine was on the highest possible level for Elemental training and you're not even winded."

I shrugged dismissively. "I'm a good runner. That doesn't really prove anything, other than the fact that you called me all the way down here in the middle of the night for a damn run."

She rolled her eyes at me. "I don't think you quite understand. Elementals by nature are strong, but to endure such strenuous labour is something many couldn't do. However, you are right, that doesn't really prove my suspicions, so can I ask you a few questions?"

"I don't really feel like an interrogation."

"Clear your mind," Elda chirped, ignoring my reluctance. "When I mention fears, what are the first ones that come to mind?"

I paused and then frowned at a sudden revelation. "I'm not really scared of anything."

"There must be something." Elda gently argued.

I rubbed my chin thoughtfully. I had no recollection of petty fears like spiders or even the normal Elemental fear of their opposite elements.

"Being useless." I heard myself suddenly say. "Never doing anything to impact anyone or anything. Just existing." Which was exactly what I've been doing my whole life. I *have* been pretty useless. No wonder my feelings of self-loathing have always existed beneath a thinly veiled surface.

Elda cocked a single eyebrow, almost as if she was surprised, but didn't comment. "You love your parents, correct?

"Yeah, of course."

"What about your friends?" I blushed suddenly, analyzing the metal molding on the walls. "I don't have many friends."

"Of course you do. You have made friends in the most unlikely place, Alyssa: right here at Magnorium." She sounded so genuine that it just might've been the most comforting thing I had heard all day. "Would you ever die for someone?"

"Yes," I answered. "I'm not afraid to die, if that's what you mean."

"Really? Not at all?"

"No," I said truthfully. "Death is inevitable, and people tell me that as a supernatural it can happen sooner rather than later. But I don't fear death as long as I don't die in vain. Why is any of this relevant?"

Elda shrugged, not looking very apologetic. "I need to understand the way your mind works, Alyssa. What brings you the most happiness?"

"Being in my room instead of here at one in the morning."

Elda glared. I cleared my throat, meeting her curious brown eyes, seriously. "That's a simple question with a complicated answer."

"Does that mean you don't know?"

I almost didn't know. I hadn't had the best experiences with people, so they certainly didn't bring me any joy, but when I thought about it, the select few people who I cared about in my life did.

"No," I assured her. "Happiness is like a contagious energy. And if the people you care about aren't happy, how can you be? Oh, and magic. There's just nothing like it; it's amazing."

"There isn't a particular place or thing that brings you joy? Money? Your home?"

I shook my head. "No. There's a difference between appreciating the things around you and being happy with yourself, don't you think?"

Elda nodded. "Indeed there is. All right, last one. What is your biggest fault?"

"Um ..." I was growing increasingly uncomfortable with the personal questions. The more she probed, the more exposed I felt. And she was no less than a stranger. But my discomfort couldn't answer the question Elda just asked. When I truly reflected, what *was* my biggest fault? I mean I certainly had plenty, but as to which one was the absolute worst, I had no idea.

"I'm impulsive," I said suddenly. "It's like I don't even think sometimes. I just act no matter the consequences. Oh and I suck at talking to people. Like I really suck at it."

Elda emitted a small laugh, resting a hand against the curve of my knee. "I definitely see that in you. But being impulsive can also make you stronger. You're quick to react. It's why you did so well in the battle yesterday."

I shrugged, trying to keep a smug look off my face.

Elda sighed, her chest rattling with even the smallest intakes of breath. For someone so small and damaged, she was fierce. "One more thing, Alyssa. I have seen many displays of your Draken abilities, but I'd like to have the honour of witnessing it up close."

I stood up abruptly from the chair. I wasn't in the mood to take my magic for a spin. "Listen Elda, I just ran a marathon for you, and then sat through an interview. I think that's enough—"

"No," Elda interrupted, a cutting edge to her tone. "Just this one last thing."

She wagged a bony finger, motioning me over to the centre of the room. I sighed, got up from my chair, headed to where she was pointing me, and heard the wheels of her wheelchair rolling on the floor behind me.

When she caught up, she stopped beside me and pointed down the room. "You see that target?"

I looked where she was pointing and saw a mannequin positioned at the far end of the room. The room was so large, the mannequin was almost hard to see.

"Meant specifically for Draken training," she supplied, before I could form a question. "I want you to hit it. From here." Then she laughed, a hysterical sound that filled the room and bounced off the walls.

I frowned, looking over at Elda's wild mass of white hair, which practically stood up on its end. From this angle, she really did look mad, confirming what most of the student body already thought. I wasn't sure if I entirely agreed, but I could definitely see where someone would get the idea.

"You mean scorch it?" I said, awkwardly shifting on my feet. "Something is morally wrong about this. Why would Magnorium encourage Drakens to burn a human-looking mannequin? It's rather creepy to practise murdering people, don't you think?"

"I think," Elda said, squinting, "that I have found another one of your faults. Avoiding things."

"A genius deduction," I said, dryly.

"Am I sensing sarcasm?"

"Quite possibly," I muttered. "You're not too bad at it yourself."

She wheeled her chair forward and paused, bringing a hand to rest in the small of my back. I jumped at the contact and more specifically at how affectionate it felt.

"I quite like you, dear."

"Thanks. Not many people do."

"Well that's just absurd then, isn't it? Do you know what would make me like you even more? If you would hit that target over there."

I drew in an annoyed breath, and then took a few steps away from her, adopting an attack stance to properly encourage my magic to flow. I peered across the room at the mannequin. I had never shot my fire that far. I doubted my aim would be accurate, but at least if I tried, it would shut Elda up.

I guided the wisps of my magic that lay dormant and it responded with a buzz. My magic was always there, thrumming beneath the surface, but it was also always explosive and hard to handle. Yesterday during the battle, I had shot fire at Amber and Haven. This was the same thing, just at a farther range. I had been successful in the battle because I was impulsively reacting to the situation. Could I do it deliberately?

I shifted my weight and swung my body forward, shooting flame from my fingertips. A long vertical blast of the hottest flame I had ever conjured burst from my hands, spiralling directly towards my intended target. The flame smashed into the centre of the mannequin's body with a hiss, and in moments the fire spread across its surface. Oddly enough, after the target was set ablaze, and I released my magic, the flames flickered pathetically and then dissipated. There wasn't even any smoke, or burn marks on the material. I guess it *was* designed for Draken training. More importantly though, I realized that I wasn't as big of a failure or fluke as I had first thought. As long as I did magic my way, it worked!

Elda grinned manically. She wheeled herself back over to me faster than I would have thought possible, and took hold of my hand, grasping it tightly.

"My heavens," she breathed, trailing her gaze up and down my body. "I was right."

"What?" I finally thought to whisper.

Elda merely smiled again, squeezing our hands together even tighter. The intimate movement was startling and I looked down at her questioningly.

"Come sit down, I'm going to tell you a story."

"I thought you said I was done after that," I practically whined, the first signs of exhaustion creeping its way into my voice. I had enough of this.

Elda shook her head, suppressing what appeared to be a laugh.

"Oh no my dear, we're just getting started."

I glared daggers across the table at Elda, as she shifted in her wheelchair getting comfortable for what promised to be a long conversation. I couldn't believe the nerve of this woman. "Alyssa, have you ever heard of the Orb?"

I frowned. The Orb? I remembered the passionate look in Professor Tate's eyes when he talked about the elusive artifact that was lost to the world.

"Yes," I said. "I know about the Orb. The subject of many Elemental treasure hunter's fantasies. It's the most powerful weapon on the planet, created by Orchins, but it's lost to the world forever."

"Yes," Elda said faintly, wringing her hands together. "Magnorium has taught you well. All over the world, supernaturals have been on a mad hunt for centuries to create the Orb. No weapon to date has ever compared to the Orb's power. Its user can literally do anything."

"Wow." I had already heard a bit of the same speech from Professor Tate, but it was interesting to see how the topic really seemed to captivate people. No one could resist the fascination.

"Orchins," Elda said with a glint in her eyes, "were a group of the finest people around. They lived only among themselves, recognizing the corruption of the supernatural world. They combined their knowledge and power to create the Orb ... before they were all murdered. With the demise of the Orchins came many complications with the weapon they left behind."

"I heard about that," I said, bringing the heels of my feet up onto the seat of my chair, and drawing my knees up to my chin. "The Orb is split into four crystals, each hidden around the world. And only once they're brought together will the crystals actually create the Orb."

"Yes," Elda whispered, looking at me fondly.

"That kind of sucks."

Elda nodded. "It rather does. The Orchins certainly didn't intend to make this quest an easy one. The Orb is *only* retrievable by an Orchin. Any other being will instantly perish if they try to remove the crystals from their resting places."

"And we need the crystals," I said, suddenly realizing it. "We need the Orb to defeat the Society ... because nothing else can stop them."

"Correct," she continued. "As you can imagine, the tension in the supernatural world is higher than it's ever been. The Elemental community has run themselves ragged trying to create other weapons to compare to the Orb's power, but have failed. They have tried countless experiments, and eventually began an extensive search for an Orchin."

"If they're extinct," I mused. "Then it's not possible for another to be born, so ..." I shook my head, baffled by what I was hearing, "shouldn't they stop looking?"

Elda shrugged, eyes darkening. "The Council's solution to the Orbs' complication was to create the Ritual. It's a test that every newborn Elemental is given to determine its element group. As you've probably seen by now, each of the five Elemental groups has a distinct and universal symbol."

"During the Ritual, the child is presented with these symbols. After a process of elimination, one element is left standing. Implemented in the fifties, every Elemental child has undergone this test; it's policy. And yes, before you even ask, you were given the test too. However, there has been speculation about the Ritual for decades. It's run by Council officials, and in the past, the Council has experienced internal issues from the Society." Elda grimaced. "The Ritual documents the number of children born to each element, and of course, as you can probably guess, they were unsuccessful in finding an Orchin. None exist."

"That's unfortunate," I said quietly. "But maybe that's what's meant to be, you know? With power often comes destruction. The Orb sounds too powerful for anyone to handle alone. Maybe it's fate that the Orchins are gone forever."

"I used to think that," Elda whispered softly. "But that clearly isn't the case. The universe must have a sense of humour, because here you are, the first Orchin in centuries sitting right in front of me, in the flesh."

I stared at her, waiting for the seriousness to drop from her expression. It didn't.

"*What*?" I exclaimed, laughing. "Did I just hear that right? You think I'm an Orchin? Oh wouldn't that be grand." I shook my head, regretfully. "Sorry to disappoint you, but I was born a Draken."

"I beg to differ," she said firmly. "I am willing to bet something interesting happened at your Ritual, because you are *not* a Draken. Orchins by nature possessed power that was incomparable to the rest of the elements. Tell me Alyssa, what do you know about their extinction?"

"Scary," I whispered, not sure if I was referring to the extinction of the Orchins or Elda's preposterous claim. I frowned, gathering any lingering snippets of information about the Orchins I could find floating around in my head.

She nodded. "It was a unjustifiable bloody slaughter by our Elemental ancestors. Orchins had always threatened the well being of the other Elementals, just by their existence, and when they recognized the threat they posed, every living Orchin was hunted down and slaughtered by their own kind in just under a month. You are the first Orchin to come along in hundreds of years. Why this is the case, I haven't the slightest idea. But the ritual does *not* falsely lead."

"Oh really," I snapped, surprised by the amount of venom in my voice. I had enough of people seeing things in me that weren't there. "Were you at my ritual then, since you're so convinced?"

Elda blinked. "No, but someone was. And I'm guessing your parents either kept them quiet or ... I'm sorry Alyssa ... but maybe even killed them to keep you safe."

"I ... I think my parents would have told me a little detail like that."

Elda shook her head. "Our world would not take such news well. You would be an imminent threat to the Society, and most likely either be locked up, killed, or worse: used to get the crystals for them." Her words seemed to echo off the walls and bounce back to slap me in the face, again and again until what she was claiming actually started to set in.

I took a deep breath and let it out, trying to diminish the dismissive and disrespectful tone that I feared would be apparent in my voice. "Is that so? Locked up, killed, or used. In that specific order?"

"I'm sure the Society could find a way to spice things up for you."

I rolled my eyes. "Elda, I didn't think you were crazy before; please don't give me a reason to. Orchins are extinct. I'm sorry, but no matter how much you people want one, I can't be made into something that doesn't *exist*!"

"That's enough!" Elda snapped. "I've been watching you ever since you first arrived at Magnorium. Let me explain the evidence Alyssa. Even before you got here, you exhibited an astounding amount of power, taking so little time beating the Magnorium test.

You've barely been here a month and have already surpassed Amber Travie, and done it dramatically with your little stunt with the *Magnus Lumen* spell. And yet, you've barely received any training in Draken magic ... so the skill does not match up at all. Also, you seem to be fearless with the other elements, unlike *all* of the other Elementals."

"That proves nothing," I breathed indignantly.

"No!" Elda snapped. There was something firm in her expression, something that told me that arguing with her would get me nowhere. Elda adamantly believed I was an Orchin.

"There's more. Even the way you *think* matches the profile. Each Elemental group has their own characteristics and tendencies. Terrans are usually free spirited and calm. Drakens are generally hotheaded, determined, and somewhat selfish. Skyros are impulsive, agile, and strong. Aqurian are usually intelligent, loyal, and kind, and tend to be more logical. You see, all four have a certain way of thinking and responding to situations. All are very different from the others. Yet you exhibit traits from all four. Of course, these traits vary depending on the individual, but no one has ever quite displayed such a wide range. You said it yourself. You're impulsive and always determined to do better. How else could you have done so well in the battle yesterday? I was watching your every move during that fight, Alyssa, and ever since you arrived here! Another Draken would *never* have jumped in front of a Power Arrow to save someone else!"

"Elda look," I said, holding up my hand to stop her, "I appreciate this elaborate and well-thought-out deduction, but an odd personality doesn't make someone a Orchin."

"That's true, but it definitely does help recognize one. Please just listen to me. You're fully capable of manipulating the other elements, and I'll show you proof!"

"How can you be so sure?" I demanded, smacking a hand down against my knee.

"I've never seen *anyone* like you before!" Elda's insisted. "Just trust me!"

"How can I?" I shot back. "I barely know you! Why should I listen to *anything* you say?"

She leaned forward, looking me in the eye, her expression fierce. "In this world Alyssa, there is either dead, going to be killed, or alive. *You* are alive. You are also a living Orchin, and *if* you are not careful, you *are* going to be killed. Now pick up that basin over there and let me help you!" Her tone had escalated with each sentence. There was something dangerously commanding about her voice. Operating on a will that I wasn't entirely sure was my own, I picked up the basin lying on the table in front of me, grasping the edges with my fingertips.

Elda nodded encouragingly, leaning back in her creaking chair. "Good girl." I only sneered in response.

"Aquarian magic is the easiest of the four to execute. Now, all I want you to try to do is freeze the water in that basin."

"This isn't going to work," I snapped.

Elda shrugged, undeterred by my increasing annoyance. "Then you will lose nothing and neither will I. Magic to you should be effortless. It's all about the visualization." She spoke wisely, and even I couldn't ignore the fact that she had years and years of collected experience and knowledge.

"Listen Elda," I said, trying desperately to get her to hear me, "I don't know why everyone keeps saying I'm something special. I'm *not*. Magic to me isn't effortless! It takes hard work and concentration."

Elda shook her head, her shaggy white bangs settling down over her eyes. "Stop doubting yourself, my dear girl. Even though you're used to Draken magic, the same steps apply for Aquarian magic."

Was this woman really being honest with me? And if so, was she just someone to dismiss as delusional? Either way, I supposed, if I proved that I was not an Orchin, it would shut her up and put an end to this ludicrous theorizing.

Still, I knew that there was insight to be found in her teachings, and so I tightened my grip around the basin. For a moment

I thought of Haven, and how talented he was at Aquarian magic. How did he go about freezing water? Did it feel as natural to him as Draken magic did to me? Haven's magic was extremely distinct. It flowed gracefully, like water. Remnants of our fight flashed through my mind ... the way he had toyed with the molecules, drawing them together, moving them about to condense, to harden, to solidify ... If that was all he had to do, then the whole process seemed almost easy.

The sides of the basin suddenly cooled to the touch and as I tightened my grip, I looked down, drawing in a gasp. In my hand, I held a frozen chunk of solid ice.

I yelped, releasing it and watching it crash to the floor, where it shattered into a million tiny ice shards. I gaped at the frozen pieces on the floor, created out of my own will. Was this actually happening?

I struggled to lift my gaze from the floor to meet Elda's proud, smiling face. I couldn't move, paralysed by my effort to understand. I didn't think I *could* understand. Question after question were itching to be answered, and I gulped, forcing them all down and trying to be calm.

"I don't understand!" I finally managed to choke out, after a few moments of shocked silence. Elda simply smiled, empathy flashing through her narrowed eyes.

"You were *right?*"

"Have a little faith in me, Alyssa. I don't make mistakes."

"But—"

Elda held up a hand, cutting me off. "You are an Orchin. I would be lying to you, if I said I understood why this is the case, or how. All I can say for certain is that you are special, and were given this power for a reason."

"What's the reason? I-I don't get it!" I felt a pulsing hysteria latching onto the forefront of my nerves. This didn't make any sense! How could I have lived my entire life without me, or anyone else for that matter, noticing this? Was this even possible? That *I* could be such a rare anomaly—a creature the whole supernatural world was after?

I took a shuddering breath, drawing my hands to my sides to stop them from trembling. "My parents told me I was a Draken. Why? If they know the truth, who else knows?"

The more I thought about this *truth*, the more I made connections to little things I had dismissed as insignificant: my fascination with all the elements; my power that, once probed, had come so easily, yet so undeniably strong.

Elda's hand shot out and grabbed my wrist, drawing me close. "You should get in contact with your parents as soon as possible. My guess is that they thought it would be best if you remained ignorant of your true nature. Disguising you as another element probably seemed like the best option. However, I assume that, if your parents were smart, no one else knows. That being said, it's imperative that this knowledge remains a secret. You and I cannot tell *anyone*. You are in incredible danger here. If *I* noticed the incongruities and understood what they might mean, I cannot say who else might have done the same."

I felt the little colour that was left in my face slowly drain away. I wondered if Elda knew about Kurt, and how present the Society was here.

"Do you know about, um ..." I took a deep breath, desperately hoping I could trust her. "Do you know about how Magnorium and the Society are connected? About Kurt Bell?"

Elda flinched immediately, looking away. "I have my suspicions but much is uncertain." She sighed heavily, eyeing me almost with pity.

"The Society is especially prominent here," I said. "I think maybe it always has been." She narrowed her eyes as I continued. "I have reason to believe that Magnorium is one of their main bases, and that Kurt is not just a member, but their actual leader."

Her eyes widened. "How do you know that?"

My heart hammered in my chest. "Haven Reeves is a stubborn, persistent person who likes to prove that he's right and everyone else is wrong. He suspected something was off, so we investigated, and found out that he was *too* right."

Elda looked grim. "It would do you both best to keep that to yourselves."

I gulped.

"Magnorium is a highly regarded institute," she said. "Putting himself in charge of this establishment allows him to keep watch on our most powerful students, and our Council. I fear the Society built this school in the first place. It's not safe here Alyssa; you must be careful." She closed her eyes for a second and then looked at me again, studying my face as if she were afraid I would disappear.

"My deepest fear is that your secret will be leaked. The Society's goal has always been the extermination of mortals and control of the rest of the world. They grow closer to that goal with each passing day. They've already killed countless mortals, but they've been looking for a stronger weapon for a long time. If they find out you exist they will use you and throw you away when they're finished with you."

Elda was right. And suddenly I was struck with a wave of anger, delivered like a slap in the face. I saw red. "But I never asked for any of this! My life before was just fine! That isn't *fair!*"

"Fair?" Elda thundered, glowering from across the table. "You're right; it's not fair. It's not fair that a completely psychotic bunch of Elementals are murdering innocent people! It's not fair that the only weapon to stop them is almost impossible to get. It's not fair that I am sitting here in this wheelchair unable to *do* anything about it! And what's *really* not fair is that the only Orchin alive is some bloody *sixteen-year-old girl!"*

"Well what do you want me to do?" I yelled back, clenching my jaw. "If you're so smart, tell me what can I do to fix this?"

Elda recomposed herself, swallowing hard. "Go find the crystals. Make the Orb. Destroy the Society."

I inhaled sharply. "Fine."

She laughed dryly. "You don't know what you agreeing to, my dear. It's not that easy. The four crystals are hidden in remote locations pertaining to the element each one represents. Mysterious unforgiving creatures—creatures that exist beyond my own knowledge—are drawn to them. The crystals are a beacon of magic, it brings things close ... just like Magnorium drew you here."

"This just keeps getting better," I mumbled sarcastically.

"Once taken from their resting places, anyone can handle the crystals. But obtaining them in the first place is impossible to do without the existence of an Orchin. But now we have you."

She placed a hand on my shoulder and I cringed. The ground washed away beneath me. Was this why I was given such power? To go and get the crystals? I wasn't a firm believer in fate, but if the supernatural existed, I'd be crazy to assume that fate didn't.

"So you need me to go and get the crystals, make the Orb, and ultimately destroy the Society," I said flatly. "You see Elda, the problem with that is, if mortal security rests in my hands, everyone is utterly screwed."

"I don't think that's true. Many have tried and failed on this quest. But you won't Alyssa, not if you try. I have full faith in that. Innocent people are dying. The Society is close to winning."

Dizzy, I jumped to my feet, dread slithering it's way up my spine. "Will I die?"

Elda gave a tight smile. "Would you like me to answer that question honestly?"

"I guess not," I muttered.

"Alyssa," Elda said gently, "sometimes a strong will overpowers sheer physical strength. Luckily for you, you have both. I know you can do this if you try."

"I can't travel the world all alone," I said quietly.

"No, of course not. I have already put a lot of thought to this. Other than you, Haven Reeves and Amber and Zack Travie are the most powerful Elementals I have ever encountered in my lifetime. Working together, you four can accomplish this quest that so many deem impossible. Unfortunately, it will require their cooperation. I would like to arrange another meeting—this time with the four of you—but that will require a bit of explaining on your part. Ultimately though, I need your consent. Will you help me Alyssa?"

"Who are you really, Elda?" I asked softly, avoiding her question and watching as a sea of emotions spilled into her eyes.

"For a while now, I have been employed by the Council to try to stop the Society. They positioned me at Magnorium to keep watch and report any sightings. All my sources and information come directly from them. I am dedicated to stopping the Society, but I just *need* you."

Her once small eyes now looked huge and were lit with passion, eyeing me so hopefully it made me ache. Maybe this was what I was meant to do, and why I was given this power in the first place: to avenge all the people the Society have killed, and to stop them before they could kill any more. If I had so much power, would it be a waste unless I used it for good? The reality was that I could die on this strange quest. But was I afraid to die? No. I'd rather die meaningfully than live a meaningless life. But how could I possibly ask my friends, people I really only just met, to do this?

"I'll do it," I said firmly. I sounded sure, even to my own ears, and then I realized that I actually was.

"You will?" Elda asked, suspiciously.

I nodded. "People will die if I don't. And it seems like I'm the only one who *can*."

Elda smiled, a sheen of tears collecting at the corners of her eyes. "Thank you," she whispered gratefully, reaching for my hand again and squeezing it. "Thank God for you."

"I won't speak for the others. I'm willing to die for this cause, but they might disagree."

Elda sighed. There was empathy woven into the deep wrinkles of her gaunt face as she looked at me. "I understand. I wish we lived in a world without darkness, without greed and power."

"That doesn't sound like a world at all," I said. "Power and greed go hand in hand. Maybe the trick is not letting power fall into the wrong hands. But there's always going to be a need for power, and people who climb to the top no matter who they have to push down in the process. People are selfish. And that's the real problem." The words had all spilled out of my mouth and I was powerless to stop them. Elda chuckled, rubbing her fingers along the metal armrest of her wheelchair. "Sometimes I forget how young you are ... how little you've seen of our world."

"Everyone keeps reminding me of that," I muttered, glancing down.

Elda sighed. "Ignorance, my dear, is not a sin. But when people *choose* to be ignorant to the suffering around them, that's where the line should be firmly drawn. For many, ignorance is survival; it's self-preservation, especially in our world. But not you. You're choosing to help. I *am* sorry though, this shouldn't be your burden to carry."

"Maybe it should be. If I don't help, no one will. Elda ..." I was at a loss for words. How could my life change so drastically in just a few weeks? I went from being a boring mortal to a powerful Draken, to an Orchin! I mean, what would come next?

"I don't know what I'm going to do next. How can I hide this?"

"For now, just get in touch with your parents. They owe you some answers."

"Like hell they do," I muttered under my breath. Answers weren't enough. I deserved nothing less than an *explanation*. They had blatantly lied to me. Again. They had known all along and never bothered to tell me, even though coming to Magnorium was potentially dangerous. I felt betrayed.

"Next, you do not breathe a word of this to anyone, with the possible exception of your three friends, *if* you feel that you can trust them. Then, on the surface, you carry on like nothing happened. Try to practise the four elements, in absolute secrecy, of course. Experience will be rewarding on the job."

I snorted. "It's not that easy."

"Alyssa, you're an Orchin. Everything's easy for you." I didn't think that was very fair. Just a week ago, I was failing all my average classes.

"I think that's enough for one night."

I only had the strength to nod. Mentally I was exhausted and needed time for all this information to fully sink in. I rose to my feet, almost stumbling as I got up, and walked away.

"Oh Alyssa?" Elda called, her voice echoing through the huge room. "Be careful please."

I turned around, nodding. "I will."

I reached the huge steel doors, and took one last look at Elda. I was still stuck in a daze as I exited the training room, in shock and worried—worried about Magnorium, about the Society, and even worried a bit for myself.

I made it about twenty feet down the hall before a hand clamped onto my wrist, forcing me backwards into the shadows. The first thing I thought was *Kurt*. The second was that it was the guards who made their rounds at night.

I opened my mouth to scream but the person's other hand snaked upwards to cover my mouth. A pair of stormy grey-blue eyes shone against the darkness, and that was when it registered: *Amber*. My heart, which had felt like it had gone into cardiac arrest, slowly but surely slowed to only a frantic beating.

I shook the hand away. "What do you think you're doing?" I hissed, shocked. "How long have you been standing here?"

Amber had backed my body up against the wall, looking absolutely astonished as she released me from her grip. "You looked off all day, so when I heard you leave, how could I not follow you?" She rushed over her words almost apologetically, then ran a hand nervously through her hair.

"You should probably know that Skyros have advanced hearing. Especially me."

I closed my eyes, sighing. Elda had said to be cautious of this secret, and here I was, ten seconds later and it was already too late. But didn't Elda think that I would eventually have to tell Amber anyway? At least Amber had made the explanation easier this way.

She looked at me and I smiled tightly, though my heart felt like it might jump out of my chest. There was so much that I wanted to say that the words hung in the air between us. But the hallway, in the dead of night, was no place to have a conversation like this, so I motioned for her to follow and began the trek back to our room.

It took us little time to get back. When we arrived, I shut the door and collapsed onto the comfort of my bed. Amber was uncharacteristically silent and merely took a seat beside me, her lips pursed. We both sat quietly, not really knowing where to start. I didn't know if I even wanted to start, because that meant I'd have to face it for a second time.

"Sorry, I followed you," she said, suddenly refusing to meet my eyes, "but I wasn't really expecting that."

"It's okay. Neither was I."

"So," she said slowly, staring at me, "you're an Orchin."

"It would appear that way," I said flatly. "But then again, maybe this isn't real."

"You really froze the water?" When I nodded, she smiled a terrible half smile. "The first Orchin in centuries! And you really never had any clue?"

It was my turn to give a dry, condescending laugh, shaking my head. "Did it look like I had any clue?"

Amber paused, but she looked more excited than grave. "Alyssa, you have more power than you'll ever know what to do with! Imagine the two of us together! I bet we alone could get the crystals!"

"You would risk your life like that?" I asked quietly, awarding her with a curious gaze.

She reciprocated the look, similar to the one she had given me on the day she started the riot. "Of course! You heard Elda! *Someone* has to fight the Society and I want to be the one to do it." Her voice deepened with passion and she suddenly went very still. "No one ever told you the story of how my family died, did they?"

"I never *knew* your family died," I whispered, completely shocked. There was something in her tone, and in her eyes, that made me stop. I moved closer to her, taking a seat on the very edge of the bed, tangling my fingers in the folds of the fabric.

Amber dropped her hands into her lap, fiddling with them. "Zack and I have been at Magnorium much longer than anyone else. I wasn't quite eleven when we came; Zack was twelve. It's true that we've received more training than anyone else, but that isn't why we're so powerful." Her voice ran cold, curdled with what seemed to be a rush of painful memories, as a nostalgic look crossed over her angular face.

"We lived in New York with our parents and they would teach us magic. Ever since I could walk they taught us magic. The Travie bloodline has always been powerful, and they tend to marry other powerful Elementals, so we just seem to grow even better with each new generation, or more powerful at least." She took a shuddering breath, which made me brace for the inevitable; her story clearly didn't end well.

"My parents were two of the most powerful Elementals of their time. It didn't really surprise me that the Council recruited them, needing them for their power. I was even proud that my parents were so important. It only took two years for them to gain status and eventually they were at the head, running the entire group. Nothing changed as they got promoted; they still saw us every morning and every night and found the time to train us." Suddenly, her dark, grey-blue eyes darkened even further until they looked like a storm cloud threatening to wreck havoc.

"Then one day they had to travel abroad, to Tokyo, for this special Council meeting. Apparently it was something important that required both of their attendance, but to this day I don't even know what it was." She laughed humorlessly.

"Maybe it was a setup. That day, the Society killed over two thousand innocent mortals and also targeted the Council. There were no survivors. A few days later, a strange man named Mondo came to our house and told us that our parents had been killed by the Society. Zack didn't want to go to the funeral, but I dragged him. We owed them that, you know? I wanted to say goodbye. It was open-casket." As she caught her breath I sat completely still, afraid to say something that would make her feel even worse.

"It was death by gunfire," she finally choked out, with a horrified look on her ashen face. "They were Elementals and were killed by a gun! I always wondered how they could be killed by something so mortal, and only when I learned more did I realize that magic *had* killed them—powerful magic that bound their hands so they couldn't fight back. Yet they looked so peaceful, so content for the dead ... there were matching wounds on their chests." Amber's whole body was trembling.

"Mondo said that when their bodies were found, they were together." Her breath caught. "I'll never forget it." Pain bled from her expression.

A sob caught in my throat, but I forced it back down. I felt her anguish; the pain of losing two parents was enough to drive anyone to the brink of insanity. But she wasn't. Amber was strong—stronger than I, or anyone else, ever gave her credit for.

"Early the next morning" she continued, "we left for Magnorium. Mondo said that we were too young, but it was going to be our home. We had no other family, and so I said goodbye to no one, and took nothing with me." Amber shuddered and then suddenly well-deserved tears were streaming over her sharp cheekbones and dripping off her chin.

I was horrified—horrified that the strongest person I knew was reduced to tears because of the Society, who didn't deserve her sorrow. I remembered how cold and distant Amber used to seem to me. Sitting there, watching her cry, I could finally see her real strength, unmasked by power. Maybe the mere act of crying revealed a person, because everyone handled pain differently. I remembered Haven and the sorrow of his loss. He didn't hide his emotions but used them to fuel his anger and make him stronger. Amber cried as if her pain was a flood, normally protected by a carefully crafted dam. Barriers never held forever though, and eventually they burst.

"I'm going to kill them all!" Amber suddenly snapped, as if only willing to allow herself two moments of self-pity. Her tears stopped as quickly as they had started. I rested a hand atop one of her clenched fists, not speaking, just offering silent reassurance that I knew could never put her broken world back together. Pain was an eloquent tragedy; it spiralled out of control and ignited the fiercest types of passion.

"I'm sorry Amber," I whispered, sincerely. "I didn't know." After a long moment, I squeezed her hand, and tried to think of something I could say to her. "You know what I said to Haven once? I told him that I don't like saying sorry to people who have lost loved ones, because I'll never know what it was like to lose them." I spoke softly. It was clear that Amber never talked about this, and so I wanted to tread carefully.

"Close your eyes, okay?" I almost smiled as Amber complied. "Now think about your favourite memory of your parents and Zack." I looked at her for a moment, watching as her eyebrows furrowed, deep in thought.

"Do you have one?"

She nodded.

"Good." I said soothingly, as if I were talking to a small child. "Would you tell me about it?"

Her eyes flashed open and she looked at me curiously, but didn't speak.

"People don't usually listen to you, do they?" I asked suddenly. "They see your power, but don't know what you've done to get there. Well, I *am* listening Amber. I promise."

"Okay," Amber began shyly. "Well ... with powerful Elemental parents, we never really got to do normal mortal things; we never got to develop any hobbies or do fun things. Our life was always about training. But I remember once, just once, it was a really nice summer day and my mother didn't want to train us. She convinced my father to take us all to the park and we spent the whole day there. We all sat in the sand and then they pushed us on the swings." She smiled. "It was the most normal thing I ever did with my parents. It was the most fun too. We felt like a family, an Elemental *and* human family. It was so nice." Now she was grinning, and I didn't think I ever remembered a time when Amber looked as beautiful as she did right then. "I miss doing fun things like that."

"You'll do them again," I said suddenly, turning so we faced each other. "With me. I'm as close to mortal as they get, and we'll do normal things together for sure. Life spent completely as a warrior isn't a life at all. And you deserve more than that—you both do. If we can ever get to be friends, I'll make sure you get all the things you deserve."

"We *are* friends," Amber said quickly, her eyes widening as if I was silly for doubting it.

"Are we?" I said gently. "You tolerate me and that's okay. But just because I'm an Orchin, I hope that doesn't make you feel like you need to like me now."

"Alyssa," Amber laughed, a sound that was half amusement and half choked hysteria. "I've *always* liked you, right from the moment you walked into that office. You treated me exactly the way you would treat a normal person, a normal *rude* person. I admired you for it, you know. You never backed down, even when I threatened you or insulted you. You're brave." Her face froze suddenly, dropping down into a grimace, as she really thought about what she had said.

"Wow, is that really how I treat the people I actually like? By insulting and threatening them? I treated you so wrong, and I am *so* sorry." She covered her face with her hands, her shoulders heaving as silent sobs tore through her. It seemed like now that her emotions had been set free, she was having a hard time getting them back under control. "God, I'm a failure—even a failure at making friends; how can anyone stand me?"

"It's all right," I said. "You're not a failure. We just misunderstood each other. We can start over; we can start completely over."

"You *didn't* misunderstand me. I'm just as horrible and as arrogant as you first thought I was."

"No!" I exclaimed, trying to calm her down. "Amber that isn't you, and I always knew there was a different you in there somewhere even when I was told otherwise."

"I can explain," she said, dropping her hands from her face and back into her lap. "Losing two of the people you care most about ... it leaves a hole in your heart, a hole in yourself that never heals. People that we love fill up those holes and once they're gone ..." she sighed. "You become wary and guarded. You don't want to let anyone in, because you're afraid of caring about someone and then losing them." Frowning and shaking her head, she went on. "I thought friends were a distraction ... that I had my brother and that was enough. Friends would be a weakness, because they'd be people too, and people can be killed. But I was wrong." She looked up at the ceiling her dark, grey-blue irises dancing in circles.

"Zack did the same thing as I did, except he shows it differently. He acts like he cares about nothing; it's hidden by stupid jokes, but sometimes I think he was even more affected by losing our parents than I was. But I don't really know. We've never spoken of it, and Zack is rarely genuine with anyone."

She smiled fondly. "I know he really likes Haven though. I think he's genuine with him. There's something about Haven. They both were so affected by the Society that their world kind of spins the same way ... you know?"

I had enough of this. Haven's brother, Amber and Zack's parents ... was it not my obligation to stop them, as the only person who could? I thought of all the people who, when urged to fight, remained indifferent, too self-absorbed to possibly give a damn about anything else. Our world was on fire and we were just watching it burn. I *had* to do something. I knew that, if I decided to venture down this road, there would be unimaginable consequences. But even so, my power couldn't go to waste. More people were going to die—more children and families were going to be hurt by the Society, and it had to end.

"Amber," I said, suddenly seething, my words holding more authority than I've ever spoken with before. She recognized the odd tone in my voice and angled her head to look at me. Waves of emotion were flooding into the grey-blue storm of her eyes, unable to find any reprieve. In that moment, I had no doubts about what to do.

"I'm going to burn the Society down to ashes and you're going to help me." Her eyes shimmered with more tears that she refused to shed. I saw her grief, reined in and endured over the years, finally untamed in this one single moment. When her words failed, she simply nodded, and then ducked her head towards her shoulder to hide an almost embarrassed look. Her nod was all the confirmation I needed. We would take down the Society together ... and I wasn't afraid to go down doing it.

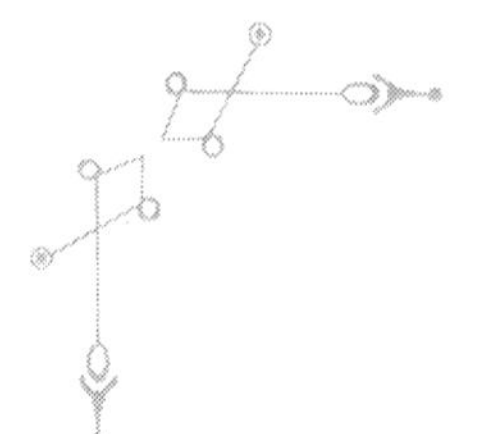
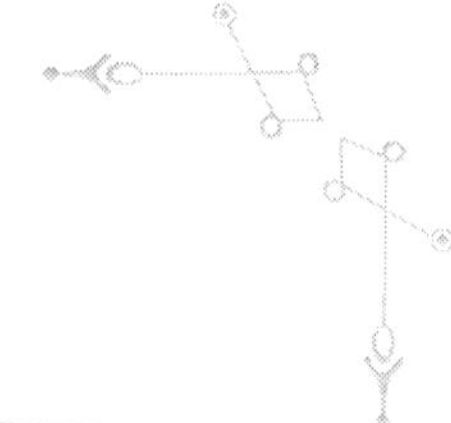

CHAPTER 12

AS THE DUST SETTLES

"So?" Amber prompted softly, as I stared down at the cell phone in my hand. It was now approaching four o'clock in the morning and there was no possible way I was getting any sleep tonight. Amber had decided to take the liberty of staying awake with me.

I was going to take Elda's advice and call my parents, but I didn't know what to say, and feared what *they* would say.

"I don't know what to say to them, Amber."

"Oh I can understand that," Amber said, nodding. "Would you like me to do the talking?"

"Are you serious?"

"Well I'm kind of thinking about it, since I have a few questions for them myself." She snatched my phone from my hand, tapped the screen, scrolled through the directory, and dialled my home number.

Then she handed it back to me. "You just needed a little push."

I winced. I almost felt bad about calling them this early, but this was an emergency.

The line rang five times before I heard a click and the sound of shuffling around. I pressed the phone closer to my ear.

"Alyssa?" My mother's groggy voice floated from the phone and I waved off Amber, who was hovering over my shoulder.

"Mom?" I whispered softly. "Do you have time to talk?" Maybe it was the seriousness of my voice, but she didn't laugh at the absurdity of the question.

"What's the matter Alyssa?" Immediate concern flooded her voice. "Did something happen?"

I bit my lip. I didn't know how to come out with a truth buried by sixteen years of lies. "Why didn't you tell me?" I figured I should just be blunt. "Did you want me to figure it out for myself? Or did you want someone else to figure it out and tell me? Because that's what happened."

"What are you talking about?" Her speech shifted ever-so slightly, her words speeding up.

I could tell, even over the phone, that she knew what I was talking about. "Don't play stupid," I accused. "I'm an Orchin and you are going to answer every question I'm about to ask or I'm hanging up."

"Alyssa—" my mom started, softly gasping.

"Don't!" I exploded harshly. "You need to let *me* talk! Why did you lie about my element?"

I heard my mom sighing. "We had to disguise you in another element." Her voice was solemn and I could almost imagine the look on her face. "It would be safer. A lot of people would be after you if they knew. We *had* to keep it quiet." She was starting to sound almost panicked. "Who else knows, Alyssa? How did this happen? We thought you would never know or figure it out! Tell me how this happened!"

"A teacher!" I snapped, gripping the phone tightly. "A teacher tested me." I looked at Amber. "Other than that, no one else knows."

"Which teacher?" My dad's angry voice joined the conversation, and I pulled the phone farther away from my ear.

"It doesn't matter. She won't tell anyone."

"You don't know that! You can't trust anyone!" my mom exploded. She sounded worried ... no, not worried ... terrified.

"I *do* know." I said, with a soothing lilt to my voice, in the hopes of calming them down. "I trust her." There was a momentary lull, in which I realized that the conversation had taken a wrong turn, with my parents questioning me, instead of the other way around.

"What happened at my Ritual?" There was no answer. "Hello?"

Finally, my mom answered. "We discovered what you were at the Ritual sixteen years ago. You chose the Orchin symbol."

"Does someone else know? The person manning the Ritual that night maybe?"

"Don't worry about the official," my mom said, sounding oddly defensive.

"Don't worry?" I didn't understand. "What happened to not trusting anybody?"

"We took care of it," my dad said firmly. I frowned, detecting something odd in his tone—almost like a nestled feeling of guilt.

"What did you do?" I probed. "What happened?"

"Paid him to keep quiet," my mom said quickly.

The second she answered, I knew. "You're lying." The accusation filled the silence that followed. Then I remembered Elda's warning about my parents doing anything to keep my secret safe. I swallowed.

"Answer me!" I seethed.

"We took care of it!"

The room suddenly tilted on its edge and I grabbed my bedside table to steady myself.

"You mean by killing him."

"It was for your own protection; the government is corrupt—"

"Someone's dead," I whispered, slowly feeling the colour drain from my face, "because of my existence. You killed an innocent person because of me!"

"No one's innocent! He could've told the Society, the Council, or—"

"You don't know that!" I shouted through the phone. "You took away a life! *A life!* Who gave you the right to do that?" My hands

trembled and I struggled to keep the phone from falling. Suddenly I was leaning against Amber for support, her strong hands on my shoulders.

"It was for your safety!" My mom was shouting at me now. "This isn't a game Alyssa! You're a threat to the supernaturals! You would've been killed! How could we have let that happen; you're our only daughter? You're an Orchin! Do you know how special you are? You can't die."

"That doesn't mean someone *else* should!" I cried.

"We love you and we protected you," she said, suddenly calm. "We do not regret our actions."

I recoiled at the warmth in her voice. These were my parents. They taught me all I knew; they raised and loved me. And yet ... they were never who I thought they were. They were something foreign. They were liars, and more than that, they were murderers. I was disgusted.

"I'm hanging up now," I said faintly, the world locking back into focus. "And don't you dare call back."

"Wait Alyssa—"

"No. You had lots of time to tell me things I didn't know. Your time is up," I said coldly, ending the call. I still had questions, but I knew that I wasn't speaking with them again any time soon. The people who had raised me all my life were murderers. I was angry ... no angry wasn't the right word. I was repulsed. Suddenly my phone was airborne, slamming against the other end of my bed with a muffled thud.

I took a deep breath and let it out. "My parents are murderers," I said calmly.

"Are you okay?" Amber looked at me nervously, as if I were a bomb just seconds from exploding. Her nervousness was fitting. I sounded eerily calm even to my own ears.

"Fine," I said, dazed. "But the person who's dead because of me isn't. How much of that conversation did you hear?"

"All of it." Amber winced. "I'm sorry Alyssa. I'm sorry. They still love you. You know that, right?"

"Killing out of love doesn't excuse it. If they think it's better to tell me nothing, then I'll do the same. I won't tell them about the quest." I tried to digest the giant lump in my stomach, as memories of who I thought were my loving parents replayed in my mind. Where did they put the body? How had they done it? Why did they think that was okay for even a moment?

"They're still your parents," she whispered gently. "Even if they did something awful ... that was a long time ago."

"Murdering someone is kind of an exception," I whispered, staring at the cream-coloured walls in shock.

"They're your family Alyssa," Amber said desperately, though her voice was faltering.

"No," I said firmly. "They're strangers ... and I don't talk to strangers."

The next morning Amber and I reached a mutual agreement that Haven and Zack both needed to be told about the quest. If we truly hoped to succeed at obtaining the Orb, bringing Haven and Zack along was necessary.

Elda had requested another meeting with the four of us, which meant that the explaining was left up to me. There would only *be* another meeting if they both agreed, but there was no way Amber was leaving Zack or Haven in Magnorium's clutches. We set out early Saturday morning, wandering the halls, which were vacant just as Amber promised they would be. Not many people were too enthusiastic about getting up early on weekends, and I was sure Haven and Zack were no exception.

I walked down the familiar halls of the school more warily than I had before, waiting for Kurt or some unfamiliar foe to strike. The man in question hadn't been seen floating around the hallways for days now, and I could only guess at what he must be conspiring with his Society.

Amber ignored any form of courtesy, and stalked up to her brother's dorm, knocking loudly on the door. No one answered, but I didn't think Amber would stand for being ignored. She knocked even harder.

Zack finally swung open the door, noticeably lacking a shirt, with hair that was adorably dishevelled, and looking incredibly intoxicated. I hadn't the slightest idea of where Zack could possibly have gone about drinking here at Magnorium, but if anyone were able to achieve this, it presumably would be him. He rubbed his face with his fist and dim recognition filtered through his green eyes as he took us both in.

"Well what brings you here so late?" he slurred, swaying against the door frame.

"First of all, it's morning, and second of all, how drunk *are* you?" Amber asked, a smile she couldn't quite contain forming at the edges of her drawn mouth.

Zack shrugged submissively, waving her off with a flick of his hand. "I've been here long enough. I can hold my liquor."

"Fair enough," I interjected, trying to reach him through his drunken stupor. "Listen Zack, we need to talk to you and Haven. It's kind of important."

Zack laughed, drumming his fingers against the wood.

"Hear that Reeves? When girls say they need to talk, it is never a good thing." A shuffling sound came from behind Zack, and Haven appeared at the doorway, looking almost as rumpled as his roommate. He clearly wasn't as wasted as Zack though, and I watched as he slapped a hand across his roommate's shoulder.

"Sit down before you fall over, idiot." Actually being obedient, Zack sluggishly tugged his drunken body over to his bed and collapsed into the wrinkled sheets.

Haven rolled his eyes, wordlessly gesturing us inside. Zack's bed and the floor around it were littered with empty cans and streamers. Haven groaned, kicking a nearby can and sending it shooting to the side of Zack's bed.

"So what's so urgent that you feel the need to wake us up at this ungodly hour?"

Amber was silent, and made herself at home, plopping down next to her brother and giving me the floor with a gesture that told me to take it away.

I didn't even know where to begin. I took a deep breath. "It's been a crazy night. You wouldn't believe me if I told you."

"Did you come across a naked Kurt Bell?" Haven asked.

"*What?*" I shuddered at the horrifying image. "Um ... fortunately, no."

"Then the night wasn't as crazy as you thought."

"That's right," Zack said. "So go ahead. Shoot."

They were both looking at me oddly by this point, putting all joking aside, and obviously very curious. Zack even managed to struggle into a sitting position.

Maybe if I showed them—since words would likely not suffice—it would be easier. I glanced around the room quickly, surveying my options for something I could use to test my magic on. So far, I had only dabbled into Draken and Aquarian magic, but now seemed as good a time as any to attempt Skyros magic. Well, assuming that I didn't hopelessly fail at my first attempt. Either way though, I wanted to try.

I spotted a small plastic paperweight on the nearby desk, which I thought would suffice. I extended a hand in its general direction and called to my magic. It responded instantly, the adrenaline helping it to gain momentum until I could feel it crashing through me like a tidal wave. I stared at the paperweight, toying with the nearby air molecules. The small object quivered for an instant, almost as though it were succumbing to gravity, but obeyed my order and rose off the desk, hovering about three inches above it. I held onto my concentration and carefully pressed against it with the invisible force of my will, sending the object flying through the air, just narrowly missing Haven's head before clattering to the floor.

It's falling hardly made a sound, but the silence in the room was thick enough to make it sound like a bomb going off. Haven's face was the epitome of shock, his jaw hanging loosely open. Zack, appearing perfectly sober now, held the same look of shock, his eyes darting back and forth from me to the fallen object.

"Reeves, just how hungover am I?" Zack asked, squeezing his eyes shut. "Because that didn't feel like Amber's magic, but it sure wasn't Draken magic either."

"Alyssa!" Haven exclaimed, and then he was laughing, a sweet dizzying sound that continued as he bent down to pick up the fallen object. "I think you are the first person, and the last, to continuously confuse me. Honestly."

He blinked at me for a moment before looking at the paperweight again, shaking his head. "You're actually an Orchin. Aren't you? The first one in *literally* centuries. Is there anything else you care to share?"

"I know. It's insane," I said, firmly this time and leaving no room for debate or questions. "But there's more."

"Am I missing something here?" Zack sputtered, jumping to his feet and rocking back on his heels. "Because the last time I checked, Orchins were extinct!"

"I don't know. But Elda figured it out yesterday."

"*Elda*? Our battle strategy teacher?" Zack's voice rose, thick with confusion. "You need to start from the top."

I dropped into the nearest armchair with a composure that surprised me.

"Two days ago, Elda sent me a letter saying that she wanted to meet with me. When I visited her yesterday, she said that she wanted to evaluate me, and thought I was special. I agreed, not really knowing what it meant. She ran a series of tests and claimed that I exceeded expectations. She sat me down, and told me she had a theory ... that the only explanation for all these anomalies is that I'm an Orchin. At first I thought she was lying, or crazy for even suggesting such a thing. But then I tried a form of Aquarian magic and was shocked when I succeeded ..." I trailed off rather lamely, considering the weight of the news, and Zack's frown deepened, forming creases in his smooth skin.

"But you're supposed to be a Draken. If you're not, what happened at your Ritual? And how come you didn't know?" He raised a good point, and I thought back to all that I knew about the Rituals. The only people supervising the Rituals were the government officials, but the one who had watched over mine was dead—thanks to my parents.

"I don't know what happened at my Ritual. But my parents told me I was a Draken to disguise me in another element. I had no idea until today. But other than the four of us, my parents, and Elda, no one else knows."

"We're keeping it that way!" Amber supplied.

"Jeez Amber, just give me a second for this to sink in," Zack said, rubbing his temples. He paused for another moment and then snapped his head back up, giving a firm nod. "Okay I think it's sinking in."

I bit back a smile.

Haven looked at me curiously. "So, this secret can get you killed and yet you're telling me and Mr. Completely Wasted over there. Why?"

I glanced at him. They were both still staring at me, as if they were afraid that, if they blinked and looked away, I would be gone.

"I'm telling you because Elda requested something else before I left that meeting. She needs more than just me. She needs the four of us for a job, and according to her, we're the only ones who could possibly ever hope to do it."

"Someone needs me for something?" Zack asked, amused. "And what would that be?"

"Oh well ..." I let my voice trail off, a small smile beginning to stitch together at the corners of my mouth. "Elda wants the four of us to go and retrieve the four crystals, make the Orb, and use it to completely annihilate the Society."

"I might be totally wrong here, but this kind of seems like an unfair bargain," Zack grumbled later that day, as the four of us sat in Elda's battle strategy classroom. The room was vacant, and so we seated ourselves civilly at a table, patiently waiting for Elda. There was a certain nervous energy in the room that was almost palpable.

I could feel Zack's need to barge into the adjoining training room and pummel something to bits and I almost felt bad about blocking the door.

"I mean," he continued, "all we have to do is go get four crystals that are really not meant to be found, put them together, and use it to completely destroy an organization that has been in power for centuries?"

"Yes," I admitted, with a nervous glance around the room. I was paranoid about someone overhearing our conversation, and since this was Magnorium, anything along those lines seemed totally plausible.

"So we're going to be out there risking our lives while she gets to sit back in her good old comfy wheelchair and enjoy the show?" Zack asked again.

I nodded.

"No," Zack snapped. "I refuse. I like it here. I can get wasted, party on my own time, and no one can stop me. And you know what other grand accommodations they have here? No monsters or people trying to hunt you down." In my peripheral vision, I watched as Amber's face fell as if it had crashed from the sky itself. She shook her head at her brother. I knew she had thought Zack would be all for this, and it surprised me as well that he wasn't, but with Zack, I guess you could never really know.

"Zack, you're coming with us," Amber said stubbornly, not taking no for an answer. "I'm not leaving you here. The school is run by the Society, okay? Kurt actually *runs* the Society. The people who killed our parents. Do you not understand how dangerous it is here?"

As Amber spoke, Zack stilled, the sarcasm completely disappearing from his expression, and a darker look brewing on the sharp curves of his face. I remembered the chilling story of their past, and the way the haunting memories seemed to seize Amber, even so many years later. Zack seemed to be impacted in the same way.

"Oh," he finally muttered, but his face was screaming a million things that were far more expressive. "That does change the ball game a bit." It seemed like it really did. I had never seen Zack say anything so seriously. "All right, I agree to go on this fantastic journey with all of you, which will probably get us all killed." The smile was back on his face again.

"That's quite optimistic of you," I said.

"Darling, I only speak the truth. I don't think you've been part of our world long enough to really understand, but this will be dangerous."

"Come on Zack, don't tell me you're afraid?" Haven's entrance into the conversation carried a patronizing tone; he was clearly trying to bait Zack.

"Of course not," Zack replied, puffing out his chest. His eyes remained rather dubious. "I just don't have a death wish ... unlike you."

"I don't have a death wish," Haven said, sitting up straighter in his chair.

"Then you're completely okay with this then?" Amber asked, quietly drawing her hands into her lap. It was true, Haven really didn't seem to be bothered by any of this, but I couldn't tell if he was out to avenge his brother or simply didn't care about his own life. I *could* tell that he wanted this—wanted to have a purpose.

"The only reason I came to Magnorium was to investigate. But this is an opportunity to change things! To save people from feeling the pain that *you* felt!"

"You've felt it too," Amber pointed out. I had never really divulged Haven's past to Amber, but the rumours about him were endlessly circulating around the school.

"Exactly," Haven said solemnly, not even bothering to deny it. "How could we not do this? It's like you said, Amber, if no one else is going to help, maybe *we* should. Alyssa is a miracle! With her, we actually have a chance!" Haven looked at me with such admiration that I had to duck away, my face flaming. He was so optimistic. I could hardly believe it. It was funny how emotions played out on different people—Haven and Amber so full of drive, and Zack so full of spite.

"I agree with Haven," I said softly. "If we do this, the Society will be gone. No more murders. No more terrorist attacks."

"I'm so glad we all agree," Elda said, announcing her arrival, suddenly appearing in the doorway. I had no idea how long she'd been sitting there. She quickly wheeled herself into the room, the door slamming behind her. I raised an eyebrow at her stealthy entrance. I guess she wasn't the combat teacher here for nothing.

"Thank you all for meeting me here today. We should get right to the issue at hand. As you can probably imagine, when I first started to suspect the truth about Alyssa, I was almost afraid to hope it might be true, and when we discovered that it *was* ..." she shook her head in amazement, as she tried to find the words, "we were understandably shocked." The wheels of her chair squeaked as they rolled across the polished floors and stopped beside me, capturing our attention.

"I'm sure she has filled the three of you in on what happened. I ran a series of tests, and thus the unfathomable was discovered. I am quite certain that Alyssa is the only Orchin on the planet. Which leads us to my next request." Elda leaned forward, drumming a single fingernail on the table.

"The Orb was created by the Orchins to ensure the safety of our kind. For centuries, many have sought out the famous crystals, that together create the most powerful weapon our world has ever known. Without an Orchin, the crystals were lost to the world ... but with Alyssa here, there is a chance. However, as you know by now, many others would do almost anything to obtain this weapon."

"The Society," Amber breathed, her eyes hardening.

Elda gave a curt nod. "For years the Society has been looking for the means to accomplish their goal: a 'purification' that would exterminate the 'weak-willed mortals'. Of course, with the help of the Orb, achieving their goal would be much easier. But they've grown restless, always looking for other methods and tools to achieve success without the Orb. They are close, and in the meantime, they execute smaller tasks, like the massacres you've heard about. If they somehow were to acquire the Orb, or find another weapon that will suit their purposes, innocent people *will* die. Our world would be left in the Society's clutches, completely under their rule. It would be chaos. I don't think I can stress it enough. This can not happen."

I didn't know Elda's exact age, but I was willing to bet anything that she had been around long enough to fully witness the Society's havoc. Suddenly I could understand just how much she wanted them gone, and how much she must be depending on me.

"But," Elda finally said, triumphantly, "now we have you lot. I am turning to you—the four strongest Elementals I have seen in my lifetime. With all of you, working together, the Orb is now accessible."

Zack frowned. "Yes but—"

Elda cut him off with a wave of her hand, too far into her impassioned oration to be interrupted.

"Please just hear me out. I want you four to travel across the globe, stopping at each crystal site. Once you've acquired one, you will travel to the next, and so on, until all four are collected. Once you have them all, assemble them to create the Orb and together ... we will annihilate the Society."

For the first few moments after Elda's plea, there was silence. Amber was first to react, shooting me a tense look. I might've been left out of the loop for a good part of my life, but I certainly wasn't naive any longer. What Elda was asking for was extremely dangerous. Elda seemed to notice the nature of our expressions and nodded.

"Of course it isn't that simple," she acknowledged. "I know this. Each crystal is hidden quite intricately, but perhaps the Eye can help. The three of you are probably familiar with it. Alyssa?" I shook my head, almost starting to get angry. There was so much I didn't know.

"The Eye is one of the famous Elemental artifacts," she explained. "It has the power to show the user just about anything: memories, lost places, real places ... as long as it exists now or did exist in the past."

I had a vague memory of Professor Tate mentioning something about this in one of his classes, but Elda wasn't finished.

"It could be used—"

"Like a map," I breathed.

Elda smiled. "Yes, like a map ... in a way. Unfortunately the Eye is very specific and tightly focused. What we know of the crystals' locations is still vague. If you obtained the Eye, it would show you the crystal itself, and only those elements that might be seen in its actual presence. However, it *could* be helpful in revealing the surrounding environment or perhaps even a key feature that would eventually give a location away."

"Gee, that's helpful," Zack said, sarcastically.

"Oh, it most certainly is. Any average person can posses the Eye, even a mortal, which is why the whole world was after it as well, for a very long time. It was acquired by the Society in the 1980s, and over time, what they learned about the crystal sites, by using the Eye, leaked out to the rest of us."

"So the Society has it," Zack grumbled. "This just gets better and better, doesn't it."

"You see," Elda said, completely ignoring Zack. "Mr. Kurt Bell plays a huge role in the Society. And in turn, so does Magnorium. Magnorium is the Society's main base, hidden right in plain sight. They have an enormous underground laboratory under the school, and that, I assume, is where they keep the Eye."

"How do you know this?" Amber asked quietly.

"I've been there dear."

"What?" I breathed. "When?"

Elda gave a knowing smile. "A few years ago, when I still could walk. As Alyssa already knows, I work for the Council. They placed me at Magnorium to investigate suspicious behaviour. Over the years, they have also asked me to gather as much information as possible about the crystals—"

"Wait a minute," Zack interrupted, shaking his head as though he couldn't quite believe what he was hearing. "If the Council knows about Kurt, and the location of the Society's main base, why the hell are they not *doing* anything about it? Where are the troops? The tactical squads? Why are people still dying?"

Elda held up a shaking hand, asking for his patience so that she could respond. "Mr. Travie, I understand your frustration, and believe me when I say that I share it tenfold. But that is not a question easily answered. At one time, the Society would have been crushed almost instantly if even a hint of their membership or whereabouts came to light, but since Tokyo ... " She shook her head. "Too many great minds and great powers were lost that day, and in trying to fill the void created by their loss ... we let the darkness in."

She sighed, looking older than I ever remembered seeing her. "Today, there are forces at work within the Council intentionally undermining their effectiveness, misplacing evidence, hindering strategic efforts, and casting doubt and aspersions on anyone speaking with too clear of a voice. Uncertainty and hesitation have become common practise I'm afraid, and so nothing that matters ever truly gets done."

"Couldn't we ask for help," I asked, "from outside the Council, maybe—"

"No," Elda interrupted firmly. "I'm sorry Alyssa, all of you ... but the other supernaturals refuse to get involved with our conflict."

Zack couldn't seem to let it go. "But that's ridiculous, if they—"

Haven cut him off. "Stop it, Zack. It won't change anything, and we don't have time to argue in circles." He paused a second, and when finally Zack nodded stiffly, he turned his attention back to Elda. "Okay, so this lab you're talking about. If you've been, then where's the entrance?" he asked, in a clipped voice.

"It used to be in a room behind Kurt's office. I don't know if the entrance is still there now."

Haven and I locked eyes. Our little detour flashed before my eyes. I remembered an archway on the back wall of the office, and being tempted to explore whatever was on the other side. Was it possible that was the entrance to the lab?

"We've been there," Haven said slowly, as if saying it aloud would make it real.

Elda's expression shifted, clearly shocked. "What? Alyssa told me something about investigating, but she seemed to have left out that little detail!"

He held up his hands defensively. "I thought Kurt seemed suspicious, so I wanted to investigate. I took Alyssa with me and we broke into his office, and then found his real one behind it. It was two or three weeks ago. I just wanted to find some information on my brother ... he went missing here."

"We never got to the lab," I added with a nod.

Elda paused for a moment, looking pleased. Proud even. "You two broke into Kurt's office?"

"Yes," we said in unison.

"Splendid. Do you think you could do it again?"

“I could do it in my sleep,” Haven answered.

“Good. Now, listen to my proposal. I want you four to break into the Society’s lab, find the artifact, and then escape the school. Know that, at this point, you’ll be fugitives in the eyes of the Society. You will need to flee the country.” She looked at each of us in turn. “Leave the school and begin the quest by finding the first crystal.”

“That’s quite a proposal,” I muttered, averting my gaze. Maybe Elda thought that, since I was a big bad Orchin now, I wouldn’t be scared about doing this. But I *was* scared. Immensely. What if I failed?

“Listen, I know this is a lot to ask of all of you. It will be dangerous. The crystals are hidden well, and will be heavily guarded by all sorts of supernaturals. But if you *don’t* do this ... hell will be released on this planet!” Elda’s voice escalated a notch, the utter desperation apparent in her tone. “You four are the last hope for everyone, from the Council to the mortals.” I could see fear settling in her eyes, and imagined that it was probably reflected in our own. “Do I have your commitment to this quest?”

I knew it wasn’t the time to take a detour down memory lane, but couldn’t help it.

I had never really considered myself very brave or strong at all; I was just some outcast. I remembered sitting all alone, seeing the suffering in the world. And it was upsetting, because the problems the world faced seemed too big for someone like me to even consider tackling. But what if ...?

What if I could create waves of change, bringing good things to those same people? What if I could help? Innocent and good people would die if someone didn’t do something. If *I* didn’t do this ... hell, I could never forgive myself. Maybe my decision was impulsive, but it felt right.

“I already said I would do this, and I meant it. Learning more about the situation doesn’t change anything. Of course I’ll do it,” I nodded vigorously, more sure of this than I ever have been of anything. “But I won’t speak for the others.” I turned to watch as the three of them weighed the decision. Were they really up to this? More than that, could I really allow myself to take them with me?

"I want to do this," I said to them. "But it will be dangerous and we *could* all die. You don't have to do this if you don't want to."

"Now what kind of friend would I be if I let you go alone?" Haven said, shaking his head.

"A safe one," I suggested.

"Safety has never really been my top priority. I'm coming."

"So am I," Amber said, almost too quickly. I smiled a bit at how enthusiastically she jumped into the conversation; I knew she had no doubts. I couldn't say the same for Zack, and I wouldn't blame him if he chose security.

He rolled his eyes at my worried expression. "Someone's got to protect you three," he nodded. "I'm in."

Elda's grin was huge; it spread across the deepest craters of her worn face, bringing light to her tired, old eyes. "Thank you," she whispered. It was by far the deepest, most heartfelt thanks I had ever received.

"I will aid you as much as I can. In regards to the crystals themselves, I can only provide you with the following information. The crystals are hidden in a particular order. The Terran gem is first. It's hidden in the deepest parts of the Amazon jungle. The second gem is the Aquarian gem, which is near the Bermuda Triangle. The third is the Draken gem, and I have reason to believe it is somewhere with strong volcanic activity, though we don't have a conclusive location yet. The Skyros gem is last, and is hidden near Mount Everest. The exact locations are unknown, but with luck, you will be able to make better use of the Eye than those who came before you, and discover new insights. Alyssa, however, will be the key." She looked at me with unnerving intensity. "You will be drawn to the magic in the crystals, just as you were drawn to Magnorium."

"Well, this will be fun," Zack said dryly, after a momentary pause in the conversation.

All three of their faces had paled as Elda spoke, and I realized that they were all imagining delving into their opposing elements.

"Before you ask, let me tell you that money will not be an issue," Elda continued. "I will give you a generous amount for the journey, more than enough to cover any travel or living expenses. I will also provide you with false identities, properly documented, so that you can cross borders without being detected or detained by anyone who might be trying to find you. Now to the matter of time. The sooner you begin your quest the better, but there are certain things that should be taken care of before you do. So, should we say a week from tonight?"

She looked around at us all for any sign of disagreement. There were none. "Very well. That night, you four will break into Kurt's lab, steal the Eye, and be on your way. Of course, I will also provide amenable transportation. A car especially for your use will be parked in the Magnorium garage. Report there immediately after you leave the lab. Do you know where the garage is?"

I didn't, but Haven nodded.

"Good. I will meet with Alyssa again to give her the money, and some supplies, and to finalize the incidental details. In the meantime, I suggest teaching Alyssa to harness and handle the rest of her elements. It would be helpful on the quest if her powers were better developed ... and I can see no better teachers for her than the three of you."

"No problem," Zack said, with a devilish smirk.

I rolled my eyes.

"More than that," she continued, "you need to build trust. You four *must* depend on each other in order for this to work."

We all gave short, somewhat mechanical nods. No one could deny that Elda was helping us, because she really was ... but in the end, the total weight of this quest would fall on us. Especially on me. Presumably, if I failed, the entire world was doomed. As well, if anything happened to Amber, Haven, or Zack, I'd hate myself for it.

But I would protect them ... no matter what. I was the Orchin. Technically, this was my mission, not theirs.

"The Eye has misled many," Elda warned. "It is small but extremely powerful. It is said to look like a clear stone, about the size of a fist. When you're in the lab, be quick. Kurt is many things and cunning is all but one. That makes him unpredictable. Be careful. I know you can succeed."

I smiled at Elda one last time before rising from my seat. The rest followed suit. Suddenly I was beyond tired. Exhausted from the day, my comfy bed seemed more than appealing right now. I knew that there was so much more to be said—to discuss, to plan, to debate—but I really had no energy to do so. I figured that, if the world had waited for the Orb for this long, it could wait another week.

I squeezed Elda's outstretched hand and then she rolled herself to the exit.

"We'll speak soon Alyssa. I can't thank you enough." She was out the door and halfway down the hallway as quickly as she had appeared.

I watched her go for a moment. I was still in the process of fully registering what exactly it was that I had agreed to.

Zack cleared his throat. "Well, I'm going to leave now, because I'm sure we'll be spending a hell of a lot of time together soon enough. Oh," he said, turning back and taking a step closer to me, "meet me in the clearing tomorrow morning at seven. You're going to get special Terran lessons from yours truly." He puffed his chest out.

"I don't think you teaching me is a good idea," I said.

"You're right; it's a great idea. I'll see you tomorrow!" He sauntered out into the hallway so casually that it was almost like the previous hour had never happened.

Amber didn't make a move to go after her brother, nor did Haven, who stood behind her.

"We're going to go do some research about the sites," she said. "Are you coming?"

I was almost tempted to go with them. I knew that planning was crucial to the success of the job, but I couldn't think of anything I wanted to do less than stare at a screen or a book for the next five hours.

"No thanks. I'll catch up with you guys later."

They both nodded in understanding and I took my leave, trudging back up to the dorms. When I got into the safety of my room, I changed into my pyjamas, and was asleep before my head even hit the pillow.

"You're tense," Zack said observantly, just one day after our meeting with Elda. "Don't you trust me?"

"Um," I opened my eyelids, which felt like they had been sewn shut, and took in the clearing deep within the forest, in which Zack and I were conducting our lesson. The last time I had visited the forest, a little Troll had jumped on me, but today the woods were quiet and seemingly devoid of life. A cool breeze was ruffling the leaves and shrubbery. Zack deemed the clearing ideal for practise as there was very little chance of anyone seeing us. Today, the school was like a ghost town. Most kids left the school grounds on weekends, and this early on a Sunday morning, no one in their right mind would be roaming around in the woods.

"Trust you?" I shifted my gaze back to him, and shrugged. "Not really, if I'm quite honest."

He laughed, which lightened up the dark hue of his eyes. "I wouldn't trust me either."

"Then I'm glad we agree," I said sarcastically.

He rolled his eyes, folding his arms over his broad chest.

"I'm tense too," Haven called, from his position about thirty feet away, "just in case anyone was wondering." He and Amber had decided to accompany me to Zack's training session, to keep watch and make sure no one witnessed me practising Terran magic. They were leaning against oak trees on opposite ends of the clearing, keeping an eye on the paths and watching our lesson with filtered amusement.

Zack rolled his eyes at his friend. "Thank you for your input, Reeves. Anyway, as I was saying, your magic isn't flowing, Alyssa. Either quit being tense, or I'll just have to *make you* stop being tense."

"Oh yeah, how are you going to do that?"

"By distracting you with my overwhelmingly good looks, of course."

I bit back a smile, and muttered dryly, "I think that might do it," but he seemed to no longer be listening.

Suddenly he was standing close—so close that I could see the individual hairs on his head, which fell gracefully over his forehead. I didn't move for a moment. I completely forgot to.

He was right when he said that he could distract me with his looks, because every inch of his face looked annoyingly perfect from this angle. His hands were suddenly on my waist, and he leaned in even closer. I finally comprehended what exactly was happening. I didn't even think about it. Moving faster than I ever thought I could, I grabbed ahold of his shoulder blade and swiped his feet out from under him. He stumbled backwards before losing his balance and crashing onto the grass. He lay still for a moment, silently gaping at the clouds and processing what I had just done.

"You're a feisty one, aren't you?" he asked lazily, putting a hand under his head.

"If you were going to kiss me, you better work on your approach." I clamped my mouth shut, but the words had already spilled from my mouth. When exactly had I become so blunt?

"I was trying to seduce you into your Terran abilities."

"I think you need a new tactic," I mumbled.

"All right, just don't attack me again." He jumped to his feet, clearly more playful than angry, and dusted himself off. "Okay," he said, ignoring what had just happened. "First of all, you look stiff. Loosen up."

I looked down at my feet and noticed that they were firmly planted together. I adopted a new stance and planted my feet shoulder length apart, working on loosening the joints in my arms.

"Now concentrate," he said. "Terran magic really is just all about connection. The earth is right there to connect with."

"So *you* connect with it!" I said, defensively.

"Shh!" Zack exclaimed bringing a finger to his lips.

"You're quite insulting," I observed. "Do you know that?"

"There's nothing insulting about me!" Zack mocked, with a look of shock. "Just stop failing miserably and connect with the ground."

I repressed a sigh. This was fun, but I'd really like to learn some Terran magic, so that I didn't look like a complete idiot out in the jungle. Reminding myself that I had less than a week to master it didn't help matters.

"All right, seriously now," he said, "you already connect with fire. The earth is the same thing. It's at *your* disposal."

I closed my eyes. Fire came to me pretty easily. I was determined to establish the same rapport with the earth.

I remembered how successful I was with my first element. I always just imagined what I wanted to happen and it happened. But I was finding that not all of the elements worked the same way Draken magic did. I was better at some elements than others, and it appeared I was really weak in Terran magic.

"Zack," I said apologetically. "I don't think I can do this; maybe we should try again another day."

Zack shook his head, his dark hair falling into his eyes. "I'm not like Haven or Amber, who would automatically tell you not to quit. If you want to stop, we *can* stop. But you'd have to get past both of them."

I quickly looked at Amber and Haven, staring alertly out into the forest, and sighed. "No thanks. I just don't think I understand how—"

"Incredibly talented I am?" Zack finished for me.

"No," I rolled my eyes, "I don't understand how to *start*."

"Oh," Zack said, but he looked thoughtful. "Well Terran magic doesn't come easily through emotions the way Draken magic does. So getting angry won't do you much good. To do Terran magic, you must be calm and clearheaded."

"Well," I said, shrugging, "it looks like I'll never be able to do it then, because if you haven't noticed, I am not the calmest person. How do you create earthquakes?"

"Come on. We've been here for half an hour. You're getting distracted," Zack remarked under his breath.

"You're letting me get distracted," I said, smiling slyly, but I knew I was doing just that. I needed to focus.

"You're a bad student," he said, amused.

"You're a bad teacher," I said, evenly.

"Then I guess I'll be the one saving your ass in the Amazon." He plopped down onto the ground, as if giving up on me entirely.

"There is *no way* that is happening," I said, glancing down at him.

I really, really didn't want that to happen. Technically, this wasn't completely my quest, but it sure felt like my complete responsibility, and that included being responsible for everyone joining me. I *needed* to be good at all four elements.

I looked at the ground where Zack was sitting. Then, as quickly as I wanted the ability to come, it delivered. The sensation of magic trickled through me like a stream, though this time it was not overwhelming, like it was with Draken magic. But it existed nonetheless. I suddenly felt locked in place, almost like I was pushing against something hard.

The ground shook, wavering beneath him. Haven and Amber looked up at me in surprise as they tried to keep their balance. I wasn't so cautious, even though I was the one who started it. The ground shook more violently, and I fell forward onto my knees. The miniature earthquake stopped as soon as I broke concentration, and Zack was suddenly on his feet, clapping.

"You're a Terran! Well ... sort of. I have no idea how I taught you to do that, but it was a good start. You'll get better in time."

I jumped back to my feet, enthusiastic about this now. I knew I could do better! I raised my arms and the ground shook again, this time focused on a specific plot of dirt, which sprung up from the ground, managing to startle even Zack. It grew quickly, jutting from the earth like a pointed brown sword before crumbling back into motionless mounds of soil.

Zack laughed. "You're doing it!" He jogged to the tree that Haven was leaning against and pushed him out of the way without a moment's hesitation. The shadow of the branches shielded half of his face, but did little to conceal his smile. I had never seen Zack quite so genuinely happy before. It was a side of him that I liked.

"Hey!" Amber called, jogging towards us. "She's doing it!"

"Amber, go teach a bird to fly or something!" Zack called, waving his sister away with a flick of his hand.

"But ... " She looked confused.

Haven climbed back to his feet, pushing himself away from the trunk of the tree. "Hey Travie, I have an idea that can probably help Alyss—"

"Hey!" Zack interjected, trying to look hurt. "This is *my* lesson! You're not allowed!"

"But I can help," Haven said defensively.

"Save it for another day, Aquarian," he replied quickly, cutting his friend off with a raised finger.

"Fine," Haven grumbled in surrender, leading Amber away.

Zack looked triumphant. "So controlling inanimate objects is a big part of being a Terran, but," he grinned mischievously, "you also can control living things; it's just harder." He stepped back and rapped a knuckle against the solid bark of the tree.

I glanced upwards. The branches from the deciduous trees seemed to climb halfway to the sky; its leaves fell lazily around us. Strong sturdy branches lunged outwards, creating a maze for the sunlight to pass through. It was by far the biggest and oldest tree I had seen in the landscape of Magnorium.

"Don't mess with this tree," I told him firmly.

"I'm not, but you are. Don't worry I can fix whatever you mess up. So ... obviously a plant doesn't have a will or a mind of its own; controlling them is very different from controlling animals." I raised my eyebrows. "Don't worry, that'll be the next lesson,"

"Can't wait," I mumbled.

"Anyway, you can't completely control living things. For example, you can't kill the tree entirely. But you can twist it to do what you want. See that branch up there?" He motioned upwards to a long curled branch, rising about seven feet above my head.

"Bring it down here,"

"I think I would prefer," I said slowly, glancing upwards, "to just climb up and get it,"

"No shortcuts!" Zack said, sounding very strict. "Remember, it won't be totally under your control. You have to compromise with the will of nature."

"I think that is the most cryptic thing you've ever said to me."

"I'm glad you think so highly of my intelligence, sweetheart."

I frowned at that.

"Oh," he said, cocking his eyebrow. "Don't like that? I can go back to 'darling', if that's what you'd prefer."

"Nature is telling you to shut up. You're interrupting our connection," I said, genuinely trying to focus on Zack's request. I closed my eyes.

Okay. I just needed to move that one single branch.

First I tried my usual tactic, which was visualizing the end result, only to remember that Terran magic didn't work that way. After five minutes I came up shorthanded, but I refused to succumb to frustration. I shifted my weight onto my right foot, opening my eyes and staring at the unmoving tree.

Move, I pleaded internally. This was harder than I thought. How did people like Zack master these things?

"You staring isn't going to move it," he said impatiently. I looked at him. It had barely been twenty minutes! Patience clearly wasn't his forte.

"You never know," I joked, before resuming my deep, brooding stare. I just had to think. I was positive I could do this. What did Zack mean by connection? It was too vague. I gave it another try, and then another, and after another ten minutes, I could see Zack growing antsy.

"Come on," he groaned, exasperated and rocking back and forth on the heels of his feet. "Alyssa, you're an *Orchin*." He said the last word quietly, almost out of instinct. "You're not allowed to take this long!"

"Hey," I said wearily. "This is kind of hard. I can't just master it in five seconds."

"Can't you?"

"No! I'm just like you. I have to learn."

"Well learn faster, would you?" He laughed, ramming his hands in his pockets. He really didn't sound insulting, just genuinely curious.

"I'm trying. You know, I think Terran magic is the hardest out of all of them."

"I'm telling you Alyssa, you just need to have a clear head."

"How do you manage that?" I asked curiously. "You don't seem the type."

He looked fake-hurt again. "Do you really think there's nothing going on upstairs? There is. I just taught myself not to care about most things; that way I could save my energy caring for the things that did matter."

"What does matter to you?" I asked curiously, completely forgetting about our lesson.

Zack glanced up at the tree, sighing. "My sister ... and having a normal life."

I tried to conceal my shock, but it was hard to keep my jaw from dropping. "You want a normal life?"

"I've always wanted one," Zack said rather wistfully. "I've always wanted to go to a normal school and go to concerts and sports games, just like other people our age do. I wanted the freedom to pick my own future and find things that I loved ... but people don't always get what they want."

"Why are you coming with us, if you want a normal life?" I was shocked. This was on my list of the last things I'd ever expect to hear Zack say.

"My sister and my best friend both seem to have a death wish and an obsession with vengeance. And then there's you ..." His voice trailed off as he looked at me, but as to the nature of the hesitation, I really couldn't tell.

"What *about* me?"

"You think you can save the world, that it's your job when it really isn't ... and you can't even move a tree branch."

I tried to ignore what he just said and stared up at the branch above my head, only to realize that it was twitching. Almost unbelievably, the branch wavered and elongated a couple feet. It lunged downwards, moving quickly, growing at an unimaginable speed. The sharp tip of the oak approached the back of Zack's head. I was so speechless that I couldn't even form a proper warning. The tip of the branch crashed into his jet-black hair and he yelped, jumping in surprise.

The small, weak feeling of my magic immediately began to fade. I could barely process what had happened, or how exactly I had done it. It all just happened so fast.

"Alyssa," Zack said flatly, holding the back of his head and wincing. "Was that necessary?"

"I can move trees," I announced smugly. "And if I can do that, then I may just be able to save the world."

"Your magic is shaky," Zack remarked, though he was grinning now. He was right. My Terran abilities *were* shaky, but they were definitely present.

"Don't worry," I answered. "I'll work on it."

CHAPTER 13

THE TIME HAS COME

It was kind of funny, that time seemed to pass so quickly when you didn't want it to. The plan had been to leave on Friday, but we'd opted to push it to Sunday so that there would be less traffic in and around the school, and therefore less chance of being seen or delayed. The week leading up to our departure basically entailed endless hours of research, training, and very little sleep. It was already Thursday, and Sunday seemed to be approaching relentlessly. In my dorm room, after school, I sat myself down to do some final preparations. Haven and Zack both sat beside me, wired up on huge amounts of caffeine, each leafing through a bundle of papers that Amber had collected.

"There's a lot of information on the first crystal; a lot of people have tried to get it," Haven commented, scanning the words on his page. "There's been records of people feeling the pull of the crystal, but the exact location is still undetermined." He grabbed ahold of his papers, anxiously flipping. "Apparently the pull *can* be felt by Elementals, but it seems to come from everywhere and nowhere all at once. So it can't really be followed."

"While that is really helpful," Zack interrupted sarcastically, "here are some of the things to watch out for." His nose was stuck in another book. "We have sightings of Trolls, some unspecified Demons, and a couple Golems."

"What's a Golem?" I asked quizzically.

"A monster made out of materials from the earth and programmed to kill. Bundles of fun, I tell you," Zack deadpanned. "But that's only scratching the surface. There's more. Things we've probably never heard of or seen. And trust me, I've seen tons."

I bit my lip and nervously ran a hand through my hair. We couldn't even afford to think about those things right now. We could only focus on the present problem: escaping Magnorium unscathed.

On Sunday night, all four of us would begin our trek down into Kurt's real office, a place Haven and I had visited just weeks ago. Once in, we were trusting my assumption that the door in the office would lead to the lab. There'd be no telling how long we would be in there for. The Eye could really be anywhere, and even with all the research Haven had done before coming to Magnorium, we really had no idea where they would possibly keep something as precious as that. From then on, things would start happening faster. Somehow we would have to circle back around the school, get all the way to the garage, and escape to the nearest airport.

From there we would be taking the next possible flight to Brazil, using the false identities' with which Elda had graciously supplied us. She had also supplied us with directions to that airport, the schedule of possible direct flights, and a list of other flights that could get us there indirectly, with as few layovers as possible. While it was essential that we get to our destination, it was equally important that we simply get away.

Our plan was extremely shaky, and I couldn't even count all of the things that could go wrong. I could only hope that it would somehow work in our favour. Sometimes hope was all you needed to run on. Today an excited sort of buzz filled the air. I think the closer we got to the date, the more we reminded ourselves that we each had something to fight for.

"I come bearing gifts!" Amber called, as she swung open the dorm room door, and then slammed it behind her. Amber carried a huge box with a sealed lid, and I could only guess what was in there, since I knew it had come from Elda.

Over the course of the week, I had met with Elda an impressive number of times, beating every detail of our plan to death. When Elda told me that she had even more supplies for us, I sent Amber to get them, because I had taken far too many trips there and didn't want to start raising suspicions. I didn't know how many illegal items I was now storing in our dorm, but I was fairly sure it was too many.

Our room had become our base of operations, since the boys still had far too many visitors in theirs. We had decided that it would be best not to change our patterns or behaviour too much, so that no one started to ask questions. Amber's room had always been fairly secluded, and so this was where we had stashed our backpacks, books, plans and anything that might give us away.

Since the expedition really was Elda's idea, she had been very generous with supplies. Stuffed in the bottom of my dresser were keys to our getaway car, cash in a variety of currencies and several false identities with passports and incredibly detailed documentation to back them up. Now that I thought about it, the bottom of my dresser really wasn't the best place to hide all of that, but I couldn't think of a better alternative.

Amber set the box down on my bed, making a loud clanging sound that reverberated around the room. I looked up curiously. The box must be heavy.

"Weapons. A bunch of them!"

She sounded so excited that I put down the papers I was examining and rose to my feet.

"You look like a kid on Christmas morning," Haven commented, springing up from the couch with a fair amount of enthusiasm of his own.

Amber grabbed a pair of scissors, split the box open, and took a deep breath. I peered inside. Tangled together were flashes of silver, odd looking weapons, and familiar-looking weapons, all heaped into one giant box.

"Wow." I exclaimed.

"Just wow?" Amber practically exploded, pawing into the box's contents and pulling out what looked a lot like Power Arrows, like the one Rachel had been shot with all those weeks ago.

"These are the newest models!" Haven said. "How did Elda get these? They're so rare!"

"Don't forget," Amber said, "she really works for the Council. They're probably the ones actually funding all this."

I reached into the box, gently picking up the nearest item.

"Careful!" Amber screeched. "Don't scratch them!"

"Amber," I laughed. "They're weapons. We're probably going to use them to kill something." She seemed to be barely listening, pulling out a sharp dagger. The metal was so shiny that I saw my own reflection.

"I want that one," I said, only half joking.

"Elda says to stock up. We've got Power Arrows, daggers, sheathed swords, a few revolvers, and a partridge in a pear tree," she laughed, separating the weapons into four neat piles on the bed. "Everyone gets one of each."

"This is very much against the rules," I commented, grabbing my fair share of the items and starting to stuff them into my backpack.

"I think what's very much against the rules is our headmaster being part of a crazy terrorist group," Haven pointed out.

Zack was looking at us like *we* were crazy. "Speaking of terrorists, do you not think we're overlooking something kind of important?"

Amber frowned at him. "What?"

"How do you think we're going to get *any* of these items past airport security? Even the partridge in a pear tree would be stopped at customs and held in quarantine for a month."

Haven chuckled at that, but Zack ignored him. He wandered over to the box and pulled out a revolver, turning it in his hands and examining it closely. I had no doubt that it was loaded. I also had no doubt that I would use it if I had to.

Amber smiled at her brother. "Don't worry, Elda has that covered too." She dug down into one corner of the box, careful not to cut herself on any of the assorted blades, and pulled out four decorative boxes. Each was about half the size of an average shoe-box, and looked like something you'd find in a gift shop. "One for each of us." She started passing them out. "You could pack a tank or an atomic bomb in there and take a guided tour of the pentagon."

I glanced inside mine, frowning for a second. Unlike the one I'd seen in Professor Tate's class, this box *seemed* to actually have a bottom.

"It's triggered by your magic," Amber explained. "Just lay your hand against the bottom for a moment and call it up."

I did as instructed, and as I felt the magic start to course through me, the bottom faded and became translucent. I could still see it, but my hand could pass through it like it wasn't there.

Amber nodded, watching as I reached my arm deep into the box. "It will stay like that until you close the lid again."

Pulling everything back out of my backpack and laying it on my bed, I started feeding the items, one at a time, into the small opening. It was actually hard to watch, seeming to twist reality somehow as large items passed through an opening only a fraction of their size. I shook my head, once again amazed at what magic could do, and wondering if I would ever get used to it.

I collected all the items from my room that I wouldn't want mortals to stumble upon, fed them into the box, stashed the box in my backpack, and then sat back, watching as the others finished up.

With all the weapons neatly sorted out, there was really nothing else to do for now. It was hard to pack for a trip when you had no idea what to expect. My single backpack, with the basic necessities, a few changes of clothes, and my winter jacket rolled up as tight as I could get it and strapped to the outside of the pack, would have to suffice. I couldn't really think of what else I might need. The trip was going to take us all over the world, but with the money we had with us, I hoped we'd be able to purchase some supplies as we went.

"We should probably split up the money between us and stash the bulk of it in the boxes," Haven suggested, almost seeming to read my mind. "A group of teenagers with so much cash will look pretty suspicious. Plus that way, if we get separated, no one gets stranded anywhere."

We were all in agreement with that and quickly sorted the money out and had it stashed. Everything seemed to be in order. Amber and Haven had studied all the available information relating to Orchins, the Orb, and the crystals themselves, specifically looking for any information on the crystal's hiding places. They had had scoured the Internet for information about the Amazon, Bermuda, and the other crystal locations, so that we could be prepared, and were surprised to find hundreds, or maybe even thousands of results online relating to the crystals themselves. I supposed it made sense though. Magic may be hidden, but Elementals were part of the new millennium as well.

We had done all we could do. No one said it aloud but no one had to. A silent piece of common knowledge passed through the four of us.

All that was left to do was wait.

When there came a firm knocking at my door late Friday night, I really wanted to ignore it and continue lying in the comfort of my bed. Amber groaned sleepily from across the room.

"I only have two more nights of sleep in this place; can't you get that?"

I turned over, squinting at my bedside clock as the world shifted back into focus. It was three o'clock in the morning! I was mentally and physically exhausted from training Skyros magic with Amber all day. I don't think I had ever worked so hard in my entire life. I rose from my bed anyway, stumbling over to the door, opening it up a smidge, and peering out into the darkness.

A pair of blue eyes shone back at me, just inches from my face, and nearly gave me a heart attack. "Haven!" I hissed, grabbing his wrist and pulling him inside. "What the hell are you doing?"

His eyes were bright and he looked wide-awake. He always seemed to be fuelled by restless energy. "You forgot about *my* training session."

I didn't want to even hear the word 'train' ever again. Amber and Zack together had managed to crunch years of training into mere days, and it was seriously wearing me out.

"We don't *have* a training session," I said, tiredly crossing my arms over my chest.

"We do now!" Haven said cheerily, flicking the light switch.

Bright light flooded into the room, and I blinked against it.

Amber sat up in her bed, glaring. "Haven, do you ever sleep?"

He paused for a moment, as if to consider the question, and then shook his head. "No time for stuff like that. Anyway, you need to come too."

She wrinkled her nose in disdain. "Definitely not."

"You don't like having fun?"

"No," she said dryly. "I'm a soulless being who experiences no enjoyment in life whatsoever."

Haven looked at her seriously.

Amber cleared her throat. "I'm kidding. I'm just not good with water."

"Well, that's just too bad," he exclaimed, clapping his hands together and making me jump.

"You won't even have to get in. Just come with us to keep watch."

Annoyed, Amber shot him a tired glance, but when she shifted out of bed, she was clearly trying not to smile.

"All right Alyssa, look alive. We don't have all night."

"Where are we going?"

"The pool obviously."

I didn't even have the strength to try to fathom how we would get into the pool area at this time of night. Haven clearly went anywhere he pleased. I looked down at my thin t-shirt and shorts.

"I don't have a bathing suit." I didn't even own one. It's not like I was expecting to ever go for a swim.

He gave me a once over, smirking. "You don't need one."

"What are you implying, exactly?"

He sighed dramatically. "You never need to get wet if you don't want to. You're an Aquarian, like me."

I stared. "What?"

"I love that Aquarian trick," Amber interrupted, putting on her shoes. "It's the coolest thing."

Haven pretended to be shocked. "Did you just say something positive about my element?"

Amber shrugged, not answering the question. "Would you hurry up, Alyssa."

"See? Even Amber wants to go," Haven announced smugly.

"I do not," she argued. "I just don't want to stand here all night."

"Oh my God," I muttered, interrupting their bickering and getting my shoes on. "Fine, let's go."

Haven was already out the door and halfway down the stairs. I followed him hurriedly out into the dark halls, finding it ridiculous how many times I'd snuck out of my room at night.

The Magnorium pool was on the main floor next to the gym. I only knew this because I had seen Haven disappearing in there plenty of times. I had never actually been there myself.

"Does Zack ever notice that you're never in the room at night?" I whispered, hurrying to catch up with him on the stairs.

He shook his head. "To be honest, neither of us are really in our room very often at night."

"Of course," Amber huffed. "Who sleeps at night anymore anyway?"

Haven grinned at her, weaving expertly towards the main part of the school, and hanging a right, stopping at the front entrance of the pool. He pushed open the pool doors softly, even though the hallways were eerily vacant.

"It's already unlocked?" I whispered, surprised that he wasn't going to bust out his collection of illegal tools.

"Yeah. I come here a lot by myself so I've convinced the caretakers to leave the door unlocked whenever they can do so without getting in trouble. Just in case, you know? Breaking in gets tiring."

The pool looked absolutely serene, lit from below with bright flickering lights of blue and green. The water looked warm and inviting, and shimmered from the moonlight that filtered though the nearby window. Haven led us inside and I could almost imagine him all alone in here in the quiet of the night, just sitting by the water.

"It's calm, isn't it?" he whispered fondly.

"Yeah."

"It's the calmest place here. Calm places are rare in a moving world; don't you think, Lyssa?" Haven knelt down to rake his fingers through the water, causing a single ripple to echo out into the middle of the pool.

"Very," I whispered, and then found that I was smiling. I liked the nickname. No one had ever given me a nickname before.

He stood up and turned to Amber, who had her arms crossed over her chest, looking uncomfortable. She looked very much out of her comfort zone. I had a sneaking suspicion that the more powerful someone was in their own element the more uneasy they would feel in the others.

"Can you keep watch outside?" he asked, then added with a grin, "Unless you want to learn Aquarian magic too?"

Amber wrinkled her nose in disdain. "No thanks, I'll be outside if you need me." She moved to the exit, her shoulders relaxing as she stepped back outside into the hallway.

"So," Haven announced cheerily, "first question: Do you know how to swim?"

"I wish. My parents never taught me."

"Great. It's always more fun that way." Suddenly, his arms were around my waist. Holding me tightly, he hiked my entire body up into the air, and tossed me over his shoulder like some sort of rag doll.

"Excuse me!" I exclaimed, mortified, pounding my fists against his back as he started walking to the side of the pool. "Put me down!"

"No," Haven said chuckling, ducking back out of the way of my thrashing legs and kicking feet.

"What do you mean *no?*" Propping myself up a bit, with one hand braced against the very top of his lower back, I frantically pushed the hair out of my face so I could see.

"No, is pretty self explanatory."

He moved easily, adjusting his hold around my waist as we approached the deep end of the pool. Starting to panic, I wriggled against his iron grip, but it was no use. He was obviously much stronger than he looked.

"I could drown, you know!" I cried desperately, as a last resort, as my bracing arms slipped and my face bounced off of his toned lower back.

"You're part Aquarian. You can't drown," he said calmly. Releasing his hold a little, he leaned back, tipped my entire body upside down, caught me by the legs, and tossed me like an anchor into the middle of the pool.

I crashed into the warm water with a start, the force of my body creating huge rolling waves that smashed repeatedly against the tiled edges of the pool. In all of my sixteen years, I had been in the water only a few times, and those had been in shallow water in which I could actually stand up.

To Haven, I probably looked pathetic, with my head sunk under the glassy sheen of the water as I kicked my legs and thrashed my arms, desperately trying to get my head above the surface.

Then, before I could completely drown, I found that I was being pulled backwards ... gliding through the water and coming to a rough stop at a shallower section. I was released and started staggering around, coughing and sputtering as I tried to get to my feet.

Haven laughed, pushing his wet blond hair out of his eyes. As he stood up, waist deep in the water, I noticed that his white t-shirt was completely dry. I blinked, rubbed my eyes for a moment, and saw that his hair was dry now as well.

If this was the "Aquarian trick" Amber had been talking about, I had to agree that it was pretty cool. I needed to learn it too. I was soaked and probably looked like a drowned rat.

"Haven," I seethed, stumbling a bit as I tried to stand up, thoroughly humiliated. "That wasn't funny!"

"No, it was hilarious actually," he corrected, parting the water with his fingers and moving closer.

"Ready to learn something useful? For real this time?"

"I would love to."

"First of all, you need to remember that the stuff your teachers told you about magic is all wrong. So forget about it. Magic," he said firmly, "is all about triggers. Emotion. Feelings that instigate something. Once you figure out your triggers, magic is easier to control. You turn weakness into a strength." He circled me, and kept talking, fervently.

"Everybody has one, even if you don't think so. For example, as only you would know, my trigger is my brother. Every time I think of him when I'm practising magic, I get this intense rush of feeling, and my magic becomes more fierce—more strong. Do you think you can think of one?"

"I don't know," I said softly, crossing my arms over my dripping form. "I don't think I have one. I don't have anything to be passionate about like you do. Is that bad?" When I thought about my fairly uneventful life, it really was just a blur of unexciting events and routine. Nothing really stood out.

Haven shook his head. "Everyone has one. Your parents? Your family? School?"

I shook my head apologetically. "I'm pretty boring."

"Come on Lyssa, you're not a robot. Grades? People? Fear?" His eyes flashed as he scrutinized me for a moment, cocking his head suddenly as if he had picked up on something. "Yours is fear?"

"Um ..." I mumbled defensively, flicking a few water droplets out of my eyelashes. "I didn't say anything—"

"You didn't have to. People speak without actually speaking, if you pay attention. So ... fears?"

Startled, I asked, "What's wrong with you?" But when I thought about it, I knew he was right. The only things that made me feel strongly and act impulsively were related to fear.

He held up his hands in defence. "Nothing's wrong with me. I'm just observant! So fear it is." He moved closer and asked me in a very quiet, but very challenging, whisper. *"So what is the most powerful person here scared of?"*

When he said it like that, I felt as though he expected me to be scared of nothing. And maybe I was, in terms of mundane things like heights or bugs or getting hurt. But looking at the bigger picture, I was scared of everything. I was scared of never doing anything to help anyone. I was scared of wasting my power. I was scared of the Society. I was scared of failing on this quest. I was scared of people dying when I could've prevented it. I was scared of my ignorance, because there were just so many things I didn't know. In fact, I was so scared just thinking about all of it that I began to tremble.

I tried to steady my hands. "I'm scared of—"

"Shh!" he hissed, cutting me off with a finger. "Don't tell me. I want to figure it out myself."

I stared. It was like everything was a game to him, including people's feelings. I didn't know what to make of this side of him.

"Now isn't the time though." He stared down into the water for a moment, as if trying to figure out the best way to put his magic into words. "When you're doing magic, think of your trigger ... your fear. Think of the way it makes you feel, and let it act as an conduit for your magic ... Watch."

He waded backwards, turning to face me. Eventually, his power must have been holding him up, as he was nearing the far end of the pool and the water never reached higher than his waist. He flexed his wrists outwards then, and I stared as the water around him begun to compact and condense. I watched the water level of the pool drop as the surface near Haven slowly pulled upwards, morphing to form a giant wall of water about twenty feet high. I glanced up at the monstrosity. The wall was transparent, glittering like crystal, and came rushing towards me when Haven motioned it to do so. It moved as if pushed by some unseen force, and luckily started sinking back down as it came until it was only about eight feet high when it slammed into my body, dunking me under the surface and sending me toppling end over end.

When I managed to pull myself out its grasp and resurfaced, with the remnants of the wave rolling in currents around me, he was there, only a few feet away from me.

I rolled my eyes at him, forcing myself to shrug it off, not wanting to give him the satisfaction of reacting. "Really? That's it? A big wave?"

"Scared of not being able to do it?" he challenged slyly.

I glared at him now, and then looked away, staring down at the swirling surface and letting my irritation at him become my starting point. Then I thought of Kurt. I thought of the purification plan. I thought of Amber and Zack—both orphans because of the Society. Suddenly my magic was there, thrumming in my ears loud and demanding. The water around me bubbled, moving together at my command and compacting to form a wave about five feet high. Nothing as impressive as Haven's but at least it was something.

"Good!" Haven exclaimed, giving my small quivering wave a once over, before waving a finger. I watched as my wave dispersed, raining back down in heavy droplets.

I smiled, looking down at the ripples the droplets made. Draken magic came to me the easiest, but maybe I wasn't so bad at this four-element thing after all.

"Haven?" I looked around, astonished to find him missing. He was here just a second ago! I looked around the room wildly, and finally spotted him. A moving blur, darting like a fish underneath the water. He was moving unbelievably fast; all I could make out was a flash of white and gold.

I cried out in surprise as a hand snaked around my ankle, yanking me under. Water rushed into my ears and nose, and for a second, I was afraid. I had this terrible urge to claw my way to the surface, but then I opened my eyes.

I saw Haven, gripping my wrist to stop me from resurfacing and looking worried.

"Alyssa," he said softly. I opened my eyes wider, astonished.

Everything looked surprisingly normal, considering we were underwater. There was no translucent fog or bubbles floating around; it was all crystal clear. The blond strands of Haven's hair were floating around his head like a halo. His eyes were open and he just kept looking at me. Other than the halo, he really looked and sounded quite natural.

"Relax. You can breathe under here. And you can hear me clearly too. Just let yourself." He was right, of course. His voice didn't sound muffled like you would expect underwater. I made myself relax, calming my beating heart and frazzled nerves, and sighed, not even realizing I had done so.

Haven let go of me, and I realized that I was breathing fine. Better than fine. It felt like breathing pure crisp air on a cool autumn morning. There was no water rushing into my nose or mouth. It was surreal.

I paddled my way to the surface anyway, breathing big gulps of air, just to be safe. Things like that were going to take time to get used to, no matter how many times I told myself I was an Orchin.

"What'd you think?" Haven asked excitedly, popping up out of the water.

"Going to have to get used to that," I laughed, raking a hand through my soaked hair. "You think I'll be okay by the time we make it to Bermuda?"

Haven smiled encouragingly. "You're doing great. By the time we make it to Bermuda, you'll almost be as good as me," he said. Then he held up one index finger and articulated carefully so as not to be misunderstood. "Almost."

I chuckled. "Of course."

"Want to see more?" he asked, wading out to the middle of the pool.

"Definitely."

"What I'm about to do is called a water lock. You detach pieces of water and command them to take on other properties. Watch."

There was a giant splash and then suddenly two long tendrils of water emerged, parting from the rippling surface. They extended into long chunky pieces of water that were so clear it was almost hard to spot them. A moment later, the tendrils were airborne, zig-zagging through the air like long flimsy snakes. They floated above me, and almost as if they had solidified completely, no water dripped from them.

Suddenly, the two tendrils shot downwards coiling around my wrists, feeling as substantial as chains. My arms were completely paralysed. Haven was fixed in concentration, holding the water lock around my two wrists and using them to pull me forward. I shot forward through the water, wrists extended out in front of me. I managed to keep my head up as long as I could, and then took a breath right before my face slammed quite hard into the water's surface and I plunged under for a moment before resurfacing once again.

Instantly, I could feel the pressure around my wrists loosen and let me go. "What the hell was that?" I asked, mortified.

"Told you. It's like a chain made of water," he said, proudly flexing his hands.

I gaped, rubbing my sore wrists. It was unbelievable how flawless his magic was; he made it look literally effortless. How could he have learned to do that all by himself?

I'd had enough whiplash for one night. "Haven," I said, wrapping my hair into a ponytail in my hands and squeezing out the water droplets, "when did you do magic for the first time?"

Haven stared at the water, his expression shifting. "When I was four. My brother thought it would be funny to see what would happen if he tried drowning me."

I sighed, understanding the sometimes-odd dynamic of siblings, even though I'd never had one. "You two must've been really close."

"Yeah. It's not like I had anyone else." He laughed coldly. "Want to know something? My parents didn't even show up to his funeral. Even Kurt was there. But not them."

"That's awful," I whispered, horrified. My parents may be murderers, but they loved me.

"It's okay. It's not like he'll be around to reciprocate the gesture when it's their time."

I was quiet as the waves rolled around us. His voice bounced off the tiled wall—in echoes of anger and anguish. He recovered just a second later, forcing his features to even out once again. It was clear that anything family related made him extremely uncomfortable.

"Tell me a good story, Lyssa," Haven requested, changing the subject and relaxing his body as he floated in the moonlit water.

"I don't know any stories."

"Wrong. You're a story. *People* are stories. I hardly know anything about you. Tell me what you were like before."

"Before what?"

"You know," he said, eyes dancing lazily up towards the ceiling. "Before all this. Before magic ..." He sighed. "What were you like in your mortal life? I never had one, so I wouldn't know."

"Oh," I said, sinking into the warmth of the water next to him. "There really isn't much to tell. I was boring. I didn't even know what kept me going. I had no purpose. You know what I mean?"

"What was that like?" he asked, sounding genuinely intrigued.

"It was exhausting. My life was a routine."

He nodded in understanding. "Living without purpose means you're just existing. There's no fun in existing."

"I was also weak. Add that to the story," I spat bitterly. The topic of my old life caused old petty wounds to resurface, along with a bucketful of humiliating memories. "I was bullied, so I kept to myself a lot. I read a lot of books just to feel like I wasn't alone ... because really I was. People thought I was weird."

"You *are* weird."

I shot him a look. "Yeah, but people talk to me here ... even though I'm weird."

"Mortals are closed minded. They don't see the world like we do. They don't like people who are different. You know, I can actually understand Kurt's logic. Why save an entire race of people when all they're doing is destroying? Starting wars. Destroying the environment. Destroying each other. Destroying what *makes* them human."

"Then why are you so against him?" I asked, raising an eyebrow.

"Because even though it seems like the human race is inherently bad, there *are* good, honest people out there who don't deserve to die. Good people are worth protecting. And no matter how messed up mortals are, there's always room for change."

"Do you think Kurt can change?"

The stillness of the room, mixed with the calmness of the water, was almost mesmerizing. Even though we were swimming in the middle of Society headquarters, I felt safe.

"No. Some people are just too stubborn to change. Something made Kurt like that ... something caused his unnatural hatred for human beings. His hatred is his trigger. It's what keeps him going. And it's very hard to change when you think what you're doing is right."

"You're pretty good at reading people."

"Sure. I mean, people leave themselves open all the time; it's easy."

I frowned. If Haven really saw people like that, I wondered if anything he had ever said to me was genuine ... or if he was just as afraid of leaving *himself* open.

"Do you only *act* genuine?" I asked him. "I mean, you say people leave themselves open. Do you do the same?"

"What do you think?" he asked softly.

I truly didn't know. I didn't know him well enough to tell for sure, and so I ignored the question.

"Read *me* if you're so smart," I said, with a challenging tone in my voice.

"I would Lyssa, but I'm too busy reading the time," he said, squinting at the giant clock fastened on the far wall. "We should go. The security guards go by here on their rounds at four-thirty." He waded towards the stairs, climbing out, and I followed close behind.

We hadn't gotten caught sneaking around yet, and I didn't want to break that streak on one of our last nights at school.

"Haven, how are you dry already?" I commented, stepping out of the pool and staring at his perfectly dried hair and clothes. He looked exactly the same getting out of the water as he had getting in.

"An Aquarian can absorb water molecules. Here." He grabbed ahold of my dripping wrist and squeezed gently. Suddenly, I was struck with an overwhelming sense of Haven's magic—a calm sort of lull that seeped into my pores. It reminded me of the time we had shared magic out in the desert a month ago, except that this time I wasn't reciprocating. I looked down at his firm hold on my wrist and gasped. Strands of dark blue seemed to shoot out in all directions under the thin skin of his wrist. It looked like someone had drawn elaborate blue lines all over his arm. In a few moments, I realized that I was completely dry.

The lines on his skin began to fade, from a dark angry blue to a lighter shade ... and then back to his normal skin colour. He gave a satisfying sigh and released my wrist, flexing his arm.

"Did you ..." I was staggered, searching for words. "Did you just ... air dry me?"

He grinned. "More like vacuumed dried actually, absorbing the water molecules, but yeah. It's easier on our own bodies of course, but even doing it for other people, it's faster than the normal way. Don't you think?"

"Very," I said, marvelling at my dry shirt and hair.

"Coming then? We need to go get Amber," Haven said, moving towards the door. I gave one last look at the flickering shades of colour that shone brilliantly on the water's surface.

As much as I wanted to, I knew I couldn't come back here during the day without raising suspicion. A normal Draken would never go near water ... much less go swimming.

I sighed. "Yeah, lead the way."

"So what happens if we can't get into the labs without being seen?" Zack asked worriedly, late Sunday evening.

"What do you think is going to happen?" Amber asked, running a hand nervously through her black mane. "Should we just give up and let ourselves be killed by Kurt? If someone does happen to catch us, no matter who it is, we do what we have to do."

I frowned, taking note of the foreign expression on her face. Oh boy, I thought. If Amber was actually nervous, I definitely had every reason to be.

"And no one," I added, just in case they forgot, "is being left behind, even if we have to fight Kurt himself."

"Don't worry," Haven announced from his seat on the couch, lazily waving his hand in the air. "We'll be quick. I promise."

Compared to the rest of us, he seemed oddly calm, especially considering we were mere moments away from beginning the job of a lifetime. I knew that things would soon be very different. I had no way of knowing if I would ever see this room again. That wasn't really a problem, though. It's the people who make a place a home, and I guess it was rather convenient that almost everyone I cared about was coming with me.

The previous few days had been particularly strenuous, with hard-core training in all of the elements, and it was safe to say that I had improved significantly. The hardest part about leaving was coming to terms with the fact that I was leaving Elda at Magnorium.

We had all said our goodbyes yesterday, and I had found it hard to face her. I couldn't fail her, nor did I want to leave her behind. But I had no choice. I couldn't bring an old woman with us, and besides, she'd made a home of Magnorium long before I was even born. Still, combine that worry with the fear of running into Kurt and hopelessly failing, and it was enough to send me to the brink of insanity. But I knew I had to press on.

I realized that it was pretty bad to already be thinking like that, considering we hadn't even started yet.

I found relief in checking myself over and assuring that I felt prepared. Strapped against one of my thighs was a dangerous-looking knife, which made me feel incredibly bad-ass, and a Power Arrow was strapped to the other. Both weapons would be stowed in our bottomless boxes before we reached the airport, but for now, they were easily accessible if needed. The others were similarly armed. Our magics would be our primary weapons, now and on our quest, but we knew that we could never afford to push ourselves too far with it, exhausting ourselves to the point of collapse.

Other than our physical weapons, we carried nothing with us that couldn't fit in our pockets. Haven had enthusiastically volunteered to stow the rest of our things in our car, and that morning had snuck into the garage to do so. We still hadn't determined who was most qualified behind the wheel. Zack was the oldest, Haven was a bit more trustworthy, and Amber ... well, Amber was Amber, so I really had no worries about letting any of them drive.

We all rose from our seats, stretching our limbs in preparations for what I knew was going to be a very long night.

"Ready?" Amber asked quizzically, tightening the straps that held her weapons on her legs.

I nodded.

"All right then. Let's move."

The restless pacing around our room was finally over. I did the honours of swinging open the door, watching the shadows leak into our dimly lit room. The others filed out, watched as I quietly shut the door, and then followed behind me as I padded down the hallway.

We decided to take the stairs, which were barely ever used, in order to be less noticeable, so after a few moments, Haven took the lead and hung a right. We trailed after him. It was crazy how well he knew these halls. In five minutes, he led the three of us back to the isolated corridor the two of us had visited just weeks before. Kurt's "office" door remained locked, with no evidence of our previous break in. Haven turned his head over his shoulder to wink at me.

"Remember how fast I picked the lock last time?" he whispered.

"About two minutes?" I suggested, with a smile.

"Well, I bet I could do it even faster." He slid the familiar jagged metal rod out of his pocket, inserting the tip into the opening of the lock. In less than a minute, it produced a soft click. He stood up, turning the handle triumphantly, and swung the door wide open.

"Welcome to Kurt's fake office," he smiled. Amber strode inside first, with Zack tentatively following. I entered next, and then Haven was last, shutting the door behind me. I flicked on the light switch, illuminating once again the very ordinary room.

"Well, this is boring," Zack said, his eyes darting around.

"Wait till you see the next one," I replied. My gaze trailed upwards to the lone painting, which concealed the pass-code screen behind it. I reached the painting first and removed it from the wall, revealing the screen and the keypad. In one quick motion, Haven punched in the same password, Asclepius, and a moment later the wall slid back, revealing the archway into another dark room.

We wasted no time venturing inside, allowing Amber and Zack only a moment to absorb their surroundings. This was his real office, the place where he undoubtedly planned terrible things, and ordered countless deaths. I felt dirty just standing here. On the wall proudly hung the symbol of the purification plan, the rod of Asclepius, with its weird-looking snake coiled around it.

The room was oddly personalized. I saw now that there were actually picture frames on his desk, and if I had more time, I would've loved to examine them closely. It was somehow odd to think that Kurt treasured things outside of his horrible mission, but as unbelievable and creepy as it sounded, Kurt had a personal life just like everyone else.

I knew that his office was big, and cluttered with odd things, but seeing it again firsthand still shocked me. The archway on the far left was the only evidence that the room led somewhere else. I gestured for the others to follow, and moved cautiously through it and down a narrow hallway. If I listened carefully, I was sure I could hear my heart thumping. Kurt's office had been dimly lit, and venturing farther down the hallway only plunged us more deeply into darkness.

The long hallway came to a stop in front of a glass door. I peered through and saw the top of a spiralling stairway that descended into the darkness. I tried the door handle, which opened with ease. It was the first door we had come across that was unlocked.

Zack courageously entered first, moving swiftly down the stairs with the rest of us following at a cautious pace. We didn't know for sure where the stairs led, other than down, so being rash probably wasn't the best tactic.

"Slow down," I hissed and Zack nodded, doing as he was told.

The farther we descended, the louder the sound of voices below us became. I was positive that we were deep underground now, having descended a hundred steps or more, which somehow made it all the more unnerving. I hated to think who the voices could belong to.

I stopped moving, as the voices became more distinct. There were two of them—both male. Zack stiffened and slowed his movements to a halt. I flattened myself against the wall, straining to hear the echoing conversation.

"Hey, did you get your paycheck for this month yet?"

"No."

"We should really be paid more; I mean this shift is the worst!"

"Quiet! Don't say stuff like that!"

"Why can't I? It's not like anyone's around to hear me!"

I let out a sigh of relief. At least it wasn't Kurt. It sounded like guards, just making small talk on the night shift. It would have been nice had the place been empty, but the fact we had stumbled across a pair of guards was actually a good thing. It confirmed that there was something worth guarding. We were in the right place.

I locked eyes with Amber, and gave a curt nod. A silent agreement passed between the four of us. There was only one thing we could do: attack.

There was no time to formulate a proper strategy. Amber rushed forward, thundering down the remaining flight of stairs. The three of us followed suit. The guards' heads snapped up, and when they saw us, their mouths dropped open.

"Hey! What do you think you're doing in—"

I could really feel no sympathy for them. They had no idea what even hit them. Before I even made it to the last step, Amber had bashed in one of the guard's nose with the point of her elbow. Then she swung her body around, as he teetered on his feet, and delivered quite a brutal roundhouse punch to his temple. The man crumpled to the ground, further smashing his face in the process, and lay still.

His partner's features were twisted in shock for an instant, and then went completely slack as Zack emerged from behind him, delivering one neat blow to the side of his head. He followed that with a kick to the man's gut. The man doubled over, wheezing and reaching for his gun in his holster. Zack struck quickly, and with a single additional punch, completely knocked the man's lights out. He fell adjacent to his partner, who had a little trickle of blood leaking onto the floor from a wound on his temple—I couldn't see his face from where I stood, and was glad of it.

A part of me almost felt guilty, but the feeling quickly passed as I remembered that these were Society employees. Suddenly, I couldn't find it in me to care very much. Sure, they would probably be sore and very angry when they woke up, but by then we'd be long gone.

I watched as Haven pulled some duct tape from one of the pockets of his black cargo pants, and quickly bound them, so that they couldn't come after us or sound the alarm if they did wake up prematurely.

Stepping around the fallen guards, I looked up and saw yet another entrance—a set of double doors. Other than the two guards, no one else appeared to have been stationed nearby. For now it appeared that we were alone, but I knew it was always better to prepare for the worst and hope for the best.

I listened for a moment at the doors and didn't hear anything. Then I tried the handles. Locked. Shaking my head, I backed up, allowing Haven to come forward with his lock pick. A minute passed, and then another. Finally, he cursed in a fierce whisper and stepped away. "It's no good. Wrong kind of mechanism."

"So what's the plan?" I asked, watching tensely as he put the tool back into his pocket.

Haven looked at me for a second and then back at the door. "Simple." He reared back and then forward, kicking the door with such a force that it seemed to rattle the very ground. The force cracked the doors right down the centre, and they sprung open.

I charged inside and the rest followed wordlessly behind, moving almost as one.

The room we stumbled into had fluorescent lighting, and the switch from darkness to light momentarily blinded me. When my eyes adjusted, the enormous room began to take form.

True to Elda's stories, it really was a single enormous lab. Countless tables were spaced throughout the room, home to artifacts, machines, and odd-looking equipment I had never seen before. There were three huge, bizarre contraptions in the far corner that I figured it was best to stay away from. I could see countless trinkets in just as many glass cases, which were likely bulletproof, and the number of files on the nearby desks was staggering. There was a huge arsenal of weapons hanging on the left-hand wall, painful-looking weapons ... weapons that were almost certainly designed specifically to bring down supernaturals. A scent wafted through the air, like the metallic scent of blood mixed with too much disinfectant. It reminded me that we were standing in the heart of the Society—the core of all things evil.

"This is crazy," Amber spat bitterly, her eyes very round. "This whole time the world has been after the Society while they've been hiding right beneath us. I bet they sit down here and laugh at us."

I could hear the rage building in her voice.

"Let's just hurry up!" Zack said, almost sounding nervous. "I'd rather not hang out in here for too long. There are probably skeletons in the closets. Literally."

"Hiding skeletons does not even begin to describe what they must do in here," Haven said angrily. He was looking around quickly, as though he were trying to drink in all the details and make sense of them.

"Split up," I finally ordered. "Anything important is in this one room, so the Eye has got to be here somewhere."

Haven narrowed his eyes skeptically. "Why isn't this room more heavily guarded?"

"I guess Kurt's too arrogant to think anyone could ever break in," Amber muttered.

"Okay," I announced, trying to get them focused on the job at hand. "Guys, you take the left side; we'll take the right."

Zack and Haven gradually migrated towards the collection of weapons, while Amber and I moved towards the odd-looking equipment. We reached the first contraption. It was oval in shape, and appeared to be hollow. A metal chain hung loosely from it, attached to the side.

"Is that blood?" Amber inquired, pointing to the chain. I gulped, giving the contraption another look. Bright red was smeared across the metal links, and without warning, dripped onto the concrete floor with a splat. In the silence of the lab, it sounded like a gunshot.

"I guess the janitors missed a spot." Amber drew her lips together in a tight line, moving away from it. I wandered over to the cluster of files, thumbing through them quickly. All held mention of theories, experiments, and future projects, and all of it was alarming ... if not extremely useful. I quickly abandoned the stack of files and moved on. There was so much to explore, so much to see, that for the next twenty minutes, we all searched in complete silence.

"I think I found it!" Amber suddenly called from the opposite end of the room. I immediately abandoned my searching and moved swiftly towards the locked glass cases where she was standing.

There were about twenty identical cases clustered nearby, each holding a single item.

I shook my head. There were more clusters of cases like this in different parts of the room. This was clearly the Society's entire collection of artifacts. And it was impressive. There were so many powerful tools here, coveted by so many people, that it must've taken years to collect them all ... and many lives taken as well.

I looked where Amber was pointing and eventually saw an artifact that matched Elda's description. Its glass case was right in the centre of the group. I leaned forward, peering at the object. It looked exactly like it did in pictures we had found in our research. It was roughly circular, about the size of my palm, and reminded me of a clear, smooth stone. It seemed to be made of some sort of translucent glass, and I had almost missed it, as it blended into the container so well. Considering that the entire world was after it, and how badly we needed it, the Eye better work as amazingly as people said it did.

"That's it?" Zack muttered, clearly not impressed.

"Yes, that's it!" Amber said breathlessly. "The Eye—one of the most powerful tools ever created."

"Alyssa," Haven said, quite impatiently, "hurry up and get the stone out of there would you?"

I rolled my eyes but stepped backwards a bit in preparation, motioning them to move even farther away, just to be safe.

With a single focused glance at the case, I obliterated it. It shattered and crumbled into thousands of tiny pieces of glass, which now carpeted the floor beneath it. The noise had been horrible—actually painful—and when the dust settled, we all realized that our hands had come up to cover our ears without us realizing it.

It wasn't just the glass case holding the Eye that I had shattered. With the anxiety building in my stomach, I had unintentionally shattered every other casing in the room as well. Amber quickly snatched the Eye, dropping it neatly into her pocket.

That was when an alarm went off.

Oddly, I was calmer than I thought I would be. The Society's lab contained countless items that would be deemed priceless, and the fact that we had gotten this far without encountering any real signs of trouble had made me nervous. From somewhere high above our heads, a high-pitched siren wailed.

I sucked in a breath. There was no immediate reaction to the alarm; no hordes of angry guards burst in. There was only the echo of an extremely annoying siren. It was so loud that I was almost positive the entire population of Magnorium could hear it. The faster we got out of here, the better.

Haven and I shared a tense look.

"I think it would be best," I said, after a moment, "if we run now."

"No kidding!" Amber hollered from behind me, racing back towards the entrance. "I've got the Eye, so let's *go!*"

I took one last look at all the treasures the Society had gathered. I would've loved to poke around and see what other wonders they kept down here. But, instead, I broke into a full-out sprint, flying across the room.

"Stop!" We were halfway across the lab when Kurt stepped through the broken remnants of the double doors, looking more dishevelled than I ever remembered seeing him. There was something almost robotic about the way Kurt usually presented himself, and seeing him look almost human was startling. His hair wasn't brushed. It didn't look slept on, just very windswept, as though he had been running outside on a windy day. His clothes were rumpled, his tie loosely undone, and there was a tired look in his eyes. I guess I had to give him credit. It was the middle of the night and somehow he'd managed to throw on a suit, and get to his lab in record time.

All four of us skidded to a halt, and froze. We were caught red handed, and there was no way around it. He eyed the four of us for a moment. The silence was absolutely excruciating.

"Now *someone*," he said at last, his shocked expression mixed with unnerving amusement, "better tell me what you are doing in here." He crossed his arms, further wrinkling his black suit. I had never seen Kurt smile, but he was grinning at me now, his white teeth flashing disturbingly.

I couldn't find it in me to be polite enough to provide him with an answer. My heart beat wildly in my chest, but despite my fear, I gave Kurt an impressive glare—a glare that only intensified as he started to a laugh.

"Oh, you are especially priceless," he said, motioning to Haven and I, widening the expanse of his grin. "First you two break into my office ..." Haven stiffened and we briefly made eye contact. "... and then *all four* of you break into my lab. Quite a nosey lot, aren't you?"

He sighed, looking around the room at the piles of shattered glass and then at each of us in turn, stopping at Amber. He looked at her for a long moment, and then shook his head. "Remarkable. I've only just noticed, but ... you look so much like your mother. Funny that I've never noticed before." He watched, fascinated, as every muscle in her body tensed, her face seeming to turn to stone. "Must be something in your expression." He gestured vaguely in her direction. I stepped forward a bit, putting her slightly behind my left shoulder—fully prepared to stop her if she did something rash that would put her in danger, or stop him if he decided to use his magic to hurt her, instead of his words.

"I met her you know," he continued. "I met both of your parents." He looked at Zack for a moment and then back to Amber. "Only the once of course." For an instant, as he stared past me into Amber's eyes, the veneer of civility slipped, and his cruelty and arrogance shone through, leaving no doubt whatsoever as to what he was referring.

"Pity," he said. Then he shook his head, and just like that, the mask was back in place. "In any case, I suppose I must give credit where credit is due; you're the first students to ever find this place. You made quite a mess, though," he observed casually. His passiveness irked me. To be quite honest, I expected to be dead by now. Somehow, the very fact that we weren't terrified me even more.

"We know you're part of the Society," I blurted, saying the first thing that came to my mind.

For a moment I saw pride flicker in his eyes. "Oh, on the contrary, Brooks, I *am* the Society," he corrected. "What was it that gave it away though? The giant snake tapestry on the wall?"

Amber growled. "Maybe it's your superiority complex."

"Why Magnorium, Kurt?" I asked. I knew Kurt played a big role in the Society but hearing him brag about his true importance was frightening. This was a man who had obviously climbed to the top by inflicting pain. He likely murdered Amber and Zack's parents and did the same thing, or something worse, to Haven's brother. And he was standing literally no more than twenty feet away.

"Hmm?" He looked at me questioningly. "Oh, you mean, why place myself at the head of a school filled with hormonal, moronic teenagers? Well, it's an important Elemental institution, of course. Gaining control of the school itself was necessary to achieving my goal."

"The extermination of all mortals?" Amber exploded from behind me. The emotion in her voice was suddenly so clear, her rage so powerful, that it made her shake. I couldn't fathom what it'd be like to come face to face with your parents' murderer.

"No. The extermination of the weak-willed, which basically describes and includes all mortals, as well as any supernaturals I consider unfit to take part in our community. And that is quite a lot of people to exterminate, I'm afraid. But what you children won't be able to understand is that I am doing this broken world a favour. The mortals will be the downfall of this planet and so I will eliminate them in order to prevent the inevitable from coming to pass."

"There is *no* excuse for killing innocent people!" Amber shouted shakily. The passion in her voice stirred up the depths of my own. Standing there in front of Kurt somehow made it easier to remember why we were doing this. There was a glint in his eyes, a hazy sheen that almost managed to hide his obsession. In that moment, I realized that Kurt truly believed that what he was doing was right and just. There was nothing more dangerous than the power of certainty paired with a person's will ... and it was clear that in Kurt both were alarmingly strong.

"I disagree." He studied Amber and Zack for a long moment. "Such a powerful family, the Travies. Your parents were brave until the end. Funny how their children have wound up in the same predicament."

Amber made a small choking sound. He was hurting her, even without ever physically touching her. I was furious.

"Kurt," Zack growled, with more malice than I ever remembered hearing from him, "I swear to God if you speak one more word about my parents, I'll rip your throat out right here with my bare hands."

Kurt laughed easily, looking at Zack with filtered amusement. "Would you like to test that assertion, Mr. Travie? I'm sure your sister over here would be rather heartbroken by the results."

"Shut up!" I interrupted murderously, before Zack rose to the bait. "I don't know about your *clearly lacking* morality Kurt, but it won't excuse mine." I didn't even notice when I stepped closer to him, my words spilling from my mouth in perfect clarity. "We *are* going to stop you." I couldn't find an ounce of doubt inside of me refusing to take on the task.

"You can't stop what's coming Brooks. Don't be naive. Even as I speak, my employees are working on developing weapons of mass destruction that will rid us of humanity, without destroying the world I am trying to save. Even if I have to tediously eliminate the problem one mortal at a time, with *my* bare hands, I will succeed. There are too many of us, Brooks. Know your place."

"I think you're bluffing," I said, curling my lip in disgust. "You don't have any weapon. But *we do*. And ours is stronger than anything you'll ever build!"

Kurt cocked an eyebrow disbelievingly.

I knew I had to watch what I said. Talking to Kurt was like treading on eggshells; he was unpredictable and that made him dangerous. But I knew as soon as the words left my lips that his curiosity was piqued. And that was enough for now.

"Now *you're* bluffing. You are powerful, Miss Brooks, but don't let it go to your head."

"You don't know anything," I continued stubbornly. Anger ran so thickly through my veins that I could barely control what I was saying. I could feel the magic rising to the surface, threatening to seep from my pores like blood. How dare he think it was right to pass judgement on *anyone!* Kurt was controlling, insane, and completely egotistical. Now I understood why he was so important to the Society. They were the perfect match.

Kurt produced what sounded oddly like a genuine, hearty laugh. "I know everything! And at this moment, I can tell you for certain that the only thing I'm not sure about is the best way to kill you. You'll have to be dealt with, of course. You understand, I'm sure. I can't let my four most powerful students escape unscathed."

Our eyes met for a long, hard moment, and I saw … anticipation. He was enjoying this. Looking forward to snuffing us out like candles, one by one. I felt the very ends of my hair stirring a bit in a wind that I tried very hard to hold back.

"You can't beat us, Kurt," Haven said, stepping forward. "Now get out of our way."

Kurt raised his eyebrows, looking at Haven with a calculating expression that suddenly made me very nervous. "Quite the big man now, aren't we?"

"Kurt," I said warningly, sensing what was coming.

He ignored me, and took a step forward. "Actually challenging me? When you *know* what could happen ...? "

When Haven moved to step forward as well, I placed my hand on his chest and pushed him back a bit. "Haven, don't."

"Yes, Haven," Kurt mocked, with feigned sympathy and innocence, "don't. You are so far out of your depth, I would hate to think what would happen to you." A small, terrifying smile curled his lip. "But then again ..." he cocked his head to one side, and I could almost feel the other shoe preparing to drop, "your brother would be *so* proud."

Haven launched himself towards Kurt, who lurched forward to meet him with arms raised and small flames erupting from his fingertips. In that instant I could see them colliding. In my mind, I saw Haven burning, bleeding ... I saw us captured and defeated before we'd even begun, and the Orb in the hands of Kurt and the Society.

"No!"

Suddenly both of them were flying backwards, away from each other. Haven slammed into Amber and Zack, who managed somehow to catch him and keep him from falling, while Kurt hit the wall beside the exit hard—and about four feet off the ground—before dropping unsteadily to his feet.

He looked up at me then ... at my long, blonde hair swirling violently around me, lifted by a wind that I couldn't seem to pull back ... a wind that lifted tiny shards of glass from the floor nearby, making it plainly visible for one long, clarifying moment as it orbited the person whose magic had brought it forth. Then it slowed, a little bit at a time, before dissipating completely ... the shards of glass dropping like frozen rain at my feet.

No one spoke. No one even breathed.

I watched Kurt as he tried to wrap his head around what had just happened. I watched him trying to fit the pieces together somehow. I was a Draken. A fire Elemental, and yet ...

I saw Haven move off to my left side. Then Amber and Zack spread out to my right.

Kurt was slowly being cornered, but he didn't even notice. Horror and fascination battled for supremacy in his expression, as the proof of what he had just seen smacked him dead in the face.

I was an Orchin. I was the thing he needed ... the thing that he had been seeking for so long.

He lunged forward with incredible speed and I couldn't jump back fast enough. His hands extended as I quickly tried to sidestep him. Something sharp slashed my back as I retreated, and I felt a thin trail of blood trickle down my shoulder blades. If it weren't for my quick reflexes, I knew I wouldn't have been so lucky.

"Well," he said, his face gleeful as he pocketed a dagger, red with my blood, "here you are." As he circled slowly back around me, putting himself between me and the exit once again, he looked mad, his face invaded by the fiercest curiosity I could ever conceive of on a human face. "Finally. And what a pleasant surprise. Your blood will be excellent for research, and you my dear ... I reckon that you will be *quite* useful."

"You will *never* use me," I said, raising my arm, and without even thinking about it, calling up a wind that lifted him, pinned him to the wall, and held him there. "We're going to get the Orb," I said, a strange calm passing over me. "And we're going to use it to destroy you, and your Society."

I moved towards him, coming to a stop an arm's length away from him. I could feel him struggling against my magic—struggling to bring his hands and his fire into play—but I held on. I didn't even know how I was doing it, I had improved significantly with Skyros magic but *this*—this was pure instinct, a reaction caused by my trigger. Without taking my eyes off of him, I instructed the others to leave.

As they started filing out, Haven paused, putting his hand on my arm. "Lyssa—"

"Go. I'll be right behind you."

Haven hesitated for a moment and then nodded and headed out.

As soon as the room was clear, I stepped a bit closer, wanting to make sure that he heard me.

"You will be the first to die, Kurt ... and the Society will fall soon after."

He smiled at that—a chilling smile that made the hair on the back of my neck stand up. "We'll see Miss Brooks." Heat started pouring off of him in waves, as his flames reached for the surface. "We'll see."

My calmness evaporated then, like a drop of water in the desert. It was time to go. Concentrating on holding him in place for as long as I could, I bolted from the lab.

"You can't run from me, Orchin!" Kurt hollered, his voice echoing up the stairwell after me.

I managed to maintain my hold on him for maybe a minute and then felt him break free. When I heard the lab door slam shut, followed by his footsteps, my stomach plummeted. He was chasing us, and I had little faith that we could outrun him.

Yet I just kept climbing, urging my friends forward as we raced back upstairs, stumbling over our own panicked feet. Just moments after we crashed back through the office doors, another siren blared, different this time, and much more noticeable. This siren roared through every crack of the building; instilling a feel of terrible dread. I bet Kurt wanted to alert every teacher, guard, and student in this whole damn school.

"Haven!" I called. We needed him to lead us now. Magnorium was a labyrinth during daylight hours, which made it nearly impossible to navigate in the dark.

"I know!" Haven shouted over his shoulder as he jetted off down the hallway. "Keep up!"

I had never moved so fast in my entire life. The harsh siren kept wailing and I could faintly hear Kurt's screaming voice in the distance as we ran. Magnorium seemed to explode into chaos. Suddenly I could hear other voices, guards and teachers who rushed to respond to the call.

"Trying to escape!" was the one coherent phrase I managed to pick out from the jumble of yelling voices.

"Hey, you four! Stop!" A guard on his night watch stood obstructing our path, his face gaunt with shock. His hand immediately went to his hip, pulling his gun from the holster—his hands wavering as he raised it in our direction. "I said stop."

Haven swore and used the guard's moment of hesitation to turn and bolt down another hallway, warning us of the sudden direction change with a quick shout. We followed, making the turn right on his heels. I recognized vaguely where we were, yet with all the panic and darkness it was difficult to tell for sure. We were remarkably silent, dissolving into the twisting shadows of Magnorium. I suspected that Amber was using her well-honed magic on the run, to somehow keep the sound of our footsteps from carrying through the air.

I could still clearly hear a growing collection of voices off in the distance, but none seemed to be in our immediate proximity. The smell of gasoline and burnt rubber suddenly wafted through the air, and I knew we were close to the garage. Haven kept running, until finally, keeping his forward momentum, he slammed his entire body weight against a large black door. The wood split near the lock, the door flew open, and we all rushed inside.

The lights came on by themselves as our presence tripped the motion sensors. The garage was large, with grey ceilings and grease-splattered cement flooring. Cars sat under green tarps, and random car parts had collected on nearby workbenches, but I had no time to ponder the purpose of the auto-shop, since I didn't think Magnorium held classes in the subject. The only piece of equipment I cared about at all was the car Elda had smuggled into the garage: the newest BMW M5 sports model. Elda was apparently extremely wealthy, or had access to people who were, and when I had asked for something fast, she sure delivered.

Our car sat on the far side of the garage, facing the exit. Elda said that teachers frequently parked their cars in that area, and that many were quite nice, so ours wouldn't look out of place. The vehicle was painted the finest shade of black the industry had to offer. I ran towards it, digging into the deep pockets of my cargo pants, and retrieved the car keys. Fumbling, I tossed them to Zack, who caught them easily. He reached the car first, and wrenched open the driver's side door, slipping inside. I jumped into the passenger seat, and Amber and Haven dove into the back. As we caught our breaths, we heard more angry shouts. I turned my head around just in time to see Kurt step into the garage, his fury appearing ready to fly off of his face and strangle me itself.

"What the—" Kurt roared, running towards us. "You're not going anywhere!"

"Zack!" I squeaked nudging him, "you said that you like fast. So go!"

Zack clenched his jaw, clearly fighting his nerves as he popped the keys into the ignition.

"Um there's a door in the way!" Haven said motioning to the sealed garage door that was obstructing our path.

"Hold on!" Zack said with a shrug, as the engine roared to life. His hands were white on the steering wheel as he pressed down the brake, shifted into drive, and then released the brake, slamming his foot onto the accelerator as hard as he could.

We shot forward so fast that I lurched backwards, pressed hard into my seat. The car smashed into the wooden garage door, reducing the door to splinters. Pieces of frayed wood flew across the hood, scratching the paint as we continued on through as if it weren't even there.

The car crashed out onto the paved laneway beside Magnorium's main building, just a short distance from the road. In the distance, I could still hear Kurt yelling out orders to the various guards. I grabbed onto the armrest of the passenger door and held on for dear life as the car kept accelerating.

The car was fast but hard to control, and I could hear Zack's nervous breathing over the roar of the engine. It was the first time I had ever seen a break in his cool facade. Suddenly the distinct sound of a gunshot exploded into the night sky and I ducked. Not a moment later, I practically jumped through the roof as another bullet hit the trunk of the car. The bullet clanged, embedding itself in the metal, and I whipped around in the passenger seat, on the verge of panic.

I shot a fast look at Amber and Haven in the back and commanded them to get down. Haven grabbed Amber by the shoulders, throwing her down onto the seat and covering her with his wide frame. I held my breath as another shot was fired at us, and then another … all hitting the back of the car. One came coming dangerously close to shooting out the back window, smashing into the passenger side mirror instead.

"I can't drive like this!" Zack yelled.

"Just don't stop!" I shrieked.

Zack executed a sharp right-hand turn, skidding onto the main road (almost flipping the car in the process) and burning rubber in our wake. He drove even faster now, pushing the gas pedal down with all of his strength. We quickly sped out of shooting range. I was afraid that Kurt was going to hop in a car and chase us down himself, and when a few minutes passed with no evidence of him doing so, I remembered something that Elda had said, about having one more trick up her sleeve, and suspected that she had somehow sabotaged the other vehicles.

At the rate we were going, the fork in the road where Haven and I made our decision all those days ago sped quickly into view. Zack slowed down a bit, executed another sharp turn to the right, towards the city, and then floored it again. We needed to put as much distance between us and the school as possible.

The chaos began to fade into normalcy, but it did little to ease the tension. No one spoke for a very long time as we zipped down the highway and back into the city, periodically looking behind us to see if we were being followed. After more than an hour of the fastest, most uncomfortable driving I had ever endured in my life, Zack clearly needed a break.

"Hey," I finally said, breaking the silence. "Zack, it's okay, you can pull over."

Zack nodded tiredly, slowing the car and steering it towards the shoulder and a gradual stop. He killed the engine and the car produced a groan in protest, almost as well deserved as his own.

He flexed his fingers, which had been tightly clutched around the steering wheel for the last hour or so, and sighed, slouching back in the leather seat. I took a moment to get my bearings with the world outside my window finally still. It was oddly peaceful, even if we were parked in the dirt on the side of a highway.

"You're welcome," Zack finally said, slowly stretching all his tight muscles.

I managed a tight smile, laying my hand across his on the centre console. "You did great."

"I never realized how Magnorium was like a prison," Amber said, playing nervously with a long strand of her hair. "It was almost like there was no world outside. They kept us ignorant to keep us obedient."

"Didn't it work?" Zack spat bitterly, turning around to look at his sister. "This whole time the person the Council was after ran the damn school! He was our parents' murderer and we didn't know!"

"Remember hearing about all those Society terrorist attacks from the teachers, Zack? I was so caught up in everything else ... if only we knew. We could've done something—"

"But you didn't know," I interrupted gently, turning around to look at them. "And neither do the couple hundred other people sleeping there right now. But now we know ... and we're doing something about it. That's what matters."

Haven nodded, catching my eye. "We need to catch the next flight to Brazil. If Kurt catches us, the three of us are dead ... and something worse would happen to you Alyssa."

Haven was right. It was best to leave the country as soon as possible. The more distance in between Kurt and the four of us, the safer we were.

I peered out the window at the wide desert road that seemed to stretch on forever. I knew we'd be on the run for a long while, but somehow even this fugitive life was better than my old one.

All I ever wanted to do was make a difference ... to make my one life meaningful. Attempting to wipe a psychotic organization off the face of the earth seemed like it would fulfil my wish pretty well. If we failed, it would mean the inevitable death of billions of people—including my three friends and ultimately myself.

I had no doubts that Kurt would come after us, but for now, in this moment ... sitting in this car on the side of a highway, we were safe. Well, as safe as we could possibly get. From now on, safe moments like these would come in small numbers. This quest would be a global game of hide and seek, and the prize more rewarding than anything I could even fathom.

If Kurt wanted us, and if he really wanted the crystals, he would have to find us. The game was on and the clock was ticking.

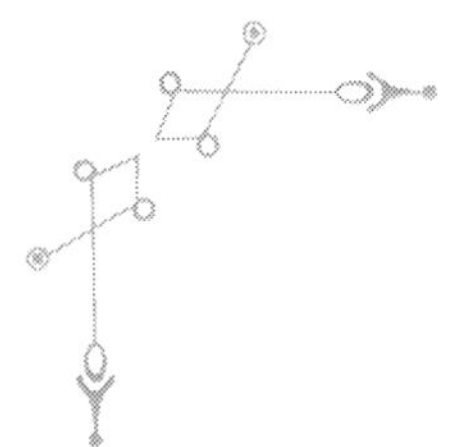
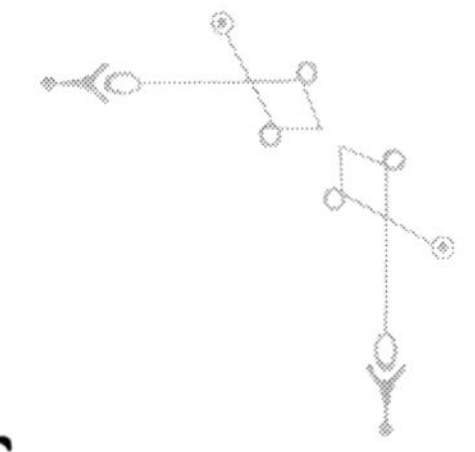

EPILOGUE

Kurt realized that sooner or later he'd have to go inside. For some time now, he'd stood loitering outside the doors of a local bar that was known to be Elemental domain. Even more fitting, the bar seemed to be a reprieve for criminals and Society employees, offering customers the luxury of escaping prying eyes.

The night was chilly and the frigid wind mussed his neatly parted, pale blond hair. He quickly raked his fingers through it, combing it back into place. Not a moment later, the wind roared rather mercilessly, and blew the blond strands across his face. His trench coat, draped lightly over his shoulders, flapping in the wind as he stood very still against the night.

He knew he'd have to enter the bar, but he'd met far too many blabbering buffoons in his day, and knew that most people turned to piles of mush whenever he was in close proximity. That was something Kurt embraced rather humbly; he couldn't help but feel proud that so many people regarded him with such admiration or perhaps fear.

The pads of his fingers met the cold metal of the doorknob, and finally deciding to get it over with, he pushed open the door and sauntered inside. The bar was appealingly empty, which was ideal, with only a few drunken fools scattered throughout the room.

Their chatter was a low hum, but faded into nonexistence as soon as he stepped through the door. Conversations fell into silence, drinks clanged back onto the solid oak tables, and all eyes turned towards him. Most recognized him, so there was no looks of alarm, just surprise.

When Kurt first joined the Society, one of the things he learned was that intimidation is key to being a leader. A good leader can persuade an audience, but an exceptional leader can strike just enough fear to inspire complete obedience. The look Kurt wore on his face was a mixture of glare and disinterest and it struck the onlookers exactly the way Kurt wanted. They went back to their private discussions and the chatter rose once more.

He surveyed the bar quickly. It would do, for tonight's intended purpose. Expensive cherry wood covered the walls. The round, wooden tables had plush chairs placed evenly around them. The most noticeable feature, however, was the huge bar that ran from one side of the room to the other. The granite counter top sparkled, and an endless selection of bottles lay behind it, encased in sleek metal racks. Kurt really did enjoy a good drink, even if he was here solely for work purposes.

He finally spotted a lone figure sitting at the end of the bar, clad in black, his face turned towards the wall. Kurt allowed a smile to pass over his face. He had always told his workers to aim for discretion. He quickly made his way around an array of chairs and tables before dropping onto a barstool next to the man.

The man turned, revealing one of Kurt's most skilled employees—someone he was forced to cooperate with whether he liked it or not. He was a young man, yet the severity of his job made him appear older. Kurt was pleased to see that the guilt which encompassed the young man the last time they spoke, was now completely gone from his face. In the end, the young man's job seemed to fit him like a glove. It was why Kurt had recruited him in the first place. He possessed an astronomical amount of skill, and wit that almost rivalled his own. The young man's jobs covered a wide range of tasks. Targeted assassinations, victim tracking, technical hacking, even strategic planning ... whatever problems Kurt brought to him were solved with ease, faster than he usually expected. This was precisely why he was perfect for this special job. Failure was *not* an option.

The young man sighed, his first movement of the evening, and ripped away the black hood that had been shielding his face. Brown hair spilled across his forehead and tumbled down to meet his shoulders. Light blue eyes blinked coldly at Kurt, who suddenly remembered how completely being part of the Society could change you. The boy had not been cold and unfeeling when last they'd spoken.

"You called me here to talk, so you better start talking," the young man snapped, running a hand through his unruly hair.

Kurt rolled his eyes and motioned for the bartender, who approached warily, as if sensing the tension. When he ordered a whisky, the bartender gave a vigorous nod and quickly went to fetch Kurt's drink.

Kurt looked at the young man's reflection in the mirror behind the bar. "I forgot how unpleasant you were, Tracker." He knew that he had to cooperate with the young man, no matter how irritating he was.

Whether or not the youth remembered or acknowledged it, Kurt was responsible for his subordinate's success. Kurt had seen to it that his talent was tested to its limits, and it was Kurt who was responsible for giving him the name that had made him famous throughout the Society: the Tracker.

Given enough information, the Tracker could successfully find and bring in anyone, regardless of whether or not they wanted to be found. Council members, supernaturals, extremely powerful Elementals, it did not matter. And when orders called for it, many of the people the young man tracked also became his victims, killed by the Society's orders and his hand.

"It isn't in my job description to be pleasant," the Tracker snapped. Kurt found it rather amusing that this man was the only one daring enough to snap at him. No ... fear was a trait the Tracker seemed to have conquered and then eradicated. If Kurt possessed any respect for someone other than himself, the youth would be a strong contender.

"Well that's splendid," Kurt said, "because your next job calls for anything but pleasant."

The Tracker frowned, the creases around his eyes crinkling in curiosity. Before he could make another comment, Kurt dug his hand deep into the bag he had slung over his shoulder, and pulled out four file folders. He neatly set them down onto the granite counter top, grabbing ahold of the first one.

"Tracker, you've been part of the Society for a while now. You should know our goal."

"Plan purification, the extermination of the weak-willed mortals."

"Someone's been listening," Kurt said, rather humorlessly. "As you know, the mortal population is growing at an exponential rate. As of now, there is only one realistic means of complete extermination."

"You mean the Orb," the Tracker said, a smile quirking at the edges of his thin mouth. "I hate to burst your bubble, but you're not going to get anywhere with that plan."

"That avenue of opportunity was closed off even to us, but not anymore."

Kurt had certainly grabbed the Tracker's attention now. His curiosity was clearly piqued and he leaned in closer, not even bothering to deny it.

Kurt ran his fingers along the sleek edges of the first folder and gently pried it open, placing it in front of the Tracker and revealing the picture of a young smiling girl, her hair spilling in golden waves down her shoulders.

"Tracker, this is sixteen-year-old Alyssa Brooks, the first Orchin in centuries."

Despite his subdued composure, the Tracker's jaw dropped for a moment. He quickly hid his shock once again behind a dismissive look.

"This kid?" he finally scoffed.

"Yes," Kurt said, looking him carefully in the eye. "'This kid' ... the most powerful person to walk the earth in generations. She is a threat and needs to be eliminated, *after* she serves a very special purpose. You can probably guess what that might be."

"You can't possibly expect this girl to retrieve all the crystals!" the Tracker exclaimed, with a hint of disapproval.

"Oh but I do. Let me explain."

The Tracker couldn't deny his need to understand this and snatched her file off the bar, his eyes greedily scanning the words while Kurt was speaking.

"Alyssa Brooks just recently transferred to Magnorium. At first, she seemed completely average but very quickly started displaying evidence of her power. She is faster, stronger, and smarter than any of the other children. It is unclear how or when she discovered her true powers, but when she did, she decided to retrieve the crystals. Of course, this isn't really surprising as she is the only one who can do so."

After a thorough scanning of the file, the Tracker slammed it shut. It was true then. An Orchin. A living one. "This kid will never find them on her own."

Kurt shook his head. "Even more worrisome, Brooks and a few others somehow discovered my real office, broke into our laboratory, and stole the Eye. The artifact is extremely valuable to the Society and is currently in their possession. It is still a matter of speculation as to who is helping her and feeding her this information."

The Tracker's thin lips broke out into a wide grin and he laughed. "I can't believe she got away with that!"

"And you shouldn't ... because she didn't. Oh no, you see Tracker, I only made it seem like she got away. I met them in the laboratory and put up a pathetic fight. It is much wiser to make them think they got away. With the artifact, her expedition is made significantly easier. We are using her in a way she is not even aware of yet. Unfortunately for us, Brooks has one main goal once she retrieves the Orb and that is to destroy the Society. Now this is where you come in."

Tracker's eyes gleamed with the excitement of a new challenge.

"Currently she is unaware of any pursuit. It is going to remain that way until the very end. I am sending you to track her down. Not to attack. I just need you to watch her closely. Follow her from destination to destination. Do not interfere. Only once all four crystals are collected are you permitted to attack, and quickly. Take all four crystals and bring them back to me. Use any means to accomplish this. Do you understand Tracker?"

Tracker said nothing for a long moment, regarding Kurt with a look he couldn't quite decipher. Then he shook his head. "You genius bastard."

"I do try," Kurt announced. "Now for the other obstacles to be aware of." He sighed, gathering two more files into his hands.

"Alyssa Brooks is joined on this expedition by three other extremely powerful Elementals. Together the four of them are the strongest team I have ever witnessed in action. I guarantee that this will not be easy."

He opened the files, laying them side by side. Pictures of two similar-looking youths greeted the Tracker.

"Amber and Zack Travie. Descendants of the Travie bloodline. Amber Travie is the strongest Skyros I have ever come across; likewise is Zack Travie the most powerful Terran. These two have a burning hatred for the Society, which is most understandable considering both of their parents fell at my hand."

The Tracker shook his brown hair, disbelievingly.

"For such a secret organization, Kurt, you sure make a lot of enemies."

"It's all part of the job description," Kurt replied rather dismissively, not even bothering to try to contradict the Tracker's observation. He had said nothing but the truth.

"Now for the fourth member, Haven Reeves. Mr. Reeves is an extremely perceptive individual, and highly skilled in many areas, although you probably already knew that. In addition to all of those irritating qualities, he also is the strongest Aquarian I have ever seen. Together he and Brooks broke into my office. Twice. You taught him well." Kurt said flatly, rolling his eyes at the picture of the smiling boy before slamming the file shut. The Tracker's blue eyes were wide, horror flashing through them for a moment.

Kurt made a noise, disapproving of the very human look on the young man's face.

"Don't tell me this will be a problem."

"It won't be," the Tracker said finally, after a moment's pause, composing his features once more.

"All four seem to have no weaknesses, except for their loyalty to each other. Take advantage of this. And when you have all four crystals, kill Alyssa Brooks, and the other three as well."

The Tracker gave a curt nod. "I understand. Follow the four of them, take the crystals at the end, and kill them. You'll have your Orb and I can go back to hiding out in scummy bars."

"Splendid. I am pleased you understand." Kurt clapped his hands together once, grabbed his drink, and swished the contents around. Then he took a swig and downed the drink in one large gulp, earning a few curious glances from the bar's other occupants. Kurt had experienced enough anguish in his life to expertly hold down any type of liquor.

"You leave in the morning to their first destination, Brazil. As of now, you are already a few hours behind them. As for me, I will issue orders from Magnorium. I still have that ridiculous job to hold down after all."

"What an exciting life you live," the Tracker muttered dryly.

"I get others to do my dirty work. I like keeping my hands clean."

The Tracker possessed the audacity to actually roll his eyes, unintimidated by the man before him.

"I will personally equip you with the newest weapons," Kurt continued. "Every necessity will be offered. This job will guarantee the future of the Society."

"I'm flattered, really."

If Kurt noted the sarcasm, he made no retort and hastily moved towards the exit, with the Tracker trailing behind him. The chatter grew quiet once again, as all eyes fastened on the two men exiting the bar.

The two men met the night's chill, the darkness shadowing their figures well. Kurt felt alive with the adrenaline and excited for what was to come: the Society's long awaited success. And he would be the one leading them to victory. He turned sharply back to the Tracker who stood silently behind him.

"We will speak in a few hours' time. Your job is essential, and success is imperative. Do not bother to come back here if you fail," Kurt said, finality practically dripping from his words.

"I never fail," the Tracker said, his facial expression unmoving.

"And that is why *I* recruited you," Kurt replied, with an impressive level of conceit. Then, without a final goodbye, he took his leave, heading back out to Magnorium.

The Tracker stood motionless, lost in thought. After a long moment, he refocused on the task at hand and disappeared into the night. The shadows engulfed him as he prepared for what was going to be his most important job to date. Failure was not an option if he valued if his life. He was almost as obsessed with winning as Kurt was. They were just four teenagers after all. He really didn't think the job was going to be that difficult, and that was perfectly fine with him.

END OF BOOK ONE

ACKNOWLEDGMENTS

This book has been five years in the making and I am very blessed for the many people who have helped me along the way. To my good friends Gregory Tucci and Alexandra Trevisan, this book wouldn't be what it is today if it weren't for your patience and ideas. To my artistic sister Julia Dickson, who provided the sketches for the book cover. To my mother Lella Conte, who provided invaluable input during the final editing.

Thank you to all my beta readers; Diana Conte, Katrina and Erica who spent countless hours carefully reading my book and took the time to put their two cents into the little world I created. To my friends, peers, and teachers who always shared my excitement on this project.

Thank you to all the people at Friesen Press for their patience and services. My father, John Dickson, you gave me the courage to start and told me to never stop writing.

Thank you, it has been a great ride over the last few years and I am glad to have had you all accompany me, each step of the way.

CPSIA information can be obtained at www.ICGtesting.com
Printed in the USA
LVOW08s0831190416

484214LV00006B/115/P

9 781460 264645